Fanged After Forty

Volume 1

A Life After Magic Mystery

USA Today Bestselling Authors

Lia Davis and L.A. Boruff

Fanged After Forty Volume One

Published by The Phantom Pen

PO Box 224

Middleburg, FL 32050

DavisRaynesPublishing.com

Cover by Glowing Moon Designs

Formatting by The Phantom Pen

This is a work of fiction. Names, places, characters and incidents are either the product of the author's imagination or are used fictitiously, and any resemblance to any actual persons, living or dead, organizations, events or locales is entirely coincidental.

FANGED AFTER FORTY VOLUME 1

Jilted at the altar a month before her fortieth birthday. Poor Hailey. Midlife really does have a crisis. Or is it that midlife is the crisis? Either way, it sucks.

Hailey Whitfield can't take any more run-ins with her ex. It's time for a big change.

She's never considered moving away, but it's her best plan yet. Bonus – her bestie lives next door! However, her new neighbor is… weird, to say the least. Extremely hot, but odd. So are his friends. But Hailey will take strange neighbors over facing her lying, cheat, deadbeat ex-fiancé all day, any day.

Finding a job in a new town is more challenging than she realizes. With her savings depleted from the move, Hailey has to suck it up and take what she gets. After taking a job as a private nurse for an injured bounty hunter, things start to look up.

Then a skip falls into her lap. Okay, sure. She was being nosy and reading an incoming fax intended for her patient. But with a little encouragement, Hailey takes on the task of tracking down the skip. It's easy money. Right?

Wrong. This skip is far more than Hailey bargained for. And her life is about to change in a very bloody and pointy kind of way. What a bite in the… Well, you know.

With the help of her witchy best friend and her new, very pale neighbor, Hailey is going to collect her bounty.

Or die trying.

This collection includes:

Bitten in the Midlife
Staked in the Midlife
Masquerading in the Midlife

BITTEN IN THE MIDLIFE

CHAPTER ONE

The day had finally come, and I could hardly contain my excitement.

I never knew starting over at the not-so-ripe age of forty would be so freeing. It was like a huge weight lifted off my whole body. I was *free*!

I didn't have to look at my ex-fiancé's face anymore. Nor did I have to watch him openly flirt with all the other nurses. I didn't have to watch him happily move on to the tramp he cheated on me with.

Jerk.

He was a lot more than a jerk, but I was *not* thinking about him anymore. Plus, karma always got back at the people who deserved her wrath. I was starting my new life in a new city, in my new-to-me house.

The best part of this move was that my neighbor was my best friend since we were in diapers.

We were celebrating this glorious day with champagne on my front porch, ogling the movers as they unloaded the truck and carried all of my things into the house.

It was a great way to celebrate on a Monday.

See? Not all Mondays were bad.

Another thing that made this move better for my sanity was that I was closer to my two older brothers. One I adored, Luke. The other was the eldest of the five of us, and…the poor guy wasn't everyone's favorite. We all loved him, but we wouldn't walk out in front of a bus to save him. Oliver was just...Oliver. He was a hard person to figure out. Oh, calm down. We'd save him. We might just shove him out of the way extra hard.

Pushing away thoughts of family and ex-jerkface, I went back to supervising the movers. It was a tough job, but someone had to do it.

"What about that one?" Kendra asked, pointing at one of the moving guys.

I hid my smile behind the crystal champagne flute she had brought with her.

My bestie had taken the day off to celebrate with me. She was a lawyer and had just won a big case, so that gave us double the reasons to celebrate.

Good times!

I watched mister tall, blond, and delicious—with rippling abs, a luscious tush I could've bounced a quarter off of, and one of those cute little man buns—carry a large box toward us.

He was young enough to call me mama, but still legal. Maybe being a cougar wasn't such a bad idea, just as long as he left before the sun was up. I had no plans to wake up beside another man, ever.

Did you hear me? *Ever.*

It would give my eldest brother, Oliver, something else to turn his nose up at and lecture me about why it wasn't a good idea to date a man young enough to be my son.

At least Luke would support a fling with the hot moving man. On second thought, Luke supported orgies and any manner of sexual escapades. That was a little too many hands, arms, legs, and bodies for me.

No, thank you. Although… maybe… Nope.

As the cutie with the man bun walked past, he batted a pair of lashes that looked like someone had dipped them in chocolate, and I glanced down at his pants, totally by accident.

No, really. I didn't mean to.

But oh, my. His pants fit like they'd been painted on. Molded to every muscle of his body, but also like they were begging to be torn off. It'd been a while since I'd had a back to rake my fingernails down.

Kendra, my bestie for as long as I could remember, cocked a dark brow, then shrugged. "I have socks older than he is."

I snorted, then giggled. It was probably the champagne, but who cared. "I didn't say I wanted to marry him."

God forbid. One bite of that sour apple was enough for me, and even if spitting out that second bite wasn't my choice, I was over the whole idea. Kendra had it right. Her love 'em and leave 'em lifestyle was my inspiration from now on. New start, new motto.

Broken hearts were a young woman's game, and I wasn't young enough to be willing to risk another. No way, buddy.

"Since when is a little bump and grind enough for you?" Skeptical was Kendra's middle name, while a smile flirted with her lips. Her skeptical part sure helped in her budding law career. Her last name was Justice, after all. Literally.

Kendra didn't trust easily, which was why she'd stayed single after her divorce almost fifteen years ago.

I shrugged and watched a mover lean against a dolly full of boxes while he rode the truck gate to the ground. Shirtless, muscular, and blond were apparently my new turn-on. Who knew I had a type? "Being ditched at the altar was eye-opening and threw my entire life in a new direction," I mumbled.

This direction's sheen of sweat, when combined with the champagne, put thoughts into my head. Fun thoughts. Sexy thoughts. Thoughts a newly single woman with no prospects had no business having—or maybe every business having them.

The best part was I didn't have to wake up next to anyone or answer to anyone. Ever. Again.

"Have you found a job yet?" It figured Kendra would change the subject to something more serious... What a way to snap me back to reality.

She was such a buzzkill sometimes.

"No, but I put in applications and sent copies of my résumé out to hospitals within fifty miles as well as every doctor's office in the greater Chestnut Hill-Philadelphia area. I also found an agency offering private nursing that I'm thinking of checking out." At this point, I had to take what I could get. My life savings had gone into the sanity-saving move.

Kendra nodded. Her approval wasn't essential, but the validation was nice. "Have you met the neighbors yet?"

She knew I'd come to tour the house and talk to the previous owner about a week ago. Kendra had been on some witch's retreat at the time.

Pointing to the house on the other side of mine, she said, "Sara lives there with her two-point-five kids and a husband who is never home. She's nice, but on the snobbish side. She is one hundred percent human, like you. Don't tell her anything you don't want the whole neighborhood to know."

Kendra had connections with the neighborhood I didn't, yet. There were two reasons for those connections. One, she was a witch; Two, she'd lived in this neighborhood for the past fifteen years. She'd moved right after her divorce to start a new life with her kids. Of course, she now had a great relationship with her ex. They made better friends than lovers, as it turned out.

It had been the same years ago for me and my ex-husband, Howard Jefferies. Our divorce had been messy and painful, mostly because I hadn't wanted to admit we'd fallen out of love with each other. I was bitter for a long time before we'd finally become friends.

"No. I've been here a couple of times, but always during the day when people are working, I suppose." I hadn't met a single soul besides the previous owner, Ava Harper, who was also a witch, and her extended family that had been with her.

Kendra hid her smile with another drink. "The neighbors across the street are," she leaned closer to me and lowered her voice, "*weird*."

"Yeah?" I glanced at the house across the street. "How so?"

It was a large three-story, modern brick house with a balcony that wrapped around the top floor. I wondered if the top floor was one large room or a separate apartment or living space.

Black shutters accented the windows, which appeared to be blacked out. The front door was crimson with black gothic-looking embellishments. There was a front porch on the ground level that was half the length of the front of the house, and the lawn was perfectly manicured with lush green grass and expertly trimmed bushes.

"You know, *weird*." Kendra cocked an eyebrow. "*My* kind of weird."

Maybe she'd had too much to drink, or I had, because I wasn't following whatever it was she hinted at. Then it hit me. Oh! *Her* kind of weird. "You mean like…" I lowered my voice to a whisper as I looked around to make sure there wasn't anyone in earshot. "Witches?"

She shook her head, and I pursed my lips. A guessing game. Awesome. I *so* sucked at those.

I kept my voice low enough that only the two of us could hear. "You said there's more than witches out there. Is it one of the others?"

This time, she tapped the left side of her nose and smiled. Kendra so loved her dramatics.

"Werewolves?"

"No."

"Werepanthers?"

"Nope."

"Bears?" I paused for another negative reply, then ran through a list. "Dragons? Lions? Cats of any kind?"

"No, no, and no." She kept her brow cocked and her smirk in place. She loved torturing me with these crazy guess games.

"Llama, dog, sock puppet?"

She burst out laughing at the latter, drawing glances from the movers. We laughed together like old times. Being around Kendra was soothing after everything I'd been through. God, I'd missed her so much.

"If we were playing the hot-cold game, I would say you were getting hot, but you're very cold." That helped so much. Not. Cryptic hints were her thing. "Brr." She ran her hands over her arms and faked a shiver. Then cackled like the witch she was.

"Zombies? Something in the abominable category?" Now I was reaching into the tundra. While Philly was cold in the winter, anything of the snow critter variety wouldn't stand a chance in a Pennsylvania summer.

"Warmer with zombies, a little too cold with the snowman."

My tone dropped to reflect my almost boredom. "Ghoul? Ghost? Alien?" She was losing me.

"Oh, come on!" She stood to her full height and leaned against the rail on the porch to stare at me. "You're dancing right around it." She let her tongue slip over her canine.

Oh, snap! No way.

"Vampire?" I whispered that one, too, because I'd read somewhere that vamps could hear every pin drop in a five-mile radius. Then again, that article was on the internet, and you couldn't trust anything on the web. At least I didn't.

I stared at the house again after her wink, indicating that I guessed right. Finally, the gothic embellishments and blacked-out windows now made a little more sense. However, the home looked normal at the same time.

"Wow." Were they friendly vampires?

"Yeah." She nodded with her lips pursed.

We both shifted to look at the truck, right as one of my boxes went crashing to the ground and the sound of breaking glass tinkled through the air.

I groaned inwardly and hoped there wasn't something valuable in that box. The movers would be getting a bill for it if it was.

Later, after the hotties had left and the sun began to set, Kendra started unpacking the kitchen while I worked in the living room. Thank goodness they'd put the boxes in the rooms they belonged in, thanks to my OCD in labeling each one.

I was knee-deep in opened boxes and bubble wrap when the doorbell rang. "I'll get it," I called in Kendra in the kitchen.

Not waiting for her to answer, I swung the door open and froze.

The most exquisite man I'd ever seen stood in the doorway.

Hellooooo handsome.

This guy was...tall. Well, taller than my five-one height, but then, most people were. He towered over me with a lean, athletic rather than muscular form. His deep amber eyes reminded me of a sunset, while his pale skin said he didn't spend much time in the sun. Light hair, something in the blond to strawberry range, brushed the tops of his shoulders. Shiny, clean, and begging for my fingers to run through the strands.

Smiling as if he could read my mind, Strawberry Man handed me a basket smelling strongly of blueberry muffins. The smell made my mouth water. Or was that him? Maybe he was Blueberry Man... Oh, geez. I hadn't even said a word yet. Had I?

"These are for you." He nodded toward the basket, looking a little uncomfortable.

Oh, yes, they were. His large hand brushed mine as I grabbed it, and I sucked in a short, quick breath. At some point, I'd become awkward. And ridiculous.

I remembered I hadn't brushed my hair all day since the movers arrived. Damn.

The porch was smaller with him standing on it, somehow it had shrunk, and I couldn't draw in a breath around him. Dramatic, yes, but so true. Or maybe he was too hot, and all the oxygen had evaporated in his presence. Either way, I found it hard to breathe and think.

"Um, th-thank you." I was like a nervous teenager who'd just met her very first pretty boy. I chuckled, hiccupped, and would've fallen out the door if not for the doorframe I'd somehow managed to catch my shirt on.

He nodded, smiling as he tilted his head. Damn if my knees didn't go weak. "No problem. If you need anything at all, I'm Jaxon. Uh, Jax, and I live right over there." He pointed to the house across the street. The back view of his head made my heart pitter-patter and my belly rumble as much as the front of him did.

"You're the…" I didn't know if he, if they, were loud and proud with their creatures of the night status, and I didn't want to take the chance of outing Kendra for telling me. Unfortunately, I thought of it a second *after* I'd started speaking. "Neighbor."

His grin hit me like sunshine poking through the clouds on a rainy day. Ironic, since vampire meant allergic to the sun in a deadly kind of way.

"Yeah."

I didn't know if I should invite him in. What if there was a Mrs. Vampire? The last thing I needed was to become a jealous vampire wife's main course.

Like the queen of the dorks, I held up the basket, gave it a sniff, then hiccupped again. "Thanks for the goodies." I wasn't usually so awkward. There was something about this guy.

As I spoke, I wished again I'd taken a moment to brush my hair or put on a clean shirt before I answered the door. Vampire or not, this guy deserved a neighbor who combed her hair.

CHAPTER TWO

Tuesday came in like a lion with a couple of bites on the message board where I'd posted for jobs in private nursing. And bingo!

One, if they hired me, they needed me to start immediately. Hope bloomed in my chest and for once, I didn't tamp it down. I didn't tell myself this wasn't going to happen. I was an optimist. Newly formed, but enthused and excited.

This was my break. Because this girl was *broke*.

Calming myself just a little, I typed a reply to the sender. **I would be happy to discuss the position at your earliest convenience.**

It sounded formal enough. I hoped.

She replied quickly. **Is now too soon?** The sender added an address and my heart leaped. One day in town, and I was on my way to an interview.

I can be there in thirty minutes.

Because I wasn't a complete bumbling idiot, I didn't tell her I'd already showered and would only need to change into something that didn't say I had planned to spend the day unpacking boxes. I was an early riser, always had been. A morning person, to the disgust of both my exes.

After changing clothes, I was in the car on my way to the Chestnut Apartments. Thank goodness for GPS. I was too nervous to find my way, and with my luck, I would've ended up in Jersey rather than Center City West in Philly.

Center City was the wealthy section of the city. At least, this apartment building was. Glass and metal and windows all the way around. The views of the city alone sold the place.

After checking in with the front desk, I was sent right up to the apartment. She must have been expecting me because the door opened before I could knock.

"Hello, I'm Tracy. You must be Hailey." The woman had long black hair and dark brown eyes. "Thank you for coming."

We shook hands, then she led me into the apartment. As I'd thought before entering the building, I could see for miles out of the floor-to-ceiling windows in the living room. The location was one of those to die for, close to everything, like my brother Luke's gallery, for example.

Tracy moved into the kitchen area, which was separated by a small island, so I followed, taking note of the large open space of the apartment and the small nook up against the wall of glass. The countertops were black and silver marble. White cabinets lined up under and above the counter; The appliances were stainless steel. Everything was luxurious.

When she had two cups of steaming tea poured, we sat at

the nook. "Cleo is my mother. She's a fifty-five-year-old bounty hunter, who probably should've stopped the stakeouts and takedowns a few years ago, but she claims to love what she does." She sighed. "And, admittedly, she was a pretty badass bounty hunter. She put hunters half her age to shame. But bullets don't care how badass you are."

Tracy shrugged and whipped her hair over her shoulder. "Her last hunt, a few weeks ago, the perp—you'll get used to Mom's lingo—anyway, the perp pulled a gun and shot her. The bullet grazed her spine." She shuddered, closed her eyes, then opened them again after a few seconds and one long exhale. "It's going to take a while before she's back on her feet, much less hunting down perps and hauling them in."

I nodded. Tracy spoke about a thousand words a minute, as if there was a premium on how much she could say at one time. "All right."

"She needs round-the-clock care, so we've broken it up into three shifts. There's morning until early afternoon, early afternoon until mid-evening, then a bedtime shift." She outlined the pay, and it wasn't nearly what I expected, but at least I wouldn't have to go asking for handouts from any of my family.

Oliver was a hard no. He was stingy with his money and often blamed his kids and wife for spending it all. My sisters never had any money. Luke had plenty and would give me a little to help make it through tough times, but I didn't want to ask him.

This job would help pay the bills. I'll just go without cable and only eat every other day. No biggie.

After a brief silence, Tracy added, "I've moved back in temporarily until she gets back on her feet, but I work full time, *and* I'm taking classes to get my master's degree."

Sheesh. Busy woman. Tracy asked all the usual interview questions. Reliable transportation? If necessary, could I stay later or come in early? What shift would I prefer?

"Day shifts." I was wide open for availability, but I liked mornings. Even when I was young, I'd enjoyed getting up early and feeling the morning sun on my face. I could get a lot of stuff done before noon.

"Excellent. The other girls are still in school; they want to split the evenings and bedtime shifts, so this is perfect." Tracy smiled like some great weight had been lifted from her shoulders. I imagined it had been. I'd seen many sick mothers in the years since I started working in the medical field. The worry alone when someone else provided the care was enough to turn a young woman old. Tracy was smart to get help.

I signed the papers authorizing the background check, and Tracy smiled. "This should just take a day or two then I'll give you a call and you can get started by the time Mom is home from the hospital."

I nodded and shook her hand again on my way out.

It was a beautiful, unseasonably warm March day, and instead of driving and having to deal with Philly parking, I left my car in the underground parking garage at the apartments and walked the few blocks to Luke's gallery.

When I arrived, my brother was in mid-conversation with a client, but he stopped talking and a wide grin spread across his face when he noticed me. "Girl*friend*!" His extra emphasis on friend made me laugh. "What are you doing here?" He toe-ran across the space and air-kissed me on each side of my face. "You look fab! What brings you so close to the action?"

"Job interview," I said. Luke's perfectly coiffed hair and Armani suit gave him the air of a man with money, a man with style, and a man with his own personal shopper. All of these things were true. The personal shopper was his new boy toy, Favio. I suspected Favio wasn't his real name, but since it wasn't a detail that mattered, I went on liking him all the same.

Luke adjusted an invisible out of place hair from his forehead with the daintiest of fingers, then smiled and cocked his head. "Let me get rid of this art enthusiast," he leaned in and whispered, rolling his eyes. I didn't have to guess that the client had zero art intelligence. "Then I'll take you to lunch."

Lunch sounded fabulous. It had been a while since we'd had a chance to sit down and catch up. I browsed until Luke was ready to go.

Of all my brothers and sisters, I saw Luke the most. Oliver never took a day off, never left his office, and from nine to six, Monday through Friday, he was off-limits. But after work, when the sun went down, Ollie knew how to get down. In his younger days, anyway. I didn't know about it, now. He'd just turned forty-five and it had hit him hard. Something about his mortality staring him in the face, he'd said. My sisters told me he was a different man, though just as hard-nosed. I hadn't talked to Ollie much in recent years. I just couldn't face the judgment of being emotionally close to him, so I'd put some distance between us quite a while ago.

"Have you talked to the girls?" I asked when we started down the sidewalk toward his favorite bistro-style restaurant.

He sighed. Luke was the hub of all familial information for the Whitfield clan. Then he distributed the gossip among each of us. "Ally called me yesterday." Allison and Avery were the twins, our mom's late-in-life children with our dad. Her *special* surprises. At twenty-six, they lived in New York and acted on Broadway. They both had quite the flair for the dramatic, and I never really knew if it was because they were the youngest or if they had some special skill.

"And?" He was building anticipation, withholding the information until I asked. The girls weren't the only ones with dramatic tendencies.

"They got a commercial, toothpaste of all things." He widened his eyes at me. "And Ollie is, of course, chomping at the bit to invest their income so they can shelter from taxes or something." He slapped a hand through the air. "Such a pain in my surgically enhanced backside. And his wife…" As well as a trophy wife, Ollie had the requisite son and daughter who attended private school and knew to hold out their pinkies when they sipped tea at the country club. As a bonus for all of us, he had an opinion he loved to share about every single thing. Everything. I'm whispering now. *Everything.*

"What about her?" Luke hated Victoria Beckett-Whitfield. In my opinion, he hated that she got a hyphenated last name, and he didn't, but I'd never voiced that concern.

"Bun in her oven." He cocked his head. "That tummy tuck? *Worth-less.*" He sing-songed the last word like it gave him pleasure to say it.

"You're so bad." Not really, and I loved him no matter what anyway.

"Yet you love me." He leaned in and air-kissed me again.

Once we sat down and gave our orders, I changed the subject. "How are things with Favio?" While Luke loved to gossip, there was nothing he liked more than talking about himself.

"O-ver." He double thumbs-downed, then faked-swiped away a tear. "He was using me for my money, my apartment, and of course my skills in the boudoir." His grimace was the punctuation for his sentence. "I'm single and on the mingle. So, if you find something luscious of the tall, dark, and delicious variety, send him my way."

I laughed. Where the hell was I going to meet anyone of the delicious variety? Well, except my new nightwalker neighbor. Now that was one delicious specimen of a man. Erm, vampire. Still man. No way was I telling Luke about him yet. No point in freaking out the family over a guy who hadn't even looked my way.

Not that I was considering dating a vampire. Maybe a nice tumble under the sheets. But nothing long-term. Not going down that road again.

Ever. Have I mentioned that yet? Never.

"Of course," I agreed, and took a drink of my soda.

"Anything from Brad?" His eyes narrowed, and his face contorted every time he asked about my ex.

I rolled my eyes. "Nothing more than the usual BS. He loves me, misses me. He's so sorry he broke my heart. Sent me flowers." I hadn't even read the card. I would have thrown the flowers in the trash, but they were my favorite—pink roses. So as long as I pretended someone else gave them to me, they stayed.

"Ugh." An actual shocking sound was a few rungs beneath Luke, but he tried, and I appreciated the effort. "I thought he moved on with some nurse from the hospital?" he asked.

I shrugged. "I'm not sure if he's just apologizing and trying to calm his guilt, or if she left him and he's trying to get back with me. Either way, I'm not interested."

Luke snarled his upper lip. "He was *so* not good enough for you."

It had taken a while for me to realize that, but I finally agreed. "I'm just glad he's gone."

Luke nodded. "Well, if you need help keeping him gone, you let me know."

"Aww, is my big brother going to kick my bad ex-fiancé's ass for me?" The idea was laughable. Probably why Luke laughed.

He held out his hand. "Absolutely not. My manicurist would kick *my* ass. I will happily pay someone to show the man who left my sister at the altar the business end of a knuckle sandwich." He grinned and put up his fists like he was going to fight, then pulled his fists in front of his face and blew his nails as if he was drying the clear polish he kept on them.

We spent the rest of lunch with gossip and laughter. Luke, with his creamy skin and blond-blue beauty, was the social darling of the family, and there was no one I would rather have celebrated my new job with.

CHAPTER THREE

By the time I'd gotten back from having lunch with Luke yesterday, I'd received a text saying that my background check came back, Cleo was being discharged from the hospital this morning, and Tracy wanted me there bright and early. So naturally, I was wide awake at 5:00 a.m., but didn't need to be there until eight.

You could say I was a tad excited. Or was it anxious? It was probably both.

I wasn't surprised that the background check came back so fast. My record was squeaky clean. Although, it had been really hard not to tarnish that record many times while working with Brad the jerkface. So, this move didn't only save my sanity, but helped keep my perfect record clean. It was the one time in my life that having no life had paid off.

I was two minutes early for the first day of my new job. I

didn't want to be too early, and I didn't want to be late. Did I mention I had a touch of OCD? Yeah, well, I did.

Tracy opened the door and smiled with a bit of relief in her features. She just didn't know how badly I needed this job. "Thank you for coming."

"I should be thanking you for hiring me." Oh, great, that sounded desperate. Well, I was getting there.

After shutting the door, she led me down the short hall into the living room/kitchen combo. I was drawn to the wall of glass overlooking the city, just like I had been the other day during my interview. The view was incredible.

Tracy gave me a short tour of the apartment. The bedroom adjacent to the living room was converted into Cleo's office. The master bedroom was the first right just before entering the living room.

"Mom is asleep now or I'd introduce you, but she's generally pretty awake and alert and she can tell you where to find things." Tracy gathered her books from the various tables in the rooms. During the interview, she'd told me she went back to school to get her master's in criminal defense. "Her medicine schedule is on the fridge, and she loves to try to distract you from making her take them." She chuckled. "She says they make her ditzy."

"I've had plenty of experience in getting patients to take their meds. They used to say I could talk them into anything." I chuckled and shoved my hands into the pockets of my scrubs.

"Also, she likes to order food delivered." I nodded as Tracy kept rattling off things. I wondered if I needed to write all this down. If so, I was unprepared. "You don't have to clean. I'll run the vacuum and straighten up when I get home. Mom is particular about her rugs." She stopped at the door and faced me. "That's all I can think of. My number is by the medicine schedule on the fridge if you need anything."

She waved and left. I shut the door behind her and headed to the living room. A few seconds later, before I'd even had time to turn around, she came back in again and grabbed a jacket. Yesterday was warm, today was cooler. Tomorrow, there would probably be a snowman next to the Rocky statue at the art museum.

You just didn't know what the weather was going to be like.

I chuckled at my thoughts, then went into the bedroom to check on Cleo and officially meet my patient. I poked my head in the door first. She was stocky with dark skin and black hair. When she looked at me, she smiled a welcoming, open grin. "Hello. You must be Hailey."

"Yes, ma'am. You must be Cleo."

That was obvious, but I was nervous and excited to have a job. I was such a goof sometimes.

"The one and only." She let out a soft laugh. "I'm sure my daughter has told you what a difficult patient I am, but I have promised to be on my best behavior." She held up three fingers on her right hand then winced as she shifted and tried to use her free arm to push herself higher. "Mm." Her eyes squeezed shut then flipped open a moment later. "Come. Sit down. Let's chat." She was the boss. I liked her instantly. "Tell me what brings you to my neck of the woods, other than the promise of a paycheck."

Direct. I did like her already.

"Oh, where to begin." My life up to this point was a mess. Mostly. That was why I needed a reboot in a new city.

She nodded. "I knew there was a story there."

"Two stories. Husband number one was my first big relationship. Howard and I fell in love in high school. Then somewhere in the ten years we were married, we fell *out* of love. I didn't even realize it until he pointed it out and served me with divorce papers." I shrugged and sat down in an armchair next to her bed.

Cleo frowned. "Ouch. What a jerk."

"That was my thought at the time. It took me a long time to get over it and trust that not everyone will just up and leave me." I smoothed a nonexistent wrinkle from my scrub pants.

"Anyway, I came to realize that he was right. I don't think we were actually in love. At least not deep love." I scrunched up my nose and met her gaze. "Does that make sense?"

She nodded. "It does. Tracy's dad and I were like that. Only it was me to point it out. He still tries to convince me to give it another go." Cleo picked up a glass of water from the nightstand. "Not happening. I have a rule I've never broken. If I was married to him once, there would be no second time."

"That's a good rule to have." I relaxed in my chair and crossed my legs. "Howard is a good guy when he wants to be. By happy coincidence, he was a bounty hunter, too. I helped him on occasion, so I know the ins and out of the business."

How had I forgotten the adventure, the fun we'd had? "We

worked well together. Until he dropped the bomb that it was over. That was the most painful and messiest time of my life, but we've mended fences and we speak now. We found out we were better friends than a couple."

She laughed. "Bounty hunters are a hard lot. Some love their jobs more than their families. Maybe he was protecting you by getting the divorce."

Wasn't that just the truth, whole truth, and nothing but the truth? "That's what I thought too. It's all water under the bridge now. He's a good man, we met at the wrong time, wrong place, wrong life. It happens."

We laughed and shared a brief silent moment before she asked, "You said *husband number one* like there's a number two?"

"An *almost* number two." The mental picture caused an ache in my gut. I still wasn't over that one. "Brad." Even saying his name brought a wave of darkness rumbling through me. "He's a doctor at the hospital where I used to work. The SOB left me at the altar. Literally. He apparently wasn't done fishing, if you know what I mean. So, this is my new start. I needed to get away from seeing him and the fish he was screwing on our wedding day."

"Reasons to leave don't get much better than that one." Cleo studied me for a long moment before adding, "Fresh starts are needed, sometimes, to keep us sane."

She was right, of course. "What about you? I'm guessing there's a really good story behind how you ended up in this bed."

"It was just a regular skip. Nothing jumped out that told

me it would go south before I introduced myself to him. He was a big bad biker daddy who skipped on a big bond. No different from any other I've taken in." She spoke with her hands, but there was pain with every move, and it reflected in the lines on her face.

"I tracked him to a bar in Fairhill." Even I knew that was the worst neighborhood in Philly, but I didn't say as much.

"I didn't even get the chance to tell him who I was before he pulled a gun and shot me." She lifted her shirt to show me a bandage, pointing to the center, which was a couple of inches above her belly button. "Bullet went in here and it tore through tissue on its way out. Missed all the important shit except a sliver of spinal tissue. Grazed it. Bruised it. Hurt it, anyway." She sighed. "Could've been way worse and I'm thanking my maker every day I'm here."

I smiled and patted her hand. "Then I will, too."

"I was in a coma for a week. Poor Tracy. That girl stayed at my bedside every single minute, praying her heart out for my recovery." She spoke with a slight southern accent, which was odd for a Philly girl and told me she wasn't from around here.

I wanted to ask her more about where she was from, but her eyelids were droopy, and her yawn full of fatigue.

Still, she continued. "I have to relearn to walk, so therapy is set up to start coming every day, starting tomorrow. I'm gonna be up chasing skips again in no time."

"I hope so." Even if it meant I was out of a job, I liked Cleo and wanted her to be at full strength. I imagined she was a whirlwind when she was at a hundred percent.

I stood because she needed her rest. "I'm going to see about breakfast and familiarize myself with your medicine. You rest, and I'll be back in a little while. Any special requests to eat?"

"Scrambled eggs would be nice." She yawned again. "But maybe in an hour or so. You are welcome to whatever is in the fridge. There's no telling what Tracy bought for food."

I helped her ease down, then left her alone and set off to take inventory of the food. As I passed her cell phone, it beeped, and a banner that said *AAA Bonds* appeared on the screen. I would've shown it to her immediately, but she needed her rest. Her injury wouldn't heal if she let herself get run down.

She awoke about an hour later, and we ate together while I asked her where she was from. She was born and raised in Tennessee and moved to Philly after she married Tracy's dad. Then after the divorce, she was down on her luck and met a bail bondsman looking for bounty hunters.

After we finished eating, I cleaned up while she settled in to watch TV. But I couldn't just sit around. I needed to be moving so I could justify charging this woman to be there. I went off in search of the laundry room to see if I could start a load for her. I passed the office first and decided to be nosy under the guise of dusting. I'd found a feather duster under the kitchen sink.

The room looked to be the same size as Cleo's bedroom. A large wooden desk that looked older than me sat in the middle of the room. Bookshelves and filing cabinets lined up against the wall that wasn't all glass. In the corner, there was a beeping fax machine with several papers gliding onto the paper tray. At first glance, the form didn't look like much more than a job application, but as it finished feeding, a picture of a woman was in the lower-left corner of the final page.

It was a bond sheet, I realized. It wasn't the same format I was used to from when I worked with my ex-husband, so I hadn't recognized it for what it was at first.

Too curious for my own good, I picked up the stack of papers. The woman had listed her occupation as an accountant —maybe Ollie knew her—and her crime was grand larceny, AKA embezzlement. The recovery fee was five grand.

Holy smokes!

Five grand to chase down a jolly-looking woman with rosy, red cheeks and a kind smile. Although I'd bet she was anything but kind.

She looked a little on the heavy side from the photo, and she was listed as only five feet and two inches tall. Just an inch taller than me.

It was too bad I couldn't go after her myself. Five grand would be a nice payday. It reminded me of when I was married to Howard. He'd brought home great money. Now I understood why Cleo had no intention to give up on her job.

With the stack of papers in my hand, I walked into Cleo's bedroom. With every word she read, her smile faded by another degree until she pushed the papers off to the side of the bed and sighed. "I wish I could take it. Sweet money for an easy skip, but it's going to be a long time before I'm up and around enough for this kind of thing."

Maybe I shouldn't have shown her the file, but on the other hand, maybe it would serve as an incentive for healing.

"Here, Hailey. Take this away. Looking at it makes me sick to my stomach." She handed me the pages. "I'm going to nap again. I swear, if I don't get out of this bed soon, I'm going to be as big as a house from all the lying around sleeping."

I walked into the living room and pulled out my smart-phone. One internet search later and my cell proved its worth. The woman in the photo had "checked in" last night on Bird-Book—the latest in social media trends—at the coffee shop just a few blocks from here. And according to her BirdBook page, her phone had checked her in again. Now.

Intriguing. So much so, I pictured myself storming the building, flashing my bounty hunter ID, the crowd parting and my skip—the aforementioned plump accountant—holding her arms out in front of her for the cuffs I would slap on. I also envisioned the paycheck with my name on the *pay to the order of* line.

By the time I finished living out my fantasy, it was time to go, and I was out the door. I could totally be a bond agent. Not like 007, obviously, but I knew a thing or three about tracking down a skip from helping Howard, so I sure could track Ms. Curvy Accountant.

CHAPTER FOUR

After I parked in my driveway, I rushed straight over to Kendra's house and pounded on her door. She jerked it open with a frown, then studied me like she was waiting for me to grow a new head. "What's up with you?"

I grinned. She always knew when I was on a mission. Pushing inside, I closed the door behind us. Kendra rolled her eyes and led the way to the kitchen. "Either you have some really good dirt on someone or you're up to something."

Laughing, I handed her the fax printout of the bounty and waited while she read every line. Once, then again. "Five grand for hunting her down?"

I tapped the page with my fingertip. "I'd forgotten how much money Howard made being a bounty hunter. I could totally do this."

Kendra eyed the page with doubt. "You're going to track down a criminal? And do what with her?"

I shrugged. "Turn her in, then collect the money." I stared back, then grinned.

"Just like that?"

"Just like that." I picked up the paper and read over the details again. "You could help. It'll be fun."

Kendra took the paper from me to read again. A slow smile formed, and I could almost see the wheels turning in her mind. "Okay. I say we do it. I'm all in."

Yes! Excitement filled me as I thought about where we'd even start to look for this woman. It was close to dinnertime so she could be home. Then again, if I had skipped out on court, I wouldn't be hanging out at my known address.

I pointed at Kendra. "You could do a locating spell."

She cocked an eyebrow. "I could."

"Then we go check it out." I wiggled my brows. "You up for the adventure?"

I loved the idea of the two of us working together. The times I'd helped Howard with his skips, I always got a thrill.

"What can it hurt? We'll see what we can find out and maybe figure out a plan?" She had a gleam in her eyes that told me she was totally on board. Not that I was worried she wouldn't be.

Kendra was always up for a little adventure or troublemaking, depending on her mood.

Following her into the living room, I sat on the floor in front of the coffee table and instantly regretted it. I might not be able to get up now that I was down. Kendra sat on the sofa directly in front of me and smirked. "You comfy?"

"Yep, let's do this." I rubbed my hands together as I watched her pull out a map of Philly and a pendulum.

As she reached for the paper, I hesitated. "You're not going to burn it are you?"

"No." She snatched it from me and laid it on the left edge of the map, then she held the pendulum above the center of the map. She whispered a few words in a language I didn't know.

Soon the pendulum started rocking back and forth, then in a circular motion. Then it stopped over downtown. I met Kendra's gaze. "Do you have a detailed map of downtown?"

She was already slipping the map out of the hidden compartment from the coffee table. "This isn't the first time I've had to scry the city." With a wink, she quickly repeated the spell over the detailed tourist map of downtown Philly.

The pendulum stopped, and I studied the area of the map. "Is that a coffee shop?"

Kendra nodded. "They have the best pastries. Their sandwiches are amazing."

At the mention of food, my stomach growled like an angry beast, making both of us laugh. Kendra jumped up and rushed to the front door. "Are you driving, or am I?"

I rolled to my knees and grabbed a hold of the table to help push myself upright. It was uncomfortable, but I did it without help. Yay me. Maybe it was time to start working out. Or maybe walking?

Maybe I could cut back on the snacks.

Maybe not.

After Kendra stopped laughing at me and got into my car, we drove across town to the coffee shop.

Reading the file, Kendra asked, "So what does a person do to get a bounty put on them?"

Seems like something a lawyer would've known. But she mostly worked in corporate stuff. I glanced at her briefly before turning my attention to the road and where I was going. I really should have let her drive because I wasn't familiar with the roads or downtown. "Most bounties are issued by a bail bondsman because the perp skipped out on a court date or a check in after being bonded out of jail."

Kendra glanced up and pointed. "Turn at the next right. Then find a place to park."

Nodding, I switched on the blinker. "Sometimes bounty hunters will get private jobs to track down someone. But this bounty came from a bondsman, so I'm not worried about dealing with shady people."

"Shady as in paranormal, or shady as in mafia?" I could just see her skeptical look from the corner of my eye.

I snorted. "Maybe both."

Sucking in a breath, she nodded. "You're right."

I pulled into a spot about a half-block from our destination and smiled. "Parking gods are smiling on us. It's a sign."

"It's a parking spot." Kendra's flat voice made me chuckle. For being a witch, she always had one foot stuck firmly in the cement of reality. "I think a sign would be like running into the woman we're looking for, and her surrendering peacefully. That would mean this is what we're meant to do with our lives."

I chuffed at her. "Where did the 'go get 'em girl enthusiasm' go? The what-can-it-hurt logic that's ninety-four percent of the reason we were on the case in the first place?"

"Ninety-four percent?" She arched an eyebrow. "That's awfully specific."

"Mama needs the money is the other six percent." I shrugged, and she laughed as we crossed at the light.

Kendra snorted. "Funny, I thought it was the other way around."

She wasn't wrong there, but I was excited about this case.

Instead of staying at the Cup o' the Morning Coffee House after we took a quick look around for our skip, who wasn't there, we decided to have lunch at a sidewalk cafe across the street and watch for her. They had chilled wine breezers as well as the best cheese and charcuterie trays in the state of Pennsylvania. And when the tray was gone, we moved onto loaded nachos, then bruschetta and pita chips. By the time we decided to give up and go home, I was in carb overload. I'd probably have to lay off them for the next week or two. I didn't have the metabolism of a twenty-year-old anymore.

"I don't think she's going to show." I sat back in the black iron chair and pushed my hair behind my ear. "I don't understand it. She was here, right? How accurate is the locator spell?"

She too sat back; her lips twisted. "Accurate enough, but that doesn't mean she couldn't have left while we drove over here."

Yeah, that made sense. Darn it.

Unfortunately for us, it meant a cold trail just when I'd been excited about being on the case. On the hunt. Doing something for once in my life. I sighed. "Well, let's go home and come up with a plan B."

Kendra nodded. We'd paid as we went along, so we didn't have to wait for a bill before we left. I stood and pushed my chair in, then looked at the number of plates left on the table. "Good thing she didn't show up. If she ran, no way was I catching her." I slid my arm through Kendra's. "Roll me to the car."

She chuckled, then stopped. Stared. Or maybe gaped was a better word. Open-mouthed gawking. No matter what I called it, she saw something and stopped, giving me time so I would see it too. I followed her gaze. "Well, I'll be damned. Would ya look at that?"

In front of us, walking as if she didn't have a care in the world, was Zara—the skip. She was wearing a black hoodie with the hood on, but no doubt, it was her. The reason she used the Cup O' the Morning Coffee House was because it was close to her house.

She made a left into a parking garage.

I glanced at the building and the street sign on the corner. "That's her building. Why on Earth would she use the address the bondsman had?"

"Maybe she's arrogant enough to think she wouldn't get caught."

Zara would have to be. Either that or stupid. I was going with a little of both.

We followed close, but not so close she would hear the tap of our shoes against the concrete. We stopped when Zara did and flattened ourselves against the wall as Zara took the stairs.

We hopped into the conveniently empty and waiting elevator and went up a level.

When the doors whooshed open, Zara was at the far end of the garage, walking through another door. This time, we followed, racing through the open air to where she'd disappeared. But before I could reach for the knob, an arm stretched out and clotheslined me. I was flung backward and landed on my ass. My throat closed up where the arm hit me, and I had to fight just to suck in just a little bit of air.

Kendra had her hands about four inches apart in front of her, summoning the energy she would need for the binding spell. She spoke the words in Latin, because it always had to be Latin instead of just *so-and-so, I bind you to so-and-so!* Or whatever the words meant.

While she weaved her spell, I took a slight pummeling as I tried to breathe. If I could get my breath, I could fight back at least a little, but being clotheslined had really taken me down.

I just had to wait for the words to work their magic but tucking and rolling wasn't doing me any good. "Ken?" I gasped as I rolled away from Zara's kick. "You got anything?"

She might've said run. Or none. Or done. I couldn't tell because all I saw was a giant hand—it was probably normal sized, but I was a teeny bit overwhelmed—reaching for me and pulling me into the darkness. Someone, or something, had yanked me into an alcove, a very very dark alcove.

But then a sliver of light from the outer garage shone on what could only have been fangs one second before they plunged into my throat.

Then the world went black.

CHAPTER FIVE

My head was being held in a vise. The vise tightened every second. The pressure pounded in my temples, which was getting worse with all the noise. Every sound was amplified to ear-splitting decibels, and I ached like I'd been hit by a train, then knocked under a falling tree.

Then the tree caught on fire before being doused with acid.

In other words, ouch.

As soon as I peeled my eyes open, I first realized I was home; then I noticed I was in my room, and it was night. Those were the things I knew for sure. The rest… I had nothing. No idea how I got home from the parking garage. No idea why my head hurt or why my house was so loud.

A flash of a memory went off in my mind. Fangs. I'd been bitten by something with fangs. What the hell was that about? It was the last thing I remembered.

Kendra's voice was loud, so damned loud. It was like I

could hear her hair moving. Really? That wasn't even possible. Whatever the noise was, it couldn't have been her hair.

Then again, my bestie was a witch with real magical abilities. That wasn't supposed to be real either. Yet here we were.

I opened my mouth to let her know I was awake, and to ask her to quiet down, but I couldn't speak. My throat was too dry and scratchy. The only sound that came out was a deep sounding squeak. Like a cow being choked to death.

Sexy.

I turned my head to look at the table where a glass of beautiful crystal-clear water sat waiting on me. Oh, thank God. I only needed a sip, to wet my whistle.

I sat up, grabbed the glass, and tipped it to my lips. Cool refreshment washed down my throat and the sandpaper eased enough so I could shout.

"Hey!"

But as soon as I spat the word, I choked the water back up and out. It dribbled it down the front of my nightgown. I must've drunk it too fast.

The door flung open revealing Kendra and Jaxon—my hot neighbor from across the street. They stopped just inside the door frame, in silhouette thanks to the hall light behind them, but there was no mistaking either one. Plus, I was new in Philly. I didn't know anyone beside these two, Cleo and her daughter. Of course, my brothers. And whatever the hell bit me.

"Why are you here?" I croaked. It was all I could think clearly enough to ask. Now, I was parched again. So damned thirsty. I reached for the glass again.

"Are you feeling okay?" Kendra sat beside me on the bed.

Jax moved around to sit on the other side. "You've been asleep for a while."

After staring at Jax for a second too long, wondering again why he was in my bedroom, I looked from one of them to the other. They looked concerned. I still needed a drink. No way was I going to be able to talk until I got a damned drink.

Kendra laid her hand on my forehead then glanced at Jax. They shared a look. "What?" I tried, but nothing came out. Again.

"Oh, tell me you remember," she gasped. "Holy shiznet, Hails. We were at the garage, do you remember?" She didn't wait for me to answer. "This woman, the skip? She attacked. Had you on the ground and my spell didn't work!" Her voice tore through my skull, but I remembered. The images of what had happened flashed through my mind. Not that it mattered, because as Kendra spoke, she waved her arms. A lot.

The one closest to me... Oh, my. It looked like the juiciest, most flavorful turkey leg I'd ever seen before in forty years of Thanksgiving dinners. I ignored the ringing in my head, the pain from her volume, everything that wasn't her delectable, mouth-watering arm.

I followed it with my eyes, with my head, until I had the moves down, and I knew what she was going to do. I reached out for a bite. Just one. It was all I needed. A nibble.

She jerked back, and I recoiled in horror, wanting to smack myself. I should've grabbed it with my hands first. Duh.

"What the hell are you doing?" Her appalled face wasn't

as intense as my hunger, and my tongue swiped across my lips.

Jax held up one hand. "It's normal, Kendra. She's fine."

"What's normal?" I whispered. My throat felt like dust. When the heck did we normalize that? Lusting for a taste of my best friend's arm? Wait. Why did I want to eat Kendra's arm?

A second after I had the thought, I didn't care. I wanted a bite. She was back to talking. "...she bit you and we had to act fast." Her arm moved left. I faded with it. "Stop looking at me like I'm lunch." She hugged it closer to herself, but then the other arm looked just as good. "Jax?"

"Right." He sighed. "She isn't going to be worth much until she eats."

"Yeah. I'm starving." I didn't know if the words made it past my parched throat or if I imagined them, but the sentiment stood. I liked the way he thought. Food.

Before I could try to speak again, Luke burst into my room and pushed between them like a bright, delicious-smelling roast beef sandwich. The closer he came, the louder his heartbeat sounded, and the better he smelled.

Wait! Why was I imagining my brother as food? Better yet, why was I so damn hungry? What had bitten me?

My mind was too muddled to put it all together, even though all the clues pointed toward only one possibility.

Luke plopped down on the bed. "I have been trying to call you for days. Your voicemail box is full, FYI." He gave a sideways head bob, then I grabbed him without a second thought, pulled him close, and sank my teeth into his soft, warm flesh. Blood spilled between my lips. Effervescent. Delicious.

Better than any gourmet meal I'd ever eaten, more satisfying than the greasiest burger or the savoriest soup. This was Nirvana. Heavenly. My own garden of Eden.

Then he jerked back—more accurately, Jax pulled him back. Luke slapped his hand over his artery. "You bit me?" He glared at me with wide eyes. *"Bit me?!"*

I shrugged. He had roughly a gallon and a half of blood in his body. No way had I taken enough to matter.

Then, I froze. As a cloud of confusion lifted from my hazy, food deprived brain, reality slammed into me. I'd bitten him. Drank his *blood.*

Horrified, I jumped up from the bed and rushed into the bathroom. After slamming the door shut, I stared at myself in the mirror. Besides the bedhead, I looked *great.* Fantastic, really. My once imperfect skin was flawless, even though it looked pale.

Then I opened my mouth, and my suspicions were confirmed.

I had fangs.

I poked at them with my index finger, wondering if they went away and only appeared when I was hungry. I frowned, turning to sag against the counter. So many questions swarmed my brain. Jax would have the answers.

I jumped out of my skin when someone pounded on the bathroom door. Then Luke screeched through the wood. "Hailey Marie Louise Whitfield!"

I giggled and opened the door. "Uh-oh. It's a full name

assault." Then I stared at Luke, who stared back at me with wide-eyes and his mouth hanging open. I darted a glance to Kendra then back at my brother. "What?"

"You bit me! You freaking bit me!" He touched his neck with his fingers and showed them to me. "You drew blood."

I stared at the tips of his fingers coated in crimson. I swiped my tongue out, catching a small drop of leftover blood from the corner of my mouth. A second wave of Utopian happiness washed over me. Lightning quick, I wrapped my fingers around his wrist. "Come here."

He jerked his hand away from me and held it to his chest, his features a mask of horror. "Stay away from me," he whispered.

A pang of sadness washed over me. I knew my actions weren't normal, but I couldn't help it. Luke had tasted so yummy. Okay, no. That was my brother. He was not food.

Brothers were friends. Not food.

I drifted closer to Jax. Surely, being a vampire himself, he'd stop me if I went crazy. At least, I hoped he would.

Luke was still being dramatic about the whole thing. He turned on Kendra and put his hands on his hips. "What the hell is wrong with Hailey? I want answers, and I want them now because I am *freaking* out. And bleeding."

"Breathe, Luke. Just breathe." Kendra led him away while Jax took my hand and pulled me toward the bed to sit down with him.

It took a second, but my mind cleared. Somewhat. Although I could still smell Kendra and Luke, I got nothing from Jax. Well, nothing but the desire to lick every inch of him and that had nothing to do with eating...erm drinking. "Why can't I smell you?"

"Because you're a freaking vampire." Kendra shrieked the words at me, waving her hands.

"A *what* now?" Luke turned to her as she sat him down and handed him a cloth to put over his bite. "I'm gonna need a bigger story here."

Kendra nodded. "Yeah." She told him everything, and bits of memory came back to me with each word until I had a whole picture.

Zara had turned me.

"She's a vampire? You'd think they'd put something like that on the bond sheet." I huffed out a breath. Then again, humans wouldn't know what Zara was because vamps and other paranormal creatures did whatever they could to live in secret, just like Kendra did.

"After you passed out, she took off. I screamed for help, and Jax showed up." She nodded to him.

"I'd been tracking Zara, too. I almost had her, but then..." He shrugged, and it didn't take a genius to know he thought we'd gotten in the way. "I got a call for help. I smelled the blood, saw the teeth marks, and I knew what she'd done."

"Holy crap." The situation probably warranted something a little stronger—something that started with an F at least—but I was all kinds of hopped up on Luke blood. And Lukey blood was *good* blood.

Jax waved his hand. "Yeah. Killing humans is a big no-no in the vamp world. So is turning them, for that matter. There's a council that governs the whole race. I didn't have any choice but to turn you." His apology was so heartfelt, it said this euphoria wasn't going to last and things were going to go south eventually. No one would apologize for this kind of rapture, the ecstasy, the bliss.

"So, we took you home and you've been asleep for the last three days." Kendra finished the story, but I stopped listening after *three days*.

"I have to go to work. Oh, God. I can't afford to lose that job, I just got it and I really like her!" I said every word in a single breath, which considering I was a vampire, I probably didn't even have to breathe anymore. Did I? I tried to hold my breath, but I was too upset.

Kendra moved closer until I couldn't help it any longer and licked my lips again. Then she took a step back. "I called and told her you'd been in a car accident."

Luke swiveled from looking at me to glaring at her. "You remembered the boss she worked for *one day with*, but not her beloved older brother?" he snarled out in a breath.

Kendra brushed him off. "I would've called, but I've been busy worrying about my best friend."

"Watching her sleep?" His volume climbed. "How busy could you be?"

Kendra puffed up her chest. "Listen, bucko, I sat at her bedside. Held her hand. Chanted a mantra so good—"

"A mantra? You chanted *a mantra*?" He mimicked her lighter tone, cocked his hip on the chair, then held up a finger. "Let me tell you something, *best friend*. I am the first call. Always."

They argued back and forth. She reminded him I was in

my forties and didn't need my brother. He said I was younger than him and would be until one of us died. I wanted to jump in with a walking dead joke, but Jax shook his head when I opened my mouth.

It was like he could read my thoughts. That was something I wasn't ready to know about at the moment.

"Some things are better left alone." He nodded to Kendra and Luke, still bickering. "That's one of them." Then he stood and ushered them out of the room, shut the door behind them, locked it, and crossed back to the empty side of my bed. He pulled back the blanket and slid in.

"Uh…" I scooted over to give him room on the bed. It was a good thing I had a king size. At least I didn't run the risk of biting *him*. "What are you doing?"

"Your body is still adjusting to the changes, and you should rest. But I have some things to explain, first." He gave me a soft, sweet, dreamy look. "You're going to need to feed often right now. And until you learn to control your impulses, I need to stay with you."

Stay with me? Yeah. Good plan, right there. How the hell was I going to focus with mister hottie vampire in my house. All. The. Time. "Okay." Maybe we could snuggle, too.

"There are rules, Hailey. Not many, but they are in place to keep the race from being detected by humans. One of those rules is we are not allowed to turn humans without the council's permission." He paused, as if giving me time to absorb what he'd said.

"I take it you didn't have permission to turn me?"

He nodded. "I did not."

My gut twisted with worry. “Then why did you?” He didn’t know me, so why risk punishment?

Jaxon rolled to his side and stared at me for a long while. “I have my reasons, so don’t worry about the council. I’ll deal with them.”

I’d do as he asked and let him worry about that. “You said there are other rules?”

“Besides keeping the existence of vampires a secret, the others are more like guidelines. I am the master vampire for the Philadelphia and surrounding areas. I set the rules for my territory. My biggest rule is to not bite unwilling humans. I own a club that is strictly for paranormal beings only. I have humans that work for me that vampires can feed on.” I must have made a face because he paused and laughed. “It’s not that bad. The humans are loyal and have full knowledge of us.”

I thought about it for a few moments. That was a handy way to deal with the feeding issue. It was a relief that I wouldn’t be going around biting random people. “What happens if one of the humans betrays your trust in them?”

“Their memories are erased, and they are encouraged to move out of town so there is no risk of their memories coming back.” His tone was so matter of fact, but there was a note of something else in his words.

I narrowed my gaze. “If their memories return?”

He sighed and brushed a stray strand of hair from my cheek, leaving chill bumps in his wake. Good to know I could still get chill bumps. “I don’t kill them unless I have no other choice.”

I nodded and stared at the ceiling, then yawned. So, he would kill a human when necessary. Would I?

Jax gave my hand a squeeze. "As your sire, it is my job to train you. But for now, you need to rest."

I smiled; not sure I could sleep anymore. After all, I had slept for three days! "Will you stay?" When he nodded, I blew out another breath.

He settled in against the pillow, and I turned to look at him. The full-on view was breathtaking. Wasn't every day I had a gorgeous vampire in my bed. Or anyone gorgeous, vampire or not.

I watched him for a few seconds. "Does this mean I can never go to the beach again?" Not that I was much of a sun worshipper, but I loved the sand and the ocean, and the smell of it all.

"You can, but you'll only get a few good minutes before you burst into flames, and maybe one more minute before you're a pile of ash. Or you could go at night." He could've just said no. But he had to go for the dramatic.

"And garlic?" I loved walking by Juliano's Eatery. They had the most aromatic dishes on their menu.

"Myth. Doesn't hurt us. Crosses are also a myth of epic proportion." He reached over to brush my bangs off my forehead, and if I still had circulation, my blood would've rushed to my heart. "You can see your reflection in a mirror."

So, the latter, I found out when I rushed to the bathroom after biting Luke. "Good. Bad hair days are okay every once in a while, but...a girl needs to see herself." I frowned. This was a lot to digest. "At least, I get the super speed, right?" Maybe I would finally run that marathon I'd always dreamed of.

"Maybe. Our kind isn't a class you can fit in a box. Some of us are strong, some can see in the dark, some are fast, others hear really well. A few of us are blessed enough to have all the…" He grinned. "Superpowers."

"How'd you get so lucky?" I wasn't jealous. More like intrigued. More so than I'd ever been.

He winked. "I'm going to help you get through this."

"As my maker?" And lover?

He smiled again. "And a friend." Ah, well.

I wanted to thank him, to be grateful, but I was a vampire who would never feel the sun on my face again. I was tired and hungry. For blood. There was a lot to unpack before I would be able to work my way around to gratitude for his saving my life.

"How old are you?" I asked. It didn't matter, really, but I was curious.

Jaxon sucked in a breath. "More than a century."

Oh geez. Talk about a May-December relationship. "I have a lot more stuff to learn, huh?"

"There's time." But even at a hundred plus years old, he wasn't a good enough liar to sneak a deception past a woman who'd already been lied to by a husband and a half. Of course, right now, I wasn't worried about the lies. I was worried that I had a gorgeous man beside me. In my bed.

And all I wanted was to drink my brother's blood.

CHAPTER SIX

I WOKE up again on Sunday, after sunset. I hadn't really given much thought to whether or not vampires slept, but it seemed to me maybe I didn't think they did. Then again, Jax had encouraged me to rest so maybe they did? But here I was, four days into a long and somewhat broken nap, and I was a vampire.

Thank God I didn't have to sleep in a coffin.

I hoped this fatigue didn't last and was just part of the transformation process. That was another thing I'd add to my growing list of questions for Jax. Right now, I needed to get my ducks in a row because, vampire or not, I still had to pay for a place to live and that meant I had to work.

I picked up my phone from the table and dialed Cleo.

She answered on the third ring. "Hello?"

She sounded strong, and not angry despite caller ID, so I hoped it was a good sign. "Hi, Cleo. It's Hailey."

"How are you doing?" The concern was comforting.

"I'm fine. I just wanted to apologize and let you know I'm going to have to adjust my shifts." Shame and guilt bubbled inside me for lying. Well, technically I didn't lie. Kendra had. For me.

"All right. I can work with that. I had to hire someone for the day shifts anyway, but we're still looking for a part time night shift person." The sound of papers rustling filtered through the line.

Relief flooded me that I hadn't lost my job. That was perfect. Luck was finally smiling on me. "Thank you." There was no way I could make it without the income from that job. I could maybe go part time now that I wouldn't have to buy food. "Thank you so much."

"Tracy has it covered for the next two nights, so how about you start back on Tuesday night?"

The next time I saw her, I was going to give her the biggest, strongest hug I could manage without injuring her.

When I hung up, Jax was standing in the doorway to my bedroom, hands in his pockets, shoulders braced against the door frame. Damn, he looked good. "Good morning."

Morning was about twelve hours ago, but in this circumstance, it made sense. "Hi."

His slow smile sent warmth burning along my nerve endings, and I would've thought I had blood flowing through my veins, but I knew otherwise. Still, the effect was the same.

He looked me up and down, then shook his head and smiled. "You slept for three or four days, and you look amazing."

"Maybe that's my vampire superpower." Not the most functional of gifts, but I could make it work.

He chuckled. "Come on. You need to eat."

At first, I thought he was inviting me to my own kitchen, but then I remembered. A wave of sadness hit as it occurred to me that I would never again eat in my own kitchen. Not food anyway. I wondered if I would miss the taste of comforting favorites like cheese and fried chicken.

Immortality was a trade-off for taste buds, and I wasn't sure I was down with it. I really liked to eat.

I stepped into the bathroom to get ready, but… my hair was full and lustrous, and my skin shone like a toddler's who'd never been kissed by the sun. Just for good measure, I brushed my teeth carefully. My fangs were still out and sensitive! After a change into less wrinkly clothes—I still hadn't unpacked them all—we headed downstairs.

When we were in the car, Jax glanced over at me. "You okay?"

I wasn't. This was a lot to take in. Maybe the sleep was my subconscious trying to hide from the reality of my new lifestyle. But telling him wasn't very otherworldly of me, so I didn't answer. Instead, I asked my own question. Avoidance was a good friend to have at that moment. "Where are we going?"

"The club I own downtown." He started the car, and within moments we were on the road.

I remembered him saying he owned a club for the paranormal during one of the times I'd woken. "Does this club have a name?"

"It's called 'Catch and Release.'"

"Catchy. Decorated in a fishing motif?" Made sense in my head.

"No." His focus was wholly on the road, as if he didn't drive much and this made him nervous. Maybe he didn't. I would ask another time. "It's more about the patrons. I opened the club with the idea to help vampires feed without risking discovery. It was more popular than I'd imagined. Eventually other paranormals started to come. It's one of the few safe places they have to be who they are without hiding."

"That is where dinner is tonight." I was okay with that. The thought of lurking in the shadows and waiting on an unsuspecting human to feed on made me want to cry. There was comfort in knowing that the person I feed from tonight would be all knowing.

"How often will I need to feed?" I asked.

Jax glanced at me, then quickly focused back on the road. "Right now, once a day or every other day. Once you're a little older and more controlled, you won't have to feed as often. Maybe once or twice a week."

How much older were we talking? Because that sounded much better than dealing with this insatiable hunger. "Like years?"

"No." Oh, thank God. "It varies. Could be a couple of months." I could live with that. "Could be a bit longer. In rare cases, a couple of weeks."

Again, too vague for comfort. "Is there anything else I need to know?"

He nodded. I knew there would be. "If you lose too much

blood or wait too long to eat, you'll go through a period where you need to eat more in a shorter period of time." I wasn't up on vampire lore. The things I knew about witches came from Kendra, but we hadn't talked much about vamps until I'd moved next door to one and then the extent of our conversations had been that my neighbors were vampires. "Feeding isn't sensual or sexual," he continued. "Though some of the romance novels make me wish it was."

I chuckled. I'd read those books, too. I could buy that as far as when *I* was feeding. But I couldn't imagine Jax doing anything and it not looking sensual and sexual. Sinful. The thought of his mouth anywhere near a pulse point of mine would've done exciting and crazy things to me… if I still had a pulse.

"Okay," I squeaked.

He smiled and gave my hand a squeeze where it lay on my lap. There was something to be said for this man's touch. He used it in all the best ways. "I only feed about once a week. It doesn't take nearly as much to satisfy me."

I totally didn't focus on the way he said, *satisfy me.* Because I was a grown woman who knew how to control herself. I hadn't jumped his bones yet, had I?

Instead, I focused on the benefit of his words.

"Imagine how much extra time you have without having to worry about cooking or eating."

I smiled, and without thinking said, "I would finally have time to plant a garden." Then it dawned on me. "Except I would have to do it by twilight." Ugh.

"I've always been partial to night blooming jasmine."

Another squeeze of my hand before he let go and resumed his grip of the steering wheel. "Moon flowers are pretty too."

Night blooming jasmine. Maybe I could plant that garden, then. I'd do my best to look on the bright side.

We pulled into the parking lot, and he walked around to help me out of the car. I didn't really need the help or expect it, and it was so very old-fashioned, but I smiled. He seemed to be the kind of guy I'd thought Brad had been. Boy, had I been wrong.

I walked beside him inside the club. I'd expected low, eardrum bursting music, but it wasn't loud at all. Instead, the club was filled with upbeat, electro-dance-type music, but not overly loud, maybe because vampires had sensitive hearing. For that I was glad. I was getting too old for a lot of noise. My ears wanted to crawl away from all the noises. The car had helped, blocking out some of the outside sounds, and surprisingly, this music helped quite a bit. Maybe I'd invest in some really good earbuds when I got a paycheck.

"The club is two-story," Jax said as we made our way to a set of spiral stairs to the right of the main entrance.

I slowed and scanned the lower level. The club had an old gothic-style look. The color scheme of the club was red and black with gold accents. *Better to hide the blood.*

There were tall, round tables with fancy bar stools at each one scattered around the dance floor in the center of the room. Booths and other casual living room-style seating filled up the space along the walls. There were two bars, one at each end of the ground floor.

Glancing back at Jax, I realized he was halfway up the stairs, so I rushed forward to follow him up.

The second level had less seating available than the first. It seemed much more private too. Groups of high-back sofas that curved in half circles about the size of a loveseat framed by matching armchairs were randomly placed around the floor.

The upper floor also had two bars, as well as an area with pool tables and dart boards.

Jaxon walked beside me, his hand at the small of my back and, whether I imagined it or not, he filled me with warmth. There was something about this guy and the way my body reacted to him. I just couldn't pinpoint why or how.

He guided me to a section above the dancefloor with plush seating and mirrored walls. Swiping out an arm to the vampires sitting in that cozy seating area said, "Hailey, this is my clan." They stood, and a man took one step forward. "Ransom, my brother and my right hand," Jaxon said.

Ransom held out his hand, and I shook it, but couldn't stop marveling at how much they looked alike and how pleasing those looks were. The resemblance was striking as far as chiseled features and pale, creamy skin. But where Jax had strawberry blond hair and blue eyes, his brother had hair the color of milk chocolate and the eyes to match.

"This is Paige." Jax indicated the woman next to Ransom.

I nodded and smiled. I'd seen some beautiful women before, but this one had cheekbones and lashes to die for. Her coal black hair was sleek and off her face. Her rich, brown skin glowed under the strobing lights of the club.

"Grim." Jax continued, nodding toward another man.

Grim stood and thrust out his hand. Smiling. I shook his hand and he nodded at Jax, then moved back to his chair. He was rougher looking; big, built like half a building with tawny beige skin and eyes as dark as a midnight sky.

"And finally, this is Nash."

Nash nodded and slung his arm across the back of Paige's seat. There wasn't much about Nash to comment on except to say he reminded me of a chameleon; his long face gave the impression he would fit in anywhere.

Maybe that was his vampire power. Blending in.

"Nash and Grim report to Paige, but they're all enforcers."

I wasn't sure what an enforcer did, but I liked that a woman was in control.

Jax led me around, helped me pick some humans for feeding then showed me how to make it happen. It wasn't much different than when I bit Luke except the humans in the bar knew what to expect.

He also showed me that to cover the bite marks, I only needed to lick over the bite and my saliva sealed up the holes like magic. Neat-o.

Jaxon included memory-altering in his brief training session. Which I would need to learn in case I had to feed and couldn't make it to the club. That was a skill I learned quickly.

When I finished feeding, I smiled at Jax. He really was gorgeous. I felt twenty years younger, stronger, and more alive for someone whose heart wasn't even beating anymore. Dear God, Jax was beautiful. Did I mention that already? I danced over to him and slid my arms around his neck.

I never did this kind of thing. Never had this kind of fun. It was exhilarating.

Jaxon cleared his throat and gently pulled my arms down. "I should get you home. Start training you."

Duty always got in the way of a good time. It didn't look like being a vampire was going to change that.

I nodded but frowned. I couldn't help it. I wanted a moment. A memory. I didn't know whether or not being changed was something to celebrate. Not for more than it had kept me alive, but I was having fun. I hadn't let loose like this in decades.

"Should we say goodbye to the clan?" I asked.

He nodded. "Sure."

Maybe I knew they would insist we stay. Or maybe I just hoped they would, and to my delight they did. "Nah, come on, Jax. Stay. Have fun," Nash said.

Paige chimed in with Nash's argument. "She's new. Let her celebrate. Find her place."

Ransom stood and put his hands on his brother's shoulders. "And what's the point in having a bar if you don't indulge every once in a while?"

Paige crossed her arms and cocked her head. "Did you tell her?" Her grin spread across her face as she leaned in. "Do you feel it? The blood from a drunk human is such a buzz. It's the beauty of Jax owning this place." She put her arm around me. "Look at them."

Bodies writhed to the deep, loud bass line of whatever music this was. Couples dancing close. Others gyrating into the air. But everyone had a drink, and everyone was smiling.

This was the life I'd missed by marrying young and not finding out who I was first. I hadn't experienced anything like this before.

I glanced at Jax, who was busy staring at me. He asked, "You want to stay?"

I did. More than anything. I nodded.

With a shrug, he sighed and chuckled. "All right. We'll stay."

And before I could rethink it, I threw my arms around his neck and pulled him down so I could press a hard kiss against his mouth. Then, I let him go like it was the kind of thing I did all the time.

It wasn't. But the look he gave me when I pulled back made it all worth it.

CHAPTER SEVEN

According to Jax, for the time being, I was going to have to feed at least once a night, although the amount I would need at each feeding wasn't too much. True to his word, when I awoke Monday night, I was hungry. Again. Apparently, it was the hunger I had to learn to control, but to start the small feedings would help. Kind of like a new diet. I'd been on enough of those to understand the notion.

At least I could use the club for feeding. Plus, it was fun.

As far as useful information, it was like DIY for new vamps, and I couldn't believe he'd left me on my own already. What if I failed?

No, I would not think like that. *I will not fail!*

I called Kendra and Luke, and when they came over, I gave them each a bracelet Jax had helped me make to repel vamps. That was when I found out that he knew a witch who had made the anti-compulsion charms. That had sparked a bunch of questions that Jax didn't have time for. At least at the moment. He'd had some kind of meeting to go to. But he promised we'd have time to chat soon.

I was looking forward to spending time alone with him.

The main reason I reached out to Kendra and Luke was because who else was I going to ask to go with me to a vampire bar? Not just a bar owned by a vampire. A bar where vampires foraged on humans for their sustenance. And what if every vamp didn't have someone like Jax to see them through the changing, the feeding? The thought made me glad for the bracelets. I didn't even know if vampires bit other vamps, but I also didn't want to take the chance.

Jax had said that vampires couldn't compel their own kind, our own kind, but sometimes a really old vamp could influence a newbie easily enough. That was enough motivation to get a bracelet for myself.

When we got to the club, the music pulsed and the bodies gyrated, but I was in a get-in-and-get-right-back-out kind of mood.

Kendra stopped and stared as Ransom approached. My new senses helped me understand Luke was about to burst from nervousness. He was like a shaking chihuahua, though he contained it. I probably wouldn't have noticed when I was human.

"Hello, Hailey." He gave each of us a quick once-over and his eyes lingered for an extra second on Luke. "Who're your friends?"

After I introduced them, we stood in an awkward little circle until Luke smiled. He'd overcome his nerves, apparently. "Hey, Halo, do they have anything here to drink that doesn't have an RH factor?" Luke nudged me, and boytoy he was, smiled at Ransom.

I glanced at Ransom, who wasn't built to be a boytoy, but he watched until Luke quit gyrating to the beat of the music. "We have a fully stocked bar of top-shelf liquor."

Kendra slipped one arm through mine and waved her free hand toward the dance floor. "See anything that looks like a T-bone? A Big Mac maybe?"

I snorted at her attempt at a joke. She was trying to be funny, and I appreciated her attempt at lightening the mood, but this was serious business. Jax had been clear. The hunger could drive me mad and cause me to lose control. Since Kendra had gone with the food reference, I wasn't seeing a bunch of twenty-something humans getting their groove on, I was seeing dancing steak and burgers.

"It's not like heading to the grocery store and picking out a cut of meat, Ken." I rolled my eyes, then leaned in close to her. "You of all people should know that vampires have amazing hearing.

Luke reappeared without Ransom, but with a frozen margarita for Kendra and a martini garnished with a green apple slice. "Sure, it is," he said. "What are you in the mood for?"

Apparently, my brother had picked up on our conversation.

Just then, a well-built male human with a polo and khakis tight enough I could see his religion walked past, and Luke followed with his eyes and the turn of his head toward me. "He looks tasty. Banana cream pie tasty."

I laughed a little as he sipped and stared over the rim of his glass. I didn't care who I fed on, but the thirst was powerful.

Instead of standing and gawking, I pulled Kendra onto the dancefloor while Luke perused the clientele, then when something of the tall, dark, and dumb as a brick variety ground into the group, I quirked my finger at him and motioned for him to follow me to a dark corner. If he didn't know what I wanted, it didn't matter. In ten minutes, he wouldn't remember me anyway. And all the humans in here had been pre-warned. That was the deal and why it had taken us a moment to get in. The bouncer had cleared Luke and Kendra. I wrapped my arms around his neck and bit, only drinking enough to slake my thirst, then closed up the holes and wiped his memory. "That was a nice hug," I said as I stared deeply into his eyes. "Thank you."

He walked away with a dumb, but happy smile on his face, though I was still hungry.

There was a safe way out of this. I could just ask one of the vampire servers there to bring me someone. Jax hired humans that were loyal to him and his clan and worked here to feed Jax's VIPs. Since I was now considered one of Jax's vamps, that included me. But I needed to learn to feed, erase, and let go. AKA Catch and Release.

Hence the name of the bar. So clever.

I scanned the dance floor while Kendra and I moved to the beat until a cute, young man caught my attention. I offered him a closed lip smile. That was invitation enough for him because he moved through the sea of bodies straight for me.

"Hi, I'm Grey. Would you like to dance? Maybe a bite as

well?" He winked and smiled at me, showing the cutest dimples.

"Sure." I offered my hand to him. "Lead the way."

Grey took my hand and pulled me out to the center of the dance floor. Just as we stopped the music switched to a slow song. Perfect! I wasn't sure why I felt the need to conceal my feeding. That was the point of the club, after all.

Gripping my hips, Grey pulled me close and began to sway. I enjoyed the dance for a little while before I couldn't fight off the hunger anymore. Not because it was trying to take over, but because I didn't want to lose control when Jax wasn't around. I needed to prove I could do this on my own—without the fanged babysitter. Ransom was here for that reason; I knew that the moment I saw him. But lucky for me, Luke was currently distracting him at the bar.

I fed from Grey and danced some more, then fed again quickly before I closed the holes and stepped away from him. As I turned to walk away, he grabbed my arm tight enough that his fingers dug into my muscle.

My gaze locked with his, and I asked, "What is your problem?"

"Don't you want to feed some more?" He loosened his hold and slid his hand down my arm to my waist. Desire flared in his eyes, and I frowned.

Grey wanted more than just to feed me his blood. Well, he was about to get his bubble burst. I flatted a hand to his chest and gave a gentle push. "I'm done."

He pouted and covered my hand with his. "Oh, come on. Just one more taste. I know you like it. I sure did." To prove his point, he took my hand and placed it on the crotch of his jeans. By the feel of it, the package behind the denim was impressive.

Too bad. I wasn't in the mood to be seduced by Grey, the blood junkie. I grabbed a hold of his bulge and squeezed, bringing a whimper from him. Then I spoke through my teeth while making eye contact. "When a lady—human or vampire—says she is done or says no in any form, she means it. Don't come on to her like a crackhead needing his next fix. You hear me?"

He nodded while swallowing hard. A slight tremble went through his body, so I released his erection before causing permanent damage. "Forget we ever met and go home to sleep it off."

With a slight nod, he walked off. That was when Kendra made an appearance. She touched my arm, making me jump. "Sorry. I didn't mean to startle you. Are you okay?"

"Yeah." I watched Grey disappear out the front door, then met Kendra's concerned stare. "I'm fine."

Then I led Kendra to the bar where Luke was chatting with Ransom. Tugging on Luke's arm sleeve, I said, "Come on. Let's go."

Ransom caught my gaze. "You did the right thing out there."

I wanted to ask him if that was normal, but I didn't want to talk about it right then. Jax was coming over for training later, so I'd ask him. "I know." I didn't need a man telling me how to handle men. I'd done it for forty years. Ransom meant well, but ugh.

Luke, who didn't seem to hear Ransom's and my exchange of words, grinned at me. "You go ahead. I'll be along later." His brow wiggle accompanied a lean-in for a hug.

After hugging him, I asked, "Are you sure?"

Ransom slid a hand over the back of Luke's chair. "I'll take good care of your brother, Hails."

Oh, I bet he would. I hesitated for a long few moments. "Okay. Call me when you get home. If I don't answer, I died a final death during training with Jax."

Luke waved me off like I was interrupting private time with his new vampy crush. Laughing, I gave him a kiss on the cheek, then Kendra and I were off.

It was just after midnight, and I was standing in front of my closet. I wasn't sure what to wear anymore. Pajamas were my daytime attire now, but it felt odd to change out of my club outfit and not into PJs.

After a little longer, I settled on a pair of exercise pants and a Bon Jovi t-shirt. Not long after I changed, Jax knocked on my door. "Come on. Time to train."

I wasn't sure I liked the way he said train. He'd mentioned honing my skills, harnessing my strength, and finding my vampire power, if I had any special ability. But now he made it sound like we were going to get sweaty, and not in a fun way.

I walked beside him to his house across the street, more

specifically around his house and through the gate in the obscenely tall fence around the back yard. And by *obscenely tall,* I meant definitely higher than the eight-foot zoning restriction fence. But the fence wasn't the reason for my open-mouth gaping. He had an American Ninja style obstacle course set up in his backyard. Water pits, giant wooden structures, plus equipment designed to enhance endurance, strength, speed, and even musculature.

"This looks intense." And frightening. I wasn't twenty-five anymore. Not that I'd done anything like this when I was in my twenties or any other age.

He shrugged and crossed his arms, looking me over, which gave me a chance to admire his masculine beauty. The corner of his mouth lifted slightly as he spoke. "We have to hone your strength and show you how *not* to use it."

"Not?"

"If a baby is trapped under a car, it's okay to lift the car. People will credit adrenaline. If you drop a quarter under the car, even though you can lift it, a passing human might freak out a little if you've got it propped in one hand while you feel around for the quarter with the other." He lifted a brow.

Okay so that made sense.

I nodded, clapped my hands together and rubbed. "Lead on, Miyagi."

He turned to look. "What?"

I chuckled. "Not big on the pop-culture, huh?"

"No." He stared at me for an explanation.

I could've explained it, maybe even suggested a viewing one night soon, but by the time the thought came to me, he moved on. "The fence protects the neighbors from the lights." He pointed to the corners where flood-lights were installed on poles that lit the entirety of the massive yard.

"Why didn't you just get a place outside the city? A place where you could light up the world and not worry about both-ering anyone." The houses on this street weren't particularly close together, but the house wasn't solitary, either. Eventually, there would be noise complaints. Especially after my first whoop of success.

"This is close to the city for the club, and there isn't much of a food supply for us out in the wilderness."

True. Unless he liked bunnies.

About forty minutes into vampire fight club, where Jax taught me how to disappear into the shadows and move fast enough to avoid his equally fast jabs, Ransom showed up, and we worked the obstacle course. I was fast. So fast I was a blur, even to me.

The action was the most exhilarating thing I'd ever done. I moved instinctually, my body automatically knowing where to go and when. Running, being fast, it was like magic. Was this my power?

By the end of the training, I could throw, quickly fade into the shadows, put the end of a dart through the eye of a needle —literally—and I could almost harness and restrain enough strength not to make a human look twice.

It was around four when Luke showed up. He knocked on the front door, and even though we were in the backyard, we all heard it. Ten years ago, when I was the queen of gossipy book clubs—I'd belonged to three back then—hearing like this would've been so useful.

Jax answered the door and brought him around back. Luke waved. "Hey, all."

I wasn't sure when I'd been relegated to "all," but I smiled at him anyway. Not that he noticed since he was busy batting his eyelashes at Ransom, and it became clear why I was now a part of the "all."

"What's up?" I moved closer to him.

"I came bearing gifts." He smiled down at me, empty-handed.

"Okay." I chuckled. "Are you hiding them?"

He laughed when I squinched my brow. "I didn't know you wouldn't be home. Your rock-and-roll-all-night status is new, and I'm not quite used to your hours."

He had showered and smelled like he'd spritzed on more than one squirt of cologne. Then again, that could've been my new vampire senses intensifying the scent. His shiny shoes and ironed shirt said he'd spent some time on his wardrobe. He always had.

I didn't mention it, though. That wouldn't have been sisterly. I didn't want him to point out that after working out, I probably looked like a dishrag.

"Sorry. Lead on, big brother."

On the way out of the back yard and across the street, Luke managed to position himself next to Ransom, who kept his side of the conversation to monosyllabic answers.

I unlocked the door, and we all filed in. Entertaining vampires was much easier than humans; I didn't have to offer food or drinks. I didn't miss any of the conversation for it, either.

Luke handed me a basket roughly the size of a hat box. "Ta-da!" He yanked the towel covering it off with an arm flourish that only he or Vanna White could make look regal and not ridiculous. The basket was full of donor bags of blood. "I figured it was like Snickers bars for you now."

"Oh, my." I mentally added Snickers to the list of things I would miss, then smiled at Luke. He really was a good brother. I loved him. "Thank you, but…how?"

"Girl! You remember Mark? The guy who thought every single day was an episode of Survivor?" I didn't, but nodded because Luke's explanations were only going to get more drawn out. "He works at a blood bank."

Jax shook his head. "A blood bank?" I could see the red flag in his mind. Everyone in a ten-mile radius could see the red flag. Everyone but Luke. "You told him about vampires? About us?"

Luke cleared his throat and shook his head. "No. Of course not. I have a personal relationship with Mark." Jax cocked an eyebrow, but Luke waved him off and continued. "He asked why I needed the blood. I didn't answer right away. After a bit, he admitted he already knew about vampires."

Jax's anger was visual—pinched face, narrow eyes, tight line of his lips. The only thing missing was an angry growl.

Luke was still oblivious. "He said he dated a vampire several years ago. Then said something about the vampires trying to compel him to forget about them, but he has a natural resistance to mind control or something like that." Luke looked at Jax, then to me.

Jax breathed in deeply through his nose, which was a total man-move because vampires didn't really need to breathe. He looked at me. "It isn't common knowledge that vampires exist. Not since the hunters supposedly took out the last one."

I didn't know the hierarchy or the lore, or even this history.

Jax leaned against my couch. "Our king is married to a witch who cleans up when someone finds out we're still around who shouldn't have. Do we need to make the call?" He turned to Luke and stared, eyebrow cocked.

"No." I stepped between them and glared at Jax. "Luke said Mark knows. If a vampire tried to compel him, surely you would have known about this."

Ransom nodded. "I remember Mark now. He dated a vampire from another clan that was visiting the area and decided to stay. Adam something. When Adam found his true mate, Paige and I went to wipe Mark's memories. That man has a strong mind. We couldn't take all the memories from him."

Jax relaxed. "This is the same guy?"

Ransom bobbed his head up and down. "Yep. Worked at a blood bank."

Jax gave my brother a hard look. "You got lucky, then. Mark is a trusted human. He is sworn to secrecy. Just as you should be."

Luke pressed his hand to his hips. "I would never do

anything to hurt my sister. I was trying to be helpful, especially after what happened at the club tonight."

Jax whirled around to face me. "What happened?"

I scrunched up my face at his tone, then glared at my big-mouthed brother. Before I could explain, Ransom cut in. "Grey happened, but Hailey handled him perfectly."

Laughing at Ransom's grin, I briefly explained what happened, and that I compelled him. By the time I finished, Jax was laughing. "I guess we don't have to worry about Grey being a problem anymore."

There was a story there, but I decided to ask about it later. I could feel the sun coming up and all my energy draining with it.

CHAPTER EIGHT

THE NIGHT SHIFT at Cleo's started at eight and ran until Tracy finished with her late evening study group. It wasn't much, but I needed the money. Despite Jax's informal request not to go, and his modest pouting, I went anyway.

Cleo was sympathetic. "Was the accident horrible?"

I hated lying, so I kept things vague. "Definitely unexpected."

The sweet woman patted my hand. "Your friend didn't explain your injuries."

"It was nothing, really. A couple of bumps. A bruise or two." I sat in the chair beside her bed, hoping I wasn't being obvious about lying. Cleo was smart, but I didn't know if she knew about vampires or the paranormal and I wasn't going to tell her. "I think I had more internal injuries than external because I slept a lot for the first few days." There, a half-truth because I did sleep for four days.

She furrowed her brow. "But you feel okay now?"

I nodded. "I feel great. Ready to go back to work because sitting around the house is driving me crazy."

Cleo laughed. "Tell me about it. I'm itching to go back to work. If you ask me, physical therapy is moving too slow. Don't even get me started on how Tracy is babying me."

Relieved to finally have the conversation shift, I took the chance to switch the topic around to bounty hunting. "How does it work? Your job. I know the basics because my ex-husband was one, but we really didn't go into the details. I mostly did research for him."

I couldn't ask him directly. That was a call I dreaded. He'd want to come for a visit, see the house, and all that jazz. He always knew when I was lying or hiding something. So, avoidance was the key when it came to Howard. He couldn't come visit me under any circumstances.

She shrugged and motioned to herself, propped in her bed. "It's dangerous. But it's also exciting and adventurous." She giggled. "I went on a date a while back and you should've seen his eyes when I told him I once tracked a skip to Colorado and chased him down a mountain on skis while he shot at me and everyone else on the bunny slope."

She shook her head and smiled. The memory was obviously a fond one. "It was treacherous. And once, I was shopping for groceries at the Bargain Bagger, and I saw my skip walking through the store like she was queen of produce. I yelled, 'Stop! I command you in the name of the law!' She threw a grapefruit at me, so I chased her through the dry goods and tackled her at the deli. The secret was keeping my body between her and the exit. So long as she couldn't get past me, there was nothing stopping me from picking up that collection fee."

This was a woman who was proud of her accomplishments. It reflected in her dark brown eyes as she told the stories.

I could do all that, especially since I was a new brand of invincible and immortal. My training with Jax was helping. After one night, I was already faster, and my reflexes were off the charts. It was so cool.

She yawned a couple of times, so I stood and collected an empty glass from the end table. "You are a woman who knows her business. I'm going to let you sleep now, and we can talk more the next time I'm here."

She nodded, and I helped her move down deeper into her bed. "I'm glad you came back, Hailey."

"I'm glad, too," I whispered.

I flicked off her bedroom light, then shut the door most of the way so the light from the living room wouldn't bother her.

Tracy came home around one-thirty, but I was glad for any time I could work.

She smiled as she hung up her jacket. "How was she tonight? She's been a little moody, kind of depressed. She hates not being able to get out there and track skips and nabbing perps and all that other bounty hunter jargon she's always grumbling about."

"She's good. We talked for a bit then she went to sleep." I couldn't imagine being laid up in bed. "How's her therapy going so far?"

Tracy shrugged, then crossed her arms, rubbed her biceps, and looked at the door to her mother's room. "She's trying, but she gets so unhappy when she realizes it's going to be a while before she's out on the street again making money."

I totally understood that. "She'll get there. I can also help with the therapy if you like. You know, get her up and walking more. I might make it a challenge for her. She seems like the type that loves to be challenged. Lying in bed is not helping her."

Tracy's eyes brightened. "Sure, that would be great, as long as she doesn't overdo it."

"I'll make sure she doesn't." I picked up my bag from the end of the sofa. "I'll see you later."

"Bye and thanks."

When I left Cleo's apartment, I pulled my phone out to call for a ride, but Ransom was already in the parking garage waiting. Because I had to make my lie about the car accident look real, I couldn't exactly drive myself until my car was 'fixed.' That meant I couldn't drive it to work for another week or so.

After I hopped into Ransom's car, we headed straight to Catch and Release to meet Jax. He was adamant that, if I had to go to work, I would meet him to feed when I left. He was being a little overprotective since the Grey incident, even though I'd handled myself quite well. Plus, I was hungry, which wasn't anything really new, it was just a stronger urge since I had only had a sip from the blood basket when I woke this evening.

When I'd had a nice long drink, I found Jax. "Can I catch a ride home with you? Ransom brought me here, but he's occupied again." I glanced at the bar where Ransom was washing glasses while talking to Luke.

"Sure." His deep, smooth voice washed over me. I ignored the shiver of awareness, the tremble when I was near him. We'd spent so much time together lately, I should've been immune, but the man was potent in the way chocolate had been before I was bitten.

We walked out to his car, and he drove us toward home while I tried to think of things to talk about that weren't my training or my hunger for the red stuff.

Fortunately, the ride wasn't long, so I pretended to sing to the radio when no topics for chit chat came to mind. It wasn't until he pulled onto our road that I saw the one thing that made my stomach clench like a cramp. *Brad.*

Well, not him actually. His car and the fact that he was not *in* his car meant he was in *my* house. And how the hell had he gotten in? I had to install a better lock on the door.

The last person in this world I wanted to see was Brad, especially while I was pale-faced and still dressed for work.

What the hell was he doing here? Did the homewrecker kick him to the curb already?

Because Jax noticed everything, he glanced at me. "You okay?"

Big fat liar that I was, I nodded. "Right as rain."

Speaking of which, I turned in the car to face him and to stall. "Can I go out during the day on rainy days?"

He shook his head. "Better not. UV rays are not our friends. Besides, then you'll get your sleep schedule all screwed up. You don't want that."

"No, I guess not." I missed seeing people in the morning, all dressed for work, ready to take on a new day. The only people I saw these days were Jax and his brother and Kendra and mine. Although, seeing Cleo and Tracy was nice.

What I didn't want was to go into the house and talk to Brad, but I couldn't say anything because I didn't want Jax to know my ex was here. Not because he would care, but because I was embarrassed to admit the guy that I hadn't been enough for was inside my dang house. He would ask why, then I would have to answer, and nothing was worse than pointing out my own flaws.

"You want to train for a while?" Jax asked.

Yes. I did. But I couldn't because… Brad. I faked a yawn I didn't feel. "I'll probably turn in early today. First day back at work…" Faked another yawn. "So tired."

If he didn't know I was a liar, he had very low standards for actors. But he nodded, smiled his pretty smile, and climbed out and walked toward his front door. I got out and stood for a couple of seconds watching, because that man had a stride worth noticing.

He disappeared inside his house, and I took a deep breath —for courage—then hurried to my front door. Brad, stretched on the sofa with his shoes on the cushion, snorted a short snore. I could've eaten him. No one would've known. Except me, and probably Jax who wouldn't be too impressed with my self control. Or probably with my selection of dinner menu.

Although, I was pretty fast now. I could bury the body before anyone saw. But I wasn't great at lying. I wonder if Jax would help me with acting lessons.

Instead of killing the cheating good for nothing jerk, I stood over him. Hmm. I thought about eating him for another second, but there were better uses for this one. He was a prime candidate for me to practice my compulsion techniques. A bonus on the front and back end. Front end—practice, back end, I could convince him to go away and never return.

I woke him by shoving his shoe-clad feet to the floor a little rougher than I'd intended because I had vamp strength now.

He startled awake and sat straight up. When he saw me, he gave me a crooked smile. "Hey, babe."

Ugh. I'd never liked that he called me babe instead of my name. It sounded so smarmy.

"Brad." I sat on the coffee table in front of him, looked deep into his eyes and blanked my mind. "You need to move on with your life."

He didn't blink. I had him. "Get over me and be glad I'm happy now."

But he shook his head and his brow wrinkled while he smirked. "What the hell are you talking about? I'm not here because I haven't moved on with my life. I'm here to check on you. Make sure you're not falling apart."

Smug bastard thought I was falling apart? That I needed checking up on? I should've eaten him. But more than annoyed, why hadn't the compulsion worked? It worked at the club with Grey.

"What are you doing here?" I asked, exasperated.

He'd already explained, but as much as I wanted to be a bad mamajamma who wasn't bothered by my ex showing up

—the same ex who'd left me at the altar—he was the reason I'd moved here in the first place. Seeing him at the hospital was too much. Then the random appearances at my place had started, and I had to get out of there.

Now he was here. Please, God tell me he hadn't moved to Philly.

Before I could make my repulsion known, the door burst open and Jax stood in the living room. His eyes flashed, then went dark. Deathly dark. "What in the hell is going on here?"

Oh, holy crap, that was the hottest entrance I'd ever seen. But Brad, being the overstuffed jerk he was, looked up at Jax. "WTF, man?" Yeah. He was the kind of guy who said WTF. He looked at me in indignation. "Who the hell is this guy?"

"Who the hell are *you*?" Jax wasn't giving up information, not because he was private. He was. Not because we didn't have anything to hide. We did. But because he had this whole mystery man vibe, and he was sticking to it.

"I'm her fiancé."

"*Ex*-fiancé," I said fiercely. It was a small correction, but important to me.

Jax made a sound from low in his chest that rumbled in his throat.

Brad pulled his head back and widened his eyes. "WTF, dude. Did you just growl?"

And when the heck did the word *dude* make its comeback? Was I so old I missed it? When had Brad turned into such a douche?

"I'll show you growling!" Jax roared, but I put a hand up to stop him. To his credit, he froze and glowered.

"Hey, could we all put our dicks away and stop trying to measure whose is bigger?" I asked. That was mostly meant for Brad, who always had to be the biggest turd in the room.

But the fool advanced, and Jax cocked his head in a come-and-get-it silent dare.

"Stop!" I stepped in front of Brad and glared. I *definitely* should've midnight-snacked him when I had the chance. "Knock it off."

Then I glanced at Jax and kept my voice low. "Can't you just compel him already? I tried and can't for some reason."

His lip curled in a sneer and his voice stayed low and grumbly. "Gladly."

The growl, like everything else, was sexy enough that I cocked my head. A lesser woman would've pictured him naked. I wasn't lesser, but I was lesser enough to picture him shirtless.

"Tell him to move on with his life and forget me, to think of me fondly, but to move on." Way on. Like into the next life on.

Jax shot me a glare. "I'd rather just eat him."

Yep, me too. But that would've just caused more questions.

I rolled my eyes. His metaphorical dick was still out, and I shot him the girlfriend glare—even though I wasn't his girlfriend. It worked. He spoke softly to Brad, then led him to the door. When they stopped so he could push Brad out, Brad turned, hand extended. "Hailey, I'm so glad to see you happy. It's all I've ever wanted for you."

To my credit, I didn't vomit. I shook his hand instead. Then he turned to Jax.

"You, my man, thank you for taking care of her." He shook Jax's hand and looked at me again. "I think I can move on now. This feels like good closure."

Jax shut the door behind my ex, hopefully for the last time.

Blech. I should've gotten points for not eating him, but since Jax hadn't smiled in a little while, I kept my opinion to myself until he turned to me. He whirled around and glared at me. "Going to bed early?" He faked a yawn, imitating me, and added a ridiculous and awkward stretch that irritated me, because I'd done the move in front of him, and now I knew what it looked like.

I rolled my eyes again, then stalked to my room. He could damn well show himself out. I was tired of it all. I especially didn't want to talk about Brad to Jax.

CHAPTER NINE

Sunset wasn't a time when I'd usually enjoyed coffee, but at least I could drink it. If I mixed a few tablespoons of blood in, it was absolutely delicious. I didn't care if the caffeine didn't affect me like it used to. I loved the rich aroma and bittersweet taste.

I was in the middle of my second sip when I heard footsteps outside. With my coffee in hand, I went to the door and opened it before Jax could knock. His sexy smirk told me he wasn't surprised that I'd known he was there. But he wasn't alone.

Paige was with him, and she seemed anxious about something. Umm, that couldn't be good. "What's up?" I stepped back so they could come in.

Paige paced my front porch, distracted, worried, and completely oblivious to her surroundings.

"What's her problem?" I crossed my arms and watched her

closely. She was much older than me so I was sure I couldn't take her. For that reason, I hoped it wasn't me that pissed her off.

Paige stopped and glared at me for a second before pacing again. "*Her* can hear just fine. My problem is that Zara has a bounty on her head." She stopped pacing again and shook her head. "It's a big bounty."

"So?" Wait, had her bounty grown? "I know she has a bounty. That was why I went after her. Granted, I didn't know at the time she was a vampire."

Paige snarled, fisted her hands, and Jax held his hand up to stop her. "It's better if we discuss this inside."

"Sure." I stepped aside again for them to enter. After making sure no one else was heading over, I closed the door.

Jax went to the kitchen, so I followed, leaving Paige to stew in the living room. He poured himself a cup of coffee and turned to face me. "Zara had a human bounty when she was human. Now, the council has put their own bounty on her."

Paige entered the kitchen and turned her nose up at the coffee. "We're going to be overrun with our kind. Not to mention the human bounty hunters out to collect. More humans and more money-hungry vamps can only mean mayhem or more vamps like you turned because they don't know who they're really going after."

Ah, yeah, I could see where that would be a problem.

Jax, on the other hand, sat down at my kitchen table and picked up the paper. He was calm, like he didn't have a care in the world. "I'm not surprised. Trying to kill a human is big business. Zara should never have been made to begin with.

They'll want her to answer for what she did to Hailey. That is, if Hailey is the only one she tried to kill."

Paige wrinkled her brow and sat in the chair across from Jax.

My mind kept churning over the words 'big bounty.' I could use the money, big or not. Jax pulled a sheet of paper from his pocket and handed it to me. I read over the bond intake form and my mouth fell open. "A hundred grand? I'm in!" No hesitation.

Jax shook his head. "Oh, hell no. Too dangerous."

"You're not the boss of me." I didn't know if that was true or not, but he damned sure wasn't in my own house. I'd been running my own life for about fifteen or so years without help from anyone else. No way was I giving up that independence now. "I'm in."

Besides, I wanted a cut of that money.

He rolled his eyes, and I wasn't sure what it meant. Neither did I care because I was an adult. With superpowers. And fangs! I could do as I darn well pleased.

I could tell he wasn't going to budge on his *hell,* not without a fight. I stared down my maker. "I went after her the first time because I needed the money. That hasn't changed. Especially now that my full-time job is a part time job. But I like Cleo, who happens to be a bounty hunter. My first husband was also one, and I learned a few things from him."

Jax shook his head, but Paige stared at me, slightly nodding as if she was forming a plan. Could she be on my side with this?

Tapping her fingers on the table, Paige said, “You know, she could help.”

“No. It isn’t safe.” Jax took a sip of his coffee and glared at his head enforcer.

“Even you have to admit her training is going far better than any newbie you’ve trained. She's quick and learns just as fast. She doesn’t have to take the case on her own. I’ll be there.” Paige sat back in the chair looking a little more relaxed.

When Jax didn’t reply right away, Paige added, “Besides, if you contact the council and tell them that you have a team on it, they will be less likely to interfere or send their own team. It buys us time.”

Frowning, I wondered why we’d need to buy time, but I didn’t ask. I needed this job. “Plus, I owe Zara for killing me.”

The crazy bitch had taken my choices away from me. I wasn’t sure I would have chosen a life as an immortal vampire. I wasn’t sure I *wouldn’t* have either. However, I wouldn’t give it back now.

A few long moments later, Jax blew out a breath. “Fine. But I’m on the team as well.” He pointed at me with a serious master vamp look. I was betting that was the same as a mom or dad stare.

“You will not go after her alone. We plan everything out. No one takes unnecessary risks.”

“Agreed!” Anything to get him to let me participate.

They left soon after that, and I did a happy dance in the middle of the living room. I was going after Zara with vampire backup. It was me she had tried to kill, after all. I knew just the witch to add to the team. A magical boost to add to the vampire strength would be the cherry on top.

As I walked from my yard to Kendra's, my cell chirped. Luke. "Hello, big brother," I greeted.

"Don't you just sound bright eyed and sparkly fanged." He chuckled at his own joke, tiny as it was. "I have some more blood for you."

Never bad news. "Thanks!"

"I could drop it by."

"Sounds good." That also sounded like an unfinished thought. I didn't have to guess the rest of the idea.

"Maybe you can invite your neighbors? The heartthrobs without hearts?" He loved his plays on words.

"I'm on my way to Kendra's. I'm going to go after a vampire who has a bounty on her head." I grinned, barely holding onto my excitement.

I could practically hear his eyes lighting up. It sounded an awful lot like a half-squeal-half-gasp. "I want to go."

A bit like a begging five-year-old, too.

As much as I loved my brother, I loved him too much to risk his safety. "I'm a vamp, Kendra's a witch. On the food scale, we're right below gods. You're just above mosquito and roadkill."

It wasn't the kindest way to put it, but I needed him to understand I couldn't compromise his safety.

"That's why I would be the perfect bait." Before I could reply, and apologize for hurting his feelings, he hung up, and I sighed.

I wouldn't be hearing the end of this one for a while. But

once I captured Zara, I could buy him something nice—a car, maybe—and he would forgive me.

I walked into Kendra's house and found her lounging on the sofa in pajamas with that Brad Pitt vampire movie on the TV and a glass of wine on the table next to her. She nodded toward the TV. "I was in the mood to interview a vampire. Seemed fitting given how your life has gone recently."

Ignoring her joke, I plopped down. "We're going to work." I filled her in on the bounty. "What do you think?"

"With your super-strength and my spells, we'll have that undead freak picked up in enough time for you to climb into your coffin before the sun barbecues your behind." She tossed her blanket away, clicked off the TV, and downed her glass of wine.

I held up my hands. "Before we get too involved with planning, I agreed to allow Jax and Paige to be on the team. Jax is being weirdly overprotective, and Paige seems to have a score to settle. Or she just wants to catch Zara before the town is overrun with other vampires and humans trying to collect the bounty." I sat down and took a breath.

"No problem," Kendra started, then added, "I can pack some things up and we can go over there to fill them in and come up with a plan. I'll get dressed!"

We packed a bag with rooster toes and eye of newt. Kendra's enhanced spells—she'd been doing research on amplifying spells for vamps—would find Zara, slow her down and disable her, while I swooped in with the enchanted cuffs—who knew?—and together we would haul this big baddy in.

As we were about to head over to Jax's house, the doorbell

rang, and she looked back at me. Of course, I knew who it was. I could smell him. But she peeked out the peephole, then turned to gape at me. "You invited Luke?"

I shook my head. "Invited is not the word I would use. I actually told him no, after I filled him in about the situation." I should have kept my mouth shut. I sighed. "Might as well let him in. He won't go away otherwise."

From outside, he said, "She's right. I won't."

She yanked the door open, and he held out a brown paper bag with a fast-food logo on the side to her and a small donor bag of B-positive to me.

I took mine and she took hers and he breezed in. I loved the smell of crispy, golden fries, and I sniffed the air over her bag. "God, I miss food."

"Shouldn't you burst into flames for saying the Big Guy's name?" He cocked a brow at me and stood back a step as if he expected it still to happen.

I huffed out a fake sigh. "Do I look charbroiled to you?"

He laughed. "You look like vampire Rambo."

I had on a camo jacket and jeans. Kendra was dressed all in black. The nights were chilly in Chestnut Hill, and I needed to look the part, as if the weather affected me, at least.

"What are you doing here?" I added just the perfect amount of boredom into my tone. "I didn't invite you."

"Can't stop me, either." If there was a single word to describe Luke, it was *saucy,* and he lived it.

He was right. Short of using the enchanted cuffs on him, there wasn't much we could do to keep him from following and screwing everything up. Maybe I could get Ransom to distract him long enough for Kendra, Paige, Jax and me to slip out.

I glanced at Kendra. She gave a slight eye roll, and I nodded. "Fine. You can go, but you're not getting a cut of the money."

"Fine." His smile widened. "Let me earn my Ransom. Can you imagine his face when I tell him that little old mortal me caught a big vampire escapee?"

I didn't correct his classification of Zara. I had more important things to do, like figure out how to find this chick.

We were about halfway out the door when Kendra snapped her long fingers. "Oh, Hails! Remember that room where she left us to die?"

It wasn't an image I was likely to forget no matter how old I lived to be. "Yeah."

"I found a necklace there. I kept it. I'm positive it's not yours. I bet it belonged to Zara. We could use it in the locating spell."

There were days luck shone on me, which was fair since the sun could never shine on my skin again. This was one of those days.

CHAPTER TEN

A FEW MINUTES later we were in Jax's dining room with Kendra's witch paraphernalia spread out on the table. The map of downtown Philly was in the center of it all. Paige and a few others stood around the table, watching. I hadn't seen Jax when we got here. According to Paige, he was in his office talking to the council.

Just as Kendra got started on the locator spell, Jax entered the dining room. Our eyes locked as he made his way to me. "Your brother is not going."

"I know that. He's a stubborn ass who wants to be a part of the action." I glanced at Luke at the same time Ransom came in. A smile tugged at my lips. "Maybe Ransom can be Luke's distraction."

Jax's lips twitched. "That can be arranged."

"Got her." Kendra smiled and pointed at the map. "Downtown. Near the club circuit."

Of course. It would be an ideal hunting ground for a rogue vamp. Lots of alleys and a smorgasbord of victims.

Jax pointed at Nash and Grim. "You two start at the north end of the circuit. Paige, Hailey, and Kendra will start at the south. Ransom and Luke will stay here with me and the others."

Luke opened his mouth to protest, but Ransom grabbed his hand and pulled him down a hallway. "We have more important things to do."

I heard something about research and giggled. If it hadn't been for Ransom, Luke would have had a fit about being stuck back at the home base.

Paige grabbed a pair of keys from a hook on the wall beside the garage door. "Come on. Let's go get the bitch."

Kendra and I rushed out the door after the head enforcer. I stopped short when I saw a shiny red sports car. I didn't know brands, but I knew darn well that thing cost more than my annual salary when I worked at the hospital.

Once we climbed in, Paige took off down the street, tires squealing as she took the corners. I laughed all the way while Kendra looked a little green.

At least we didn't have to worry about getting pulled over. Paige would just compel the officer to forget he saw us.

We hit the first club on the street. Club 36. I didn't know what the number was about, but the entire place was strobe lights, loud music and grinding hips. My sensitive vampire hearing was begging me to leave. The music in combination with the people inside the club yelling over it hurt my ears.

Paige slipped something into my hand and leaned in to

speak into my ear. "These will protect your hearing from the club noise and serve as a radio."

"Oh cool. Thanks!" I opened my hand to see tiny earpieces. When I slipped them into my ears, I sighed in pleasure. The music was silenced to a tolerable level.

Zara's scent filtered through the crowd, and I snarled. I'd know that scent anywhere. "She's here."

Paige and Kendra asked at the same time, "You sure?"

Their voices came through the earpieces like stereo. "Yeah. I'll never forget that cheap knock-off perfume she wore when she killed me."

I followed her scent to the back of the club with Paige and Kendra on my heels. We found her with her head buried in the neck of some poor sap who probably thought he was getting lucky but was likely one or two breaths from death already.

She looked up, and our gazes connected. I glared at her, wanting to knock that smug look off her face. She knew as well or even better than we did that while inside a club with so many humans our hands were tied. Kendra couldn't throw a spell, and I couldn't use my vampire speed or strength to get to her. Because we were law-abiding vampires.

Zara, not so much, because she took off at vamp speed. She wasn't at all worried that the guy whose neck she was sucking on was about to bleed out on the floor or that people could see her vamping.

Freaking great.

I stopped and healed the bite mark then knelt in front of him. "You're feeling ill. You must've eaten some bad chicken.

Go home, drink a sports drink and rest. You'll feel better in the morning."

Kendra and Paige stood around me so the crowd wouldn't gather. Through our earpieces, Paige gave orders to Nash and Grim.

By the time I finished making sure the rogue's victim would live, Zara was gone. I glanced at Kendra. The three of us hurried out of the club at human speed, but the rogue skip was nowhere to be found. It was like she'd vanished into thin air.

I looked at Kendra. "Did we bring the necklace? The map?"

She shook her head. "Sorry."

It wasn't her fault any more than it was mine. "No big deal. We'll head back and try again."

Although, it was getting late. Dealing with my brother and his antics and filling our supply bag, scrying for Zara's location, then finding her in the crowd, had all taken longer than I realized. But the sun was about an hour from rising.

Boy, was I feeling it.

As we pulled into Jax's driveway the front door opened and Jax and Luke rushed out.

Jax opened my door and pulled me out. "What happened?"

"She got away." I was too tired to explain and hungry. I hadn't eaten all night except for one blood bag with my evening coffee.

I turned and walked across the street to my house, hoping I made it inside before I dropped into a vamp coma.

"Hailey, stop!"

I did, but only after I got my door open. Jax crossed the space between in a flash. I looked up into his eyes and gave a weak smile. "We failed. I failed. She got away. But can we talk about it later tonight? I need to eat before the sun comes up."

Jax motioned for me to go inside. When I did, he followed, closing the door behind us. "Why haven't you eaten?"

"Forgot?" I walked to the refrigerator and pulled out a couple of blood bags. "You guys came over with the news about Zara, and I got distracted wanting to catch her."

I popped the bag into my mouth, let my fangs puncture it and blood rush into my mouth and down my throat. A sigh slipped from me as I drank.

"You shouldn't go so long without feeding." Jax leaned against my kitchen counter, watching me.

I rolled my eyes because if I removed the bag, blood would go everywhere. That would be a waste and a mess I didn't have time for.

When the bag emptied, I removed it and tossed it into the trash bin. "I said I didn't do it on purpose. Anyway, Zara was in a human club. So, we couldn't do anything to bring too much attention. Meanwhile the rogue vamp was sucking some poor guy dry right there!"

I started to give him a play by play, but he handed me another bag. "Finish that one and go to bed. I'll get the details from Paige."

He waited for me to finish the second bag. After tossing the bag in the trash, I said. "I feel like I failed tonight. We jumped the gun a little."

"You think?" Jax's tone was teasing even though he didn't smile at me. He didn't smile a lot. Always the serious vampire master. I was learning to read his body language and his eyes to see what his mood was. Right then, he was concerned but relaxed.

"Do you feel the effects of the sun?" I asked.

His eyes snapped to mine, then he studied my face, reading me as I was him. "Not as much as you. I can stay up all day if I want to. Then again, I'm older than dirt."

I snorted then slapped my hand over my mouth while laughing. His joke had taken me by surprise. It was unexpected. When I was able to breathe without laughing, I said, "I'm sure you are not *that* old."

He smiled then, and it felt like I leveled up somehow. "Maybe not. The point is, as you age you will not be ruled completely by the sun. I can't tell you when because it's different for everyone."

I nodded, and we fell silent again. As tired as I was getting, I was enjoying Jax's company, this little bit of private time we were currently sharing. "So, what's our next step with Zara?"

"I'm not going to get you to walk away from this, am I?" he asked.

"Nope," I said, popping the *P* in the word.

He sighed and stepped closer. "I know for a fact that Paige is at home handing out assignments. At nightfall, she will have enforcers and scouts out gathering information on Zara. We need to learn her routine and set a trap."

Wow. I should hang out with Paige more often. She could

teach me a few things. "Okay, so I should ask her what she needs me to do?"

Jax nodded.

After a pause, he said, "I'll give you money if you need it."

His voice was soft and gentle, but I wasn't a woman who wanted to be cared for by a man. A woman who wanted him to swoop in with his cape and fangs and bail me out of my money trouble.

"I don't want your money." There was a sharpness to my tone I didn't mean. I sighed before continuing. "I'll work for my money. I've already been thinking about getting into bounty hunting and catching human skips that would be super easy now that I have all this power."

He was silent for a few long seconds. "I would be okay with that." Softer, almost in a whisper, he added, "But I still want to give you some money. To tide you over."

"Jax…" I didn't want to sound ungrateful. "Why? Why would you want to give me money?" Then it occurred to me. "Because you made me?"

He nodded once. "As your sire, I'm obligated to take care of you."

At least he took his obligations seriously. Even if a part of me had hoped he was doing it out of concern. "I'm an adult, Jax, even if I'm a baby vampire. You can help me learn how to be a vampire, but you're off the hook for everything else. Deal?"

He simply nodded, but I could tell he wanted to argue.

"Deal, but only if you will agree that if you so much as get your lights shut off, I'm giving you a monthly allowance."

"Deal." An allowance? Did he think of himself as my parent?

He leaned down until we were almost nose to nose. Did vampires ever get bad breath? Not that Jax ever would... "My obligation to you has nothing to do with being your maker."

Then he left. I stood in my kitchen breathless and confused. What the hell did that mean?

CHAPTER ELEVEN

THE SOUND of my phone ringing non-stop woke me from a dead sleep. Pun intended. *No, I know I haven't been asleep all day.*

Rolling over, I grabbed my phone and checked the time before even seeing who it was. 3:00 p.m. Someone had better be bleeding, or I was going to vamp out on them.

I answered because I was awake now. "Hello?"

If I sounded snippy, that was on them. As a human, I hadn't liked middle of the night calls. As a vampire whose nights came during the day, I liked them even less.

"Hey! It's me." Kendra sounded excited. Oh goody. "I've located Zara and have been checking in on her all day. Before you ask, yes, I can do that. Anyway, she is holed up in an apartment building on Vine Street."

She sounded like she'd drank a few more than normal

espressos. "If we can get there in daylight, we could catch her while she's sleeping."

"Great, but I've given up my daylight walking rights." At the moment, I was bitter about it.

"It might be worth asking Jax if it is possible for you to go out." Seriously, how much caffeine had she had?

"Fine." I growled, low and guttural, then hung up. I already knew the answer, but it really was a good opportunity to catch this rogue.

Yeah. Because talking to Jax was exactly what I wanted to do. Except it wasn't. Of course, it had to be today that we had a hard line on Zara's location during daylight hours. I had to be a vampire, so the sunlight was no longer a friend.

Some midlife this was.

I dialed Jax's number, staring at the ceiling while I waited for him to answer. Like me, he was sleeping—or should've been, but he answered right away. "Hailey? Are you okay?"

The concern in his voice touched me more deeply than I was willing to admit. I still didn't know what he meant about feeling obligated to me, and it had nothing to do with being my maker. I really didn't want to think about it too hard.

"I have a line on Zara, a place where she's staying right now. But I kind of need to go right now." In case he was confused, I added, "In the daylight. Is that possible?"

It probably wasn't. Probably being a vampire was going to cost me my portion of a hundred grand. Just another thing lost to being a creature of the night.

"Yeah. You'll need to wear long sleeves, and gloves." He

paused. "Every inch of exposed skin has to be covered and shaded. Do you have a wide brimmed hat?"

"I think so." It wasn't Rose from Titanic wide, but it was fit for a Mint Julep at the Kentucky Derby.

"Get ready and I'll be there to get you shortly."

I hadn't invited him along, but I couldn't very well refuse the help, either. "Fine."

I hung up and shot a text to Kendra and Luke. **Get ready! It's on!**

A second later my phone pinged.

LUKE: Bitch, please! I'm already at Kendra's. You get ready!

I yawned twice. I had become a day sleeper and it was daytime—the equivalent to three in the morning if I were still a human. I'd always been a morning person, but this was too early when I still had a few hours before the sunset.

I hurried to the closet and rooted through the boxes and bags until I found the hat. Then I rooted around for my winter gloves and other things that would cover every inch of my skin. I looked absolutely ridiculous. It beat being deep fried by the sun.

I hated answering the door when I looked like a case study from "What Not to Wear," but Jax and everyone else was going to see me soon enough.

Yet, I need not have worried because I wasn't the only vampire who needed a fashion consult. Jax stood on my covered porch wearing a cowboy hat, pants tucked into his motorcycle boots, leather gloves and a long-sleeved gray button down. "Ride 'em, cowboy!" I crowed.

It slipped out before I could censor myself.

He laughed. "Better than pan seared."

I moved back, still giggling about my outburst and his outfit. "I don't feel bad about the way I'm dressed now."

He faced me with amusement in his features. "Listen, we can be in the sun completely covered for about fifteen minutes. Less is ideal because at sixteen, even covered, the blisters come. Longer than that…" He shook his head and mimed an explosion. "Not exactly blown apart but burst into flames. If you go out with bare skin, you have three minutes, max."

That was comforting. "You are just a ray of sunshine...er moonshine? No, that's a drink. Moonbeams."

He chuckled. "Are you done?"

"Yeah. I need coffee." I turned to the kitchen, but Jax gripped my arm and pulled me to the door.

"No time. We need to catch her while she's asleep. Plus, the caffeine doesn't affect you anymore." I hated that he was right.

We walked out of the house and ran to the SUV. The windows were tinted dark, and I sat in the back row of seats. Jax was next to me. A large black duffel sat on the passenger side of the back seat, so Jax and I were hip to hip and shoulder to shoulder.

My skin prickled, and I took a deep breath. Being so near him had dizzying effects on my body. Lord, he smelled so good. I almost leaned in for one of those long, deep inhales, but caught myself.

Paige was in the driver seat with Ransom riding shotgun.

Kendra and Luke sat in the middle row and were the only two who looked normal.

I was so jealous. They were the only ones in the car not dressed like confused clowns without makeup. Kendra looked at me over her shoulder and smirked.

Another yawn fluttered out of me, and my eyelids drooped another fraction closer to closed.

Paige took off and drove straight to the apartment building. It was close to Luke's gallery, and he directed us into the hidden parking garage under the building. Smooth sailing so far.

We hit the elevator and rode up to the apartment she'd rented in her own name. Hey, I didn't say she was the smartest skip out there.

Kendra used a spell to unlock the door and we entered, silent and determined. But we could've stampeded in like the bulls in Pamplona and no one would've cared, because the place was empty. Didn't that just figure?

Because she didn't make the same mistake twice, Kendra pulled out her map of the city and the necklace before she began to scry.

When the necklace landed twice more in the same spot, Paige clicked her tongue against her teeth. "Is there a way to narrow it down? If she's here, she has to be in a different apartment."

Ransom, the man of very few words, spoke. "We could check to see if there are any vacant apartments. Maybe she uses one of those as her sleep space."

Jax nodded and slapped Ransom on the shoulder as he

walked back into the room from wherever he'd been searching. "Right. She's new, so she'll be tired."

I could testify to that and swallowed another yawn only for it to escape a second later.

"Easier to sneak up on," Jax said as he eyed me.

I went to the kitchen. There were times a girl needed to just act for herself. This was one. I needed caffeine, and I wasn't leaving without it. It didn't matter if it didn't work on me like it did when I was human. I had to try.

I rifled through the cabinets until I found a collection of coffee pods to fit in the machine next to the stove. I walked over and clicked it on.

"What are you doing?" Jax's voice, gentle and kind, on any other occasion would've elicited some not so annoyed response, but fatigue made me grouchy.

"I'm making coffee." To my credit, I didn't add *Einstein.*

"For whom?" Who did he think?

"For me. You wouldn't let me make any at the house, and I figured we had a few minutes to kill." I raised a brow at him, and he just shook his head as he walked off.

Kendra hung up her phone. "All right. They have two units open. One on the top floor, and one just above the garage on the ground floor, which is actually just below the ground. No windows. Much cheaper than this baby, let me tell you."

"That's gotta be it." I said as I came out of the kitchen with a travel mug I'd found in the cabinet full of rich, sweet, *amazing* coffee.

As a group, more like a stampede than like a bunch of covert bounty hunters trying to sneak up on a skip, we filed into the elevator, and I leaned my head back against the wall and didn't move until the doors opened and we started into the downstairs hallway.

Kendra led because she knew the apartment number and because she had to unlock the door. But we might have just as well stayed upstairs since this place was empty, too.

The ride to the penthouse was longer, and because I was so mercifully still, I snoozed a bit, until Jax nudged me with his elbow. "Are you seriously sleeping standing up?"

He was losing his hotness factor in the daylight. "I'm an infant. We need our sleep."

He chuckled, and I let my eyes fall shut again. The beauty, aside from resting, was my body continued taking unnecessary breaths, and with each one I got a big whiff of Jax. There were benefits to having him along.

When Kendra opened the door, we spread out in the apartment and Jax waved me over when he opened a closet door. There she was. Sleeping like a mean-ass rogue baby. Blanket over her. Hair splayed on the pillow like she had a lover coming to wake her and she wanted to be beautiful.

"How do we get her out of here?" It was a reasonable question, but Kendra gave me a side-eye.

"Concealment spell. We went over this, Hails."

"Infant with zero memory," I snarled, amending the description of myself for Jax's benefit because my need for caffeine or sleep overpowered my kindness gene.

Zara jerked awake and stared up at us from one to the next, because we were all in her sleeping space, and it was probably a bit startling. When she got to me, she smirked. "I thought I killed you."

I growled, and Jax put a calming hand on my shoulder. "I saved her. You *almost* killed her."

She sighed. "Sorry about that."

No, she wasn't. I narrowed my eyes. "Worst. Apology. Ever."

It was like she didn't give a damn that she ruined all my bucket list plans. No vacation in Cabo so a cabana boy could rub lotion on my back. No hike through the Grand Canyon. No Teacup ride or stay at the Cinderella castle. She was lucky I didn't stake her and take my chances with landing on someone else's skip list.

"Right?" Luke sidled closer to me and threw a protective arm around my shoulders. "You're going down, girl. No one messes with my sister and gets away with it."

"Come on. I would like to get back to bed sometime today." I wanted to cuff her and drag her out into the sunlight, but probably only because I was so tired. Maybe, once I had a nap, I might've been kinder.

Jax shot me a questioning glance with a scrunched brow and pinched lips. I shrugged and yawned.

We brought her to the car unhindered by human or vampire involvement. Considering the bounty on Zara's head, that was quite the feat, in my opinion, which no one seemed to care about since they all wanted to throw questions at Zara. They essentially each asked the same question—Why?—in different words.

She slumped, defeated. "I was bitten, turned, then left

alone. Abandoned. I didn't know what to do. I was scared and so hungry." Hell, right then she was licking her lips and eyeing Luke's throat like it was T-Bone. She snapped out of it when I poked her and glared. "I don't want to kill anyone again. I know it's not right, but I can't fight it."

Bloodlust. That was the only explanation I could come up with. Jax had told me that was how most vamps turned rogue. They gave into the hunger and fed so much that they became addicted to the blood and the kill.

Even though she didn't say as much, I knew it was true. So did Jax. I glared at Zara again. Jax was my maker, and I wasn't in the mood to share with her. She could tough it out or find someone else, and damned sure, she could stop watching him with all that blatant interest flickering in her eyes.

Paige pulled the SUV into my driveway. Thankfully, the sun was low in the sky. I ditched the hat and Jax nodded. "I'll take her back with me. I have a dungeon I can keep her in."

Of course. What vampire master wouldn't be complete without a dungeon. "What now? You have a what?"

He laughed. "Not a dungeon exactly. Just a light-tight place where I can keep baby vamps or ones who've gone rogue. As the eldest US vampire—"

"I thought you said you weren't an elder." I was sure he'd told me that.

"I'm not an elder. I'm the eld*est*." A distinction without a difference? But no. "Elders are the…council, for lack of better word. I'm the oldest vampire in the United States, so I'm in charge." When my eyes went wide, he shook his head. "There aren't that many of us left in the states. We're international...more European since that TV show came out and every American with a saltshaker and silver cross likes the idea of Winchestering us."

American or not, I liked that he was catching up on his pop-culture references. "Oh. Still, glamorous."

"Not really. It only sounds cool that I have the title of eldest."

"So, you're the King of America? Does that make me a princess?" I was already picturing my tiara.

But he rolled his eyes. "I'll get in touch with my maker to arrange the hand-off and for the bounty."

He walked Zara from my house to his, and I watched because tired or not, he had a walk that deserved appreciation.

Ransom and Paige turned to follow, then Luke hugged me close and said, "That is one sexy vampire."

"Yeah," I replied.

I was over this entire day. And even though I was about to be richer, it was going to have to wait until I finished my nap.

CHAPTER TWELVE

My nap took me well into Friday evening, and I woke up starving. My fangs fully out, poking into my lower lip, and I had a vague recollection of dreaming about blood. Jax had been there.

What the heck?

My stomach cramped. That was when I remembered I'd slept through Thursday night *and* all day today. I'd only had two bags of blood while talking with Jax in my kitchen. Talk about sleeping like a baby.

On that note, I needed blood. Now.

Out of habit, I reached for my glasses on the bedside table and slipped them on. Instead of becoming clearer, the world went blurry, and I took them off. Put them back on, then off again.

Holy crap, I could see. Without glasses.

I wasn't sure why I hadn't noticed before now, other than

my life since turning into a vampire had been one distraction after another.

But I could see. Everything. Every speck of dust, and every fallen hair that had ever fallen from my brush to the carpet. I needed to clean, geez, but first, I needed a minute to revel in my perfect vision. 20/20 baby.

I was starving. I had just enough time to drink some of the gifted blood bags from Luke before I showered, getting ready for my shift at Cleo's.

When I finished, I sighed. I was probably going to be hungry again in an hour since I went almost a whole night without feeding. I didn't need to be tempted to suck on my patient's neck. So, I put a couple bags into a lunchbox before I left for work.

When I arrived at Cleo's, I put the bag into the fridge and went to check on her.

I knocked once and slowly opened Cleo's bedroom door. "Hey."

"You have a little something…" She swiped her finger over her own lips and when I did mine, I pulled back a smear of blood from my hand.

"Must've bit it." I averted my eyes, focusing on the carpet.

"What big teeth you have today. I hope you're not planning on eating me. I'm not Red Riding Hood." She laughed, but the humor never quite reached her eyes.

I chuckled, too, but this was as close to being discovered as I'd been, and I wasn't sure I could ensure her safety if she knew for certain what I was. But how could she possibly know what I was? Most supernatural creatures didn't even know vampires existed anymore.

I excused myself and went to the kitchen because sure enough, I was hungry already. I warmed my blood and poured it into a mug—less conspicuous, and less savage than drinking from the bag.

I caught movement from the corner of my eye and jumped when Cleo walked into the room. Hey! She was walking.

"What are you doing?" I shook my head but beamed at her. "I'm happy to see you moving, but why are you up?"

"The therapist gave me the green light. Obviously, I'm not running marathons, but..." She shrugged and moved her feet from side to side, then front to back.

"Well, now you're just showing off." My smile this time was guarded. As happy as I was for her, I had half a mug of blood behind me.

It was a big accomplishment. A woman like Cleo—vibrant and athletic—wasn't meant to be stuck in bed recuperating. I was glad to see her up and about.

She waved her hand in front of her face. "Yeah, yeah. Enough about me. Are you a vampire?"

Holy crap. "Psh. What?" I danced from one foot to the other. "*What*? Vampire? No. No!"

"Are you lying?" She eyed the empty blood bag still on the counter. Ah, crap.

I followed her line of sight and dropped my shoulders. "Yeah. That's me being a big fat liar. How do you know about vampires?"

I thought we weren't common knowledge. The story that'd

been passed around was that the supposed last vampire was killed by a hunter. Vamps had lived in secret since.

"Oh, come on. I've been around the block a time or two." When I cocked my eyebrow, she laughed. "I dated a witch once."

"Wow. The supernatural world isn't as secret as I thought it was."

"How long?" she asked.

"My 'car accident,'"—air quotes—"was more of a blood draining, then a guy bit me to save me kind of thing."

Cleo nodded. "Yeah. You didn't look much like you'd been in an accident when you came back to work."

She was right. I looked stronger than ever.

She sat at the table, and I pulled out her stash of cookies to set them in front of her. She chewed thoughtfully. "I wondered at the change to night shifts."

"Yeah. Now, I have to find something to make up the income. I thought I would try my hand at bounty hunting." I shrugged. "Once you're on the go again, you won't need me here."

She nodded. "It's good money, and there's always some butthead who thinks he's smarter than the hunter so…steady work isn't ever an issue."

"I'm super strong now. Fast. Give me a cape, and I'm Superwoman." I flexed a deceptively pathetic-looking muscle in my arm.

I eyed my patient. "Anyway. I was thinking we could partner up. You have the connections. My friend Kendra has a serious location spell, and I have the brute strength." Not something I ever thought I would say. "What do you think? We could tackle twice the skips as a team as you can alone."

"But I would have to split the money." Cleo cocked her head as if she were thinking about it.

"But the earning potential is greater because with all three of us, we could work faster. Haul in more bail jumpers and larger bounties." I'd heard Howard use the phrase a few times.

She considered me with her head cocked. "Right now, I need the help."

I didn't nod or move. I just sat and waited with bated breath.

"All right. I'm in." She held out her hand, and I gave it a solemn shake.

With the pressure off, we sat and chatted about what it meant to be a vampire until Cleo was tired and went to bed. She was better but still not at full strength. It would take a while.

When Tracy came home, I left and headed to my neighborhood, but instead of going to my own house, I went to check in with Jax. I was thirsty and almost out of Luke's gift bags. I thought, hoped, we could head to the club for a drink.

I didn't need him going with me, but I wanted him to. He was nice to be around.

I knocked and Ransom opened the door, a pained scowl on his face. Tension rolled off him, and I frowned. Oh God. What was I walking into?

I stepped further inside, and he shut the door behind me. Jax sat stiffly on a chair opposite a man I'd never seen before. They both stood when I entered the room, old-fashioned style.

The man looked Italian with dark hair and eyes. He was well built but not grossly muscular, wearing a well-tailored suit.

Paige stood on the other side of the door by Ransom, like they were on guard duty.

"Um, hi?" I wasn't usually tentative when greeting anyone, but the air in the room was tight and tense and my usually bubbly self wouldn't have fit in with this lot.

I really wanted to just leave, but I was there, and the new guy had already seen me.

Jax stared at me for a second, then extended his hand to me. "Hailey, this is Dominic." He paused for the space of a second, then lowered his voice and added, "My maker."

Dominic motioned to the seat beside Jax. "Please. Sit. Join us." He spoke in a Scottish accent. It would've been sexy if he wasn't so intimidating.

He was cool. No. He was *cold.* Very formal with a deep voice and pale, olive-toned skin. If Anne Rice based her characters on real guys, this dude was Lestat. He reached to pick up a duffel beside his chair. "The bounty."

He tossed it so it landed between me and Jax. I looked at Jax, and he nodded like I'd asked if I could open it. If there was some sort of honor system for vampires, a trust in one another, I wasn't privy to such details yet. Nor did I care. I might have been a hundred-percent vampire, body-wise, but my trust instincts were still a hundred percent human. And American.

I pulled back the zipper, and my eyes widened. I'd never seen a hundred grand in person and had no idea how many stacks of bills it would take, but there were a *lot.* Different denominations. Stacks of tens, twenties, fifties, even some ones.

"No worries. I can get it laundered." Jax's voice was calm, like normal people sitting around in their living rooms with their makers and discussing washing the filth off duffle bags filled with cash.

I was not of the same opinion. To me it was a big deal, and I was sure my wide eyes and pinched brow said what my words didn't.

Jax cleared his throat. "How was your trip over from Scotland?"

"The air strip,"—Dominic looked at me as if I'd asked another question. "The elders have a private air strip in Edinburgh, and we schedule flights to land after dark to avoid suspicion when we are unloaded if we travel by coffin."

His voice had the lilt of a Scotsman with a bit of an English purr. I loved accents and could recognize most. I could tell an Italian from a French, from a Spanish, from an Irish and Scottish. Sometimes, I could even mimic them if I tried hard.

But I had to say *travel by coffin* didn't sound nearly as appealing as window seats and first-class flutes of champagne. Of course, my days of flying commercial were likely over.

I nodded at Dominic as he continued speaking to Jax, but I ignored their conversation, instead adding another item to the things being a vampire had taken from me.

Dominic looked at me. "The elders thank you for your part in apprehending Zara."

I didn't know what to say so I nodded.

He shook his head. “That was a bit of distasteful business we’re happy to have squashed.”

Squashed? I didn’t ask because Jax laid his hand over mine and gave a squeeze, then pulled away. Either he wanted me to be unable to find words because he’d touched me, thereby wreaking havoc on my thought processes, or he was trying to tell me to shut up, which he didn’t have to worry about because of the first thing.

“Do you have to go back right away?” Jax spoke when my words failed. He stared at Dominic, and I wasn’t sure which answer would make him happier.

Dominic shook his head. “No. I’ll be staying in your quaint little town for a couple days.”

Quaint little town? He sounded like a posh British ass.

Paige stepped forward. “Hailey, what do you say we go get a drink and let these guys catch up?”

“Sure.” I stood and walked outside with her, glad to have the excuse to leave. Plus, my stomach was gnawing at me.

I was three steps from the curb when I realized I’d forgotten my purse. It was on the sofa next to Jax. “Hang on. I’ll be right back.”

I opened the door and went to get Ransom’s attention but stopped when Dominic spoke. “I hope he won’t be a problem.”

I didn’t mean to listen, but Dominic wasn’t whispering, and the house had straight lines that allowed sound to carry. Especially arrogant Scottish sounds.

“No, that’s all ancient history. I’m sure he’s going to avoid me while he’s here.” Even from a room away, it was as easy to picture Jax's confidence as it was to hear it in his voice.

"Good. That's settled then."

I wondered who they were talking about, but I didn't know enough about Jax to know who or what was all ancient history.

Deciding to leave the purse, because there was no way I wanted to face Dominic again, I walked outside, unnoticed, and to the car where Paige waited to take me to Catch and Release.

As I climbed in and buckled up, Paige started the car. After she'd driven a mile or so, she spoke. "We'd hoped to get Zara out of here before Dominic learned about you."

I wasn't sure why it mattered, but she continued. "Now, we have to hope Jax can convince him to keep it quiet."

"Why?"

Paige shot me a glance. "Turning new vampires is against our laws." Jax had told me that much. "There is a process each human has to go through, and the Elders need to be aware of the potential turnee and approve them." Paige frowned.

My stomach soured. "So, Jax broke the law when he turned me."

Why would he take such a risk? Why me?

We spent long enough at the club for me to have a couple of drinks, then she dropped me at home. I wasn't in the mood for partying, just needed to feed. After unlocking my door, I stopped short when I opened it.

At first, I wondered if Brad had come back to annoy me. But it wasn't Brad sitting on my sofa. It was Dominic.

He rose grandly. "Miss Whitfield." When he added a bow, I cocked my head. "I was rather hoping you would like to go to dinner with me tomorrow night."

"Do we eat dinner?" As far as I knew we couldn't. The water I drank when I first woke as a vamp hadn't stayed down. Then again, I was now able to drink coffee.

He chuckled. "Among our kind, *dinner* is said as a polite word for hunting."

"Uh...I don't, that is, I haven't…" Hunting wasn't really something I wanted to do, but I needed to learn, I supposed. "Sure. I'd love to go to dinner with you. Tomorrow…tonight?"

Way to show you're a newbie vamp, Hailey.

There was no way I could go now because there was only about an hour left before sunrise.

"Splendid." He swept past me and out my front door.

Yeah. Maybe for him. He wasn't the one who had to tell his maker he was going to dinner with me.

CHAPTER THIRTEEN

I WALKED into Cleo's the next night, and she was already waiting for me, a stack of pages in her hand. "I printed out some skips I think you can capture easily. They're cases I've had trouble tracking down, and they have higher payouts."

Oh, nice. "Yeah?"

I took the stack and read a few reports. There were a couple of assault suspects, a retail theft, but an assault with a deadly weapon was the one I stopped to read more completely.

The woman had a couple of kids and lived in the area. By all accounts—at least by the one who'd signed the bond sheet on the woman's behalf—this woman was a good mother.

"I don't think she would leave her kids. Doesn't strike me as the type," Cleo said, noticing which one I was reading.

If that was the case, shouldn't she have been able to find this woman?

As if she could read my mind, she shook her head. "But I've never been able to pin her down."

"Maybe if we work together..." Kendra would need something personal of the woman's. I glanced at the paperwork. "It says they sent over her watch and cell phone?"

Cleo nodded and walked slowly into the other room, then came back a few minutes later with a plastic bag marked with the woman's name. "She was in such a rush to leave the police station so she could run out on her bond that she forgot her junk."

"Her loss is Kendra's scrying tool." I pulled out my phone called Kendra, tapping my foot as I waited for my best friend to pick up. When she did, I filled her in. "So, if you can meet us here, maybe we can track her down."

"I'll be right over," she said excitedly. "Text me the address."

When she arrived with her city map, Cleo and I sat back and watched. It didn't take long. Once Kendra had a location, I nodded at Cleo. "Isn't that just something?"

We both nodded in glee. "That witch I dated didn't know the business end of her broom." She laughed at her little play on words. "No way would she have been able to figure out this kind of magic. Didn't have any Houdini Hardware whatsoever."

I didn't bother correcting her that Houdini was a magician who relied on sleight of hand and illusion. What Kendra did was a whole other ballgame.

Cleo sat up. "Okay, you two. I'm fine here. You go get that woman and make us some money. Assault with a deadly should be about a fifteen-grand bounty. I'll take twenty percent off the top as a finder's fee."

Fine by me. We wouldn't have even thought of doing this without Cleo. Of course, if not for Cleo and this job, I'd still be human, but still.

She looked again at the address Kendra had written out. "But that's a sketchy part of Philly, so you gals are going to want to be careful."

She picked up her purse and pulled out a stun gun, a pair of cuffs, a pen light, and a pistol. I took the cuffs and Kendra took the stun gun. We ignored the actual gun.

I looked at Kendra who was already staring wide-eyed at me. "Wow. What do you think?" I was pretty excited.

She grinned. "I'm not worried. I've got a vampire guarding my body and a taser if my vamp gets lazy." She chuckled. "What do you think? Feeling strong?"

Confidence rushed through me, along with excitement and a surge of adrenaline. "I can handle myself."

Plus, I'd been training in all my overnight hours with Jax.

"All right then." Cleo nodded. "What are you waiting for? Call me when you have her in custody."

She made it all sound so easy, but I was a bundle of nervous energy. I climbed into Kendra's Prius and studied the booking sheet while she backed out and put us on the road to the address.

Cleo wasn't lying when she said the neighborhood was seedy. Broken and boarded windows were featured on every building on the street, and the graffiti on the house fronts seemed to be the new numbering system.

Kendra pulled in front of a small apartment building, shut off the car, and clenched the wheel with both hands. "We're doing this?"

"You bet we are. We're going to kick some felon bail-jumper butt." My optimism lacked the enthusiasm of true belief, but it was enough to spur her into action.

She climbed out and waited for me to gather our supplies from where we'd stowed them in the console. I handed her the taser then tucked the cuffs into my waistband, one dangling over the top.

We knocked on the apartment door and Kendra called out, "Pizza delivery."

A woman with long, curly hair pulled the door open and stood in a velvet jogging suit from a bygone era for about half a second before she tried to shut the door.

Not so fast, lady. She couldn't get it shut faster than I could move. I pushed my way in and backed her toward a disgusting gold sofa with stained cushions and a flat pillow back.

That was all it took. She sat heavily and buried her head in her hands. "How did you find me?" She huffed out a breath, and neither Kendra nor I answered. "Please. I have little kids who need me."

"You just have to go downtown and arrange for a new bond," I said. "You'll be out and able to go home by morning."

It was how Cleo had explained the process. She'd also said telling skippers how it worked sometimes was enough to convince them to come peacefully with us.

The woman sighed. "Please!" A tear slipped down her cheek followed immediately by a flood of them. I believed her and looked at Kendra.

"Maybe we should let her go," I mouthed at my best friend.

Kendra looked sympathetic. I'd half made up my mind to pretend we'd never found this woman before she pulled a knife from between the cushions and made a wide, slicing arc through the air in my direction.

"Are you freaking kidding me right now?" I shook my head and dodged her second attempt to end me with her kitchen knife.

Not that it would end me, but it would piss me off.

She wasn't getting a third chance. I took the knife and forced her down. It was…easy. I hadn't had a chance to measure my strength against a human. Jax was stronger than me. Paige and Ransom were stronger. But no human was going to overpower me, for sure.

More than marveling at my own strength—impressive as it was—I was tired of dealing with this woman. I wanted to be finished with her, collect the bounty, and bask in the glory of it.

Without much more fanfare, we loaded the trussed-up woman into the Prius and drove to the precinct closest to the apartment building. Skips could be turned in at any station since the warrants issued were statewide.

Once I had the recovery verification slip in hand, I called Cleo. "We did it!"

"I knew you could!" Her excitement rang through the phone.

The only other thing I needed to know was where to go to collect the money. I was pretty sure we couldn't just pop into the ATM vestibule and expect a payout. "Now what do we do?"

She rattled off an address downtown. "The front door will be open, but Jordan will be asleep in the back room. Hit the bell on the counter until he comes out. He'll take care of you. Just tell him I sent you."

I didn't want to trust some random stranger with our money. Especially since it was so much. "Who is this guy?"

"Only the best in the business. He trained me." She sniffed. "Mostly, he's retired now, but he used to go after the skips, and no one *ever* got away from Jordan." There was a note of hero-worship in her voice. "He trained me to be the hunter I am today."

All right. If he was good enough for Cleo, he was good enough for me.

Kendra drove us to the address, and we walked in. The place wasn't much more than a dingy office front with giant windows next to the door that let passersby see inside. There was a wide counter with an old-style hotel bell that I slapped a couple of times.

It was quiet except for my incessant ringing, and Kendra and I looked at one another. After Cleo's high praise, I'd expected something grander, something more elegant, but this place was little better than a hole in the wall.

I'd pictured Jordan as a big, buff mountain of a man like

the TV hunters. He would *have* to be super big, and super tough to earn the kind of awe I'd heard in Cleo's voice.

The back door opened, and light poured out into the front room. My nerves clenched. The moment of truth.

I couldn't stop my jaw from dropping as a teeny-tiny, half-bald man walked out. He was more leprechaun than mountain.

I cleared my throat, ready to assert myself with tone, but I squeaked because nerves behaved that way. "Jordan?"

"Who's asking?" He had a Danny DeVito as the Penguin walk and the hairline to match. His voice, though, belonged to Michael Jackson before puberty with a southern drawl.

I stepped forward, still not convinced this was the amazing bounty hunter who never lost his mark. "Cleo sent me. I'm Hailey and this is my associate, Kendra." I smiled hesitantly. "You're *the* Jordan? The one who owns the bonds office? Who trained Cleo? The best bondsman she's ever worked with?"

He put one hand on his hip. "Of course, that's me. What? Expecting Rambo?"

He probably got that reaction enough to expect it, but if so, his sharp and somewhat bitter tone said he didn't quite enjoy it.

Mini-Rambo held out his hand, and I thought he wanted to shake. I shifted the bond slip to my left hand and gave him a firm, professional shake. He rolled his eyes, then sighed. "Bond receipt?"

His accent said southern United States. Maybe Tennessee. He had an Appalachian twang.

Oh. "Sorry."

I handed it over, and he pulled out a large binder checkbook, then wrote a check. To *me*. Holy crap, I'd never made this kind of money. Not for one night of work, for sure.

"Thank you," I said. "We hope to do more business with you in the future."

Jordan waved me off, so I took the check and walked out, keeping my composure until I was around the corner then, and only then, did I dissolve into the fit of laughter that had been bubbling inside me since he'd first opened the door and stepped into the light.

Kendra leaned against me, chortling.

Fifteen grand! Now this was a payday worth working for.

Chapter Fourteen

By the time I got home, after chasing the skip and celebrating my first takedown with Cleo and Kendra, it was too late to hunt with Dominic. I called and politely rescheduled. He was, thankfully, gracious.

When I walked out my front door Sunday night to go to work, Dominic was poised on my doorstep, hand lifted to knock. "Miss Whitfield. You look lovely. Are you ready for our hunt?"

When I'd spoken to him yesterday, I'd told him I would have to take a rain check, but I never mentioned when. Certainly, I hadn't said *tonight*. "I have to work." Cleo's daughter had a date tonight. She was trusting me. "Maybe we can go tomorrow night?"

Dominic shook his head. "I'm leaving tomorrow evening."

"Oh." There wasn't much I could do then. "Maybe we can

go the next time you come to visit." I certainly couldn't bail on Cleo when she was the source of my future work.

"I'm afraid if we don't go now, we will lose our window of opportunity." Everything he said sounded as if he stole the phrasing from the BBC. "Perhaps you can call your employer and tell her you have an obligation." He said it as if he believed I did.

Even though I *wasn't* obliged to the man, I was curious. I pulled out my phone, dialed Cleo, and promised to work over for taking a few hours off tonight, even though my shifts really didn't work that way. If she noticed, she didn't mention it. I hung up and sucked in a shaky breath as I looked at Dominic. "Okay, but we should try to hurry."

"Splendid. Now, shall we go?" He offered his arm. Today, he was dressed in black slacks and a black shirt that made his pale skin look lighter, with a blood red tie. He could've been going off to a night at the office, or a club, even.

I didn't want to go, not really. Hunting sounded so savage when I didn't have to, not when I had a club and the ability to cover the marks and my tracks with a good glamour. Plus, the humans at the club knew about us and were trusted to keep all knowledge about vampires a secret. "I think I would prefer to go to the club. Hunting seems so barbaric."

There, I said it. I even lifted my chin a little, proud of myself.

Dominic looked at me without a trace of emotion on his face. He was a man of staunch expression. "Do I need to remind you that Jaxon was not supposed to turn you?

Normally, I would be obligated to report his breach to the elders, but he's asked me not to. Right now, I'm inclined to go along with his request, but I would hate for anything to change that."

"Anything?" I didn't care for the implied threat.

He blinked slowly. "I need to make sure you can hunt without going rogue. Then I will be more comfortable keeping the information to myself."

"What does going rogue mean?" If I was going to end up rebelling, I should probably have known what it meant. Did he mean bloodlust? For all I know, his definition would be different from mine.

He shrugged. "It could be as simple as someone defying the rules or as severe as a vampire who has given in completely to his bloodlust, which jeopardizes our entire race."

He made it sound so clear-cut. But if there was one thing this vampire business had taught me, it was that nothing in the entire world was as straightforward as it looked.

But I nodded because he expected me to. I didn't need Jax to get in trouble.

He motioned for me to continue down the path. "We're going to venture out and find a house."

I didn't like the sound of this.

"Then I want you to gain entry so we can feed from the inhabitants."

"What?" I didn't know what I'd thought hunting was, but this wasn't it. Now that it was down to it, I really regretted not at least mentioning this to Jax. I assumed he knew, but what if he didn't? Dominic was his maker, after all. Butterflies plagued my stomach.

He sighed. "All the old tales about vampires being unable to enter a house without an invitation are true. Did you not know?"

"I don't often go into places I'm not invited." He had to be wrong. "You came into my house without me inviting you." Everything he said was suspect. His accent didn't make him sound trustworthy. Sexy, sure. But even an ogre sounded hot with a Scottish accent.

"You're a vampire. That changes the rules a bit." With his hand at the small of my back, he guided me to the car, then helped me inside before walking around to the driver side. When Jax did it, it was sexy and gentlemanly. When Dominic did it, it made me feel oppressed. Plus, I no more wanted to go hunting with Dominic than I wanted *anything* to do with him, but there I was in the car, buckled up and riding quietly beside him. He had a very persuasive personality.

He parked in a small subdivision on the other side of town. I was new to Chestnut Hill, and hadn't spent much time learning the neighborhoods, but this one was average. Split level houses with siding and brick, some landscaping, and a well-kept yard—but nothing like the shaped bushes and brick mansion we'd passed to get here.

"Off you go." What was I supposed to do?

When we walked from the street where he parked, up the sidewalk to the door of a nearby house, he moved to stand with his back against the wall, hiding as I knocked.

The door opened slightly, and a woman whose face was partially hidden by the door said, "Can I help you?"

"Hi. My car broke down and I was wondering if you had a phone I could use? I fooled around and let mine die." I chuckled, but her eyes narrowed.

There were ten houses on this street. I didn't know why he'd picked this one, but the woman wasn't having it. She pulled an old flip phone out of her pocket and handed it to me. "Here."

"Oh…uh, thanks." Well, damn. That hadn't gone as planned. I dialed my home number, listened to the answering machine, and looked at the street signs as I pretended to speak to a tow company. When I "finished," I closed the phone and handed it back. "Thank you."

Dominic stage-whispered, "Use your compulsion."

I stepped forward and looked the woman in the eye, waited a second so she would get the idea, then spoke slowly and clearly, the way Jax had taught me. "You're going to let us in."

"Why would I do that?" The woman's brow creased as she stared at me. I'd not compelled her at all, and I had no idea why it didn't work. I glanced at Dominic and gave him a small shrug.

"You have to mean it. *Feel it.*"

She pulled back. "Who are you talking to?"

I looked at the woman and refocused my efforts. "You're going to let us in."

She blinked a couple times, and I had her. But then she shook her head before pushing the door. "I'm calling the police if you don't get in your car and get the hell out of here," she said as it closed.

If I was her, I would've called the cops already. But I focused again, harder, so hard, I thought I might fart. I pressed my palm to the door and kept it from closing all the way. "You're going to open this door and let us in."

This time, she nodded and swung the door open so Dominic and I could enter. "Very nice job."

I didn't even break wind.

She led us up a small flight of steps to her living room where her husband was seated watching football, a beer on a TV tray in front of him next to a half-eaten plate of fried chicken and mashed potatoes.

I maintained my focus on controlling the woman. "Sit down."

She did. This was the kind of wrong I didn't want to be, but I didn't have a choice. I sat beside her and fed while Dominic fed off the husband. I was careful not to drain her. Careful to heal her the way Jax had shown me.

We left without any fanfare or incident. Thank goodness. I just wasn't up for any drama. I felt like an ass feeding off of them in their own home as it was. When they felt fatigued and weak tomorrow, at least they wouldn't know why. I hoped not, anyway.

Dominic opened my car door. "Nicely done. Your restraint was magnificent."

If I was the kind of girl who needed praise, I would have enjoyed it. But I wasn't, and I didn't. Disgust bubbled inside of me at both of us and what he'd forced me to do when we had a club for this very purpose. It would take a pretty dire situation before I ever fed off a human in their own home ever again. From now on, my hunting would be limited to the club. Period.

CHAPTER FIFTEEN

I WENT to work after my disgusting dinner with Dominic feeling dirty and angry at him, but more at myself for going along with it. I hadn't had a choice if it meant keeping Jax out of trouble. I had to prove I wasn't going to go rogue and embarrass or screw over the entire vampire race by bringing our presence into the light, so to speak.

I wrestled with guilt as I walked down the hall to Cleo's apartment. When I went in, she had her feet up on the coffee table. She spotted me and kicked them down, then winced. When I moved to help her, she held out her hand. "Too much, too soon. I keep forgetting to go slower."

But she had another stack of papers in hand. "I think you should go after the one on the top." When I took the pages from her, she did a quick recap. "He's a puny little nudist who embezzled money from the clothing optional club he started. It's a fat bounty, and not a lot of strain involved."

Maybe this was how Jordan got so good. Going after the tiny skips until he earned the reputation for the big ones. I sure as hell would have complied if puny little Jordan showed up, and I'd heard he was the best of the best. I would also wonder what hidden talent he had that compensated for his size to make him the best. *Especially* after I heard his voice.

Cleo was right. Embezzling brought a high bounty fee because the bond was ridiculous.

I nodded. "I think this is our guy."

Stanley Kubnick, PCA.

While we waited for Kendra to show up—we didn't have any personal items this time, so she was going to have to use a location spell without it—I considered my image.

I needed a persona. A tag line. I pictured myself, handcuffing the skip, hauling him out of his apartment, turning to my imaginary cameraman, and saying, "I just took another bite out of crime," or something equally quippy and witty. Too bad I couldn't flash my fangs at the camera.

Of course, there was no camera and probably never would be, and I certainly didn't want to get into the habit of flaunting my creature of the night-ness, especially if I got so good at this that they gave me my own reality show.

Hey, a girl could dream.

When Kendra arrived, she laid out the spell ingredients, mixed them up, then closed her eyes. The Ouija board planchette she'd brought moved across the map to a spot across town near where I'd fed with Dominic.

"What do you think?" I looked at Cleo, then at Kendra. "Wanna try it?"

"He's a nudist who uses a computer to steal money. We can pick this guy up in our sleep." Kendra glanced at the photo again.

Cleo held up one finger. "I want to ride along this time. I haven't been out of the house except for hospitals in months, and I don't feel right taking a cut of the money just for sitting here reading files and faxes."

I hadn't discussed field trips with Tracy, but Cleo was a grown woman, and if she wanted to go on a skip trace with us, who was I to say no?

When I didn't answer right away, she huffed out a breath. "I can damn sure decide for myself if I sit in a car and watch you catch a perp."

She was right. She was an adult and she obviously knew the risks.

"Fine," I said. She pulled herself up and leaned on her walker. We moved a little slower because she had to take it easy, but what could it hurt to let her sit in the car?

"Shotgun." She moved a bit faster toward the elevator. "I want to be able to see out the windshield."

Kendra and I exchanged a grin. It was the least I could do. Besides, it would've been really hard for Cleo to maneuver into the back of the tiny vehicle.

When we got to the car, I climbed into the back seat. We had to get a bigger car. Maybe we should have taken mine. At least it was a four-door.

Once Cleo was in, Kendra drove her Prius to the neighborhood I'd just left with Dominic.

The sick feeling settled in my gut at the memory. I shook it because I didn't want to talk about it. Ever.

Kendra handed me the cuffs from her bag, and she pulled out the stun gun and a can of pepper spray. Cleo took the small spray can back. "Girl, you do not want to use this. It's hard to get a good aim, and the blowback could get you. Then it's a bitch to catch your skip." She put it back into Kendra's bag. "That stunner will do you fine."

Kendra nodded and squared her shoulders. "Let's do this."

As we walked up to the door of the colonial home, I glanced at the windows. There were lights on all over. "I think I want a catchphrase."

She glanced at me as we stuck to the shadows. "A catchphrase?"

"You know, like 'I'll be back!'" My Schwarzenegger impression left a bit to be desired, and she quirked a brow. "Or 'How you doin'?'" I had to speak her language.

Her eyes lit up. "Oh! Yeah! We totally need one of those."

"Right?"

I chuckled, and Kendra lowered her voice adding, "'If it weren't for you meddling kids' or 'Is that your final answer?'"

I nodded. "Both are valid."

She looked over her shoulder at me. "Let's do this."

I couldn't tell if we were mimicking catchphrases still or if she was ready. "Like really let's do this or is that another one?"

She rolled her eyes, shook her head, and looked at the house. "Let's go."

"Fine. I'm going." I headed closer to the house's front door. "I thought maybe you were trying out a new one."

I shrugged, and then I heard it. A kamikaze yell. A scream and two feet landing on the ground.

Then, a blur of flesh so pale it made me look like *I* was tan streaked past me. Naked as the day he was born, Stanley Kubnick ran from the tree toward the house. He turned with a paintball gun locked and loaded. But I was faster than he could shoot, and his paintball sailed past me. It turned out, I wasn't faster than he could yell, though. "Aim and fire, Darlene!"

Luckily, Darlene's aim was bad, or I could've ended up skewered at the end of a wooden arrow. One foot higher than my left butt cheek, and I would've been a dead vampire. Instead, I had a hunter's arrow sticking out of my rump.

"Ow! You jerk!" I yelled at Stanley. Darlene was nowhere to be found.

He stood up and displayed his…goods. As impressive as they were, or rather, weren't, I wasn't here for his junk. "We're defending our home from invaders."

"You're trying your hand at hiding yourself from the long arm of the law, liar." I reached around to yank the arrow from my ass—thanking the heavens it was a blunt tip—then tossed it to the ground. "You're now also guilty of assaulting an officer of the bond agent who paid for you to be out of jail."

I didn't know if that was such a thing since I had crossed onto his property uninvited, but I made it sound official. "Now drop your weapon and call off Robin Hood."

When he made no move to comply, I pulled the paintball

gun out of his hands and bent it in half. Hallelujah for super-strength.

When Darlene came down from the treehouse I hadn't even seen, Kendra aimed the taser at her. "Put it down, or you aren't going to like what happens." She had a spell she could've used—and I wouldn't have minded—to turn this chick into a toad, but I didn't know if she was threatening to use it or the taser. Either one would've made me happy. But honestly, my butt cheek had already started healing. It tingled.

Kendra nodded toward Darlene. "Slap the cuffs on him, and I'll keep this one back."

I yanked them from my waistband and smiled as I yanked his arms behind his back and clicked the bracelets around his wrists.

Darlene threw up her hands and stomped toward the porch. As she passed us, she spat toward Stanley. "Coward."

"Could you at least get me a pair of pants?" he asked weakly.

I agreed, and so did Kendra.

"Please. I don't want his junk on my car seats," Kendra said, and followed Darlene inside, soon returning with a pair of sweats we carefully slipped over Stanley's hips, trying to keep as much distance as possible.

Once he was no longer totally nude, off we went.

This was a big night for our team and as soon as Jordan saw us, he cocked a brow. "Well, well, well." He hugged Cleo, who insisted on coming inside with us. "Look at you, up and walking."

His hair stuck out in Einstein waves and curls, and his shirt

—a Hawaiian luau print—was buttoned wrong. Cleo looked him up and down. "Who you got back there, Jordy?" She tried to peek around him but winced when she stretched to do it.

"Mind your beeswax, Missy. My social life is my business." He yanked the bond receipt from Kendra's hand. "Which one of you amateur sleuths am I writing this out to today?"

CHAPTER SIXTEEN

BY THE TIME I returned home, it was so near dawn the sky was pink toward the east side, and I was exhausted from the dinner to the skip trace to dealing with Jordan and Kendra trying out every catchphrase she could think of. This was all new to me, and I still hadn't quite gotten used to being awake when the rest of the world slept.

I pulled into my driveway, and before I could open the door for myself, it was pulled open and Jax stood over me. His scowl was deep, and yet still extremely hot. I had a feeling my new catchphrase was going to end up being, "What did I do now?"

He huffed out a breath. "Why didn't you call me?"

"I didn't even know I was going to go. I mean, he'd told me, but I guess I figured you were involved. Then when it came down to it, I didn't have time." Never had a truer truth been spoken. Not this day, at least. "He ambushed me as I was leaving for work."

I assumed he was talking about Dominic, because I already told him about working as a bounty hunter for the humans.

"Come on." He turned and walked across the street to his house. I gave the sky another quick glance, estimated I had about ten minutes for a butt-chewing, then I would need to be home, tucked in my bed.

I followed, slower, and he waited for me at the door. I walked past him toward the sofa. When he shut the door and turned, I held up my hand. "Hold on. If I'm going to get yelled at, I need to be comfortable. It's been a long night." I pushed the button for the reclining end.

He sighed. "I know how Dominic is, and I'm not going to yell at you." His voice was softer than I thought it would be, like a warm purr that vibrated through me. "But there are things I have to make sure you know."

I nodded because he'd come to sit on the coffee table in front of me. His cologne made me want to take a lot of deep breaths. "Like what?"

He sighed. "I broke a rule by making you, by biting you. It's punishable, should the elders decide not to justify your existence. To make a new vampire, there's a process and it's strictly monitored. There's paperwork and petitions and a census in the area has to be taken. Every new vampire has to be justified by the elders before they're made, then again after they're trained. Of course, there are exceptions, but they're rare and it takes a trial to clear the maker who creates a vampire without going through the proper channels."

It was all similar to what Paige had told me. But Paige had left out the part about Jax going to trial.

"Why? Wouldn't increasing the number give vampires strength? A position in society?" God, I hoped so. I didn't want to have to keep moving from town to town because everyone else aged, and I didn't, like in that vampire movie.

Jax shook his head. "The problem from before is that we were overpopulated. It made it too easy for the hunters, screwed with our food sources, and too many baby vampires went rogue. The elders live in fear of it happening again."

It all made sense, but I wasn't the one who made me. There had to be something he wasn't saying. "Okay, but I'm already made. So, what can they really do?"

He sighed. Whatever he was about to say was not going to be pleasant. "If they decide I stepped out of bounds, I'll be punished with silver bonds for a while, or something equally as physically painful." That didn't sound fun. But he wasn't finished. "But they could rule that you'll have to be destroyed."

"Destroyed?" My voice squeaked as I said the word and sat straight up. No matter what it meant, it didn't sound good.

"Staked or decapitated." Okay. Yeah. Dead.

I nodded when his words registered. "What now?"

He sighed again. "That's why we have to be careful. The rules are strict."

"How often has the newly made vampire been destroyed?" Before I started to worry, maybe the number was low, something I could investigate as to the reasons the elders acted the way they did.

"I don't have statistics or anything..."

"Jax." He knew. There was no way he could deny it with all the guilt written on his face.

"I don't know of any who've been allowed to live."

Well, hell's fire. "Oh crap."

This was a situation that probably would have warranted a sturdier swear word, but I wasn't about to screw with karma, or the Big Guy, or whoever decided what action fate took in a situation.

I stared ahead at the ray of sunlight coming through the kitchen door. Jax followed my gaze and held out his hand. "Come on, you can stay here. All the bedrooms are light-tight. You can have a spare."

If I was honest, I missed the sun...I missed being human, sleeping at night, and enjoying daylight, and even if I wasn't three sniffles into a good wallow, the chances of my brain shutting down enough so I could even doze, after I knew I was likely going to be *destroyed* soon, were slim.

This wasn't fair. I hadn't asked to be made a vampire. I hadn't planned to give up my life or my ability to get a suntan, but a group of vampires I'd never met before were going to decide whether or not to end me.

I slipped my hand into his and the old familiar tingles rushed up my arm and bloomed in my chest. At least I wouldn't die without knowing this kind of raw attraction to another person. Not that I hadn't been attracted before, but this was more...everything.

He stopped at a doorway. "Wait here a second." He disappeared inside the room and came back a minute later with a t-shirt.

I should've gotten extra bonus points for not burying my nose in the fabric and inhaling it when he handed it to me. It smelled like him, so the restraint it took not to embarrass myself was an astounding amount.

At least, until he showed me to another room then walked out and shut the door behind him. Then I inhaled long and deep. Oh God. I was going to be wrapped in his scent while I slept in a bed in his house.

I crawled into bed, and was almost passed out when he knocked and poked his head in. I waved and he walked toward the bed, stood over me. "I came to tuck you in." After a second, he sat beside me, so his hip touched mine through the blanket. "I know you're probably worried, but I'm not going to let anything happen to you. I have a plan and will not let them take you."

I swallowed hard. "Because you're my maker?"

It took several seconds before he spoke. "No. That's not why." His smile was soft, as was the finger that brushed the hair off my forehead.

So badly, I wanted to ask why. I wanted to hear him say the words, but then he leaned in and pressed his soft, full lips against my cheek, and I couldn't have spoken if I tried. By the time I could speak again, he would probably have been asleep for a couple of hours. But I managed a smile.

"Sleep tight."

I was lying in this man's guestroom, wearing his shirt,

wishing I was braver, brave enough to ask for a real goodnight kiss, but the moment was gone, and he was at the door, his finger on the light switch.

I waved. Because that was what I did when a beautiful man kissed me goodnight, even if it was only on the cheek.

CHAPTER SEVENTEEN

When I woke, it was dusky outside, and I needed to get home, shower, and change before I went to work. I didn't necessarily mean to leave without saying goodbye, especially after our moment when Jax had tucked me in, but I didn't have a lot of choice since I didn't know where Jax was. Besides, I didn't want to look like I was snooping around his house.

When I walked outside, a long black stretch limo sat in the street and Jax and Dominic were climbing into the back. Paige stood at the edge of the yard watching, so I walked over to her. "What's going on?"

"Dominic is going home and he's taking Zara with him." She crossed her arms and watched them leave.

I nodded because I was glad to see Dominic go. After what Jax had explained, with Dominic gone, I would be able to breathe again. For a little while anyway.

Instead of sticking around with Paige, I walked across the

street to my house. There would be time later to talk to Jax about everything he'd told me and to thank him for letting me stay at his place.

When I checked my voicemails on my phone, I saw that Cleo had called and said she didn't really need me to come in if I wanted to stay home. That sounded great to me. Two skips in as many days and all this news from Jax had put my mind into a whirlwind. No way was I turning down a night I could use to decompress.

My fridge was nothing more than a magnetic bulletin board now, and Luke had made sure to attach cards for each of the openings at his gallery. There was one he'd been bugging me to come to. A new artist I was "just going to fall in love with." I doubted it since my taste in art wasn't nearly as sophisticated as his, but it would be nice to get dressed up and be among people.

I called Paige and invited her, and Ransom, then called Kendra. "Gallery opening tonight. Want to go?" I didn't even bother with a hello when she answered. These days, we were way past pleasantries.

"Formal or casual?"

"You know Luke. Everything he does is formal. He's probably wearing something from the Liberace library, and we'll be expected to sparkle to match." I loved Luke's style, but he outshone the art almost every single time.

"Give me thirty minutes."

"Excellent." I took those same minutes to shower, and blow dry my hair, then to exfoliate and shine. Whatever anyone said, becoming a vampire was good for the skin. Mine had never been clearer nor my pores smaller.

As a group, we were elegance personified. Kendra and I had on our little black dresses. Mine had gold roses embroidered across the low neckline. It fell off the shoulders and had three quarter sleeves. The body of the dress hugged my curves and stopped just above my knees. I'd worn my black, strappy heels.

Kendra's black dress was accented with lace and a long flowing skirt that fell to about mid-calf. She wore a sexy pair of stilettos.

Paige had on a sleek navy-blue pantsuit with a red cami under her jacket, and heels that matched.

Ransom had opted for a suit that I guessed was designer and cost more than the last bounty I collected. Maybe. Did suits cost that much?

Ransom had arranged for a limousine, which seemed to be one of his feature functions today, and we piled into the opulent ride. He'd also arranged for tulip glasses of "wine"—blood laced with wine, actually—and the flavor of the grapes didn't make me want to vomit, so I drank and smiled while Kendra drank a glass of unlaced Chardonnay.

We arrived in style, and since it had been a while since I'd had anything more flavorful than AB negative, I was a bit tipsy, but not sloppy. Just happy. Happy to be among friends and seeing my brother's place in all its glory.

Luke, ever the social butterfly, flitted from guest to guest and when he came to me, he threw his arms out and wrapped me in a hug. The abrupt ending of said hug sent me shoulder first into a wall so Lukey-poo could fawn over Ransom. Ransom's cheeks flushed with color. I didn't know if I was imagining it because a lot of people reacted to Luke this way or if it was real, but I nudged Paige. "I love when his cheeks do that." I'd sort of figured vamps couldn't flush.

She nodded. "Kind of makes him a real person, which I sometimes seriously doubt. Most vampires don't flush. It's a Ransom thing."

We chuckled and Kendra eyed up the bartender, then hid her face behind her hands. "Oh God. It's Xander."

Even I remembered Xander. He was an ex who'd cheated on her with another witch from a coven she'd been scoping out. Needless to say, she hadn't joined that coven.

"I didn't know he was a bartender." I couldn't remember what his occupation was, but surely I would've remembered it being bartending.

"Yeah." She rolled her eyes and turned away so if he looked our way, he would see a lot of shoulder, a few inches of spine, and her hairdo.

There was another bar on the opposite side of the gallery. "I'm going over there."

She linked arms with Paige and off they went while I stared at a deep blue painting. It looked like broad strokes of blue paint spread unevenly over a canvas. I didn't get it.

"Hello."

I looked left then right. I didn't see anyone, so I moved to the next painting because a crowd had formed around "Blue."

As I stepped in front of the next painting—multicolored splashes I couldn't make sense of—the masculine "hello" voice said, "I love the way the artist used red to show anger in the skyline of the city."

Oh! A city! "I didn't recognize that it was a city."

We chuckled together, and he used his finger to point out the lines of the building. But I'd moved on from the painting to the man. He was gorgeous. If Jax was Brad Pitt, this guy was George Clooney. Curly black hair, gray eyes, a body designed to be worshipped. He was scrumptious.

As soon as I had the thought, my heart raced—my body still reacted despite my back-from-the-dead lack of heartbeat—then guilt powered through me. I'd had a moment with Jax. Here I was drooling over this guy. But, oh my. There was a lot to drool over.

Not to the exclusion of his voice, either. "I'm Blake." He held out his hand and squeezed mine softly. More heart pounding action ensued, and I was there for it.

"I'm Hailey. Nice to meet you."

"So nice to meet a fellow art connoisseur." Now he was poking fun, but I could roll with it. "Want to know the truth?"

I nodded. He could've quoted me a line from the Pennsylvania State Constitution, and I would've stayed right there and listened to the richness of his tone and soft cadence with which he spoke.

"I've been waiting to talk to you since you came in, but I couldn't figure out how to strike up a conversation about a plain blue canvas." He was a northerner, but not New England-ish or New York or anywhere I could've placed him by the slight accent. I was normally so good at accents.

I couldn't concentrate wholly on the words, or I

might've embarrassed myself with a swoon, and in these heels, I could've broken a bone. While healing might've happened with the swift speed of a vampire, the initial fall would've caused a scene. Besides, being a vampire didn't remove pain.

"Really?" I could just see his fangs when he smiled and paid careful attention to the pale skin. "Are you a"—I lowered my voice to a whisper—"vampire?" He nodded and wagged his eyebrows.

"Do you know Jaxon Parsons?" I asked.

He smiled. "Yes. We've met." His gaze burned up my body.

I turned for a second to see where Paige and Kendra had gone. It could only up my cool quotient for them to see me standing with this guy, plus the intensity of his attention was a bit overwhelming.

They were coming my way. Close. I turned back to Blake, but he was gone. I scanned the crowd. Standing on my tiptoes, I looked for the deep black of his hair. His height was easily taller than most of the folks in the room. But it wasn't like he'd just found me boring and walked on. This guy had *vanished.*

It took almost an hour of pretending to like the paintings with Paige and Kendra before they moved on while I stared at a pumpkin landscape—a field of actual pumpkins.

"You know, you shouldn't stand so close to the paintings. You make them seem dull and without life."

I turned again, and there he was. Blake. This time, I was the one flushing with color. It was a line, but it was a good one, and no matter how hard I tried not to be, I was the kind of girl who fell for all the good lines.

I breathed out because I didn't want to tell him that underneath the makeup and updo, the sparkly dress and four-inch heels, I was a normal, rather plain woman, but not telling him seemed deceitful. I had enough strikes in my naughty column.

"I don't usually dress quite so...fancy." I motioned toward my dress.

"Good." He pulled his bowtie and it hung loose, the black making his crisp white shirt all the more stark and pristine. "Me, either." He grinned. "Would you like to get out of here and go get a drink?"

It had been a *super* long time since anyone had asked me for drinks. But it felt disloyal to Jax. What did it say about me that I could go from lusting after one man to immediately lusting after another? "I really should stay. It's my brother's gallery." The lie rolled easily off my tongue. It *was* Luke's gallery, but that wasn't why I didn't want to go.

Speaking of which, Luke laid his hand on my back. "Little sister. Who is your new friend?"

"Blake, this is my brother Luke, the owner of this beautiful establishment. Luke, this is Blake." Had I really not caught his last name?

"It's a pleasure to meet you," Blake said. His voice was more smooth than maple syrup stirred with melted butter as he shook Luke's hand. "This is a stunning exhibit."

Blake winked at me, and I wasn't sure if he was talking about the artwork or me. The words said one thing, but the look said something else. My heart skipped and stuttered. The effect this man had on the muscle memory of the human I'd been was almost as potent as my reaction to Jax.

Luke cocked his head at me and widened his eyes out of Blake's view, then smiled when I turned back to include Blake in whatever conversation I managed to have around my awkwardness.

From the corner of my eye, I caught sight of Paige and Ransom coming our way. As I was about to mention to Blake that he was going to be quite popular with my friends, he was gone. Again. This guy was some kind of vampire escape artist.

For the rest of the evening, we puttered around the gallery, staying until most other people were gone.

As we waited for the limousine to pick us up, I felt his eyes on me, and I turned to give a little wave.

Paige nudged me. "Who are you waving at?" She craned her neck in the direction where Blake had been standing, and again, he was gone.

I chuffed out a breath, frustrated. The one time a really hot guy paid attention to me, and I couldn't show him off because he kept disappearing. "I met a guy named Blake, a vampire. Although I'm starting to wonder if he's real or a figment of my imagination."

Maybe I even imagined Luke meeting him. Wouldn't have surprised me considering all the new things going on in my life. A bout of crazy hallucinations that made me a sex object wasn't as out of line as I hoped it would be.

Why was no one applauding that I'd met a man? Paige looked around with interest, her face a little puzzled. "I don't know a Blake," she murmured.

Ransom walked beside me. “Hey, I’ll meet you guys back at Jax’s house.”

There wasn’t further explanation, but there were red cheeks and a slight pep to his step as he turned and headed back to where Luke was standing, beaming at him.

I sat in the limo while Paige and Kendra gossiped over the clothes they’d seen, hairstyles, men. I thought of Blake, those eyes, that deep black hair. It wasn’t every day a man looked at me and spoke such flirty words. Not that I needed the validation. I was happy in sweats and jeans and didn't care much if anyone liked the way I looked. But there was something about a man in a tuxedo comparing me to art and me winning that made my heart pitter patter. It had been a good night.

CHAPTER EIGHTEEN

I SIDE-STEPPED A JAB. "Heard you went to the gallery opening the other night." Jax's voice sounded casual, but something was off. He didn't miss a lot of footwork, and he stumbled like he'd misjudged a third foot.

"Yeah."

"I heard you met a vampire." His voice went hard, and this jab was designed to maim, but easy to redirect. "Blake." He fourteen-year-old-girl mimicked.

"Wow. Are you jealous?" There was a new flutter in my belly, and it had Jax's jealousy written all over it.

He scoffed. "No. Of course not. This is my territory and if a new vamp is in town, he needs to let me know."

"You keep a register book?" I asked.

He shot me a bit of side-eye that meant he didn't appreciate my question. I got it a lot with him, so it was easy to recognize these days. "No, wise guy, but since the population of vampires in any area is monitored, I need to know when mine changes."

Made sense.

"Any vampire who isn't an *infant*"—he threw that word around sometimes when I did something he didn't like—"knows to give me a courtesy heads up."

"Oh. Sorry." Probably not as much as I should've been, but I wasn't completely buying his story either.

"That's enough for today." He jerked off his boxing gloves and stuffed them into the equipment bag in the corner of his basement, then stalked toward the stairs. "I'm going to hit the shower."

There was no invitation involved, so I stowed my stuff in the locker he'd assigned to me, then I went home. Would've been nice to have a shower with Jax, but whatever.

I didn't remember whether or not I locked the door, because sometimes when I headed over to train with Jax or Ransom or both, I left it open. But I never left it unlatched, able to be pushed without turning the knob.

When I walked inside, I knew. Someone had been in my house and might've still been there. The unlatched door was my first clue, the second was my living room looked like a tornado had gone through it. I picked up the glass bowl where I normally tossed the keys with the intent to use it as a weapon. It was heavy and could do some serious damage.

After a minute, I walked out onto the porch because there was nothing in my place that hadn't been touched, rifled through, disturbed, and set askew. I dialed Jax's number and told him what had happened. I couldn't call the cops because I didn't know what or who was in my house. Or who could still be there. It'd be terrible for a cop to die because he came upon a vampire in my home.

What the hell? This was nuts.

I stood near the steps and waited, still holding the crystal bowl and ready to strike and didn't relax until Jax appeared on the steps.

"Wait here," he growled. Whoa. Jax did *not* like my house being ransacked.

Whatever. Didn't mean I was doing as he said. I was freaked out, but I was still bad to the bone.

I followed him inside and bumped into his back when I gasped at the streams of shaving cream on my bathroom floor. After I bumped into him, and he stepped a foot into the mess, he turned and narrowed his eyes at me. But I continued to stare at the floor. "That's just rude," I whispered.

"I told you to stay outside." He tried to intimidate me with his glower, but it didn't work.

I shrugged.

"You can't stay here. You shouldn't be in here at all." He arched one handsome eyebrow.

"I live here." This was my sofa and my table. My clothes were in the bedroom.

"You can stay at my place." He moved out of the doorway and stepped backwards into me this time. "Okay, this isn't going to work."

"I could walk in front of you?" Anything to be helpful.

He glared, and I took a step back.

"Listen, Hailey, I can't get a sense of anyone. That means

it's either a witch or a very old vampire." If troubled had a look, Jax was wearing it—narrowed eyes, tight mouth, ticking jaw. "If you won't stay with me, let me send Paige to stay with you. Train every night whether you have to go to work or not." He wasn't playing. This was serious. "Let her stay until we figure out who was here."

I nodded; I didn't have another choice. Plus, I would sleep better if someone else were here. If that someone was also a vampire, especially a badass like Paige, sleep wouldn't be a problem.

Since it was still early enough after we cleaned up the mess in my house, Paige and I went online, and I showed her how to look up the skip traces. Cleo had given me a password into Jordan's system, so I could keep track in case I wanted to work on days I didn't have a shift at her place.

"Ooh. Look at this one." I didn't often check the crimes, I just looked at the bounty receipt fees. This one was huge.

"He's a murderer." That incited a smile as wide as I'd ever seen on a person, human or otherwise.

I dialed Jordan. When he answered with a "Hidey-ho!" I started in.

"I want Aaron Hightower."

He clucked his tongue. "No way. You can't handle Hightower."

He was almost six inches taller than I was. Shamefully, he was about twenty-five pounds lighter. I hadn't gone after a skip yet I hadn't brought in.

"I can handle Hightower. I'm a Bond Girl." Just that quick and easy, our new enterprise had a name. "I am one third of

Bond Girls Recovery." It could have been a twelve-step program or a skip trace agency.

"I think 007 might have a problem with that," Jordan drawled.

"Let him sue me. Now can I have Hightower or not?" This was serious money. Big cash.

"You're quite the steel magnolia, aren't you?" he drawled, then sighed. "I suppose, but if he eats you up and spits you out, don't come crying to me." He hung up before I could answer and that was okay. My reply probably would've changed his mind.

"Bond Girls?" Paige chuckled. "I'm not wearing a bikini top with my leather pants."

"An ejection seat would be cool, though. Life changing if we're honest." I smiled and called Kendra. When she answered the phone, I sing-songed, "We've got one."

It was all I had to say to get the reaction I wanted. "I'm on my way."

She hung up, and Paige and I waited the ten minutes it took her to arrive. Five more for her to get us a location with her spell and about thirty more to drive to within a few blocks from where we'd found Zara. I didn't believe in coincidence, but this was a little close for me. A bit easy.

I had a job to do, though. Money to collect when we finished. I glanced at Paige. "You mind watching the back?"

We were at an apartment building right beside a coffee shop. How I would've loved a place like that back in the day.

She nodded. "Yup." Kendra went to hand her the taser and Paige smirked. "I think I'm okay without it. You keep it."

In Kendra's defense, I'd taken the taser once and I had the same superpowers Paige did.

I filled Kendra in on the Bond Girl situation, and she smiled. "Heck, yeah. I'll be a Bond Girl."

As I rounded the corner to take my position at the front of the building, Blake walked out of the coffee shop, a cup marked K-Macchiato in one hand, a newspaper in the other. He stopped short and it was good the cup had a lid, or I would've been covered in scalding and aromatic coffee.

"Hey, Hailey." He tucked the paper under the arm with the coffee and slid his now free hand down my arm. "How are you?" He spoke slowly with his brow wrinkled, as if he was surprised, or like he thought maybe I was stalking him.

"I'm doing great. How are you?" He eyed Kendra while I spoke, then focused on me again, and my skin warmed under his gaze. "This is my friend Kendra."

He smiled and gave her a slight nod, then looked at me again. There was something about this guy that spoke to mystery and intrigue and such beauty I could hardly breathe. For a second, I wondered if he knew how pleasing he was to look at. Then I wondered where such silly thoughts came from. They certainly couldn't be mine since every other minute of the day, I was busy thinking of Jax.

"I'm so glad I ran into you." I'd run into him, but whatever. "Would you want to go to dinner with me tomorrow night?"

I was a vamp. He was, too. I didn't like hunting for my dinner. What did he mean by going to dinner?

Kendra nudged me. "Hails, we need to go. Business?"

She was right. I glanced at Blake. There was nothing to do but let him down gently, so he didn't kill me in the street. Men like him probably didn't get a lot of rejections, and I needed to be prepared in case he took it badly. I braced myself. "I can't."

Not because of Jax, but because I preferred to dine at the club. It was easier and way less savage. Not that I wanted to explain it to such a suave and sophisticated vampire.

"Another time, then." He leaned in and kissed my cheek then pulled back, winked, and smiled. Then he walked away like he hadn't just set my world upside down.

"Holy hot guy, Batman. Who the heck was that?" Kendra's mouth gaped open as I opened the door to the apartment building and walked inside to the stairwell.

"I met him at Luke's gallery. He must live around here or something."

"Well, aren't you just a man-magnet these days?" She shook her hands out.

I hadn't even told her about Jax tucking me in the other night. I shook my head. I had no idea what was going on. Maybe being a vampire had made me more attractive, or maybe I was attractive to vampires because there was a rule or a law or some elder edict that said they couldn't date human women. Or maybe there was a shortage of vamp women. I didn't know, but neither was I going to shun the admirers who'd chosen *me* to admire.

I walked to the second-floor apartment and knocked on the door. "Aaron Hightower?" He was in his thirties, accused of killing his wife; his uptown, socialite, society pages wife. He'd pleaded not guilty according to his bond report. I couldn't believe they'd let him out on bail. Of course, a guy who killed his wife uptown where the mansions were on acreage the size of Chestnut Hill got treated a little differently from guys who killed their wives in the projects downtown.

Furniture scraped against the floor inside the apartment. This guy wasn't putting it in front of the door so he could let us in. Kendra stepped back and made room for me.

I pushed the door open like it wasn't made of more than a few feathers and found Hightower trying to make a run out of the window to the fire escape. Before I made it all the way into the room, he jumped, and I ran to the window and looked down. Paige had him on the ground and was hog-tying him with a cord she'd brought with her, which looked suspiciously like the nylon cord I used to hold my curtains open.

Whatever, it was fine. She had him. As fast as we could, Kendra pulled the car into the alley so we could load him in and take him to the precinct for our receipt.

"Bond Girls ride again!" Kendra fist pumped the air, and I smiled. This was a brilliant partnership. We were going to succeed all the way to the bank.

By the time we went back to Jordan, roused him from his sleep and collected the payout, it was almost dawn again. He was suitably impressed. "I might have to start throwing some real action your way," he said as he signed the check.

I dragged myself home, and again found Jax outside waiting for me. "You cut dawn close," he said. But he smiled.

"What are you doing here?" I'd been very into my skip tracing.

He lifted his hand as if to touch my arm, but let it fall again. "I thought maybe you should stay at my place."

Not this again.

"What about Paige?" Her staying at my place had worked out pretty well. Not as well as me staying at his since *that* night I got a kiss. Chaste as it was, it counted in my book since it was the only one I'd had in months.

"She'll stay there, too." His place was huge with so many rooms, we wouldn't have ever run into each other had he not put me into a room close to his. "But I need you to be safe." He cocked his head. "I watched your house all night to make sure no one went in or out, but I don't want to take the chance of them coming while we're sleeping."

It made sense, but I couldn't stay at his place indefinitely. Much as I might've wanted to.

With a sigh, I relented. At least for now. "All right." I walked across the street with him just as the first rays of daylight streaked across the morning sky.

CHAPTER NINETEEN

Since I didn't have to work tonight for Cleo, I planned to sleep in, but the phone's shrill ring had other ideas, or at least the person responsible for the ringtone had other ideas.

I answered even though I didn't know the number. "Hello?"

Smooth baritone floated over the phone line. "Good evening, Hailey. I was hoping you would be free to join me for dinner this evening."

I knew the voice, recognized it as belonging to Blake immediately. As flattering as his invitation, I couldn't go to dinner with him when I'd just woken up at Jax's house.

But more important, he was giving off a vibe, even over the phone. "How did you get this number?" I asked.

I remembered our every interaction vividly and at no point had I provided my number. If Luke had given it to him, we were going to have yet another boundaries talk.

Blake chuckled, and even down the line, it sounded hollow. It hadn't sounded like that when we met the first time, I would've noticed. I was almost sure anyway. "I have money, and money gives me choices, opportunities, and options." I wondered which of the three categories I fell into. His answer told me nothing.

But I moved on. "I appreciate the offer, but I'm involved with someone."

Kind of. Close enough, anyway. I was sleeping in another man's house. The fact didn't escape me because the whole place was scented with Jax's cologne. His room was across the hall from mine.

I wasn't sure what exactly we were, but I wanted us to be more. We definitely had the chemistry for it. The tingles. The delicious magic that made my body behave like it was still human when he touched me, or gazed at me, or when we trained. When he wrapped his body around mine, I could feel every muscle and rippling valley as it touched mine.

If only he would stop pulling back when we got close.

Thinking of the devil, he knocked softly and poked his head in the door. I held up one finger. "Thank you for the offer, but I have to go."

I didn't wait for a goodbye or even a reply before I hung up.

Jax smiled and walked fully into the room. "Everything okay?"

I nodded and took a second to take him in. This guy had a way of wearing jeans that made me grateful for denim. He had eyes like a chameleon. Yesterday, I'd been sure they were hazel. Today, they were more turquoise that matched his shirt. His hair had that perfect mixture of tousled and textured that made it look like he'd just raked his fingers through it. There was nothing not to like.

"Yeah," I said. "It was Blake."

His voice changed—gentle to gruff—and his eyes narrowed. "Blake the vampire?"

I nodded. "He asked me to dinner."

Calling it dinner rather than hunting sounded deceitful to me, but I let it go for now. I wasn't going to change an entire race's verbiage, nor did I care to try. But it annoyed me anyway.

Jax shook his head and scoffed. "Presumptuous bastard."

I hid a smile by pulling my lips between my teeth until it went away on its own. I couldn't stop the question though because I wanted an answer. "Are you jealous?"

"No." He didn't even blink when he said it, but he didn't look directly at me either. "Jealous." He rolled his eyes. "Whatever."

I nodded and didn't tell him he had all the classic signs. "What's the problem then?"

He narrowed his eyes again, staring at me hard for a couple of seconds, then shook his head again. "I'm the guy he needs to register with. Everyone in this city and the surrounding area knows it and would tell him."

Oops. Was I supposed to have told him? "He still hasn't?" It was obvious, but sometimes I needed to hear my own voice to remind me not to stay locked in my own head. Plus, I didn't want Jax to realize I'd missed an opportunity to tell Blake he needed to see Jax.

Wait, but I did ask him. At the gallery. "I asked him if he knew you, and he said you've met. So, I assumed he had."

Jax shook his head. "No. He has not. I don't know any vampire named Blake."

That was odd. Had this guy given me a false name?

"That's why you're angry?" I wanted to hear him say it. More, I wanted him to tell me he was jealous, but I mostly just liked his voice, whether he was angry or happy or joking or bossy. Maybe I wanted him to deny being jealous, because his protests and denials spoke the truth his words did not.

"Yeah." Again, he didn't look at me. "Absolutely." A second later, "It's a matter of respect."

"Respect. Right." But my cold, dead little heart leaped because he was lying, and there was no denying it.

He sighed and shook his head, then glanced up at me and waited a second before he spoke. When he did, his voice was softer. "Do you want to go to the club?"

I imagined his invitation as a date more than my maker taking care of my nutritional needs. I nodded.

He motioned to a small piece of my luggage sitting inside the door. "I had Paige go to your place and get you some clothes and some of your personal stuff." He shrugged and put his hands in his pockets. "I wanted you to be comfortable."

It was thoughtful. His kindness was sexy. I couldn't help but tease him. "As my maker?"

His head bobbed up. But he said, "No."

He backed out of the room before I could ask any further

questions, and I snuggled under the cover for a few seconds, letting the fact that he'd considered my comfort wash over me. I wondered what he'd been like before he was a vampire. Who he'd been in that life. I wanted to know more. So much more.

The club was hopping. For a Wednesday in the first week of April, the place was crowded with gyrating bodies and intoxicated humans. I glanced at the crowd, scoping out my dinner, and I recognized the black hair, and the smile when it aimed itself at me coupled with a wink. I elbowed Jax, making the mistake of taking my eyes off Blake. "He's here."

"Who?" he asked absently.

"Blake." If only I could get his attention so easily when I hadn't messed up at training or when I was just being my normal self.

His head snapped toward the dance floor. "Where?"

I looked back again and pointed, but Blake was gone. Again. "This guy…" If he wasn't a descendant of Houdini, someone had messed up the family tree.

But more, what was Blake doing here?

"Stay here." He waved Paige over and she stood beside me. It was a little embarrassing, but I didn't protest.

I waited quietly, watching Jax as he moved through the crowd, as he circled the floor, as more vampires came out—

where they'd come from, I had no idea—and blocked exits, checked the clientele, and watched Jax for cues.

Jax came back a moment later. "He's gone." He swore the big one and slammed his hand against the bar top. The sound reverberated along the wood counter.

I nodded because all my heebie-jeebies had gone away.

"Did you tell him where you were going?" Jax stared into my eyes, trying to compel an answer.

It didn't work. "No. I didn't. You didn't ask me to come here until after I hung up."

He nodded at the bartender, then handed me a glass of blood. "Drink up. We're out of here."

I sighed—the dreamy kind—because he shielded my body from view as I drank which put him very close to me. So close that if he had body heat, I would've felt it. I was never going to complain about that.

CHAPTER TWENTY

In the car, he informed me, like I had no choice in the matter, "You're coming home with me."

I wasn't arguing because seeing Blake there, smiling at me, then his smarmy wink, had freaked me out enough I didn't want to be alone. There was something off. I could feel it.

I shivered, and Jax slid his hand over mine as he drove. He'd left Paige at the club with Ransom to talk to anyone who might've seen or spoken to Blake. The windows of Jax's car were blacked out with tint, and it was almost midnight on a night with no moon. If not for the dashboard lights, I wouldn't have been able to see at all.

"Thank you for everything." It felt inadequate, but if I started pouring my heart out right now, there was a chance it would never end, and I couldn't risk it.

He gave my hand a squeeze and when he pulled to a stop light, looked at me. "It's my pleasure to take care of you."

The words were hot syrup, and I was pancakes. It made sense. Syrup was tree blood, and now I loved blood. Something inside of me clicked. "Your pleasure?"

"Mmm." Oh, heavenly hotness. That sound settled in my belly and spread heat—the fiery kind—through me. "My pleasure." This time, when he spoke, his voice was low and deep, so darn sexy I imagined his breath against my skin as he spoke, his hands caressing, mouth tasting.

My pleasure.

I wasn't worldly or sophisticated enough with men to know how to react, but I hoped he couldn't read my mind. Well, all but a very tiny sliver of my consciousness hoped he couldn't. The little part of me who hoped he could, who wouldn't have minded him knowing what I wanted so I didn't have to ask for it out loud and risk his rejection.

He pulled the car into his garage and shut off the engine. We sat for a second, neither of us looking at the other, his fingers still threaded through mine. "We should go in."

I nodded, unable to form words, because the huskiness of his voice along with the naughty thoughts in my head had me imagining all kinds of new experiences. I'd never made out with a man in a car. Not even when I was a teenager, and I was expected to do things like that.

We weren't inside for more than a few seconds when the doorbell chimed, and I glanced at Jax. His shoulders tensed. Paige and Ransom lived there with him, so they didn't knock, and he didn't receive a lot of other visitors in the middle of the night. Vamps who wanted to see him often met him at the club. Or called to schedule a meeting.

He walked to the door and swung it open. Blake stood in the doorway. "Miss Whitfield." He nodded to me as he walked past Jax. When he winked again, that same freaky feeling crept over my skin.

Jax shut the door and turned to watch Blake as he sat on the sofa. I probably shouldn't have stood there gaping, but I didn't have anywhere else to go.

"Blake Winslow, Mr. Parsons." He glanced at Jax then held out a hand Jax took and probably tried to squeeze until the bones crushed. When he let go, he stepped back, and Blake smiled again. "I went to your club tonight to meet you, but I didn't want to interrupt your evening."

"Yet here you are." Jax was more ungracious, harder than I thought the situation demanded, but I wasn't a centuries old vampire who was in charge of all the other vampires in the area. Maybe this was his way of asserting his power. Who was I to judge?

Blake smiled. "Yes. Here I am." He added, "Finally." His voice dropped and he lowered his head as if he was trying—and failing—to sound chagrined that he hadn't arrived sooner.

Jax clenched his jaw. "I have to wonder why the delay if you knew where to find me the entire time."

The back door opened, and Paige and Ransom walked into the living room from the kitchen. Blake and Jax were locked in a stare-off that Jax won, because Blake blinked and smiled, then chuckled.

"I'm ashamed to admit, but I suppose I need to make this right." Suddenly, he was pouring on the slow southern charm. I hadn't noticed even the hint of an accent before, then a slightly Yankee one, but now he was giving Miss Scarlett a run for her money. “As much as it pains me to admit it, I was a coward. Intimidated by the legend of Jaxon Parsons. Your lore is widespread and well-known among our kind.”

I might’ve bought the intimidation line had he not sounded like he was about to clutch his pearls and shout that Atlanta was burning. Jax was intimidating in ways not all men were or could ever be. He had power in every pore of his body. What a body!

Jax turned away and rolled his eyes at me, then walked toward a credenza in the corner of the room away from the sofa where Blake had perched. “What brings you to Chestnut Hill? To Pennsylvania at all?” He opened a drawer and pulled out a ledger book, then flipped to the back and pulled a pen from the desk.

“Visiting friends.” He glanced at me and smiled again. “Met a pretty girl. Thought I would try my luck.”

I wasn’t a prize to be awarded to the lucky winner. Though his words were the kind designed to make a girl swoon, I wasn’t swooning. I looked away from his smile, from the wink I suspected was coming. How had I found him charming at first?

Jax shot me a look, then glanced back at Blake. “How long will you be staying?”

“I don’t have a set itinerary, but I’m thinking a week, maybe two.” He looked me up and down again. “There are various factors involved in my decision.”

“Various factors?” Jax cocked one eyebrow, and a growl rumbled low in his chest.

Blake grinned. "I should let you get back to your evening."

But when he stood to leave, he walked toward me, took my hand in his and brought it to his mouth to press a kiss against my knuckles. I pulled back and wiped my hand on the fabric of my skirt against the side of my thigh. Then he was gone. A ruffle of curtains and papers in his wake.

"He just showed up here?" Ransom scowled as he passed me to close the still open door.

It bothered me, too, that Blake seemed to have access to a lot of information I wasn't sure he would've been able to come by easily. My address and phone number, for example. Although, since it was expected that he registered with Jax, maybe coming into a new place supplied him with the subliminal information he needed. I still wasn't sure how all this vampire mumbo-jumbo worked. Yet. I seemed to be learning on the slow curve.

"Like he owned the place." Jax might've been exaggerating, but not by a lot.

Blake had breezed in, sat before us like he was invited, and had spoken like he was the man in charge, though his words were sufficiently deprecating.

"You buy that whole *you intimidate me* crap?" I wasn't sure if Paige was asking me or Jax, so I stayed quiet.

Jax shrugged. "It's lame if it's true."

"Yeah. Something's off." Ransom crossed his arms and his chest looked broader, thicker than I noticed before. "Maybe he's about to go rogue?"

Jax nodded and puffed out a breath. "Maybe."

I edged toward the door. I needed a night away from Jax.

A minute to clear my head and catch my breath because I was in danger of falling hard for all his manly-man vibes and uber-protective-ness. While I could and would take care of myself, it was intoxicating to have someone who *wanted* to take care of me. Until I knew for sure he wasn't this way only because I was his 'infant vampire,' I wasn't letting myself risk falling any harder or crushing any more than I already was.

"Where are you going?" He stopped me as I reached for the knob.

I dropped my hand and turned. "I thought I would spend the night at home."

"Why?"

No way was I coming forth with *that* truth.

"I, um, I-I-I planned a sleepover with my girls and Luke." I glanced at Paige hoping she would jump in and save my horribly executed lie. When she didn't, I smiled at her, probably looking like I was trying to pass a kidney stone. "Right, Paige?"

It took her a second after Jax looked at her. "Right! Yeah. A sleepover." She nodded a bit more enthusiastically than the situation required. But neither Jax nor Ransom stopped us when we went outside and across the street.

When I got inside my house, I decided to make my fib a truth and called Kendra and Luke. For one night, I'd had enough of being a vampire and enough of being a Bond Girl. I wanted to be normal, with friends around me who could make me laugh and for a few minutes forget the crazy twists and turns my life had taken over the last few months. If I could get one normal night, all the others wouldn't have been so shocking. I hoped anyway.

Paige and I would be sufficient to protect us while Jax worked on who Blake was and why he was here. That would do for now.

Luke arrived in furry slippers and pajamas with fur, a Chanel bag full of snacks over his arm, and wine for them and a few packets of blood for me and Paige. Kendra came a few minutes later, and we spread pillows and blankets on the floor in front of the TV.

Conversation flowed, and even Paige told stories about her vampy ex. "My last one was pathetic and hated the fact that I worked with Jax. At first, I thought he was jealous of Jax. Then he applied to be one of Jax's enforcers."

"Really?" I frowned, and knew at that moment I would never understand men. It didn't matter what species they were.

Paige nodded. "Yeah, but when Jax made it clear that he'd have to take orders from me, the jerk pitched a fit. So, I threw him out on his ass."

Kendra raised her glass in the air. "Good riddance!"

Paige clinked her glass with Kendra's. "That's what I said. He wasn't my true mate anyway. Just someone to pass the time with."

"True mate?" I asked, not hearing that term mentioned among the vamps.

"Yeah. Every vampire has a mate. The one destined to be their perfect match and to spend their very long and lonely existence with."

I fell silent and sipped my wine laced blood to hide my

reaction. At least I hoped it did. Jax had a mate out there somewhere. That meant I could never fall for him because he would leave me like the other men in my life did.

This was why I was resolved not to get into another serious relationship ever again.

Luke, the talker, the highlight of every party, changed the subject. I was glad. "Oh, ladies. You have no idea what it's like to be a mere mortal man."

I chuckled. "Do tell."

"Well, I'm dating a vampire. I work all day because... hello. I'm human and that's when the gallery's open. Then, I play all night."

Paige chuckled like she had information the rest of us didn't. "Ransom can play all night long." When we all turned to her, she shook her head. "I don't know it first-hand, but there's been talk."

Luke feigned shock. "Talk? Does that mean my boy has a naughty past?" He batted his eyelashes, pulled a bowl of popcorn onto his lap, and pretended to rapt attention while he shoved in the over-buttered kernels. "Dish, darling. Lukey needs to know."

I laughed. "Oh Lord. Give him something or we're going to be listening to third person Luke all night."

CHAPTER TWENTY-ONE

SINCE IT WAS my off night, I cleaned the kitchen, cleared out dust bunnies, cobwebs, and all the other stuff that had been neglected lately. Thanks to my new nightly activities I hadn't had much time for cleaning.

I really didn't mind all the distractions. I liked staying busy and didn't love cleaning so much.

The latter was why I was thankful when the phone rang. Cleaning kept my hands busy, but it allowed my mind too much free-range Jax time, and I had to pull that back quickly. Not picture those chameleon eyes of his, or the breadth of his chest, the strength in his hands when he clasped mine.

Thank goodness the phone was persistent so I could snap out of my mind musings. "Hello?"

"Hey, Bond girl. Jordan has a skip he wants you to track. A big one. Says he needs his best team on it." Cleo sounded excited about this one.

The praise shot a bolt of pride through me. We were three for three. About to make it four for four.

"Should I call him, or do you have the info?" If she had a fax, we could go off of, there wouldn't be a need to deal with Jordan's big personality more than after we caught the skip.

"I'll shoot you a screenshot." She hung up.

As far as business managers went, she was aces. I didn't have to worry about anything but catching the skip, and the increase in my bank accounts that she made sure happened.

I dialed Kendra, and she did the tracking spell, so we knew where we were going. I picked her up to drive into the city. The bond price on this woman was a big one, and I wanted to make sure we caught her. Plus, I liked being the team Jordan went to when he needed a skip caught. I didn't want to jeopardize our status.

We drove to the apartment, knocked on the door with a *delivery* for her and she answered. Kendra took her into custody, and I cuffed her while I explained the procedure once we took her in. Easy peasy.

Kendra drove to the station while I sat in the back with the skip. Then, once we picked up our bounty receipt we drove to Jordan's.

"Well, well, well. You guys are like Pippen and Jordan." I wasn't sure of the reference but smiled. My blank look must've demanded clarification because he rolled his eyes and scrubbed his hands over his face. "A dream team? You don't watch basketball?"

Kendra frowned. "Not basketball from the 1980s." She

shoved the receipt across the counter. "We prefer Bond Girls, not dream team."

Jordan nodded. "I do love that name." He pulled out the checkbook. "Should I make it out to the Bond Girls or to one of you?"

Cleo had opened our business account after our last payday. "Bond Girls is fine."

Without much more conversation—it was a late night even for Jordan standards—we walked out.

And ran straight into Blake. I was beginning to wonder if he was tracking me.

"Well, hello, beautiful Hailey." He spoke quietly. "I have quite a surprise for you lovely ladies."

I could've done without all the syrupy weirdness. I looked at Kendra. She looked at me. Maybe it was instinct, or maybe his weird vibe, but we mouthed, "Run!" and as we were about to take off, Blake moved with his speed of light quickness and had his hand on Kendra's throat before I could react.

He lowered his voice. "If you scream, make a single sound, or try to fight, I'll rip her throat out. We both know there's nothing you can do to stop me."

To have that kind of speed, he was obviously old. Obviously strong, too. I nodded.

Blake grinned. "Good, then. We're going to go for a little walk, and you're both going to behave yourselves, or I'll kill you in the street and disappear before your little boyfriend even knows there's a problem. Understand?"

I hated people who needed clarification that I was paying attention. "Of course, I understand." I snapped at him because he might've had the power, but he wanted us alive. Probably needed and I was willing to bet my bad attitude on it.

He took his hand off of Kendra's throat, but kept a firm grip on her arm, although to any passersby, it probably looked normal enough, especially in this neighborhood. I wanted to signal Kendra to let her body go limp, but I couldn't without alerting this jerk face since he'd stationed himself between us.

"What do you want from us?" I asked. "Who are you, really?" But he didn't answer. Instead, he walked us toward a warehouse with enough graffiti and broken windows it looked as if it belonged in some sort of scary movie.

"Shut up and go inside." I did as directed, all the while trying to think of a way out that wouldn't compromise Kendra's safety. Maybe if we got inside, and he let her go, she could do a spell or a chant to subdue him, to at least give me a fighting chance. Or maybe she could summon a coven to help. I didn't know if her powers could do that. I only knew mine were no match for his.

It turned out the graffiti on the walls were runes. My guess was spell dampeners which would keep Kendra from her magical abilities.

"Who the hell are you?" Kendra demanded as he shoved her, and she fell to her knees.

"I'm the guy who compelled your friend Jordan so he would tell me right where you were." Not a stellar feat, since I was pretty sure Jordan was the kind of guy who wouldn't be all too resistant to a good compulsion.

Not many humans could.

"What do you want with us?" My voice came out high-pitched and shrill.

I knelt down beside Kendra to check on her, but the jerk face lifted me up by my hair. "Stop it!" I screamed.

He cackled a laugh. "You are pathetic and stupid, and I cannot abide such in a member of my race."

Oh, Lord. He was one of those. A zealot. And an idiot. Not a winning combination. And with one flick of his wrist, the glamour that made him gorgeous fell away and he was just an average looking vampire. Nothing to write home about, for sure.

He lifted his arm and backhanded me across the cheek. He knew I couldn't be killed by beating me to death, but I was willing to bet he was going to try.

"Allow me to introduce myself. My name is Kalon. I'm sorry to interrupt your night, but I needed you to lure your little boyfriend here." He jerked my hair again. "Now, I need you to be very scared, very injured so he feels it."

"Why would he feel it?" I wasn't well acquainted yet with my connection to Jax.

"Oh, for goodness' sake. Pathetic *and* stupid." He shook his head and twisted my hair again around his fist. "He's your maker. He can feel all your emotions. Might even be able to read your little mind. So, call for him."

When I didn't flinch, he struck me again. Pain blossomed in my cheek, and I would've fallen if not for the hand in my hair. "Do I need to convince you?"

And he started with a punch to my stomach. After a few punches, Kendra rebounded and jumped on his back.

"How did I not feel your magic?" she grunted, yanking his neck back with both hands under his chin. He threw her off easily without ever letting me go. She crumpled onto the floor.

"I have a very talented witch in my pocket." He grinned, and evil rolled off of him in waves. It was blatant and dark. Chilling in ways I didn't care for. I jerked, trying for freedom, but he held on.

That was when I opened my mind and called out to Jax. I wasn't sure I was doing it right. I hoped so. Because I needed my maker to come and teach Kalon some manners. Or I was going to die here tonight. For real dead.

CHAPTER TWENTY-TWO

He continued to try to torture me with a couple of kicks to my stomach, a few punches to my jaw, and more than a few times, he pounded my head against the concrete floor. But I was young and healing almost as fast as he inflicted the punishment.

That didn't stop the pain.

Growing frustrated, Kalon went in for the kill, to rip my throat out with the strength in his fingers, but before he got a good grip, an overhead door pushed up and Jax, Ransom and Paige stood at the edge of the loading area.

Kalon let me go, and I fell to the ground as Jax advanced, stalking Kalon with his fangs bared and murder in his eyes. His fists clenched at his side. "Run, Hailey."

But I wasn't going anywhere.

Kendra was against the wall scraping a rune from the concrete, and Ransom went to stand beside her while Paige helped me up and we moved to Kendra's side. "Help me," she hissed.

I scraped with her. She needed the runes gone so she could work a little magic. Help out the good guys.

Jax pounced on Kalon, and they battled, throwing one another into posts that held up the building, rolling on the ground into walls that dented, and crumbling the concrete under their strength. The whole place smelled like a sewer and there was no telling what had been done in here before we arrived, but I was glad for a moment to recover. The punches hadn't done much more than hurt, but they had been powerful. I'd lost a lot of blood in the few minutes Kalon had beaten me.

More vamps poured in through the open doorway—followers of Kalon's who attacked Ransom and Paige while I gave my body a minute to heal before jumping into the fray. I was young in terms of vampire strength, but I'd been training like a prize fighter lately, and there was no way one of these asshats was taking me down.

I punched. Kicked. Sidestepped a biter.

A woman with long robes tied at her waist by a gold cord walked through the room, a whirlwind of energy around her. Papers and debris from the floor swirled in serious tornado action while she walked closer. I wanted to stop her, but I couldn't. I had two vamps taking pot shots at me, and I was in an advance-retreat mode of defense.

In a moment of distraction, I took a hard right cross to the jaw and saw a couple of stars before it cleared. Rage poured through me. Why they were fighting for Kalon, I didn't know, but they were my enemies now, and I had to prove I could handle myself.

I glanced at Kendra. Whoa. She was glowing, levitating a couple of feet above the action and the walking witch struggled, kicking her legs as Kendra pulled her off the ground. Their fight stayed in the air while the vamps fought on the ground. Paige roared while Ransom beat his attackers back with a steel pipe, he wielded like he'd taken batting practice with the majors.

But I kept my body squared where Jax would never be far from my periphery. I wanted to be able to see him. Not that I could do much against a vamp like Kalon, but if Jax fell, I would be there, fighting to the death, no matter what I had to do to get to him.

I worked my way into the corner and to a broom. I broke it over my knee and created two pointed stakes. I jabbed one of my vamps through the heart and stepped back as his body imploded. Now I just had the tattooed vamp he'd brought with him. She was long haired and glassy eyed. When she knelt, distraught, to run her hands through the mess of blood and guts her little friend left behind, I grabbed her by the hair, lifted her chin and staked her. "You got staked." No, that wasn't a good catchphrase. I'd come up with something eventually.

As I ended my vamps, I looked over my shoulder at Jax just in time to watch him rip off Kalon's head. As literally as one could be ripped off by the bare-handed grip of a vampire. Jax threw the open-mouthed skull to the side.

Like they'd been released from a spell, the remaining vamps stopped fighting, stood, and turned to bow to Jax.

Above us, the fight between Kendra and Kalon's witch raged on. Kendra shot a ball of fire, and the witch moved to the side. She sent a bolt of power at Kendra and missed. Kendra advanced, took the other woman by the throat and wrapped the cord from the woman's waist around her neck.

She murmured a few words in Latin and the woman fell, hitting the ground hard.

When Ransom moved to stop her from running out, Kendra called out. "Let her go. I stripped her power."

He stepped aside and the woman limped to the big door before she picked up her robes and ran.

The battle was over. For now.

I stood beside Kendra as Jax and Ransom rolled Kalon's body into one of those blue construction tarps. They loaded him into the back of a van. I didn't ask where it came from, because this was very likely one of those need-to-know situations and after careful consideration, I didn't need to know. I also didn't want to know.

"Why didn't his body explode?" I asked.

"He was too old," Jax replied as he held the door open for me. "He'll slowly crumble."

I sat beside Jax, who told me to stay close while Ransom drove the van and Paige and Kendra brought the Prius to Jax's house. Jax held my hand, stroking my palm with his thumb, but didn't speak. Every once in a while, he glanced at me, but whatever he might've wanted to say, he kept to himself.

"What're you going to do with his body in the meantime?"

My voice sounded small and weak, but it was what I could manage.

"Are you sure you want to know?" Jax asked.

I nodded, not sure at all. "Of course." I said it like I was a badass, but if the answer involved disemboweling or cutting him up for spare parts, or feeding off of him, I was out. So far out it would take a shuttle and a team of astronauts to get to me.

"I have a cremation chamber in the basement," Jax said simply.

I laughed. Maniacal. Disbelieving. "Oh sure. I bet that was a big selling point for the realtor." I laughed a little more. "Blackout windows, fully stocked bar, and a dungeon with a cremation chamber. Really drove the price up, I bet."

His voice was calm, soothing, soft. "It's going to be okay, Hailey."

I asked the question I hadn't wanted an answer to before, so I'd never let myself consider it. But now I had to know. "What happens if I don't get the hang of this vampire thing? Am I going to end up in the basement barbecuer?"

He narrowed his eyes. "No, of course not." He ran his finger from my temple to my jaw then around to my chin and lifted so I was looking into his eyes. "I will never hurt you. You're a part of me."

I could've drowned in his eyes, in the sincerity in his voice, in the emotion stirring in my belly. I nodded, and he pulled me to him and kissed the top of my head.

Ten minutes later, Ransom pulled the car around the back of the house, through the fence Jax opened for him and pulled shut when the van was hidden inside. When Ransom parked at the back door, Jax lifted Kalon's body and tossed it over his shoulder in a fireman's carry. The unsecured head rolled out and Ransom picked it up, easy as pie.

I gasped. Kalon's eyes were wide and colorless, his lips parted, fangs dangling now.

"Go on inside. I'll be up in a few minutes." Jax nodded at me as if he was telling me it was all going to be okay, and when he said it, I believed it. Until he walked down the steps to the walkout basement door.

Then the nerves came back, and I stood watching. I just couldn't stop myself from walking down and peeking in the window. Jax opened a metal hatch and pushed the body inside, then hit a button so a fire burst up and lit the tarp. Ransom threw the head in, and they stood for a minute as the skin bubbled, then shut the hatch and turned. I ran up the steps and was inside on the sofa before they made it to the basement door.

Jax came in and sat beside me. "You okay?"

I nodded.

"You don't have to be tough right now. It's just us, and I know I was pretty messed up the first time I saw a body burn." I didn't acknowledge the fact that he knew I'd been watching.

"I'm fine." I wasn't, but I would be so long as he kept touching my hand, soothing me with his soft voice and steady fingers.

"I have to call Dominic and let him know I killed Kalon." He laced his fingers through mine then pulled them back and stared while he slid his palm against mine, back and forth.

"Why do we have to tell?" Good riddance in my book.

"I need to get to Dominic before any of the vamps who had known of Kalon's plan do. Their spin will be a lot harsher than the truth. I'm already on the radar for affecting the vampire population. This will be another strike." He spoke as if he'd done something wrong by killing Kalon.

"Even though you killed him to save us?" Certainly, there had to be some concession for killing one vampire to save three. And a witch. And what about the vampire I killed? Will they hold me responsible for that?

"Yeah." I didn't know if it was his worry I felt as much as I heard or if it worked the other way. I only knew his emotion was palpable. I was swimming in it.

CHAPTER TWENTY-THREE

It took a couple of days to scrub the sight of Kalon's burning body from my mind. But once I did, I was back to myself as much as I could be during the waking hours. We'd just captured a particularly well-paying skip, so I was in the mood to party.

I called Luke. "Party at my place. Bring your dancing shoes and your iPod. I'll handle everything else."

Luke couldn't resist a good party. "What are we celebrating?"

"Why does it matter?"

He chuckled like I was the dumbest woman he'd ever spoken to. "I need to know whether we're going formal or California casual."

"It's a middle of the night party under the stars. Dress for mosquitoes." I smiled, then hung up and called everyone else.

An hour later, we all stood around with drinks raised. "To the Bond Girls Recovery Agency!" We were officially a company staffed by me, Kendra, and Paige. Cleo said she would work with us, but she wanted her freedom to work when she wanted and vacation when it suited her.

Paige drank her glass of blood like she was throwing back a shot of tequila. "Hell, yeah."

"You already have a job as head of my enforcers." Jax stood beside me, and I absorbed as much of his closeness as I could while he spoke to Paige.

She chuffed out a breath and shook her head. "Oh, ye of little faith. I can do both."

Ransom grinned. "I don't want to be known as a Bond Girl, but I can help out every once in a while, too."

Jax leaned down so his breath was warm on my ear. "You're stealing all of my employees."

Before I could reply, the back gate swung open and Dominic stood staring, bobbing his head as if he was counting before he walked through.

He stood at the edge of our little talking circle and nodded at Jax. "Jaxon. I was sorry to hear about the death of Kalon. Furthermore, I was surprised you left such a dangerous message on my voicemail." Jax didn't react more than to tense his muscles.

Even I could see there was more coming. I motioned for Luke to go inside and compelled it with my mind. If some supernatural punishment was coming, I didn't need my brother to see it. He walked inside as Dominic continued. "The elders demand your presence." He paused. "There is much for you to answer for."

"Who?" I had to ask in some slim chance he wasn't talking to me.

"All of you." When I turned, he tapped my shoulder. "It's time for you to meet the elders and be justified."

STAKED IN THE MIDLIFE

CHAPTER ONE

Vampires sweat. I had no idea. But here it was, nine on a Saturday night, and my drenched self was chasing the criminal version of Usain Bolt through the streets of Walnut Hill.

Such was the life of a bounty hunter.

And coincidentally, at nine on a Saturday, the seven p.m. showing of the new Clooney blockbuster had just let out, coinciding with a bar crawl, so with people left, right, and center, I couldn't use my super speed to catch the creep. I had to run like a common human, darting and dashing around bodies. Well, not *dead* bodies, living ones that were pretty much all drunk, high, or both. Or maybe just drunk on Clooney, which was understandable.

It took a lot more strength than I would've thought to control my speed. Hence, the sweat.

We'd circled the same block twice, and I was a gnat's eyelash from saying eff it and using my vamp speed to take him down, witnesses be damned. The night was slightly chilly for early April, and the sweat combined with the wind made me want to shiver.

Kendra Justice, my BFF since childhood and fellow Bond Girl, had put the word out on the street that we were looking for Foley Breck—the skip's AKA, which sounded more worthy of a Bond Girl chase than his real name, Herbie Goldsmith. I snorted thinking about it. Herbie.

I'd been surprised when we'd gotten a hit within an hour.

Then again, Kendra had connections, and those connections knew how to spread rumors in the underground crime sectors better than the busybody grapevine operators.

Apparently, Herbie wasn't very popular among his law-breaking peers. They'd been all too eager to throw him under the bus. Too bad they hadn't literally done so.

He turned another corner and looked over his shoulder at me, then ran full-speed into a brick wall, bounced off and twisted to catch his fall, but failed, and landed face-first into a puddle. I winced but kept running after him.

Ouch. He'll definitely feel that later.

It was about time I'd caught a break with this guy. Without hesitation, I hopped onto his back, but he bucked like we were a PBR team. Of course, I didn't have cuffs because I'd lost my fanny pack somewhere between our last block and our second or fourth or maybe hundredth turn around this building, so I used my vamp-strong thighs to hold him down. "You already made me chase you fourteen blocks and two laps. Stop resisting before I drown you." I gritted my teeth and tried to get ahold of his arms without making it super obvious I was way stronger than he was.

I channeled my mother and gave his head a little shove into the puddle again. Not that my mother would have drowned me, but I'd been on the receiving end of the occasional slap on the back of the head for mouthing off. She hadn't been afraid to discipline on the fly.

A small crowd gathered while Herbie and I struggled, and with them, Kendra finally arrived, shooing the lookie-loos away from the scene. "Nothing to see here! Move along, you Nosey Nellies."

As per normal, no one listened, so she rolled her eyes and handed me a pair of zip-tie cuffs. I slapped those babies on Herbie, maybe with a bit more strength than I should've, and gave him one more shove into the water for good measure. My vamp side was in the mood to drain the bastard. But noooo. I couldn't do that because us vamps had rules about killing humans. I'd managed to avoid it so far. The only being I'd killed had been a psycho vampire who'd wanted to kill me.

When I stood, I glanced at the nearest cell phone videographer, cocked a brow, and hauled Herbie up beside me. "Hailey Whitfield. Bond Girl."

Someone nudged me from behind, and I stumbled, tripped over Herbie's outstretched leg, and fell. Now, we were both dripping with rainwater, but to my credit, I sprang up like my boobs had springs attached.

I didn't look to see how many cell phones had caught my clumsiness. I'd be a GIF by morning, but not much I could do about it.

I pulled Herbie to the bus stop, and we sat. I'd left my car fourteen blocks back and even if I hadn't, this jerk was covered in slop. He was *not* getting in my vehicle.

A month ago, I was an unemployed, jilted at the altar, almost bride. Now, I was a bounty hunting—makes Bond Girl all the more clever now, right?—vampire who worked with my witchy BFF, Kendra. We were a team, and our jobs sounded a lot more glamorous than they were, truth told. Especially with the sweating and the face plant onto the sidewalk.

We had a third Bond Girl, but she had a full-time job as Jax's head enforcer. Paige was a dark-skinned goddess—beautiful, tall, and slender; a total badass. She'd been turned in her twenties, so human college guys hit on her all the time. Some older men hit on her as well.

When the bus came, Kendra paid our fares and I dragged Herbie to a seat. The bus was crowded so Kendra couldn't cast a binding spell or even one that would shut this yahoo's pie hole.

"Help! I'm being kidnapped!" He implored the woman across from him, but she turned her nose back into her well-worn copy of a popular romance novel and ignored him. He tried again with an old guy who was either deaf or uninterested, and once more with a guy who was young enough to be my son. If I had one.

The kid winked at me. "If you want to let him go, I'll let you handcuff me without complaint." He winked, and I almost fainted. He was cute, but I wasn't interested in becoming a cougar on top of a vampire. I'd had my fair share of immature men who thought they were a gift to all women.

"Yeah. Take Romeo." Herbie knocked me hard with his shoulder, and I slid to the edge of the seat, one butt cheek hanging off.

I scoffed while working my jaw and moved back to my spot. The image of me knocking him out flashed into my mind. It was so tempting. I resisted. If I did that, then I'd have to carry his ass off the bus and into the police station. I wasn't doing it.

"This isn't about romance, Einstein. This is about *you jumping bail.*" I raised my voice for the benefit of the other passengers. The last thing I needed was someone actually believing the outlaw and playing the hero. I didn't have time to call in vampire reinforcements to wipe the memories of everyone on the bus when I used my strength to apprehend another person.

Geez. This whole night had been crazy since I'd picked up the perp's trail. And it wasn't even half over.

Herbie was about five-foot-nine-inches of unbathed asshat, with stringy brown hair and dull blue eyes. He lived in a house that should've been condemned ten or twelve years ago, and I would've bet a week's pay he was still a virgin.

Did I say he was an asshole already?

"I wouldn't romance you, Hailey Whitfield, if you were offering dollars for dicks."

I laughed. "Well, *Herbert*, I heard a dollar's about all yours is worth."

The kid laughed like I was doing stand-up. He almost fell off his seat.

I rolled my eyes as the bus rolled to a stop outside the police department. "This is us, Herbert." I hauled him to his feet and just about dragged him off the bus and inside the station to collect my bond sheet.

Next stop—payday at Jordan's Bail Bonds.

Jordan Leslie was *the* man in the bail bonds trade. At least in our area of Philly. Mr. Leslie was ninety percent leprechaun, and ten percent Danny DeVito's comb-over, though even that wasn't stopping the rapid northerly ascent of his hairline. He treated his office like a giant garbage can, and I was pretty sure, despite city ordinances, he was using his back room as his living quarters. But he paid, and in the order of importance, pretty much nothing else mattered.

He dragged himself out of the backroom and unlocked the front door to let us in. Jordan was used to middle of the night appearances from us, but this was a bit earlier than our normal after-midnight calls. It wasn't even midnight yet. Still, he dragged his shirt over an obscenely hairy chest for a guy who still shopped in the little boy section at Target.

"Lady luck is my favorite kind of luck, and you broads have it in spades." He said it in his Michael Jackson-esque voice as he gave Kendra an up and down that should've peeled her skin off, but somehow didn't. It took a couple of seconds before he noticed her scowl, then pulled his checkbook from under the counter. "Bond Girls…" He spoke as he wrote on the Pay to the Order of line.

We brought in a lot of skips these days and so we were all

making the big bucks. I eyed the amount and nodded at Kendra. This one was enough to get her the down payment on a new Kia she'd been eying, Cleo a couple of weeks in LA, and me a tidy little nest egg. I wasn't peeing in my pants with joy, but I was pretty excited.

Bounty hunting wasn't my first or even third choice as a career. But I'd needed the money when I first moved to Philly a few months ago. I already knew a lot about what it took because my ex-husband, Howard, was one, and I sometimes used to help him with the leg work of tracking skips down.

When I'd started working for Cleo as her in-home nurse, after she'd been shot on a job, I took one of her easy cases that she wasn't yet up for. That turned out to change my life. The skip turned out to be a vampire and she'd nearly drained me to the point I was dying. Kendra had called our undead neighbor from across the street, and he'd saved my life.

Of course, that had involved turning me into a vampire. Once the shock wore off about my new lifestyle, I found out that there were rules about turning humans with the permission from the elder council.

Now the two of us were going to have to face the council for judgment, which Jax and I were trying to put off as long as we could.

The sound of paper tearing drew my attention back to Jordan as he handed over the check. Kendra took it and tucked it in her bra—she was the accountant for our group, the business-mind. Without missing a beat, Jordan handed me a couple of files. "Like your breasts, these aren't big ones, but…"

Did I mention he was funny? At least, he laughed at his own jokes.

I checked the names. No one I knew was on that list, which was always good news, and no big money, but enough to see us through the end of the month. I tucked the folders under my arm. "Thanks, Jordan."

"You ladies have been burning up the wire. Cops have stopped looking for the skips. They just leave it to the Bond Girls." Word was spreading. "Maybe you'll get one of those reality TV shows like the Swamp People."

God, I hoped not.

Kendra smiled. "Maybe."

Things had been going really well for us. I didn't have to worry about money anymore. Cleo was almost back at a hundred percent since the shooting that had almost paralyzed her. And Kendra wasn't stuck collecting billable hours for bottles of champagne. We drank champagne whether she won her cases or not now. Though she tended to win.

Bond Girls Skip Trace Agency was really starting to take off. And it turned out being a vampire wasn't so bad either.

CHAPTER TWO

Home was across the street from the house occupied by the vampire version of Brad Pitt, Jaxon Parsons. He was also my maker—the guy who had turned me from a dying human who'd been sucked dry by a skip, to a vampire.

The guy who had to face the council with me.

He had a smile that had panty-dissolving powers, super strength and speed, and years of vampire knowledge. I was hoping that knowledge would be enough to keep us from dying at the hands of the council.

Just thinking about him made me sigh. But I wasn't doing relationships. Not now and no time in the immediate future. Plus, as my maker, Jax and I had a bond, and I wasn't sure if it was the bond that made my knees go weak and my skin to heat when I was near him. I didn't want to start something with false pretenses. Although, I had been very attracted to him that time I met him before he turned me. Urgh, I didn't know. After all my failed relationships, I didn't trust myself, my judgment.

When I reached my porch, I frowned at a note taped to my door telling me to pop into his place when I returned home.

I debated on taking a quick shower before heading over, but I was tired. Showering and putting on clean comfy clothes would only make me lazy. After all, I had planned to catch up on some reading or watch a movie the rest of the night.

No, I better go see what Jax wanted first.

I walked across the street on a teenaged cloud of anticipation about him wanting to see me. At the same time, anxiety filled me, because my shirt was caked in what I now suspected hadn't entirely been rainwater in that puddle. Ugh. Blech.

I should've gone into the house and changed first, but I was already at his door. He'd have to take me as I was. After the second knock, he answered and gave me a solemn look.

Even solemn on Jax looked like a seductive invitation, and I pressed my lips together to keep from puckering for a kiss. I wasn't sure why the man had such an effect on me. The maker bond had something to do with it. Or it was me.

I really had to stop going over and over and around and around about this. Yeah, right. Like I'd be able to stop.

"Hailey, you remember Dominic?"

Crap. Craaaaaap.

Of course, I did. Was I likely to forget the guy who never smiled, who could one minute sound like Sean Connery and the next like Captain Jack without the drunken charm? Heck, no. Not to mention the insane hunt he'd taken me on the last time I saw him. Also, he made Jax so, I should've probably been sending him a thank you card a day.

However, Dominic's visit wasn't a friendly one. And I'd been dreading the day he'd come back for a not so friendly visit.

Crap. Crap. Crap. I'd hoped we'd have more time to come up with a plan or something. We'd been avoiding answering the council right away. Not really avoiding. More like pushing them aside for a bit.

Waiting for a written invitation that hadn't come.

We'd have to face the vampire elders at some point to see if I would be deemed worthy to stay alive and to see if Jax would be punished for breaking the rules. It wasn't like I was a menace or anything. I, for one, was quite proud of what I'd achieved in a short time. I didn't even have to worry about blood lust. Jax lust...well that was a whole other avenue that I keep missing the exits to.

My point was, I was doing good by using my abilities to take down criminals. That had to count for my case, right?

"As I was saying, the elders are waiting. You should've been there already to speak of what you've done." Dominic shot me a glance then motioned with his head.

"I don't understand why Jax has to be punished for saving my life." I glared at Dominic.

Jax shook his head at me, but my opinion mattered as much as anyone else's in this room. And since it was my head on the block in a most literal way, I wasn't going to sit quietly and let them discuss me like I wasn't in the room.

"You're not wholly innocent in the eyes of the elders, young lady." Dominic cut a narrow glare my way.

My jaw dropped in surprise. How in the absolute hell did any of this come back on me? He'd said something before about the council, but I'd assumed he was messing with me or that I'd just have to *meet* them.

I couldn't imagine, but I also couldn't imagine why I was supposed to be afraid of these elders. I wasn't even going to entertain his accusation by asking what I'd supposedly done. Existing?

Instead, I asked, "Why is Jax being punished?"

Dominic held my gaze and sighed. "He broke the rules. It is not our place to go around saving humans who are dying." He rolled his eyes and threw up his hands. "They die all the time! We have to be selective about whom we turn and bring into this life. And they have to want it for the right reasons. There is a process that must be followed."

I understood what he was saying. If master vampires went around turning just any old human, they ran the risk of having more rogues and that led to more exposure to the hunters. It was pointless to argue about it anymore.

"Who are these elders?" I tried to relax but the tension in the room was thicker than oil. And I was dirty. And tired. And so dirty.

Jax's eyes fluttered closed at yet another question from me. Or was it because he just wanted Dominic to leave already? I ignored my maker and waited to see if Dominic would answer.

A slight lift of one corner of Dominic's lips told me he

enjoyed answering. Intuition told me he would make a great teacher. Despite the fact that the man scared me to death the first time we'd met and still made me uneasy, I was warming up to him. I definitely was more outspoken now than the last time he visited.

"There are five elders. Each from one of the oldest bloodlines. They're different. Intimidating. And they're *old.*" Dominic winked at me and drifted to the mini bar in the corner of the living room and set his glass down.

"How old? Are we talking Charlton Heston as Moses or Moses as Moses?" I needed a frame of reference. A barely audible groan reached me from Jax's direction.

"Soran is five thousand years old."

The air whooshed out of me. Holy mother of the universe that was old. Even Moses wasn't quite there yet. "So, God created light, then he created Soran?" I couldn't comprehend five thousand years.

Jax smiled, then coughed as if covering a laugh. At least he wasn't irritated with me. "Something like that." This man had a murmur like a warm whisper against my ear.

"How old are you two?" I wagged a finger between them, still reeling from the five thousand years.

"I'm 546, and Dom is around fifteen-hundred." Jax watched for my reaction.

"Wow." It took me a second to really wrap my mind around it. Five *hundred* years older than me. That meant they'd both lived through the American Revolution. They… they might've known Magellan. King Henry VIII. Oh, the memories they each must have. I racked my brain for things that happened five hundred years ago. Chocolate was invented about that time. Shakespeare lived five centuries ago. *Shakespeare*!

My mouth fell open as it sank in. And for a collective two thousand plus years between them, vampirism had been better than a fountain of youth. They looked good. Brad Pitt and Michael Douglas weren't as pretty as these two. "And I was worried about turning forty." I scoffed and tried not to look totally gobsmacked.

"Forty is the new twenty-five," Jax said. I would have to remember to tell my brother, Luke, as much.

I smiled at Jax anyway. It was a nice consolation.

In terms of their years, forty was practically newborn. Did they see me as a fetus? Plus I was even younger as a vampire.

Dominic cocked his head at Jax, then shot me a fresh scowl. "You'll have to stand trial."

It took a hazy second for his words to register. "Me? For what?" Panic flared. Like a literal trial?

Getting bitten happened without my consent. And getting turned was a whole lot more than I had bargained for when I woke up that fateful morning.

I glanced at Jax, and his smile was, as usual, breathtaking. If my heart still beat—and I preferred to imagine it did—it would have been throbbing now.

Why was he smiling? Did he *want* to be punished and for me to lose my head? Before I could shoot a snippy remark his way, he leaned in and whispered, "Don't worry, Hailey. I've got a few tricks up my sleeve."

Although it was a lovely sleeve, I doubted it knew how to

keep me alive. Well, unalive. I wasn't sure if that was a thing, but I was rolling with it. However, I kept my opinion quiet in favor of a cocked eyebrow. "What are they? What tricks?" I needed to know. Probably.

"I'll tell you when the time comes." Maybe he didn't have a fully formed plan. Maybe it wasn't a plan at all. Or maybe it was just him showing off for Dominic, but it wasn't like I could go in and pull the words out of him, so I let it drop when Grim and Nash—two of Jax's enforcers—walked in.

I nodded at them with a frown. I wasn't frowning *at* them. It was just my mood at the moment. Chasing down a skip that was more a being caked with mud, and the universe knew what else, had annoyed my vampire side. My fangs pressed against my gums, telling me I needed to feed, now.

Grim gave me a tight-lipped smile. His midnight eyes watched me carefully as if questioning the tension in the room. I shrugged slightly. Grim's appearance was as dark as his name. Dark brown hair that fell to the tops of his shoulders in silky waves seemed to match his dark eyes, skin, and wardrobe.

Nash was the opposite of his friend and fellow enforcer. He had short light brown hair and gray eyes, plus an aura that said he could blend in almost anywhere.

"Hey, Hailey. Someone just pulled into your driveway." Nash pulled back the curtain so I could see. Sure enough. I sighed. Sensible gray sedan because gray cars get less tickets. A surprise visit. Nobody called anymore. Or even texted.

"It's my brother." I couldn't keep the regret out of my tone.

Ransom, who'd been seeing Luke—my good brother—for a little while now, perked up, but I shook my head at him. "My other brother."

No one was ever happy to see Ollie tapping his foot, arms crossed on their doorstep. I would've bet not even his wife, Victoria. That had to say something about my big bro.

CHAPTER THREE

I RAN across the street like my ass was on fire, which would've been less painful than a visit with Ollie, who was nothing like Luke—the fun-loving, gallery-owning brother who did YouTube makeup tutorials on his Tuesday night vlogs.

Ollie was serious, stern, and a *drag*. He meant well and as the oldest, he looked out for all of us, all five of us. Ollie, Luke, me and our twin sisters, Allison and Avery. The twins lived in New York and worked as Broadway actors, living their dreams, far away from Oliver and his fatherly ways.

Why had I come back to Philly again? Oh, yeah, Kendra. And to get away from a douchebag ex-boyfriend who'd decided to leave me for a young nurse *on* our wedding day.

Sometimes it was best to humor Oliver and tell him only what he needed to know, and that was the path I'd follow today.

My big brother judged everything we did and didn't hold back when he wasn't pleased with our life choices. Boy, was he going to be pissy about my new lifestyle. Not just the vampire part. The bounty hunter part, too.

Ollie had probably come out of the womb frowning and hadn't stopped since.

"What are you doing here, Ollie?" His real name, Oliver Bradshaw Whitfield, was too stiff, even for him.

"It's Oliver." Not. "And I waited for an invitation that never came. It's been months."

An invitation. I almost snorted. Sometimes he spoke like he was Dominic's age. Fifteen hundred plus.

And he was quite an exaggerator. The tone, the scowl, the arms crossed, all meant I would be a fool to open the door, but what choice did I have? I couldn't teleport or time travel, so aside from running screaming away, I was out of options.

Alright, Hailey, pull up your big girl pants.

I sighed and unlocked, then walked in. He stayed on the porch, waiting for a formal invitation. "Oh, for goodness' sake, Ollie. Get in here." My patience was thin.

And I was *still* dirty from chasing down that butthole of a skip.

"I'm just saying, Hailey. You could've called." And he would be saying it until one of us died, or I compelled him to forget, which as tempting as it sounded, it seemed like an abuse of power. Right now, anyway. I couldn't say he wouldn't push me to it.

"Why?" It was a stall question but telling him meant I'd

have to listen to his disapproval. Stalling wasn't going to make this visit any easier.

He tapped his foot. "So I know how you are."

I smiled, touched that he was worried. "I'm fine." He wasn't open minded enough to understand *how* I was, so the lie made sense. It really wasn't a lie. I *was* fine and would be, right up until I had to face the firing squad.

"I can see that now." He looked me up and down, then frowned. "You actually look quite fit." He wrinkled his nose. "Dirty. But fit."

It was as close to a compliment as I had ever gotten from him. I'd take it.

"So, what are you complaining about?" I shrugged. Would it be rude to leave him to shower? I was starting to smell myself.

He huffed out a breath while I tried to get him to look at me. "You exhaust me, Hailey."

I knew the feeling. I exhausted myself. But what had I done this time? I would've called him at some point.

He walked toward the kitchen, and I followed. If I still had a pulse, it would've been going wild. "Where are you going?"

Maybe he was heading out the back door.

"I want a bottle of water." Despite his impeccable manners, we were the kind of family who helped ourselves. I wouldn't have hesitated at his house to open a cabinet and help myself to a Pop tart. Well, in the old days when Pop tarts had appealed, anyway.

But I didn't have food or drinks these days. I had blood. Snack sized vials of B positive and flat packs of O neg.

And contrary to popular belief and what was seen in movies, it took a couple of steps to build up to vamp super speed. I didn't have enough space and despite the shove I gave him, Ollie beat me to the fridge, pulled it open and looked inside. Brow pinched, mouth thin, normal Ollie.

He picked up one of the flat packs, read the label, and looked at me.

Oh crap. This wasn't a 'smile my way into his good graces without having to explain myself' kind of moment. It was more of a 'wait and see what kind of tantrum he would throw' moment, but it gave me the opportunity to come up with something reasonable. If I didn't, he would camp out, and it would require something of the forklift or crane variety to get rid of him.

"Hails, why in the H-E-double hockey sticks"—he must've been on another stop swearing kick— "are there blood bank packets in your fridge?" He put on his big brother scowl. It paired nicely with his angry, adult-fisted hands. "What the hell have you gotten yourself into?" So much for not swearing.

Vampirism was supposed to be a big secret, but this was my brother. And I had to explain this somehow. Besides, I could compel him not to talk about it.

I popped my fangs down and almost squealed in delight that the pointed teeth actually obeyed on the first try. But there was nothing to jump for joy for at the moment as I displayed them for my brother's benefit.

"No!" He held out his hand like a cop stopping traffic. "I forbid..."

I waited, curious as to how he planned to finish. To my knowledge it was a little late for him to give me permission to be a vampire. This should be interesting. "Go on."

He opened his mouth, then closed it. He looked at the blood bag still in his hand and back at me. "How?"

He stood with his arms crossed while holding the bag and the fridge door standing wide open, staring at me like I'd grown a third eye or a second nose. Thank goddess I still had a reflection, or I might've worried that I *had* grown extra body parts. Besides the fangs.

His lip curled into a sneer, waiting, but there were details he didn't need to know. Ones he wouldn't understand.

I had to give him something if I ever wanted him to go away. "Well, you know how Kendra and I started the Bond Girls Recovery Agency?" I cocked my brow, ready to give him a *Hailey Whitfield, Bond Girl* TV commercial—if we ever got one—pose but took a look at his deepening scowl and cleared my throat instead. Better not push my luck.

"*You're* a bounty hunter?" Here we go. The double whammy.

He shook his head, and I didn't let his incredulity insult me. Not much anyway. "I read the email, but I thought you were joking."

In reality, he'd hoped I was joking.

It would've been an elaborate joke since I'd sent copies of my business card and a video of Kendra and me walking a perp into the police station. "Yes, I'm a bounty hunter. Pretty successful, too."

And that was not a brag. It was the truth. "Anyway, I got bit, then drained, and I was about to die."

"You let one of your…" He grimaced. "…prey bite you?" Yeah, sure. I *let* her alright. I was starting to lose my patience. Then he shook his head and added, "*Sounds* successful." Oh, the brotherly sarcasm.

He had no idea the strength of a hungry vamp. But if this kept going, I would happily show him. The jerk.

"I didn't *let* her do anything. She bit. I was dying. And a friend who happened to be a vampire saved my life."

His nostrils flared and his eyes went wide. "By turning you into a monster?" He huffed out a breath and turned to toss the blood bag back into the fridge and slammed the door shut. "And you didn't think to tell me?"

Was he serious? The current situation was the exact reason I hadn't told him.

"I wasn't sure how you'd take it." Anyone who knew Ollie knew exactly how he would take it. Little fib.

"Why? It isn't like I don't know about Kendra."

There were a lot of negatives in that sentence to unpack, but I had the gist. His mouth turned down and he looked away. He was upset.

That was true. He's known about Kendra since we were kids. If witches existed, then it wasn't that unbelievable that vampires and other beings did as well.

Relaxing my whole body and drifting over to him, I laid my hand on his arm. Hurting him had never been my plan. "I know, but to tell you about me, I would've had to tell you about them." I meant vampires in general. "And there are hunters out there that want to kill them, and me. Any exposure is dangerous."

"I'm not a hunter." And the hurt came back full force, as real as his anger. My heart squeezed.

He wasn't likely to forgive me or ever forget that I hadn't shared this with him. Thanksgiving dinner for the next twenty years wasn't going to be pleasant.

I pointed to the table. "Sit."

For once, he listened and sat ramrod straight in the kitchen chair. "You should've called, Hailey. Does Luke know?"

The answer to that question wasn't going to make him any happier. *Of course* Luke knew. Since forever, I had always confided in Luke before anyone, our parents included. I nodded, and he scoffed. Loudly. I swore it echoed off the walls. Jax probably heard from his house. "Figures."

"Luke is a busybody who waits for no invitation, and we have a different relationship." It all sounded lame to me. "Plus, he came over when I was first turned, and I bit him. There was no keeping it from him after that." Excuses. But Luke didn't judge. If he did, it was on a much more superficial basis. Clothes. Hair. Taste in men. He left the life decision criticism to Ollie, who carried the torch like an Olympic runner. "Ollie, this is all very new to me, too."

True enough.

I put on some water for tea and waited for the kettle to whistle because Ollie needed a moment to pout, to put it all in a neat little compartment where he could deal with it and pull it out when he was stronger.

I poured the water into his cup and watched him dunk the

bag a couple of times before I poured a small vial of blood into mine.

"What about kids, Hails?" He'd softened his voice and his attitude.

"I'm forty years old, Oliver. That ship is leaving the harbor, and I'm not on it." I'd never really wanted kids anyway. Well, once upon a time maybe, but at my age, a pregnancy would be traumatic. Fraught with worry. Plus, if I got pregnant right then, I would be fifty-eight when the baby graduated from high school. That wouldn't have been the worst thing in the world by far, but I just couldn't imagine myself with a kid.

It was a moot point anyway. Whether I wanted one or not, it was too late.

"Do you really want to live forever?" He spoke like I had a choice now. And hearing him, his words, knowing the age of the elder Soran, and Dominic, and even Jax, was a new kind of agony I hadn't let myself consider. But now, I had a lot to defend. My family, my friends, both new and old. "I-I'd prefer *not* to die."

"Yeah, but *ever*?"

"Not now, at least." Jax was 546 years old. And the elders made him look like a child. Even five centuries was a long time. I would have to watch my entire family die. Who the hell wanted that?

Damn. When reality bit, it really sank its teeth in.

"And I know we're not particularly religious, but aren't vampires damned by God?"

I didn't answer. He didn't give me the chance.

He moaned. "This is going to kill mom."

I couldn't think about it. "Let it go, Oliver. I can't change it. And you will *not* tell mom. Ever."

I hadn't had a choice about being turned or anything that had happened after it. But the last thing I needed was him to throw our mother in my face.

I sighed. This was my life now, and all I could do was make the best of it.

CHAPTER FOUR

By the time Ollie left, sadness had bubbled inside me, and anger hopped on board for a free ride. A tear had the audacity to slide down my cheek while my chest tightened. My big brother meant well, but he didn't always see what his judgmental words did to us. Me anyway. Nothing ever seemed to bother Luke much.

I stood frozen in the middle of my living room, staring at the carpet. Emotions washed over me, and my mind whirled with all the crap that had happened since I moved here. Entwined with those thoughts were Ollie's words of critical wisdom.

Yes, I'd live longer than him, my sisters, Luke, and Kendra, but that didn't mean that I couldn't make as many memories as I could until their time came. On the other dark and gloomy hand, I could be sentenced to death by the vampire Elders within a few weeks.

I sensed Jax before he knocked, and I closed my eyes. The last thing I wanted to do was see anyone or let them see me like this. Taking a deep breath and exhaling slowly to calm my ocean of emotions, I swung my front door open anyway.

Jax brushed past me and stood inside as I closed it and turned to face him. "What are you doing here?"

He pulled his lower lip between his teeth, took a couple of steps, and tilted his head. He was scenting the air and most likely reading my emotions. "I'm here for you." Then he wrapped me in a hug, surrounding me with his body, his scent, and his strength. And it was almost overwhelming. Almost. "I could feel how upset you are."

I looked up into his eyes, at his face. He was truly, by every definition, a gorgeous man, with his strawberry blond hair that hung loose to brush the tops of his shoulders and his big hazel-blue eyes, which were more gray than blue at the moment. At least I thought that was what they called his eye color. Jax's eyes changed in various shades of blue, gray, and green depending on his mood and the color of his shirt.

My personal favorite was the baby blue when he was relaxed, which didn't happen often.

His fingertip brushed my temple then down to my jaw, and there was nothing I wanted more than to pull him down for a kiss. To feel anything but the confusion Ollie had left me with.

Desire flared inside my stomach. This was stronger than simple lust, more than admiration for his body or because he was beautiful. This was…more. It was like I was drawn to him. At that moment, I believed we were meant to cross paths. I was exactly where I needed to be.

His eyes searched my face, and my fingers curled into his hair.

It was about to happen. I was going to kiss him.

Then he dropped his hands, took a step back, cleared his throat, and ran his hands down his pants leg. "I've put this off as long as I can."

I shivered from the absence of his warmth. He sighed and turned away from me. There was some satisfaction in the turn, but I couldn't wrap my head around the words.

"No need to put it off any longer." I stepped closer, and he backed off again. I stopped and frowned, my heart sinking to my feet. "You don't mean a kiss."

He shook his head, a slight frown turning his lips. I could've sworn I spotted desire flashing in his irises for a nanosecond. But then it was gone. "No."

"Oh." I blew out a puffy-cheeked exhale, trying to cover up my desire and disappointment. I had no idea what he'd put off. Certainly wasn't a kiss, despite my being puckered and ready.

Before I pressed the issue, I needed to know what we were talking about. "What then?"

"We need to go to Milan and face the elders."

I knew that, but we could've as easily gone with my lipstick on his mouth. He continued moving away when I got closer. This was the worst game of tag. Ever.

His Adam's apple bobbed as he swallowed. "You'll need to arrange for some time off work."

"Okay." I nodded. I knew it wouldn't be a problem. Cleo didn't need twenty-four-hour nursing anymore. I still went over there a few times a week to compare notes to see if she needed help with anything.

And the real breadwinner job, bounty hunting, didn't have set work hours or days. I had enough savings now to survive going without those checks for a few weeks. If the council decided I wasn't fit to carry on this vamp life, none of it would matter anyway.

Great. Now Ollie was wearing off on me. Gloom and doom.

"Maybe Paige can fill in for you with Cleo while we're in Italy?" he asked. The effect of the softness in his voice was a full body shimmy I couldn't suppress. But I focused on his words rather than the low timbre of his voice.

"Paige. Good idea." Cleo had met Paige before, when she went with me to talk about Herbie/Foley. They'd gotten along well enough. I couldn't imagine it would be a problem.

"I'll get a hold of her. Can you get me a work schedule?" He was handling all the details I wouldn't think of.

I nodded. "When are we leaving?"

"Tomorrow." This wasn't a romantic trip. This was so I could stand trial. *Trial.* I gulped as he continued. "We'll leave around five-thirty in the morning, so in just a few hours. We have to be on the plane so they can put the UV shields in place by dawn."

That was pretty much all I needed to know. And like he hadn't just had me in his arms, he walked to the door and pulled it open. We weren't anything except what we were. Maker and made. Not more. I leaned against the wood when it clicked shut behind him.

My heart would've been near exploding if it still beat, but I ignored that. It wasn't a literal thing, just an emotion I still attributed to my physical heart.

I was going to need someone to remind me that this trip wasn't a trip abroad with Jax as a couple. And that person would need to remind me often and with gusto.

On that thought…

I yanked the door open. "Hey Jax!" He stopped, turned and the full force of his beauty hit me again. Damn. I quickly exhaled. "Can I bring someone?"

"Yeah, of course. We have a private jet."

Oh, didn't we all?

But then he was gone, down the walk, across the street and into his house.

Pushing away the feeling of being rejected, I rushed inside and took a quick shower, making sure the water was on its hottest setting.

It wasn't like Jax had rejected me, not exactly. He was probably trying to keep our relationship professional because he was my maker. I had no idea why that thought stung more than it should have.

Pushing all sexy thoughts of my maker away, I scrubbed the grime off my body and out of my hair until everything squeaked from how clean it was. Once I was dry and dressed, I went to my room and flopped on my bed.

I picked up my phone from the end table and dialed Kendra. The moment she answered, I announced, "Pack your bags, grab your passport and be here by four-thirty. We're going to Italy, baby." Feigned enthusiasm was still enthusiasm. And I did *not* want to go alone.

"Hell, yeah, baby!" It was a good thing she was happy enough for us both. It was also a good thing that her vacation had officially started. I wasn't sure she would've been able to get time off on such short notice. After all, she still had a day job with rules.

As soon as we ironed out the details and she stopped squealing, we hung up and I dialed Luke. He was probably home and in bed. But when he answered, the heavy throb of a bass drum pulsed in my ear.

When did the man sleep?

"Hailey!"

More enthusiasm, but I couldn't let him find out I'd left because he popped over for a gawk at Ransom disguised as a visit to me.

I didn't mind being used for purposes of lust. It meant I got to see Luke more often. Did I mention he was the fun brother?

"Luke!" I shouted because he had, and it sounded like the right thing to do. But he must've been walking outside because the music died off in the background. "I'm going to be out of town for a couple days."

No point in giving him anything other than the best-case scenario. If it ended up being longer, I would explain when the time came.

"Where do you think you're going?" He did insulted, haughty, busybody better than anyone I'd ever met.

"Milan." I wasn't usually timid, but the last thing I wanted was to tell him why.

He didn't care why. "Little sister!" His voice went sharp, missing the intoxicated slur I would've expected for the time of night. "If you think for one minute that you're going to the fashion capital of the world without me, you've got another think coming." He paused, then continued, "And yes, it is *think* and not *thing*. Look it up."

I knew the think-thing thing, but I should've known he'd want to go with me. "I wasn't sure if you would be able to get off work."

Then again, he *owned* his work—the gallery.

"What is your flight number?" He clucked his tongue. "And upgrade to first class because this diva doesn't do coach unless it's a handbag."

I sighed. But I was glad he was going along. "Just grab your passport and be at the private gate at the airport by five."

"I'll meet you at your place by four," he retorted.

Of course. That was his way of making sure I didn't leave him behind.

I hung up. It was time to pack. What did one wear to appear in front of the elder vampires who wanted to take one's life?

CHAPTER FIVE

AT FOUR A.M. on the nose, Luke and Kendra showed up at my place, giddy. We gabbed about Italy while we waited for Jax. Kendra had brought over coffee for her and Luke. The rich aroma filled the air, and I wished I could taste it.

I yawned a few times, because my body was past its acceptable amount of stress for the week. Plus, it was getting close to sunrise and baby vamps' bedtime was when the sun woke up.

But when Luke spotted Jax coming out of his house, he smiled. "Ransom wouldn't happen to be waiting in the car?"

I opened the front door before Jax reached it and eyed my brother. I hated to burst his bubble. Before I could answer Luke's question, Jax did as he bent to pick up my bag. "He's staying behind. I need someone here I can trust to take care of matters, and he's my second in command." He was almost apologetic and for a second, Luke's face fell.

That made me wonder if Ransom confided in his own brother like I did mine. It could be that Jax was very perceptive. He didn't miss anything.

Then like a switch had been flipped, Luke clapped his hands together and smiled. "Oh, well. I'm going to Milan."

Rolling my eyes with a sad laugh, I touched his shoulder. I loved his enthusiasm, but this was serious business for me. "Luke, Jax and I are going to be on trial because of Kalon's death and because Jax *made* me."

"Rightly so." Luke supplied while studying his nails. He wasn't worried about the trial, and I wished I had half his confidence that everything would work out.

I agreed that we'd have to face the music for breaking rules, but I feared the unknown. "Jax turned me without an edict from the loyal order of..." I looked at Jax as he walked into my house once more, picking up the last of our bags.

"An authorization from the elder council," Jax offered, then exited the house to stow the rest of the luggage in the limo trunk.

"Oh." Luke fell silent as we locked up the house and headed to the car. I waited for it because a blind man could've seen it coming. This was Luke, and I was sure he invited dramatic. His smile burst across his face. "It's Milan, Hails. I bet even the prisoners in Milan wear Prada. And I'll worry when it's time. Right now, I'm going to Milan, baby." I didn't tell him that I wouldn't be going to a prison if they found us guilty. That wasn't for him to worry about, not now. And maybe he was right about not worrying about it at the moment.

Nash and Grim climbed into the stretch, quiet and solemn as was their usual. Luke bubbled. Kendra read a travel guide for witches. Jax held out his hand to help me inside. For a split second, I thought about running, but he was in trouble because of me. I didn't want to make it worse.

Luke chattered, filling the limo's interior with his happiness. "Oh, Hails. The fashion. The shopping. If I had a weaker bladder… mmm, girl. I probably should've worn some adult underpants." He was one chuckle away from an implosion. "But I promise nothing once we arrive on those golden Italian shores."

I didn't know about the geography of it—never one of my better subjects—but Luke was prone to exaggeration to prove his points, and I loved him for it. I laughed with him; well aware I might not get many more opportunities to do so.

But Jax shook his head. "Hailey won't have time for shopping."

Luke clicked his tongue against his teeth. "If you think I'm letting my baby sister leave Milan without at least twenty new garments, your little vampire brain is on the fritz." He head bobbed. "I know her size and her MasterCard number." This time his chuckle was half-laugh, half-squeal. "You're going to be the best dressed bounty hunting vampire in history."

In a rare moment of socialization, even Grim laughed. "You probably already are."

My skin would've flushed with color if my body still worked that way. Praise from Grim was an anomaly, and I didn't take it for granted.

The next hour or so was spent making our way to and

through the airport, boarding the plane and getting situated. We left Kendra and Luke with the stewardess, Luke gushing over the accommodations and Kendra triple checking the strength of her seatbelt.

Jax, his enforcers, and I went to the back of the plane where two bunks were attached on each side of the cabin. This place was luxe, in every aspect with plush blankets, memory foam mattresses, and a pillow that cradled my head.

Spare no expense. I just didn't know if this flying condo was Jax's or the Elders' expense.

Nash and Grim took one side of the cabin and Jax climbed on the bunk above mine. At that moment, I yawned. It amazed me I'd managed to make it this long. Then again, it wasn't every day I got to ride on a fancy private plane.

I kicked off my shoes and crawled into the lower bunk. After my shower earlier, I'd dressed in yoga pants and an oversized t-shirt because I knew I'd have to sleep on the flight. I had little choice about that.

The scent of Jax's cologne mixed in the air, and I drew it in. His nearness, knowing he was only a couple of feet above me reminded me of that moment when he'd almost kissed me. Or I'd almost kissed him. The desire rushed back like a lost puppy. Then, the sound of a duffle bag being unzipped reminded me there were two other vampires in the room.

I darted my gaze to the other bunk. Grim sat facing me going through his bag for something. I watched him for a few until he lifted his gaze to me, and he smiled knowingly.

Of course, he smelled my desire. I rolled my eyes at him and turned over, giving him my back. Now everyone on the plane knew I wanted Jax. Oh craptastic. That also meant Jax knew too.

"You okay, Hailey?"

Damn it. I forgot he was all tuned into my emotions. As my maker, we shared a bond, the one all makers and their progeny shared.

Okay was a stretch, but we weren't alone. Nash and Grim were too close for these kinds of thoughts. The inappropriateness was as startling as it was nerve wracking. I pulled lint from the blanket.

"I'm fine."

I didn't trust myself to say more. But he spoke, instead, voice soft, a mesmerizing purr. "There are five elders. Soran, Tobias, Gretchen—and you have to watch out for her. She looks like a princess, but she's a spoiled, selfish, evil vampire who loves destruction and misery. She's volatile. Then there's Amaya, and she *looks* scary but she's actually quite sedate. And finally, Dominic."

Oh. Interesting. I hadn't known that Dominic was one of the elders.

"Soran is the eldest. Dom is the youngest by quite a lot. The others are older than him by centuries, by millennia." Jax shifted on the bed above me, making the bed creak.

"I didn't know Dominic was an elder." There'd been plenty of prior occasions to mention this, and he hadn't. Neither of them had. I didn't concentrate on why, but the thought was a whispered wonder in my head.

"He's the newest. The youngest. His maker walked into

the sun about a hundred years ago." Jax took a long pause. "Dom inherited the position."

"Does that mean you will, too?" Oh, holy mother earth. I could do that math. Dom inherited. Jax inherited. I would inherit. But for me to inherit, Jax would have to be dead. I shuddered. Hell, no.

"Yes." His voice softened. "You're the first I've turned." Shit.

"In years?" The idea staggered.

"Ever." The boards to his bed creaked as he shifted again. "You're my first heir. My only."

"Holy crap." It was a lot to take in. "What happens if they punish us with death for…" I didn't want to call it crimes, so I let the sentence dangle.

"Then they would authorize Dom to create another vampire to extend his line." He sighed. "One day, the next eldest vampire in the states will become king. But the position on the council is hereditary." Meaning, one day it would be me. The gravity of the situation did nothing to ease my nerves. My breath stuttered, and my hands trembled.

"Just try to relax for now, Hailey. I'm not going anywhere. We have many lifetimes before you have to even start wondering about it." Had we not been in a tiny cabin with two others, I might've fallen victim to the softness of his voice. Might've even invited him to my bunk. Thank the goddesses for Nash and Grim.

That was one way to look at it anyway.

"We're going to be on the tarmac for a while, so we'll arrive in Milan at dusk." This guy could've read me the phonebook, and I would've listened, would've melted into the depths of his tone. "Try to go to sleep."

Whether he'd used his voice to compel me or whether I was just tired, I closed my eyes and didn't wake until the plane rolled to a stop at the gate in Milan.

CHAPTER SIX

There was an enormity to this whole thing. The trial, meeting the elders, and traveling outside the US was overwhelming. None of this was my usual.

But I wasn't worried as much as I was anxious. I was nervous about meeting the elders, but only because I didn't know the etiquette, and I didn't want to embarrass Jax by bumbling through the whole thing. Plus, my stomach was queasy, rolling, and I felt light-headed.

Jax said my physical afflictions were mental because vampires weren't generally troubled by physical failings unless they were too attached to their human selves. In my defense, I'd only been a vampire for a short time. He'd said it faded after a while, but I hoped it didn't. I like my emotional human side. And the fact they were caused by my inability to let go of my humanity made me feel a bit more human. It also didn't make them any less potent.

When we landed and deplaned, we climbed into a shuttle and watched the city pass by as we were carried to the hotel. I would never see Milan in the daylight. Never sit at a cafe on the sidewalk. Never see the fashion district while it was open. The loss of what I'd never had shuddered through me.

The hotel loomed in the distance. Large and old, stone and glass. The lights inside shone into the semi-darkness of the city.

I could only think, "Wow," even as Luke oohed and Kendra aahed beside me.

We passed a palace on the way and another bit of melancholy ached in my belly. This place was too beautiful not to see in the daylight.

As if he could sense my sadness again, Jax turned to me and smiled. "You okay?" he mouthed the words, and I nodded. And maybe I would be, but right now, I just wanted to get all of this over with. Milan had lost its allure already.

The hotel was opulent and ornate with its marble floors and crystal chandeliers and the old-fashioned bellhop inside the elevator who activated buttons when we climbed in. Jax handed out key cards. Kendra and Luke had a suite on the fourth floor and the rest of us were UG2. The UG meant underground because… of course, it did. It was good to know the hotel was vamp friendly.

Stepping off the elevator in the basement, I followed Jax down the hall, still mopey and silent. He stopped at my door, took my key, and slid it into the slot. "Get changed. They'll be expecting us."

A spike of alarm shot through me, but I squashed it. It

made sense to get this over with. I sighed before I nodded, and he smiled sympathetically. "It's going to be okay, Hailey. I promise."

I didn't nod because I believed him. I nodded because I *needed* to believe him.

He came for me a half-hour later, and with Grim and Nash, we walked out of the hotel to the nearest subway line.

I glanced at Jax when he took a seat beside me. "What? No limo?"

He smiled, but there was a tenseness to his entire body. His shoulders were stiff, his knuckles white where they curled around the bottom of his seat.

We had the car to ourselves, and Grim and Nash were only interested in the video playing on Nash's phone.

My stomach rolled. "Jax, are they going to… terminate me?" I supposed it would be fair considering I'd cheated death once when Jax saved me, but it was kind of a waste if they were going to end me now.

"I won't let that happen, Hailey." He threaded his fingers through mine and gave a gentle squeeze. "Come on. This is our stop."

We emerged from the underground train into a mildew-laden station. A mountain of a man stood at the corner. He wore Armani and pushed away from the wall when Jax approached. "Jaxon."

They shook hands, then he ignored the rest of us as he turned. He walked beside Jax on the left, with me on the right until we filed through a turnstile that led us to a half wall.

There was something quietly eerie about the big guy. He

was too well dressed to be hanging out in a subway which smelled like it did double duty as the country's sewer system.

He pulled a badge from inside his jacket, waved it in front of an electric eye, and a gate opened or maybe a wall pulled back. I wasn't paying attention enough for my mind to make sense of what my eyes were seeing.

We walked through the open archway and waited. When I opened my mouth to ask our destination, Jax squeezed my hand. Apparently, we were waiting in silence. Okay, then.

The reward for such compliant behavior was a stroke of his thumb over my skin as a single train car slid up the track to stop in front of us. It was long and white, marked with PRIVATE in English and Italian over the windows.

The doors folded open and Nash and Grim stepped in first. Then Jax turned and held out his hand for me. The big guy came in behind me.

This was a bit odd, even for four vampires. "Jax?" I wasn't usually so needy, but a month ago—just one short month—I'd been living a normal life. Looking for a job. Finding Cleo.

Now I was on a creepy train in a country a couple thousand miles from home on my way to be seen by a council of elder vampires who could very well sentence me to death. It was all too far in motion for me to stop it now.

The rail car rolled to a stop at the door of the Vampire palace. The stone entrance of the underground vampire palace seemed to melt into the walls of the subway. The architecture of the door and half of the building was neo-classical with gothic flair. Black veins of what I guessed was onyx etched through the dark gray stone like tree roots seeking nutrition.

There was no other station, and I glanced down the dark tunnel from where we came. "Is this a private section?"

Jax nodded with a hand on my lower back and leaned closer as we walked. "The palace is directly beneath the Royal Palace of Milan." He smiled and my blood heated. "*The Palazzo Reale*." Oh, the accent was spoken perfectly. My belly tightened as desire flared once again. "It was built at the same time the Visconti family built the palazzo."

"Were they…" I shrugged. I wasn't sure how much I was allowed to know as far as history. But then again it wouldn't matter if they were going to sentence me to death.

"Not vampires, but vampire sympathizers."

Ah, that was interesting. "Like trusted humans?"

"Exactly. Back then it was hard to trust outsiders."

We walked through the front door into a massive interior with stone floors and a high ceiling. My footsteps echoed, but the rest were silent. I had to learn how to walk without making a sound. Was there a magical technique for it?

As we walked into a bigger room, Jax started again. "All vampires used to be ruled by kings and queens. Not like the one in the American system now where each territory had a ruler. A king and queen sat in total power over all the vampires, all territories."

"What happened to them?" I kept my voice as low as his because I wanted to hear the story the way he whispered it—low and close to my ear so his breath warmed me.

Jax sighed, and I could've melted, but I waited for him to speak again. "He got too big for his britches."

"My mom used to say that." For all I knew, she still did.

Thinking about her now wouldn't help my nerves. Not when I might never see her again. Maybe I should have paid her a visit before we left. Then again, I hadn't had the time.

I pushed away the unwanted emotions and focused on the low timbre and cadence of Jax's voice. It claimed me on a level I didn't understand.

"There was a mutiny, and he was overthrown. Then the elders were appointed."

"By whom?"

"I don't know. Maybe through agreement with the king? I only know this part of the story because Dominic insisted I know. He might have told me when I lived as his apprentice but back then I wasn't interested in the politics of it all." Jax shrugged and we pushed through another doorway into a large space, there were people inside. "This was his throne room."

A pair of gilded chairs sat on a dais, roped off at the far end of the room. Tapestries behind them depicted a gruesome and bloody vampire attack on a naked woman whose rapture was glorious and graphic. Silver stanchions and velvet rope kept everyone away from the thrones.

Below the dais was a series of big, ebony desks and a conference table laden with laptops, fax machines, cellphones, and printers that made this room less throne-like and more office-like. People stared as we walked in.

Silence fell and hands stopped working. Voices went silent. We had officially arrived. My whole body trembled, so Jax rubbed circles on my back, comforting me.

While Jax stood at my side, Nash and Grim waited at the door with the big guy who nodded in greeting as we entered.

A man so thin he was almost bones advanced toward us. His skin was pale with a hint of Slavic ancestry. This must be Soran. He stopped in front of Jax and shook his hand. Each moment was slow, calculated, and *creepy*. "Nice to see you again, Jaxon."

Jax half-bowed. "If only it was on better terms." Jax motioned to me. "This is Hailey Whitfield. Hailey, this is Soran."

I bowed my head in greeting but didn't speak. I didn't trust my voice or what would pop out of my mouth. In situations like these, it was best to not speak unless spoken to.

One by one, each of the elders came forward for introductions. Tobias was next. He was thin, but not like Soran. He was dark-complected and looked Middle Eastern with his dark brown eyes and black hair.

Amaya was next and looked every bit as scary as Jax had said. She wore a long, black corset dress cut low in front to contrast her milky white skin. A back cape was tied at her throat, and she lowered the hood to reveal inky black hair. She glanced at Jax and pursed her full red lips which matched her bloody red nails. Her dark eyes glinted.

This wasn't just any gaze. This one was dark with lust. One of a lover. Or a former lover. She stared at me, then moved on without acknowledging my presence whatsoever.

In all of his speeches and chatter about what to expect, he'd neglected to mention his former lover was one of the elders. I tried not to hate her off the bat. It wasn't easy.

I had no right to be jealous, but here I was.

Gretchen, the one who looked young and sweet, smiled at

Jax, and leaned in like she wanted a hug, but didn't reach out for him. Wait, did she? No. Surely not. I could've sworn she hissed.

I hadn't expected her to be a Marilyn Monroe look alike, but despite what Jax had said, her mean streak wasn't hidden. She glared, displaying it proudly. Volatile wasn't an overreach.

Soran, who seemed by strength of tone and point of action to be in charge, moved to the opposite side of the conference table and cleared his throat. "Shall we begin?"

CHAPTER SEVEN

Once we were all seated around the table, the trial began, informal as it was. There was no jury or lawyers to plead our case. Nope. Just Jax and me against the five elders. It was our word against their laws.

No pressure. Oh, I was going to be sick.

Jax and I sat together on one side and the elders were on the other. It was a good thing too, because if I had to sit next to one of them, I really would get sick or faint. Or both.

My maker reached for my hand under the table and gave it a gentle squeeze. When he didn't let go of it, I relaxed a little.

Amaya slid another longing kind of gaze at Jax, then narrowed her eyes at me. I narrowed mine back. That earned me an evil smirk. Just as fast as that smirk appeared, it was gone, and she was all business. "Jaxon, you are accused of creating a vampire without the permission of the elder council."

I blew out another breath because being sentenced to death by Bad Girl Barbie wasn't something I ever thought would happen to me. But here I was, staring down the barrel of her unvarnished hate.

Gretchen scoffed. "Isn't it cute? She still breathes."

I wasn't offended by her tone. Technically I didn't need to breathe—being undead and all, but I liked breathing. I wasn't going to stop just because the rest of them didn't find it necessary. Blarg.

"I made her to save her life." Jaxon still held my hand under the table. As he spoke, his thumb traced over my knuckles while his words were matter of fact.

"We're not saviors of the human race." Soran's tone was coated with disgust. "We do not interfere with human affairs."

"She would've died." Again, Jax's statement came without emotions. I liked that he argued for me even if it did make Gretchen's scowl deepen.

"Humans kill humans all the time." Her voice was sharp, like Freddy Kruger for vocal cords.

I sniffed, unable to stay silent. "It wasn't a human. It was a vampire. The rogue, Zara. I believe you have her maker still in your custody, who *also* was a rogue." Jax's fingers tightened around my fingers, and I felt his annoyance through our bond.

It didn't seem to make much difference, though. Maybe if I'd said it with a bit more conviction someone would've paid attention. Then again, I was the one they wanted to end.

As if knowing where my thoughts had gone, Jax gave a slight head shake. I was supposed to sit down, shut up and let the council decide my fate without any defense on my part. My stomach churned.

Soran cast a glare at me and brought up the other reason we were on trial. "Kalon was also a victim."

I begged to differ. Kalon had tried to kill me. And Jax. And Nash, Paige, Grim. He even sicced his wicked witch on Kendra. Kalon was no victim. He was a villain and had gotten what he deserved. I wasn't sorry about that. "I killed Kalon. He was trying to kill all of us."

"If he'd succeeded, he would be in your chair right now." Dominic broke his silence, and I frowned at him. He wasn't getting any brownie points.

One thing was for damn sure. If I was gonna die, I was gonna die running my mouth.

"I doubt that." Jax stared as if he could take them all on. As if he wanted to. I understood because he'd done something heroic, I thought so anyway, and they wanted to punish him.

But it was the first time I'd seen or heard him be definite or argumentative.

"Jaxon." Dominic wasn't having insolence from his heir.

I wondered if his being Jax's maker made him my grandfather, which made me smile. Boy that couldn't have been more ill-timed. But my mind wandered off like a toddler with ADD sometimes. I couldn't help it.

Gretchen stood and smacked a hand on the table. "Do you find your maker's crimes amusing?"

If she could've shot lasers out her eyes, I would've been a hole in a chair. But I sobered. "No. Not at all. I simply don't find them to be crimes."

"*Human*."

She said it in the same tone I wanted to use to call her a bitch. But I refrained. It wouldn't help. Jax squeezed my hand again. Harder. It almost hurt. That time was a warning.

"I just want to get this straight before we pronounce judgment." She paused, a true theater actress, then smiled and cocked her head. This was fun for her. Less likely to be fun for me, but I waited because I didn't know what else to do. "Jax killed Kalon to save your pitiful human life, then he saved you again by giving you the strength and power of a vampire."

"The order is backward." I narrowed my eyes. "And it was *me* who killed Kalon. To protect my maker and friends." If we didn't include the details, which took some of the bite from the story, maybe it wouldn't hit so hard.

I didn't know if they somehow managed to communicate without speaking or if my "punishment" for being made without authorization had been pre-decided, but I'd also never seen anyone quite so joyous about pronouncing my sentence.

Gretchen smiled, and she really was pretty. Could've been standing over a storm grate when a rush of air blew her skirt up and it would've been as remarkable as when Marilyn did it. "You, Hailey Whitfield have no reason to exist."

"Excuse me?" I had a lot of reasons. My job helped people. I took bad people who jumped bail off the street. It was something. *I* was something.

"For a vampire to be made, it is our law that a vampire must have a purpose in order to earn his or her fangs." The she-devil smiled at Jax. "Your maker, for example, keeps peace and order in your country. You are pathetic and useless to our cause."

Vampires had a cause? "Okay. Give me a purpose." I could prove I was worthy of their vampire-ness.

The rest of the elders sat in silence. Was no one going to step in? Even Dominic? My grandvamp?

"Fine. You may prove your purpose." Gretchen wasn't screwing around this time. She sat again, folded her hands in front of her, and smiled. "We have a vampire gone rogue. You will bring him down."

There was a catch. Had to be. There was *always* a catch. But I let her continue.

"We have an idea of where he is, and we were going to dispatch a team today, but if you want to prove you're worthy of joining us, this is how you do it."

It was a double dog dare. A triple dog dare with a cherry on top. But it wasn't like I could pass on it. The only other option was to lose my head. Literally. "Okay. I'll do it."

It really couldn't be any harder than tracking down a skip. I'd tracked down one rogue and killed another. What was one more added to my vamp resume?

"Hailey." Jax pulled my hand to his lap and laced our fingers together. "Hang on. What resources are you going to give her? She's barely a month old."

Gretchen's smile was a pure kind of evil. "I think you might be confused about your power here, Jaxon." She was mean-girl haughty. "She didn't need resources to be made."

"Any other vampire would have help at their disposal." Jax's temper was slipping out of his carefully controlled shell.

"That is true." Soran was the anti-Gretchen. Calm and quiet when he spoke. There was no hint of malice. "But she can't have help from you. As a matter of fact,"—I hated when people said that—"you'll be staying here with us until your progeny either succeeds or fails."

My heart fell to the floor. They couldn't hold him. Okay, so maybe they could. I was trained to fight, to hunt, to kill if I needed to. Jax had made sure of that and so had Paige. I could bring down one rogue vampire.

"Are there any other rules?" I asked. My confidence was hidden behind a wavering voice, but it was there. Their doubt made me stronger. Tougher. Meaner. I was a goddess compared to these people.

Maybe that would be the new company motto. The Bond Girls. Strong, tough, mean goddesses.

The council looked at one another. Gretchen to Soran, Dominic to Amaya, Tobias to Gretchen.

Amaya nodded. "You have four nights to complete your challenge."

Ah, so this had become a *challenge* now. My stomach did flips but it was too late to back out now.

"Including tonight?" If so, it was unfair since I'd already wasted this much of the day being judged for crimes I'd not actually committed. Well, I had committed one but that didn't count.

Soran leveled a gaze at me. "No. Your time starts tomorrow."

Gretchen looked at Jax. "Remember, no help from you."

I had Kendra and no way was Luke going to sit on the

sidelines. He would want to be in the thick of it. I wouldn't be able to stop him. They'd said I couldn't use Jax. They said nothing about Nash or Grim.

Jax's help would've been nice. Plus, working with him meant he would be close and that thrilled me. But if I had to do it without him, I would. I didn't have a problem with it.

"I accept your challenge."

CHAPTER EIGHT

JAX'S ROOM at the palace, the one where they were putting him up for the next four days, was stocked with books. It had a large bed, big screen, an overstuffed sofa, and even a video game console. At least he wouldn't be in a dirty cell like I'd imagined. So that made me feel a tiny bit better.

I still hated leaving him here.

"Stay a moment," Jax said. "They're bringing me dinner."

I chuckled and sat on the sofa, the picture of awkwardness. "I don't have much time."

He inclined his head. "Of course, but I find I'm reluctant to have you leave me."

How sweet. I smiled at him and opened my mouth to tell him I'd be fine, but someone knocked on the door.

Jax opened it, thanked someone I couldn't see behind the door, and when he turned back into the room, he held a platter with two champagne flutes on it.

"I don't know what they think we're celebrating," he grumbled.

The liquid in the flutes was blood but looked cut with something. Likely champagne. "Is this safe to drink?" I asked.

Nodding, Jax handed me one of the crystal glasses. "Yeah. They don't do that sort of sneaky stuff. If they want us dead, they'll find a legitimate reason, or a fake reason they'll make seem legitimate. The sneaky stuff was what landed Kalon in hot water and ultimately dead.

With his blessing, I sipped the liquid. Oh, my. It was delectable. "You need to serve this at Catch and Release."

With his lips wrapped around his glass, Jax grinned. "We do," he said once he'd swallowed. "If I'd known you'd like it, I would've ordered you one every night we went."

Well, then. I wasn't going to turn that down.

We finished our drinks while pretty much just staring at one another. I would've thought it would be awkward, but somehow it wasn't. It was sweet. Lovely.

But then it was over. And I really needed to go.

He stood in front of me with his hands curved around mine, his thumbs stroking my skin. "Hailey, the only rule is that *I* can't help you." He tilted his head and gave me one of those soft looks that made my toes curl and my belly clench. "Use Grim and Nash. They're the strongest of my enforcers next to Paige. And call her in if you have to."

There was something in the depths of his hazel-blue eyes I never thought I'd see. Anxiety. He didn't like this situation. The rule of not helping me kept him from speaking of it. Times like now, I wished I could read minds. Then he wouldn't have been helping me. And I would've taken the info and run.

However, there were no telepathy mind control powers there. I could barely compel a human. Maybe I wasn't the ideal candidate for a vampire.

I'd have to fake it.

He leaned his forehead against mine. I sighed at the feel of his warm skin. To a human, he probably would've felt like ice. The maker bond teased my senses. This was one potent man. Jax's eyes locked onto mine when he pulled back and again, I thought he might kiss me, but he just continued staring.

"Don't be scared." His soft voice held the slightest tremble. He was so worried about me. My proverbial heart squeezed.

"I'm not." I had a plan. I was going to be okay. And I'd come back and get him when it was all over.

"You can't let yourself get hurt." Maybe I imagined the huskiness of his voice, the desperation, the emotion, but I committed the sound to memory anyway. If I could prove myself, then we would go free.

"I won't." But something bothered me. I backed up and met his gaze. "Jax, earlier, you said you had an ace up your sleeve. What does that mean?"

I wasn't looking for grand gestures because we weren't at that point in our relationship—if it even *was* a relationship. Beyond him being my maker. With my luck I was crushing on a man who viewed me as a sister or daughter. Ew. Surely, I wasn't misreading the signals *that* badly.

He smiled and nodded like I'd asked a yes or no question,

rather than for clarification. "I can still use it if I have to, but it's going to be better if you prove yourself without me interfering."

I puffed my cheeks and blew out a short, fast breath and gave a quick nod. I didn't care if breathing was not a vamp-like thing to do. So, I did it again and laughed because I couldn't break down. If I failed this challenge, *then* I'd break down. Good thing I didn't plan on failing. "I can do this, and I have a team to help me."

"I have faith in you, Hailey. You can do this." He spoke almost the same time I did, which meant he wasn't really listening to me. His worry was worrying me. But I wouldn't stress over that yet.

"Thank you." I stepped back, putting some distance between us, and turned to go. His loyalty was like a balm to my soul, a boost to my confidence.

I hadn't made it two steps when he took my hand, pulled me back, and spun me into his arms. His chest was broader, firmer than I remembered from when he'd hugged me against him after I'd killed Kalon.

When I focused wholeheartedly on his neck so as not to get my hopes up that this hug would be more, he swiped the back of his index finger up my throat to my chin, then tilted my head up.

Jax's gaze searched my face and drifted to my lips and back for a moment before he moved in. His eyes closed a split second before he brushed his lips over mine.

The shock froze me into place and scrambled all ability to

think. And just as I thought a lip press was all he would do; he deepened the kiss.

A groan slipped from me, and I wrapped my arms around him. He traced the seam of my lips until I opened them, and then his tongue caressed mine.

My body flew into a frenzy of sensations and electricity. At least it felt that way. This man sparked off an electrical storm inside me.

If I lived to be five thousand, I would never forget the intensity of this moment, the passion, the delicious decadence of kissing Jaxon Parsons.

It felt so right. So perfect.

He pulled back, and I kept my eyes closed for an extra second. I wanted to savor everything about it. I finally staggered back and smiled, almost cool from the absence of his embrace. One would think that I'd never been kissed before.

In my defense, I hadn't. Not like that anyway. Not even close.

"Hey," he said as I inched toward the door. I looked at him over my shoulder. "Come back to me, okay?"

If I was Scarlett O'Hara, I would've been flat on my back, swooning on a chaise. But I was a badass vampire with a rogue to hunt and four days to do it. A good swoon would have to wait.

"I will." Then I eased out the room. If I didn't leave now I might not ever. Or at least not all night. And I needed every spare minute to prepare.

Nash and Grim were standing guard a few feet from Jax's

room. When they heard my heels click against the tile floor, they nodded and led me up to ground level where a limo waited. It was odd to be followed by two enforcers. They didn't walk beside me. They flanked me, one on either side about two steps behind me. I've seen them do the same to Jax when he went out in public.

I wasn't Jax or anyone above them, not even as high as Paige, so I didn't understand why they did it. Jax must have told them to keep me safe, so I didn't bother commenting on it. And it was pretty damn cool.

When we reached the back doors, Dominic stood with his arms folded and one leg crossed over the other, too cool to be fifteen-hundred years old. Or maybe he was that cool because he was so old. I didn't know, but he was pulling it off.

"I'm rooting for you, Hailey." His Sean Connery vibe was strong tonight. "I can't help you either. As your grandmaker, I think the council would frown on it."

Oh! That was what it was called. How cute. Grandmaker.

I nodded. I wasn't sure I trusted him enough just yet to ask for his help anyway. "I get it, Gramps. We can't have the council hating on all three of us, right?"

Gramps curled his lip. "I don't care for that moniker." He was the kind of guy who used the word *moniker* when *name* would've done just as well. And I'd expected he wouldn't care for it. That was the point.

But something he'd just said made me think. "They would frown, but it isn't forbidden?"

He narrowed his brow. "No. I can't help." He handed me an envelope. It wasn't thick enough to have more than a couple of pages inside. “This is the information we have about the rogue.”

I nodded. “Thank you.”

He opened the door for me. “Good luck, Hailey.”

I threw my arms around him for a hug, and immediately knew nobody ever hugged him. He went rigid in my arms—even more so than he’d already been. I smiled against his chest and kept on hugging. After a few very tense seconds, he hugged me back. When awkward turned into pained, I pulled back and looked up at him. “Thanks, Grandpa,” I whispered.

He shook his head, but he was smiling. “Oh, make it stop.”

I chuckled as I climbed into the limo. I had no idea where I was headed or what I was supposed to do, so I opened the envelope and a slip of paper fell out. It was Dominic’s phone number with a note. *Just in case.*

Aww. Grandpa really did have a heart. I really, *really* hoped I wouldn’t have to use the digits.

CHAPTER NINE

The hotel was a welcome sight, even with it's over the top lavishness. I'd spent long enough at the vampire palace, longer than I thought anyway, and it was getting late.

Kendra and Luke had spent whatever time they'd had shopping, enjoying a five-star restaurant or something in the Michelin category. Luke had told me all about it via the million texts he sent with pictures and emojis. It was a good thing I'd turned my phone off before the trial. Three seconds after turning it on in the limo, it'd started blowing up.

There were four garment bags on my bed and if I hadn't been so tired, I would've fawned; would've given them the amount of attention they deserved. Honestly, it looked to me like they'd come from the shop in the lobby of the hotel, but it didn't matter.

I didn't care if they'd bought them from a bag lady. They

were my size, created by an Italian designer, and they were exactly my style.

Any other time, any other place, I would have dropped everything to try on each one. But with only four days and these few bonus hours to achieve what the council had previously planned to dispatch an entire team to do, I didn't have time to waste.

I dialed Paige. It was evening in the States, so she would be up.

"Yo." It was her customary greeting.

"Paige, it's Hailey." She probably thought I only called when I needed something. The last couple of times I'd called, she was right. I would make it up to her later. Now, I truly needed her help.

"Yeah. I have caller ID. What can I do for ya'?" She snapped her gum half a world away and it sounded like we were in the same room.

This was the kind of side trip my brain took when I was tired, and I shook it off. I had to focus. "I was wondering if you could come here and help me out. I have to find some rogue vamp and Jax isn't allowed to help me."

The words tumbled in a rush on a single breath, but without Jax, I felt a bit lost. I'd been arrogant to think I could do this without him. What was I thinking?

"Yeah. I'm already covering you at Cleo's." She paused. "Cleo says hello."

"Tell her hi. And I wouldn't ask, but I'm in trouble here. I only have four days and not a whole lot of information." If I sounded desperate, it was probably because I was. I didn't know enough about vampire rogues to even guess where to start.

I'd thought I had this, now I'm having second thoughts.

"Hang on." In the background, Cleo and Paige discussed. Cleo said she didn't really need Paige to sit with her at night since she was so much better, and they could hold off on skips since we'd been doing so well lately. Paige came back on the line and some of the tension left my stomach. "All right. I'll get the first flight out on the spare jet."

She'd just told me they had a spare jet, and I didn't question it. Didn't bat an eyelash. I just nodded like she could see me, and I'd known all along about the spare jet. How much money did Jax have?

Shaking out of my thoughts, I said, "Thank you. Thank you so much."

I felt better. Not great. I wouldn't feel great until I was back with Jax. Ideally, with his mouth all over mine, but that wasn't a requirement.

"I'll be there by sundown." Her assurance eased even more of the stress the vampires were probably counting on. They probably wanted me to fail.

While I didn't believe most of the elders wanted me to fail, I knew for a fact Gretchen did. I would've bet she had something to do about the lack of information on the rogue. They apparently had been tracking him for a while, yet there is no documentation that they'd ever tried to catch him. That didn't sit well with me.

I heard voices in the connecting room where Grim and Nash were staying, so I knocked on the door. Kendra opened and grinned at me. I frowned and entered the room. "Why are you still up?"

She winked at me. "I have been working on switching my sleeping routine. Plus, my magic keeps me going. I don't need as much sleep as a human. A few hours a night with a nap in between. *And* a certain vampire likes to call me at all hours of the night."

I ducked my head to hide my guilty smile. I did call her at all hours. It was a habit. She was my bestie. "As my best friend, you're on call twenty-four-seven."

Luke nodded. "That goes for brothers too. Unless you're Ollie. Don't call Oliver at two in the morning unless you want to doubt all your life choices."

I snorted because that was so true. "You sound like you speak from experience."

"Girl…" Luke rolled his eyes and went back to flipping pages of a magazine.

I glanced at Grim, stretched out on his bed with the TV remote in his hand, flipping through channels, and Nash on the sofa by the balcony. "I called in Paige."

Nash and Grim had read over the papers on the ride over, and Kendra had them in her hand, going through them as we spoke. That saved me from having to explain everything.

"Do you know of *anyone* else who could help?" Kendra looked at Luke, Luke looked at Grim who looked at Nash and as a group, they looked at me.

"What about Ava?" I didn't wait for anyone to agree with me. Or to tell me what a fabulous idea it was.

Kendra shrugged. Luke gave me a confused look. Nash and Grim nodded in unison.

Ava Harper was a necromancer and the person I bought my house from. She had the ability to control vampires, which might be a problem for the council since, according to Jax, vampires didn't trust necromancers.

I dialed Ava's number; fingers crossed. "Hello?" Oh, thank goodness.

I spilled my story in a rush before I even said hello, then waited. "Oh, sorry. This is Hailey. I bought your house."

She sighed and said, "I'm so sorry. I can't get away right now, but…hold on." She must've muted the phone because the sound went dead. I checked, but I was still connected. A few seconds later, she returned. "Hailey? I know someone who is *definitely* going to be a big help. Text me the address."

And we hung up. Whatever was keeping her so busy obviously didn't leave time for small talk, which was okay. I appreciated her efficiency in this situation. I didn't have any time to waste either.

As I typed out the address, I sat on Nash's vacant bed and Kendra stood to use the in-room microwave to warm me a cup of AB Positive. "Thank you," I said as she handed it to me, but we froze when a bubble of light appeared in the center of the room. I gasped, and Nash and Grim drew their weapons while Luke gave a squeal. A man appeared.

The mystery guy who'd just materialized in the hotel room held up his hand and Nash and Grim fell backward onto the bed, immobilized.

Holy cannoli.

"Nothing holy here, darlin'." The man's smooth British accent drifted through the room.

Had I said that out loud? I didn't think so, but maybe I had. I shook my head and stared at him. The intruder had dark brown hair, broad shoulders, narrow hips, and looked great in a trim black suit. His dark gaze was full of mischief. "Ava sent me. No need to be alarmed."

I wasn't *alarmed* or afraid. Although I probably should have been. Intrigued was more the word I might've used. Nash and Grim looked pretty furious, though, while Kendra and Luke were just shocked. Luke looked like he was having the time of his life.

And I would be sure to make a lot of time for emotions later, but right now, I had to get the details worked out so I could get some sleep before I had to start this search.

Standing, I held out my hand to our guest. "I'm Hailey. Thank you for coming."

He had a smile like the devil himself, but the touch of an angel when he slid his palm against mine then cradled my hand between his. "You can call me Luci." When I stood and stared for a second, he smiled. "Point me at the problem. I have some other things to get back to."

"Oh. Right." I led him to the coffee table, and we all sat around it. The hotel rooms weren't as nice as Jax's at the palace, but we had a sofa, a couple of chairs, and my own coffee maker which I'd recently discovered I could still drink if I put a bit of blood in it.

Kendra pinched the back of my shirt and whispered in my ear. "He's powerful. Like... really powerful."

When I glanced at her, she widened her eyes. So, I widened mine back.

"Shall we?" Luci prompted. And like he heard Kendra, he smiled and winked at her.

Luke scooted closer to Luci and smiled. "Well, hello, handsome." He clutched his heart. "Hails, you'd better call God. He is missing an angel."

Luci laughed out loud, throwing his head back. "You don't know the half of it."

Luke knew an opportunity when he heard one and no way was he letting this one pass him by. "Why don't we head to the bar, and you can tell me all about it."

"Son, you couldn't handle all this." Luci's grin was either the most angelic thing I'd ever seen or the most devilish. I couldn't decide. I couldn't get a read on him. Not that it mattered. If he was here to help, I didn't give a fat rat's butt about his politics or his religion.

"You didn't by chance lose a golden violin to a redneck, because you are devilishly handsome." Luke laughed at his own joke, and I shot him a stare attached to a sigh.

Then I snapped my figures at him. I needed him to get with the program. I was screwed in T-minus four days. He could flirt on his own time. "Luke...Ransom?"

He waved me off. "I'm not serious. Luci here knows that, dontcha big guy?"

He winked at Luke as I handed Luci the packet. He thumbed through it then passed it around the table for everyone to have a glance at what was essentially no more useful than sunscreen in a rainstorm. It had a description that could've been one in a couple million guys in London, which was the locale provided.

It said his last location was London. A six-foot-one guy with dark hair from London. And there was no picture attached. The report said he'd been draining humans at an alarming rate.

But this was doable. We had his last known address and from that we could get a name. Do a search on the computer or scry. "It's like finding a skip. We just need to get to London."

"Yeah. I guess we could submit a flight plan for the jet. Wait for the Italian airport to give us clearance to take off. Won't eat up much time." Grim was grimmer than normal. His sarcasm was on point.

"Do you have a better suggestion?" Nash threw a pillow at Grim, which he caught and tucked behind his head.

"A drive would take at least fifteen hours and car transport." Luke had lost his sparkle. Probably didn't want to leave Milan until he was finished maxing my cards.

"Oh puh-lease. Let's all just all hold hands, and we can sing a round of Kumbaya and be friends again." I hoped Luci was kidding but he had his hands out, waiting. When he gave me a pointed look, I shrugged and took one. Luke rushed to take the other then we all formed a circle. Once everyone was touching everyone else, before I could blink, we were somewhere else.

I staggered back, looking around. *Holy cannoli.*

"Welcome to my humble London abode." Luci gave a slight bow. Nothing about Luci or the *abode* was humble.

It was, at least, a mansion. A gigantic living room in that mansion to be exact. Maybe it was a palace. White and silver marbled floors stretched throughout the ground floor. Each piece of furniture looked more expensive than my car, and it all matched. This room was decorated in white and navy blue with silver accents.

Luci motioned around the room with his arm. "Make yourselves at home while I speak to the lady in charge."

When I didn't move, he curled his finger at me for me to come closer. Oh, he was talking about me. I was the lady in charge.

"Let me see the packet again?" he requested politely.

I'd been busy holding his hand. I hadn't brought the packet. Crap. "This is a great place." My voice came out tinny, even to my ears.

Luci rolled his eyes and chuckled. "You forgot it?" At least he didn't sound angry. Or like he might smite me. Although, I wasn't sure he could. "I'll be right back."

And like he was made of some sort of dissolving, air soluble material, he disappeared again.

Kendra stood beside me. "What the heck is going on here? What kind of witch can teleport?"

I didn't think we were dealing with a witch, but I wasn't going to say that out loud. Besides, he reappeared two seconds later with the packet of information and held it up.

He winked at Kendra. "Wouldn't you like to know?"

I personally didn't care who he was. He'd already helped with the transport to England and given us a place to stay. At the moment, he was my favorite person.

I yawned and felt my pocket. Oh, I had my phone. Yes! That would be helpful.

But the sun was about to come up, and I needed to sleep off this day. Er, night. I needed to prepare for tomorrow, erm, tonight. I'd be worthless without at least a few hours.

"Come, my little vampires." Luci held out his arm for me, and I slipped my hand through. "Let me show you all to the bedroom."

Nash and Grim followed.

Luci pushed open the door to a windowless room. The king-sized bed allowed us enough space to sleep, and I trusted these guys. I didn't have a reason not to.

"All right." I nodded to my enforcer friends, but they shook their heads so fast I was afraid they might rattle something loose.

"No way, Hailey. Jax would kill us. He said watch you. I don't think he means that close." Grim turned to Luci. "Do you have an extra blanket and pillow? I'll sleep on the floor."

"Oh, come on, the bed's big enough for five people. I trust you guys." The protectiveness rolled off of them. Did they ever turn it off?

"Just go to bed, Hailey." Nash pulled a blanket from the end of the bed and layon the floor.

Luci snapped his fingers and a large air mattress appeared on the floor beside the bed along with blankets and pillows. Then he looked at me. "If you really want someone to snuggle up to…" He wagged his eyebrows, but I didn't answer. I could picture Jax, and he was all I wanted. "No? Okay. Can't say I didn't try." He walked to the door as I stared at the thick comforter and the pillows. "Go to bed. We'll talk soon."

I jumped on the air mattress before the guys could argue about it and ended up jumping too hard. I bounced, right off the mattress and onto the floor. Luckily, I landed on my butt, which had a bit of extra cushion.

While Grim and Nash stared with unhinged jaws, I climbed carefully onto the air mattress and fluffed the pillow like nothing had happened. They'd get the big king bed and could just forget they'd seen anything. And I was so tired, as soon as my eyes closed, I wouldn't care about…

CHAPTER TEN

When I emerged from the cave of a bedroom Luci had put us vampires in to sleep, Paige was there. She sat in an armchair glaring at Luci. I hadn't a clue what that was all about, but I needed a wake-me-up. My senses told me I'd overslept. I'd wanted to get up as soon as the sun set.

Grim and Nash were already up and hadn't seen fit to wake me so I could get to finding the rogue. There was a lot to do, like brief Paige on everything and come up with a plan to find the rogue. I hated not knowing what I was getting into.

I was grumpy and stiff. I'd slept like the dead, but I hadn't had a single dream about Jax and where was the justice in that? Come to think of it, I had slept pretty hard. Maybe they'd tried to wake me and couldn't.

I glanced at Paige as I entered the living room. She looked refreshed and wide awake. Me, not so much. "How was your flight?"

Her mouth pinched into a slight pucker, and she narrowed her eyes at Luci. That made me look over at him.

He shrugged. "I was trying to help." Another shrug. "Saving time."

"What?" Apparently, I'd missed something, which was highly possible.

"I was sound asleep on the flight from home to here. Minding my business." She hadn't stopped glaring at Luci, although I'd never seen anyone less bothered by a woman's anger before in all my life. He was checking his nails, rubbing his hands together, shoving them into his pockets.

Paige shook her head. "Did I mention I was sound asleep?"

I nodded. "I think so, yeah."

"This asshat reaches in, grabs my arm and pops me here. It was already dark. Already on the tarmac. No need for this guy to interfere because I had a car arranged to drive me." Oh, yeah. She was salty about the whole thing.

His chuckle told me he liked it. "Oh sweetheart, if I didn't interfere every once in a while, you would've wasted valuable time traveling. Overpaying for a taxi." He shook his head, his smile hidden beneath a pout. "But does anyone appreciate old Luci and all his hard work?"

She sighed, recognizing the argument was going nowhere. "You're right. I'm sorry."

He pulled out his cell. "Could you say it again? I want to set it as my ringtone."

Movement at the arch leading into the living room drew my attention to Luke. He had bed head but a smile on his face.

"Good morning, my beautiful sister." Either he'd maxed all of my cards or he'd found a way to get lucky while I was sleeping.

I tilted my chin, and he kissed my cheek. "So, baby sis, I've been mulling this over. We should go to the police station and one of you should compel an officer or two to tell you about the victims. Maybe if we trace the victims, we can narrow down a location."

"He could be anywhere." Paige wasn't buying it, but I liked it. Luke didn't spend *all* his time watching Project Runway. He also watched true crime and read about all the big cases. When we were younger, he used to make his own case files. And more than once, he'd predicted the killer before the cops.

"Yeah, but he's a hunter, and it's harder for a hunter to hunt if he doesn't know the area. The safe spots. The places where he could take his prey and not get caught." Luke was more than a pretty face. He could be uber smart when he wanted to be.

Paige pursed her lips and nodded. "Maybe."

Luke wasn't talking *maybe*. He wanted praise. Deserved it, too.

I gave him a glowing smile. "He's right. If we can see where the attacks happened, establish a pattern or an area, it's a good start. More than what the council gave me."

In any case, we didn't have a better plan or a place to start. I was hungry and the urges to eat were strong. I needed to eat and get on the job. The clock was ticking.

Paige laid her hand on Luci's shoulder. "Maybe you could

pop us back to Catch and Release for a quick nibble?" Her fangs descended and Luci moved away.

"Oh, I don't know. I'm pretty drained from all this *popping* here and *popping* there." His emphasis didn't go unnoticed. "I might need to use what power I have in reserve. My strength isn't limitless, you know."

I didn't know his process or have reasons to doubt him. Ava had vouched for him, so who was I to argue?

He clicked his tongue. "Making portals and moving people across long distances really is a lot harder than I make it look. I give it a certain style and grace." He was as dramatic as Luke when they'd canceled America's Next Top Model. "Popping in and out of hell, however, takes virtually no energy."

"I knew it!" Luke pushed a finger into the air like he was Sherlock Holmes solving the mystery.

"Yes, aren't you the clever one?" Luci wagged an eyebrow at Luke and color flushed into his cheeks.

In the meantime, while they hashed out identities and proper names, I shot a text to Dominic. **Hey Gramps, I need a bite to eat. Don't want to end up on Scotland Yard Radar. Help a sister out?**

I meant for it to sound casual, if familiar even. This wasn't the favor I might need later, and I wanted to keep that one in reserve. I would ask formally if the time came.

Take Piccadilly Circus to Leicester Square. Find the Blood Garden. It has what you're looking for. And stop calling me Gramps.

I smiled, picturing his gruff face as he typed his message.

When he spoke, he sounded like Connery, but I read his texts in Johnny Depp's Sparrow slur.

"Dominic said we should go to the Blood Garden."

Paige nodded. "Yeah. That's his London version of Catch and Release. But he has clubs all over Europe. Just like Jax plans to expand across the US. He's worried about the hunter population. He needs it to dwindle a bit, since they believe vampires to be extinct in the States." I didn't know how long any of these guys had been with Jax, but they all knew a lot about him, about his plans, his habits, his life.

It made me a little envious. I wanted to know, too.

We left together, except for Luci who claimed he had business back in hell, but he promised to see us later.

The place definitely had the same vibe as Catch and Release. I couldn't tell what was real from what had been glamoured. Maybe because it was dark, and the slow, sensual music was loud, pulsing through me, or maybe because I just wasn't good at telling glamour from the real thing. Who knew?

The corners and shadows were occupied, but we were greeted by a woman who pulled us deeper into the club, seating Nash next to Grim, next to me, next to Kendra. Luke was already on the dance floor with Paige. He loved his TikTok dances, and they were already leading a group through a series of bumps and grinds, waving and booty shaking. So long as no one played 'his song,' there was a chance I would be able to pull him out of there before my four days expired.

As soon as this was all over, I was going to dance, too. Maybe with Jax. I hoped so.

"So, what's the difference between hunting a rogue versus hunting a skip?" Kendra asked.

I looked at her blankly. "Honestly, I have no idea."

Nash leaned forward. "Not much, except the fights won't be anywhere close to as easy when you finally catch the son of a bitch."

I snorted. "They're not always easy."

Grim stared at me…well, kinda grimly. If the shoe fit, geez. "Your human catches are irritating. This will be dangerous. You might not survive, and even if you do, you or someone you love may be hurt. This is no human bond skip."

My shoulders slumped as I waited on the waitress to come take our order.

Way to kill the buzz, Grim.

Freaking appropriate name.

CHAPTER ELEVEN

The precinct wasn't too far from the bar, but it was far enough that two taxis were required, so I didn't eat into my time by walking. It wasn't like we could vamp-speed through the city with Kendra and Luke and about a thousand-night owls out for a Tuesday night on the town.

The Charing Cross police station was four stories of smooth, white facade with windows built onto a corner where the roads narrowed to a point. We walked in the front door, and I advanced to the desk like I was on official business. I had practice at this point from all my skips. My timid days of fearing the police had long since faded. They were people. Just like I was, well, just like I'd been once. Some were good. Some were bad. All were compellable and edible.

The officer behind the desk smiled at me. He was charming in his dark navy uniform and position of power. Not as devilishly handsome as Luci, or as strikingly gorgeous as

Jax, but he wasn't wearing a ring, so I bet he got his fair share of action.

"Hello," I said with a professional smile, meeting his gaze.

"Good evening, Miss." His up and down appraisal of me only confirmed what I already thought. This guy was a player. His accent and voice were a bit Pierce Brosnan. I had a thing for accents.

"Hi. My name is…" Real or not? "Charlotte Dupre. I'm a bounty hunter in the United States. I have traced one of my skips right here to the UK, to London." Oh Lord. Why had I mentioned that? "*Anyway*, I was hoping I could see the detective who is investigating a series of murders here in London." He eyed me, met my gaze, and I held onto his. "I need to see the detective. You're going to get me the detective."

He blinked, and his mouth thinned. "I don't think so, Velma."

Velma? From Scooby Doo? Most certainly not. I was about twenty years older and had way better hair—if she was converted from cartoon world to real people land. What the hell?

Bah! I need more practice with compelling people.

Paige stepped forward. "Officer…" She leaned in, let him get a whiff of her perfume then pulled back. "Dunwiddy." She smiled, and I could've sworn I saw her push her boobs up. Damn she was good.

But then she stood at her full height, put her finger under his chin and forced him to look up at her. "Take us to the detective in charge of the murders."

He smiled like they'd shared an inside joke, and his cheeks

flushed as he stood and gazed at Paige. I didn't know how her powers of persuasion worked, but men who looked at women like that were either very hopeful they were going to get to know one another better, or they already knew. That was the power of Paige.

"CI Felber, these folks wanted to talk to you." Obviously, we were catching him on his way out. He had a briefcase in one hand and an umbrella in the other.

"Make an appointment or see the desk clerk." Felber was gruff, looked like he belonged in a Pacino movie with his thick black hair, broad shoulders, and thick, meaty arms. I sure as hell wouldn't mess him if this wasn't so important. Life or death kind of important. And since it was my life on the line, I stepped up.

"Detective Felber—"

"*Chief Inspector* Felber." His correction was strong. "Damned Americans."

I smiled sweetly. "I'm sorry. Chief Inspector Felber, I'm in a situation, and I could use your help." His gaze met mine. "I need you to show me the files for your murder cases."

"And I need to win the lottery." He tried to brush past us, but Paige stepped in again. Thank goodness.

It was obvious my compulsion ability was broken.

"CI Felber." Her voice was low and husky and I watched as she compelled him into a blush and a smile just as she had Dunwiddy.

She *so* needed to show me her secrets.

Felber moved back around his desk, and I tried not to be jealous of how advanced her abilities to compel were compared to mine. His office was huge, nothing like anything I'd ever seen in a police station in the states. He had three file cabinets behind his L-shaped desk that faced into the room. There was a window on the side of his desk that looked out over the street below and he had a picture of himself with the queen, Princess Diana, and Prince Charles back in the royal heyday when Diana and Charles were still married. Impressive.

I wished I could ask him about it, but I still wasn't sure how compel worked or if there were rules about talking to someone while they were compelled. I could fight like a badass, but the rest of vamping was still over my head.

He went to the file cabinet and pulled a few files from one drawer. They were rubber banded together. Then he opened another drawer and added a few more to the stack.

"These are the ones we've connected." I took a file, and Kendra and Luke each had one. The CI continued to ogle Paige and she continued to let him. "There are seven in total."

"What connects them?" I asked while committing the file to memory. It was something I'd learned I could do now that I was a vampire. Slowly, I was starting to get this stuff down, though most of it was still a work in progress.

"Location. The exsanguination of the victims despite no blood at the scene. The bite marks." Felders' voice was matter of fact and I wondered if Paige was keeping him under compulsion.

This was definitely our guy. "Are there more that you've discounted for one reason or another?" I asked.

He laid his jacket over the back of his chair. "Some had

bite marks but were too far away. Serial killers usually stay true to their comfort zone."

Luke looked at me and wagged his brows as he gave a little told-you-so head shake. I stuck my tongue at him before I asked, "But the victims were bitten and drained?"

"Ye—Drained is an interesting word." The detective cocked his head at me. "Why did you say drained?"

"I don't know. It is just the word that came to mind." Drained. Shit. I sure hoped Paige could erase his memory when we were done.

"We discounted some because they were beaten with no bites."

I looked from my file to Kendra's to Luke's for the specific detail I wanted. "Could I see a couple of those files?"

Felber nodded as I started opening files to the page I needed. B positive. B positive. B positive. All the victims who'd been drained had a B positive blood type.

"What've you got, Hails?" Luke came to stand beside me at the edge of the detective's desk where I had a stack of yellow folders opened, pages flipped.

"He's discriminating by blood type." I opened one of the beaten files. "O neg." And another. "AB neg." By the third, I was convinced I was right. "A Positive." I pointed to the line on each page in the files as I set them on top of one another.

"Okay." Felber nodded. "Good catch. Maybe he's collecting the blood for a purpose then. Transfusing it?"

Oh, if only. He was choosing by tastebud, but I didn't tell the detective that because I didn't want to have to kill him.

I went back through the files. "Can I have a piece of paper and a map of the city?"

I looked at Paige who had Felber once again under her spell. He handed me a yellow legal notepad, and a felt-tipped pen, along with a faded map of London. "All right." I handed the marker to Luke. "Put a dot where I tell you." Then I glanced at Felber. "Show him where."

I went through every file, calling out where the bodies of the B positive victims had been found. "Do you have a different colored pen or marker?" But I could already see a cluster of dots. Felber handed me a red pen I handed to Luke. "These are the ones who have the wrong blood type." I called out more addresses. Only one was too far off our area to belong to my rogue vamp. The rest formed a cluster around Kensington Palace.

"Maybe it's someone who works there." I studied the map.

"Maybe it's the crown prince. Wouldn't that be delicious?" Luke tasted scandal.

I shook my head while rolling my eyes. "Or maybe it's just someone who lives close by. Someone who takes this way home from work." I handed Kendra the notepad. "Now we need to chart times."

"We don't know when they were taken. We only know when they were found."

Without blood, body temp was useless for determining time of death. I wasn't sure how I knew this. Probably one of those true crime TV shows. "It's the best we can do. We have to be able to find the patterns and see what we can predict from there."

I was sure the police had already done that, but they didn't know the killer was a rogue vampire. It was possible that if they did get too close the vamp would just compel them to forget and be on his way.

Felber nodded as the door opened. I glanced at Paige, who immediately stood and walked toward the man poking his head in. "Nothing to see here. Felber's working late and we're his friends." She tilted her head and smiled. "You can go now."

The officer pulled back, then shut the door.

"Make columns. We'll put times in one, how long the medical examiner thinks they were dead in another, and where they were last seen in another. We need as many parallels as we can." And if it all worked out, the information might lead us to my rogue. Otherwise, it might go nowhere, but it was the only start we really had.

CHAPTER TWELVE

Paige stepped around Felber to take a call from Nash while I continued working with Luke and Kendra. "All the victims are female," I mused.

Kendra nodded and added, "They also have the same blood type. But how would he know?" She threw a file on the table. "It's not enough to go on. Not yet."

It was a vampire thing. I could tell the difference between blood types, between markers in DNA that would make one bite more attractive than another, but it certainly wasn't something we needed to talk about here. Not in front of the fuzz.

Aside from anyone overhearing, since this office had become busier than Grand Central Station in the last few minutes with officers poking their heads in, probably for no other reason than to get a look at Paige, who spent a lot of time honing her compelling skills, there was still Felber. And sure, we were going to wipe his memory, but I didn't want to take chances on even a sliver of recall leading to my arrest or whatever. And I damned sure didn't want to think about *whatever.*

As I thought about it, another officer stuck his head in. "Anybody need anything?"

Paige was busy on the phone, so I stepped over. "No," I said, doing my best to compel him. "We just want to be left alone. Spread the word."

Oh, my stars, it worked. He went a little glassy eyed and nodded. "Yes, ma'am."

Hot dog.

Paige hung up the phone with Nash. "The apartment, last known address, is clean. Empty. But they're checking with others now."

Jax trusted Nash and Grim, so I trusted Nash and Grim. If there was anything to be found, they would find it.

I had to concentrate on the case files in Felber's office. We'd have to leave soon because of how busy it had gotten. The fewer people who saw us, the better.

Another officer walked in. "Felber, this fax just came—" He stopped short and stared at us as if he'd had no idea anyone was in here with the CI. "Uh."

Paige stepped in his line of sight. "We're helping with an important case. We really need to be left alone. It's of the utmost importance. Can you make it happen?"

The new guy nodded dumbly and whirled to leave.

Almost as soon as he shut the door, he was out of my mind. I had far more important things to think about. "Okay, so if he doesn't like to ea...I mean, kill men, is there something other than blood type that connects these women?"

Luke smiled.

I needed to watch my phrasing. "A place they all go or a hunting ground for our va… very vain killer." He shot me a look. If I could flub the wording, I sure as hell wasn't going to bitch about him doing it. At least he caught himself before revealing too much.

Luci appeared in the room. And it wasn't subtle, like a quiet appearance. It happened accompanied by a cloudy puff of smoke and a small flame that licked up from the floor. Very unnerving, and I jumped, probably even yelped.

By his amused smirk, he'd done the visual effects for the show and nothing else.

I rolled my eyes. "Good lord, please don't do that."

"I *am* a lord, I suppose. Not good, though. More dark. A war lord. Lord of the dark wars." He nodded. "Oh, I like that. Do take care not to tarnish my reputation with words like *good*." He faked a shiver. Or was it real? Either way, his theatrics amused Luke, who chuckled.

Luke looked at me. "I'll bet he's good." He paused. "At being bad."

Luci wagged his eyebrows at me, too, as if I was the conduit for their conversation. Then he nudged Luke with his hip. "What do we have here?"

Kendra explained the dots on the map while I continued trying to figure the patterns. Luci shook his head. "It isn't about the palace. It's about the churches."

I looked up. "What?"

"Trust me, sweetheart. This isn't about anything Windsor royal. It's about the Big Guy. Or His places of worship, at least." He shook his head and waved a finger and, on the map, almost directly over every dot, was a small three-dimensional building that looked more like it belonged on a Monopoly board than as an indicator of a church. "Your little friend is eating his women—and not in the fun way—just outside of hallowed ground. Because he can't kill on hallowed ground. He can't even go there."

Did that mean I couldn't go to a church? Couldn't step foot in a cemetery?

Paige glanced from Luci to me. "That's not true. We are not affected by religious items or hallowed ground."

Oh, thank goodness. I really needed to take the time to ask Jax more questions. Why hadn't I known that? "So why kill them near churches?"

Paige tapped her nails on the desk. "He could be young enough to not know."

I nodded and Kendra said, "He could feel remorse?"

"Killing them at the churches would be his way of saying sorry?" I frowned. Crazier things had happened to be honest. Criminals came up with all kinds of excuses about why they couldn't follow rules. From what I understood about rogue vampires, they tended to be at least borderline insane.

I leveled a steady gaze on Luci. "I need to go to these churches to see if we can find anything that we could use to do a locating spell with." I waited for him to reply. There could be clues the cops overlooked, something I might've been able to see that they couldn't.

He breathed through his teeth in a hiss. "Darling, if I walk into a church, I might get struck by lightning."

He laughed at his joke, and I shot him a glare. He stared down at the map again and sighed. "So, what do we know about little Louis de Ponte du Lac?"

Luke clutched his heart. "A fellow Pitt fan? Be still my aching loins. I would let that man do me in a lion's den while Simba himself licked his lips."

Luci chuckled. "You do have a way with words. But I'm more of a Rice fan than Pitt."

Luke laughed and winked at Luci before focusing back on the cases. "The times of death all add up to the killer taking the women just after dark." Luke cocked his head at me like he'd just solved the case, but we were dealing with a vampire, so his nugget of commonality didn't mean much. Of course, he killed right after he woke up for the day. That made sense.

Kendra was focused on a brown box—one with the removable lid that was commonly used for file storage. "What's this?"

Felber looked up. "It's evidence."

I thought it should probably have been in a locker somewhere for chain of custody, but I remained silent and thought how fortuitous it was that the evidence was in this room.

"Maybe..." Paige nodded. "Maybe he's targeting virgins. That's huge with…" She glanced at Felber. "Guys like… the one we're looking for." She cleared her throat. "Serial killers."

"Maybe he's eating them for sport?" Luke asked.

"Eating? What?" Felber looked at me. Shit. Last thing we

needed was to have to terminate the chief investigator on the case because he heard my faux pas.

"I said *killing*." It was a bad lie, but Paige covered it with another layer of compulsion. By the time we left, this guy was going to be so wrapped in Paige's web, he would probably struggle to remember his own name.

Kendra pulled out a baggie with a piece of fabric. "Victim number one's torn shirt. Found it attached to a gate, like she'd been trying to climb the fence to get away." So, she was chased. That was interesting. Our guy should've been fast. Even vampires who didn't get the gift of superspeed were naturally a lot faster than humans.

"And this?" She held up another plastic bag with a paper inside. "It's a receipt."

She handed it to me. It was marked with the third victim's name. "Time stamp is eight ten p.m." It had been used to establish that the third victim was taken later than the rest.

"And what's this?" Kendra walked a piece of evidence over to Felber at his desk.

"A button we think came from the perpetrator." It sounded so regal in his accent. "It was clutched in a victim's hand, and it matched nothing on her person or her handbag."

Kendra's expression morphed into a big smile. "It's all we need, Hails. Let's go."

We gathered our stuff, all the brilliant deductions we'd made, while Paige wiped the CI's memory and Luci teleported us back to his place.

CHAPTER THIRTEEN

Kendra sat at the table in Luci's formal dining room, which I'd commandeered for the reams of paper we'd collected with Kendra's reproduction spell. My bestie never failed to amaze me with her magical abilities. I had no clue she could do a spell to replicate the case files we'd looked over in the CI's office.

I spread out the copied pages on the mile long table while she worked on the location spell that would lead me to my rogue. The problem was that there was more than one person's emotional signature left on the button, so she had to try to separate the two…or something like that. I didn't understand all the details of magic. That was why she was the witch, and I was the vampire.

But I couldn't sit still and stare at the words in the files for even one more minute. I missed Jax, which was odd in itself. Every time I closed my eyes, I felt his kiss, his hands, his breath mingling with mine. I know he doesn't breathe. It was a fantasy. And I didn't have time for the distraction.

Not now. I had to get my head back in the game. "I'll be right back." I needed to walk it off, clear my mind. Tracking humans was normally easy because there was almost always something of the skip left behind. Or maybe Kendra could just hone into humans easier.

Plus, I wanted to explore the huge house, see what secrets Luci kept hidden in his much-larger-than-it-looked-from-the-outside mansion.

Seriously. This place was unnaturally large. Probably ten thousand extra square feet than what it should've had. The hallway had about twenty doors and seemed to stretch as far as I could see when I walked. It had to be an illusion, but it was a good one.

I opened one door and pulled it shut. It was empty. Nothing to see there. Next to it was the one where I'd slept with the enforcers. All these rooms and we were still going to share? A smaller bed had been brought in and I smiled, closing the door behind me. Now Nash and Grim didn't have to worry about sleeping in the bed with me. I still didn't see what the big deal was because once the sun touched the horizon, I was out like someone flipped a switch.

Jax and Paige had both told me it wouldn't always be that way. Thinking of Jax made my insides heat and the loneliness return. So, I pulled my phone from my back jeans pocket and dialed my maker's number.

He answered on the first ring. "What's wrong?"

His panicked voice made me smile. "Nothing. I...um, just miss you." Ugh. Why'd I say that? "Is that clingy?"

A soft chuckle filled the line. "No. How is the case?"

"Good as one can be with little to no information, but I didn't call to talk about that." I opened the next door which led to a giant room full of mailboxes and other memorabilia. If we talked about the case, they might somehow know. I didn't want to jeopardize our chances of appeasing the council by breaking their rules.

"Where are you?" Jax asked. He sounded like he was bored.

"At Luci's house in London."

This one room had more square footage than my entire place back home—but again that would make the mansion disproportionate to the outer size of the building. There was some sort of enlargement spell going on.

"Oh." There was a pause, and I knew he wanted to ask about the case. "Who is Luci?" he asked instead.

"Luci is Ava's friend. You remember Ava?" It was a silly question because Jax never forgot anything, and she'd owned my house for years before I bought it. I was just trying to make conversation while I studied the room.

"Yes, the necromancer."

I swore I heard a shudder in his voice. Vampires and necromancers had a past. A long, long time ago necros enslaved vampires because we were considered undead and one of the creatures that necromancers could control with their powers.

"I don't think Luci is one. I'm not sure he's even a witch.

But he has this room in his house that has the largest stamp and mailing supplies collection I've ever seen."

The walls were lined with glass display cases with postal service uniforms through different eras and from different countries. He had sheets of old stamps from all over the world —all of Europe, the Middle East, Australia, America. "That's not too odd. Everyone has a collection." Jax paused, then asked, "Are you being safe?"

"Of course, I am. I called Paige over to help, so she's here." I almost slipped and asked him if he were a rogue, where would he hide in London? But I couldn't do that. It would be my luck that the elders had a way to spy on our calls to make sure we played by the rules. I wasn't going to give them reason to not trust me. "Don't worry. I have three of your best enforcers at my disposal."

He chuckled, but I sensed his anxiety even over the phone from a different country. I wasn't sure if that was normal.

I picked up on Luci's scent only moments before he appeared in the door of the room. He watched me, and I watched him back while talking to Jax. "I just called to hear your voice and to put your mind at ease that I'm fine. I have to go check on Kendra and that locator spell. I'll call again soon."

He sighed. "Be careful, Hailey."

The man melted my insides. "I will."

I hung up and slid my phone into my pocket and motioned around the room. "This room is a philatelist's dream."

"Yes, it really is, but my interests are vaster and more varied than a simple collection of stamps." Luci waved his arm toward his impressive compilation of relics. "As you can see."

He walked in and slid his hands into a pair of white gloves he pulled from a drawer. Then he walked to a corner display and ran a finger over a leather saddle. "This is an authentic bit of history, from the Pony Express." He smiled and caressed the leather like it was a lover more than an artifact. "It belonged to Johnny Fry, the first westward rider of the Pony Express. He was killed later as a Union soldier in the civil war between the states, but I saw it, and I had to have it."

"Shouldn't it be in a museum somewhere instead of your…" I didn't know what to call this.

"My mail room?" He chuckled. "Get it? *Mail* room."

I got it. I didn't see why he thought it was funny, but I chuckled along so as not to be rude.

He sobered and spoke sharply as if I was trying to sneak the damned thing out under my shirt. "It's mine, and I'm keeping it." He moved on. "And this is the mailbox that stood outside the Ipatiev House where Nicholas II and his family...died."

I didn't even know they had mailboxes back then.

"They didn't." He had a most unnerving habit of answering questions I hadn't asked out loud. "This came later. Before they tore the place down."

Ah, that made sense.

He moved on. "And this one was the first mailboxes ever used in the United States. It was invented by Albert Potts."

Who knew a guy like Luci had such a unique—and kind of nerdy—hobby. I let him give me the tour of the room, which was much more in-depth than any museum tour, and certainly more detailed than the one he'd given us of his place when we'd arrived.

"Thank you for showing me your things." I smiled at him when he pulled the door shut behind us. Then he crowded me against the door. "Is there anything else you're curious about? Something you've always wondered? Maybe you want to see now?"

Every word was like an invitation to his bedroom and his bed. His voice dripped with seduction and if not for my attraction to Jax, I might've been tempted.

I appreciated the hospitality, but I wasn't paying him with my body. Aside from probably not knowing exactly what to do with it anymore, I was saving myself for… in case… ah, well. I was just saving myself.

"Can't blame a guy for trying." He gave me an up and down look that seared my flesh, and the temptation grew to a full-on longing before it dissipated and disappeared. "He's a lucky man, your vampire friend." He brushed my hair back and tucked it behind my ear then leaned in, so his breath was hot against my skin. "I guess I'll just have to find another way to amuse myself."

He stepped back, and as soon as he moved, I could breathe again. Then, I was alone in the hallway. Holy macaroni. If things didn't work out with Jax…

He chuckled from somewhere else in the house. "I can hear you!" His chuckle morphed to a full-on laugh.

Damn.

I rushed out of the hallway, back to where Kendra was working.

"I think I've got it, Hails." The button moved across the map. "No. I know I've got it."

Thank goodness. "Then tonight"—dawn had come with a burning sun—"we'll find him."

I hoped so. Now more than ever, I missed Jax and couldn't wait to get back to him.

CHAPTER FOURTEEN

I STOOD next to Kendra in Luci's dining room, sipping on a bag of O positive through a straw like it was a juice box. It was officially my favorite way to drink blood, so I made a note to get some reusable straws when I got back home. I hated paper straws. Blech. Metal would do nicely.

Kendra drank coffee, which smelled amazing, while she took a little extra time on this spell. Since it'd been a whole day since she first cast the spell, while I slept, I hadn't expected the rogue to have gone far. He had to sleep and if he was new like me, he didn't have a choice.

Need built inside of me. I didn't really understand it. It wasn't like a normal pull, either, not a craving. This was powerful and almost painful. Being separated from Jax was an actual ache, or at least I thought so, and I wanted to make it stop, to get back to Jax, to wrap my arms around him and let whatever happened happen. Maybe calling him the night before had made it worse?

Plus, I didn't want to think about what would happen if I didn't succeed. I couldn't. I stood beside her, watching the button on the map. It hadn't moved in a while, and we were almost right on top of it.

"Where are Grim, Nash, and Paige?" I asked.

"They went to the last known address, again. They said to call them if we need them." Luci nodded toward Kendra. "I think she's got something."

Kendra spoke the incantation once more and the button moved to a nearby church, just as Luci had said. I finished off my blood bag and tossed it on the table before saying, "Let's go."

Luci stood. He'd been at the end of the table, looking bored. In a blink, we were standing outside the church. There was a service going on, so the doors were unlocked. There weren't all that many people there that I could see. Although they could've been in another part of the building. We weren't going inside just yet. I wanted to look around the outside. Criminals liked to hang out in dark places.

And despite his fear of being struck down by lightning for entering hallowed ground, Luci walked beside Kendra and me. I rolled my eyes but couldn't help but smile. Luci was an odd duck for sure. I was about to comment on that thought, but stopped suddenly and grabbed Kendra's arm, then pointed at a woman slumped against a bag of garbage next to the dumpster.

"You know I'm going to take the blame for this." Luci shook his head.

"You have an alibi." *Us.*

Kendra was on the phone with 999–the UK's 911– while Luci spoke to me. Probably to keep me calm since I was only a few feet from the body of another victim. "Oh, darling. I don't mean Scotland Yard. I mean…" He pointed toward the sky. "You know who."

I needed to look at that body before the cops came and sealed this place off and kicked us out. Or whatever they did to the people who found a dead body.

I moved closer, Luci beside me, while Kendra stayed back just a step as she spoke. "Is she breathing?"

Aside from my own, I'd never seen skin so pale. Not even other vampires tended to be as light. Nearly translucent.

I crouched, studying her. I didn't need to touch the woman to know she was dead. The lack of a heartbeat told me that. I looked back over my shoulder at Kendra and shook my head. "No."

She dropped her phone and moved closer, way closer, then moved to crouch beside me. "Oh, no."

"What?" Dread sank her claws into my spine.

"There's something we missed. Something that wasn't in the police reports." I didn't want to correct her, but if it wasn't in the police reports, *we* hadn't missed it. *They* had.

Instead, I watched her move the woman's head from one side to the other. "Can you see it?"

"See what?" Maybe if she told me what I was supposed to be looking for, I would know where to look at least.

"We have to get out of here." There was an urgency in her voice that told me she wasn't antsy about the cops finding us. I also smelled fear on her. What the heck could have scared Kendra like that?

She stood and wiped her hands on her pants fast and back and forth more times than was necessary unless she was trying to use friction to burn her own skin off. It was more than trying to get whatever it was off her hands.

"Okay." I curled my fingers into her shoulders. "Calm down, Kendra." Maybe I could compel her to tell me what was going on.

"Stop that." She twisted away from me and laid her hand on Luci's arm. "Come on, big fella. Get us the hell out of here."

"Your wish is…" And we were gone.

For a second, unbearable heat pounded against me, and a flickering bright light. I closed my eyes against the assault, but then I heard Luci's voice. "Probably didn't mean actual hell, did you?" He sighed. "Ho hum." And then we went back to his house.

"Kendra." I watched her pace the living room while mumbling about how it didn't make sense. How none of this made any sense. I was right there with her on that one. "What did you see?"

"It was so horrible, but it doesn't…" She couldn't finish a sentence.

Rushing to her side, I grabbed her shoulders and looked deep in her eyes. "Calm down and tell me what you saw." This was getting ridiculous. I hated guessing games.

Her eyes glazed over, and she nodded. "I saw a witch's mark." I almost didn't hear her in my glee that I'd compelled her to be calm.

Then it registered. "A witch's mark?" I looked at Luci. "Could you see it?"

He nodded. "You couldn't?"

I could not. But I wasn't a witch or a hunter. All witches were born with a mark that only other magical beings could see. "So, what does it mean?"

Luci shrugged. "Could mean a lot of things." He cocked his head when I sighed. Just once I needed a straight answer.

"It means that your rogue Lestat is taking out witches like our beautiful friend, Kendra, here."

This time it was Kendra who took offense. "Someone found a way to kill a woman who had the power to blow more than your mind, Luci." While she was frustrated, she scrunched her brows and focused on him. "And what kind of name is Luci anyway?"

He smiled one of his serene smiles and avoided her question. "Oh, I do love a passionate witch, especially one who doesn't mind talking about a good blow job."

Kendra scoffed and sidestepped. "I didn't say anything about a blow job, you pervert. I said she could blow your mind."

Luke walked in. "Who's talking about blow jobs?"

Luci pointed at Kendra.

Her nostrils flared as she clamped her jaw together on a substantial inhale. "I didn't say anything about a blow…"

But Luci smiled like he knew damn well what she said, and he was enjoying her frustration.

"Moron."

"You're exquisite when you're angry." Luci pulled her against him, and she shoved against his chest.

"This is serious." She shook her head. "I need to figure out if the other victims were marked. But I don't know how without seeing the bodies."

"We don't have to check out the other bodies. I doubt we would've been able to anyway." I glanced from Luci to Paige. Nash and Grim had left before I got up to see if they could dig up information from the underground crime groups and more staking out of the last known address. I didn't even want to know how they knew who those people were.

Kendra pulled the button and map from her pocket—she'd kept it there for traveling so it didn't get lost—and closed her eyes and spoke in Latin.

The button shifted across the page, moving to the downtown area of London. Luci looked at the spot where it stopped. "Oh, you have to be kidding me." He shook his head, disgusted.

"What?" I glanced from him to the map and back again.

"The bloody bastard is in Heaven."

"Like…?" This time I pointed upward.

"No. The nightclub in Charing Cross." He rolled his eyes.

Luke smiled reading about the club on his cellphone. "Oh yeah, baby. Listen to this." He slid his finger along the screen, and I'd never seen him smile bigger. "Heaven is a superclub in Charing Cross London, long associated with LGBTQ scene and is home to gay night." He chuckled. "Finally. A place among my peeps."

I smiled. He was enjoying this, and I wanted him to have a good time, but this was more than Luke being able to experience the nightlife in London. Still, my time was ticking down, and I didn't know if I was ever going to get to see him like this again. I linked my arm with his and pulled him down for a kiss on his cheek.

"Let's go see your peeps."

And hopefully, while we were there, we could find my rogue, and this could all be over.

CHAPTER FIFTEEN

We made it to the club a few hours before dawn, which was a little too close for me. I just hoped these few hours would be useful.

Luke took my hand and pulled me inside. He was more excited to be going to Heaven—the bar—than the trip to Milan or when I'd handed him my plastic and told him to buy himself something nice. As if he would've actually used my money to buy something for himself. He had plenty of his own moolah.

The bouncer didn't even make us stop or go through the line, though we probably pissed off a lot of people by skipping ahead. Damn, were we that hot? There were some perks to being undead. Luke was used to it. He got in everywhere. Kendra, too. She was gorgeous.

If we hadn't been under such a frantic search for the rogue

and to save my life, I would've really been tempted to dance. This place was packed with writhing, heated bodies.

"Luke," I yelled over the music. He paused and stuck out his ear for me to yell into. "This place makes my *primal* side want to go crazy!"

He pulled back and looked at me with wide eyes, then tapped the side of his nose. Taking my hand, he guided me around the dance floor, keeping our distance from the writhing bodies. He kept moving until he found what he was apparently looking for.

I looked back to make sure Luci was still with us, but he'd disappeared. No doubt he'd have no issue getting into the club. Maybe he had to use the bathroom. Even if he'd tried to tell me, I probably wouldn't have heard him.

Luke spoke to a man in an all-black ensemble, and the next thing I knew we were being led up a set of narrow stairs. The stairs opened up into a much quieter sitting area, about half full of well-dressed, attractive humans. Their blood smelled wonderful, but not like being down in the club.

"Now we can watch out this window," Luke said. "See what we can see." A big, tinted glass window ran the length of the room and looked out over the club. All the gyrating bodies still made me want to let my fangs out, but the scent of blood and pheromones didn't overwhelm.

"Thanks, Luke. Good idea." I smiled at him but moved my gaze back to the dancers quickly. "If he's here, he's almost definitely down there getting sips and nibbles."

"I would normally agree," Luci said.

I jumped and whirled to look at him. "Where'd you come from?"

He shrugged. "I've been here the whole time."

He most certainly had not, but I let it go, because he looked like the cat which caught the canary.

"What is it?" Kendra asked.

Luci narrowed his gaze on me. "Can you not sense another?"

I shook my head. "Maybe in a less stimulating environment."

With a tap on his nose, Luci nodded his head to the other side of the VIP section. As a group, we turned our heads to see a man and woman in the corner, absolutely going to town. Necking, making out. I believed the Brits called it snogging.

"Look closer," a voice in my mind said.

I narrowed my eyes and gasped. "He's drinking."

Crap. The rogue heard me. The vamp hearing, which I'd gotten good at muting somehow, must've been working full strength for him. His head jerked up, shaggy dark hair falling across his forehead. Even in this dim light, I saw his face like a beacon of light. Light brown eyes, almost gold, and a bone structure to give the great artists inspiration.

And two fangs, dripping blood.

It took me half a second to react. Everyone else moved even slower. Except Luci, who had been expecting this.

Half a second was all he needed. He used his vamp speed, leaving his victim moaning against the settee, and disappeared down the stairs. I kicked it into high gear, but as soon as I hit the dance floor, my senses went haywire. I looked and looked, but he was nowhere to be found.

And worse still, I felt the sun coming.

Luke grabbed me on one side, and Kendra on the other. I'd somehow ended up in the middle of the dance floor, just looking around, lost. When had I moved this far into the room?

"Come on," Luke yelled.

Kendra reached over and pulled one of my hands up to slap it over my mouth.

Oh, no. My fangs were out.

I shoved my head down, kept my hand over my mouth, and let them lead me out the front door, where Luci waited for us.

"He's gone," Luci said. "Even I can't track a vamp at full speed. He doesn't care about being exposed." He kicked a rock, obviously frustrated. "Don't worry, we'll get him."

Back at Luci's place, barely beating the sunrise, I fell into the single bed in the windowless bedroom. Disappointment mixed with a bad case of the sleepies had succeeded in making me bitchy and pouty. Chasing a rogue vampire through the streets of London and failing hadn't helped. If it weren't for the dang sun coming, I'd still be out there searching for the rogue.

I climbed in bed and snuggled under the sheets. They smelled like sunshine and flowers with a special dash of clean and fresh. The comforter was like a cloud, and I slept like I hadn't in months.

When I awoke, I walked into the kitchen and poured myself a glass of O-neg. Luci had brought in a gallon jug for me. The liquid had been humanely donated. At least, that's what he'd said. But the bags from the day before hadn't been tainted, and he was Ava's friend, so I gave him the benefit of the doubt. I took a sip then walked around and sat at the counter with Nash and Grim. Paige sat at the table with Luke and Kendra.

"He was right there," I moaned. "Right there! I reacted so slowly." I moaned and sipped, ready to slap myself for my foolish behavior. "How'd I not see him *feeding* in the corner?"

"None of us did," Luke said. "We're all to blame."

"I have a line on this guy, Hails." Kendra looked down at her map and the button then up at me. She pointed to the button. Thank goodness. I needed the uplifting news.

I downed my drink like it was a shot of whisky—which I missed more than I would've thought—and stood.

We assembled. Nash and Grim were going back to keep an eye on the last known address. Someone had been there since the first time they'd gone, and they wanted another look, even if they had to call a cab service to get there while the rest of us teleported to the location.

It was no surprise that the rogue was at a church. We walked around the side to the back of the church where an alley ran between the courtyard and another building. The body was against the other building this time. We couldn't get very close because the cops were already there.

Damn! We missed him again. "These killings seem to be his breakfast."

Paige nodded. "I've noticed."

And it didn't help that I was a later sleeper. We *had* to make sure there wasn't another killing. I just didn't know how quite yet.

I stepped up to Kendra, who was on her tiptoes, trying to see the body without the cops noticing. "Is there a witch's mark?"

She grabbed my hand and nodded, fear in her eyes, in the clench of her hand around mine. "Come on. Let's go."

I understood her fear. She was a witch. If the vampire had a witch fetish, then Kendra could be a target. However, I still thought it had something to do with the blood type. Paige's theory on the victims being virgins wasn't ruled out either. Again, we had no way of knowing that either.

I pulled her away, and we went to the Blood Garden. I needed a drink, and she needed something of the alcoholic kind. Then it occurred to me that I might not have been asking the right questions. "What's your blood type, Kendra?" I was pretty sure I knew based on her smell, but…

She sighed. "All witches are B positive."

Huh. I learned something new every day. Apparently so did Luci because he slid off the stool next to me and moved around to stand behind me as Kendra hung her head. "I should've known."

Luci took her by the arm. "Let's get you out of here." He

teleported her somewhere that wasn't here, and I sat at the bar with Paige. She slid into Kendra's stool and patted my hand.

"Jax says hello."

I lifted my head and looked at her. "You talked to him?"

"Yeah. He's worried, but he knows you've got this."

I didn't point out that those two things couldn't both be true, I simply basked in the happiness of knowing he'd asked about me, spoken about me. It was a warm fuzzy moment.

She eyed me. "Are you going to get all gooey now? Because you really need to keep your head in the hunt."

She was right. I nodded at her. "Absolutely. I'm on it." As a matter of fact, we needed to literally get back to the hunt. I didn't know if Luci was coming back or if I should arrange for a cab. Before I could confer with Paige, Luci and Kendra popped back in with Luke.

"He's here, Hailey." Kendra pointed at the floor to indicate the rogue was inside the bar.

Holy crow. "The rogue? Here?"

She nodded.

Luci had a hand on her arm. "Glinda here thinks that we should let her be bait to draw him out."

I shook my head. No way. This was my fight, and I wasn't letting her do anything foolish. "No. Kendra, it's too dangerous."

"He likes B positive." She pointed at herself. "I'm B positive. He likes pretty girl witches."

Luci looked away and Luke held up both hands. "Don't look at me, sweetheart. I think Leonardo DiCaprio is pretty."

She huffed out a sharp breath. "Listen, fools. I'm doing

this. These are my own kind, my sister witches getting zapped by Dracula, okay? He's attracted to female witches, so all I have to do is a little bit of magic, draw him out, you guys can off him. Easy peasy."

In my experience, nothing that ever looked easy peasy turned out to be so. Ever.

I sighed. I didn't like using my friend as bait. The risk of losing her was too high.

"Look, I can do this with you guys backing me up or without. Your call." She pulled the tough girl card today.

"All right. If this is what you want, fine, but you have to promise not to do anything brave that could also be interpreted as stupid." I'd made the same promise to her once. As much as I wanted to protect her, I also had to remember that she had magical powers and wasn't helpless.

She put her hands on my shoulders, pointed a solemn gaze at me and nodded once. "You know I can't do that, but you also know I can handle myself. And with you guys backing me up, there's no way he's getting me out of any door."

I hated this. The part of me that still rebelled against authority wanted to know by what right the vampire elders had to force me to do this. What were they going to do? Kill me?

Luci shook his head. "No. They'll make your boyfriend do it. He who created, kills. It's their way." He scoffed. "Come to think of it, that seems to be the way of a lot of species."

I wished he would stop snooping around in my head, but he spoke with such conviction I didn't doubt the truth of his words.

I glanced at Kendra and smiled against a tug in my chest.

She was my best friend, and I was letting her go into the valley of the shadow of death with my hands shaking. Never a good omen.

"You ready, Hails?"

No.

I nodded. If she wouldn't listen to reason, mind her sense of danger when it screamed for her to stop, look, and listen, then I would back her up. We weren't just friends in the easy times.

As casually as we could, we all got into position to catch this SOB. I stood at the edge of the bar. Luke waited by the door. Paige went to the back by the bathrooms and the hallway that led to the alley. No one was getting past us. At least now we knew what he looked like.

Luci stayed close to Kendra, who gyrated in the center of the dancefloor and waved her hands. A kaleidoscope of butterflies swarmed the area, flapping in time to the techno music playing through the club's speakers, courtesy of Kendra's magic. Had we not been trying to catch a killer it would've looked pretty cool. But right now, I focused on Kendra, not wanting to lose sight of her.

Kendra danced for a long time, but nobody remotely resembling the rogue approached her. She came off the dance floor and started walking toward the door. Hardest thing I ever had to do in my life was stand there and let her pass me. But this was our last shot in catching him, hoping he was waiting to get her outside.

Luci walked out behind Kendra and before me. He stood against the building, smoking a cigarette when I finally sauntered out, as casual as I could make it. Kendra was half a block down. We waited twenty minutes, her standing there playing on her phone, then she came walking back toward us. Paige and Luke joined us from inside where they'd been watching the exits.

When Kendra got back to me, I wrapped an arm around her. "Thank you for trying, but don't ever do that again." The anxiety wasn't less for my supposed lack of physical reactions. "I bet he recognized you or us. He got away."

Instead of heading back to Luci's place right away, we walked the city until it was almost dawn. Kendra kept trying to trace him, but he'd covered himself somehow. He wasn't coming up on the map.

More than two-thirds of my time was gone. What the hell was I going to do now?

CHAPTER SIXTEEN

I HADN'T SLEPT WELL. Although I supposed it didn't matter, because if I didn't catch this rogue tonight, the elders were going to kill me. So, lack of sleep probably didn't mean much in the overall scheme of things.

Was there such a thing as caffeinated blood? If so, I needed to stock up on such a supply. I'd mixed blood with coffee, but straight up caffeinated blood would be fab. Not today, because my anxiety was keeping me in tip top, wide awake form.

I showered, then walked out of the bedroom and found everyone, including Nash and Grim, in the kitchen. Luci poured me a cup of O Neg then leaned across the counter to look at me. "Someone smells nice."

Well, if I was going to fail at my mission and die today, I didn't want to do it smelling like the inside of a London night-club. And Luci spared no expense on shower gels.

I sipped from my blood trying to think of what I could do to convince the elders to give me more time. I could find him if I just had more time.

Luci opened his mouth, probably to tell me they would never agree because he'd been nosing through my thoughts again, but I held up a finger. "No."

He lifted both hands in surrender. "All right, if you don't want my opinion."

It wasn't that. I wanted his opinion. I just wanted it to agree with what I wanted. "Thanks anyway."

He chuckled because he didn't have to worry about dying today, because he was exactly who he was meant to be, exactly the jerk he wanted to be.

He leaned in to whisper. "I can't help that I hear your thoughts, but try a little kindness, love. A fella's got feelings."

I knew. I'd added the last part for his benefit, and he laughed now. "I think we're going to be good friends, Hailey."

"You see the future, now Luci?" I looked down into my cup, drank the last of the blood then went to the sink behind him. He turned to look at me and waited until I rinsed the cup and loaded it into his dishwasher.

"I don't see the future, but I have a good feeling about you, Hailey."

Kendra nodded at me, then at the map. "I have another location."

I sucked in a deep breath. This was probably my last chance. And even if I found him, I would have to figure out how to take him down, then how to get him to the elders by the end of the day. Night.

My tasks suddenly seemed insurmountable. And I needed them all to know how much I appreciated all their help. "Guys, I want to thank you for all you've all done to help me with this. Having my back. Helping me with the spells." I nodded at Paige and Kendra. "The transport has been invaluable. Plus, your general badassery." I grinned at Luci. "For being with me through all the big moments in my life." I glanced at Luke and my resolve to stay strong broke when he laid his hand over his heart and his eyes filled with tears.

Luci hugged me then Luke hugged us both, I suspected as much to help me get through as to hang on to Luci. Kendra piled on, too, while the others stood back.

Luke sniffed, but Luci stepped back and cleared his throat. "We need to go. Our target might not stay at this locale for long."

I extricated myself from the group hug and nodded. "He's right. We should go."

Of course, it was another church in case you had doubts. We went through the routine and searched the alley. The nooks and crannies left by the old-time architecture.

I had my moment in pity-ville, but it was over now. It was time to focus on this task, on finding the rogue. But he didn't want to be found. Obviously.

"Maybe we should check inside?" Kendra looked over her shoulder at me. We'd looked everywhere else, and she was standing with her map and her button, and it was still showing this guy on site.

My stomach churned and my eyes burned, but I couldn't

let my apprehension stop this mission. Whether or not I succeeded, I still had to try.

I looked at Kendra. We each took a deep breath, then I pulled open the door. We rushed in like we were fearless, like we knew we were going to win. Think positive. Plus, we had Nash and Grim at our backs.

And instead of big bad vampire villains, there were humans. Not a fang among them, but they were ready to fight. And there were a *lot* of them. Probably forty to our seven. Six, since Luci was still outside.

Most of the humans had weapons, and there was some magic inside the church blocking Kendra's spells. The fight came to each one of us, and I watched out for Luke, who was holding his own. He had Ollie for an older brother, so he'd learned how to fight at a young age, even though he morally objected to laying hands on another as an adult.

And, yes, our stuck-up, fun-sucking older brother knew how to fight. He'd taken all kinds of classes when he was younger, dragging each of us—the twins included—along to learn to fight and protect ourselves. Especially Luke, since he'd been subjected to bullying a lot in school.

Today, Luke's choice was to either lose the objections or be killed. But I was trying to shield him from danger as much as I could. He threw a punch as I fought off a couple of the humans on the attack. The bibles here were hard backed and thick. I flung one at a human's knee with all my super vampire strength and his knee bent backwards. Gruesome, but he was fighting out of his weight class. I used a hymnal—also a hard back—to smack the jaw of another.

Nash and Grim held up the other side of the room, but they were covered up with humans. Sure, any of us could kill all of them in a hurry, but these humans were under a spell. We couldn't just murder them. We had to incapacitate them, which was far harder.

A woman came at Luke with a cane—yeah, she was sixty if she was a day. He nudged the bottom of her cane, so she toppled. With a curse, then he sucked in a breath and dove on top of her to protect her from the onslaught of the other humans.

They were fighting like we'd done something to them on a personal level, but I looked closer. They had the hazy eyes of someone compelled. They weren't fighting because they wanted to, but because they had to.

The hair on the back of my neck stood, and I turned in time to watch the rogue—fangs and all—yank Kendra out of the melee and throw her over his shoulder. Luci was still at the back door, I presumed. I doubted if he even knew there was a fight going on.

Hey, you handsome devil. He loved compliments. *Kind of outnumbered in here. Could use a hand.* I sent out a telepathic signal, or hoped I did, then thanked every lucky star I'd ever wished on that he was plagued by my thoughts when he ran in seconds later.

Luci joined the fray and the effect he brought to the fight was divine. Bodies fell. People screamed. I didn't know what they saw, but I didn't have time to figure it out.

"Paige! With me!" She was the only one not covered up

with humans. As soon as they went down, they got back up and fought again.

Watch Luke!

"Go!" Luci shouted behind him as two humans pounced. But he was having a blast. His laugh followed us out as Paige, and I ran for the bell tower.

CHAPTER SEVENTEEN

THE BASTARD HAD KENDRA. Paige and I crossed the courtyard to the stand-alone bell tower. I went up the stairs first, but she was coming in hot behind me. We were the Bond Girls, and we were a trio. This guy had one of us and we weren't taking it. If I had to kill him right there, I would. Consequences be damned. We weren't losing to this guy again.

The stairs were spiral and steep, but when I got to the platform at the top, he was there, feeding on Kendra. She was weak in his arms, trying to cast a spell, but unable to. She slumped back.

Fear sliced through me like a hot knife. Helplessness flooded me, but I pushed it back, allowing my anger to rise. My own fangs lowered and the only thing I saw was the rogue.

I lunged and pushed him away from Kendra. She fell to the floor. "He's mine," I snarled.

Paige went to my best friend in the world while I dealt with the rogue. I couldn't be distracted, or he'd get away.

Oh, please let Kendra be okay.

He backhanded me, spun me around then shoved me toward the stairs. I hung onto the rail and channeled a Jackie Chan aerial move to keep from falling down the stairs. Hot damn, training with Jax was paying off. Then I drop-kicked this guy, pressing both of my heels into his neck. He yelled out and stumbled back a few steps.

I didn't give him a chance to recover before charging forward. When I grabbed his neck, he shoved me back, and I slammed into the wall behind me. This jerk was *strong*.

Ignoring the pain vibrating up and down my spine, I charged him again, but never got good footing and tripped on a raised board a few feet before I got to him. It looked like I meant to ram the top of my skull into his stomach. On a human, it would've been an effective move, but vampires didn't breathe so the air whooshing out of him didn't matter much.

He grabbed me in a headlock, and we both went crashing toward the floor. I put my hands down to keep my face from hitting the wooden planks. He landed on his ass. When we both climbed to our feet, he slapped me as I delivered an uppercut and then he tried to sweep my leg.

But I didn't see Roadhouse eleven times in the theater and probably eighty more once it came out on cable and video for nothing. Patrick Swayze said it didn't matter how big the guy was, if his knee got smashed, he was going down. I was willing to test that theory.

So, I lined him up, aimed, let him get closer, then kicked his knee backward. The sound of bone and cartilage giving way was loud in the space.

I lost focus for one minute to sneak a look at Kendra. She was on the floor, with Paige trying to revive her. "She's been drained." A one second pause. "Hailey, look out!"

I turned to get out of the way of a stake. A stake? Seriously? This hoosier was going to try to stake me. Me!

As I spun out of the way, I used his body's momentum and ended up behind him, put my hands in the middle of his back and then used *my* momentum to drive him into the wall. The stake fell out of his hands and over the rail to his left. It took a good four or six seconds for that thing to hit the ground below us. We were fighting on a six by eight platform with the rope attached to a bell suspended ten feet above us hanging down and a sketchy rail around the edge where the steps came up.

He turned, lifted me around my waist, and moved me toward that rickety rail. I brought my hands up and pounded his face. Over and over until he dropped me.

"He's too strong, Hailey." Kendra was behind me, still weak, but Paige had moved her to the corner, set her up and now it was one semi-broken rogue against a vamp and a half. At this point, I had more broken parts than working, but I wasn't going down without a fight.

"Just relax, K. We got this." I tried to sound strong but holy crap.

Paige glanced at me as we stood between the guy and the stairs. "He have any weaknesses?"

"Being an asshole doesn't count?" I asked.

She shook her head.

"Then none that I saw."

I just needed a second, a recharge, but Paige was ready. If she got her hands on him, he wasn't going to know what hit him. Paige wasn't just one of Jax's enforcers, she was the one he trusted most, put in charge of Grim and Nash and whoever else he had working for him.

She lined him up and kicked. Powered him with a flurry of punches. One after another. And when she pulled back, I went in. Fast. Hard. I didn't move fast enough. He grabbed me by the throat then shoved Paige so she tumbled down the stairs, and I couldn't see how far she went because he lifted me. By. My. Throat.

I clawed his hand, but he kept walking. Shoved me against the wall, and I kicked but couldn't make contact. I tried prying his fingers away, but this wasn't a young vamp. This wasn't some young, freshly turned like we'd thought. He was old. Stronger than I'd ever faced. I could just see Kendra, passed out against the wall, chin lolled against her chest. Paige was down the stairs somewhere.

My vision blurred to a single point of light.

It wasn't looking too good for the Bond Girls.

CHAPTER EIGHTEEN

He had his back toward the stairs now, and I was weak and foggy, but I saw what I saw. And I knew it was going to hurt, but Luke was here. He was going to save us.

He snuck behind the rogue and went for the rope. Luke reached high and pulled down hard. The bell swung, and the rope shortened, then went long again with the winding of the wheel beside the bell, and the clapper hit the lip.

A deafening toll rang through the small space, and I fell, writhing in pain. Damn my sensitive vampire ears. I screamed, though I couldn't hear my own voice. A flutter of activity happened next to me, but I couldn't do more than hold my ears closed.

When I pulled my hands away, I had blood all over my palms.

It would take a few minutes before I healed, and so I

suffered, opened one eye, and watched Paige moan and twist against the pain.

Luke knelt next to me. His mouth moved, but I couldn't make out what he said. He pulled me close, hugging me tight, and I looked up with his comforting arms around me. The rogue was trussed to the rope bell, hogtied on his belly. I looked from him to Luke. "Did you do that?"

Inside my head it sounded like, "uh, oo, oo, ah," but each syllable took a lifetime because of the pain. But I was healing because I could *almost* hear myself again.

He nodded.

"O-ey shi-i-i-."

My ears popped and his voice blared to life.

"Without going full TMI, let me just say, I am a gay man who can tie a knot, baby."

I heard every word, even though the pain hadn't completely subsided. I could have lived the rest of my *long* life without the image of my brother tying up his boyfriends. "It won't hold him," I warned.

If I was healing, so was he. And that old timer could break a knot like he was Houdini on crack.

As we sat, Kendra stood, slowly, as gingerly as she could. "I got this," she growled. She staggered toward the rogue. A string of magic wove around the knot.

"Genius," I muttered. He wouldn't get out of that easily.

She used another spell to remove him from the bell so we could transport this guy and the elders could get over themselves.

"You all right, K?" She was bent, almost on her knees by the time Luci, Grim, and Nash made it up the stairs to us.

Luci knelt beside me on the side opposite Luke while Grim checked on Paige and Nash checked on Kendra.

I stood and Luci put his hand on my shoulder. "Easy, Hailey."

"I'm fine." I stood, healed enough and ready for round five with the rogue. First, I gave Luci a withering glare. "Where were you?"

"Those humans had to be quelled," he said. "I didn't want them to hurt themselves, and this guy is *strong*. It took a minute."

As far as excuses went, that one wasn't so bad.

I moved toward the source of our pain and aggravation and flipped him on his back. "Who the hell are you?"

"My name is Jude McNeill." For a guy with so much violence inside him, he had an incredibly deep voice, but had a lisp. His *is* sounded like *ith.*

"Hailey Whitfield. Not so hot meeting you, bud. Probably not going to be friends, gotta say." I shook my head and raked my hair back. "What the hell is all this about? Why are you killing witches?" Not that any reason was good enough.

He blew out a breath and tried to twist to his side. "My father is Bishop Sean McNeill."

"A Bishop?" Luke asked with a sneer. "So?"

"After my mother was killed, he turned to the church."

"Your mother was killed?" Didn't have to be a genius to see where this was going. I looked at Luci who nodded. The guy was telling the truth. I didn't ask how Luci knew, but I trusted that he did.

"By witches."

"Of course." I didn't say it to taunt him, but it was honest agreement, an understanding.

"I know you don't believe me, but the church knows." He turned and sat up, despite his ties. Kendra added a little more binding to her spell and he winced, but he was restrained and that was all I cared about.

"I didn't say I don't believe you." It was easy enough to verify. "But why did you leave them at the churches?" It wasn't an important detail. We both knew what the elder council was going to do with him. We all knew it.

"For their souls. I was feeding off of them anyway." His fangs glinted off the moonlight coming in near the bell. "It made sense. I had to eat. They were… evil killers."

"And what did you do?"

"An eye for an eye." He shrugged like he hadn't had a choice.

Kendra walked over, crouched in front of him and swung her arm in a wide arc to slap him. "You almost killed me. I have never done anything to you or your family."

"You smelled so good." He snarled and eyed her neck.

I could understand. On occasion, I had the same problem, but I fought the urges. Made a conscious effort not to eat my friends and family. I wondered if there was a time when my humanity, my senses of right and wrong, would fade and I wouldn't care anymore.

I couldn't worry about that at the moment.

Luci helped me stand. "You heard enough yet? It's almost time for you to return."

I was ready. Definitely ready to see Jax. I nodded. "Yeah. Let's get out of here."

We didn't bother heading back to Luci's apartment. None of us had anything there. Luci popped us back to Milan, without a complaint for draining his powers moving us all over the continent.

He wasn't so bad, whoever he was.

CHAPTER NINETEEN

We arrived in Milan with time to spare and a rogue in custody. Jude looked at me and nodded. "I'm ready."

There was defeat in his dark gaze, but he seemed sorry for what he'd done. Where his life had gone. In his special kind of crazy, he'd believed he was right and serving justice. Like I said, the guy was insane.

"I'm sorry for what your mother went through. And for the hurt it left behind. That still doesn't give you the right to kill innocent women." I wasn't sorry he was going to be punished for what he'd done. He knew what he'd done and that they weren't going to let him get by with it. He was prepared.

As soon as we entered the vampire palace, a couple of guards took the prisoner away, and I sighed. McNeill would die thinking he'd avenged his mother. The witches would know the vamp who killed so many of them was paying for his crimes with his life. Everyone involved would be placated. And I got to keep my life.

Win.

Win.

Win.

Except for the dead witches.

Luci stood in front of me and twisted his grin. "Well, aren't you something?"

I smiled. "Back at ya." Without him, I couldn't have done this. "If I can ever help you…"

He nodded. "I'm very glad to have known you, Hailey. And I'm sure we'll see each other again soon." He winked then kissed my cheek.

"Hey," Kendra said. "Something's been bugging me."

Luci paused in the act of turning to leave. "Yes, little witch?"

"I've been watching your powers. You're not a witch, but you're obviously ridiculously powerful. Just your home alone proves that. So why didn't you just go grab this rogue and bring him back?" She put one hand on her hip. "You can't deny it's in your abilities."

Luci pursed his lips and narrowed his eyes. "And where would've been the fun in that?"

We all sputtered and gaped at the mysterious helper, and in a flash of smoke, a little flame across the floor, Luci was gone.

I smiled at Luke, whose eyes went wide as he pointed behind me. "Look out, Hailey!"

Every time someone said that I ended up in hand-to-hand combat, and I was usually outnumbered. This time was no different. When I turned and saw my welcome wagon, I held up my hands. I didn't have enough fight left in me for ten vamps—the exact number surrounding me.

"Hailey Whitfield?" This guy was dressed in combat gear with a stake gun in his hands.

I nodded. "Yes."

"Come." He turned, a precise military heel-turn, and I followed while his troops filed in behind me.

Luke walked beside me. "Why do I feel like we're the main course of a very slow and painful meal?"

I didn't comment as they led us down a long hallway, and the dude with the stake gun stopped and pushed a door on the left open. I walked in, expecting this to be a holding room where we would have to wait until the elders assembled to see me.

Instead, Jax stood, tossed whatever book he'd been reading into his chair and closed the distance between us. "Hailey." He spoke softly, but he threaded his fingers through my hair, urged me closer and pressed a gentle kiss against my mouth. It lasted only a second before he pulled back and stared at me, then lowered his head again. This time, there was nothing gentle about the kiss. It was lined with all the desperation, all the need, all the fear that I carried in my stomach.

"I didn't know if I was ever going to see you again." I couldn't catch a breath…then I remembered I didn't need to, but I didn't want to stop trying. I wasn't ready to surrender that part of being human.

He smiled and leaned his forehead against mine. "I would've played my card before I let that happen."

"Are you ever going to tell me what that card is about?" I whispered.

"Maybe after you tell me what happened."

Well, I supposed he deserved to know. "It's kind of a long story. How much time do we have?"

He grinned. "Time for the Cliffs notes version."

Luke, Kendra, Paige, Nash, and Grim filed in. The enforcers took up positions of security.

"If I condense it, you're going to miss some mighty fine details." But some of those I didn't want to relive so soon.

"Do what you can." He led me to a sofa with pillows on each end. "I just want to hear your voice."

And sometimes he said the sweetest things. I scooted closer as Luke and Kendra crowded us on the couch. "Well, first, we got the file from the council. All the file was, literally, was tall, dark and deadly used to live at this one address but he moved, and we don't know where he went, but here's that other address anyway."

"So, I called anyone I could think of. And with everyone's help, we got it done."

He listened to my recount with a smile on his face. "So, you met Luci, huh?"

I nodded. "Is he really…?"

Jax shrugged. "I don't ask questions."

"Did you know who I was looking for?" It didn't really matter. Especially now that I'd found the rogue, but I was curious.

Jax shook his head. "No." He stood back, looked at me for

a second, then pulled me against him again. "I'm so glad you're okay."

Warmth purred through me. "I'm glad, too." Really glad. "I wasn't always sure it was going to end well."

I wanted to melt into his touch, even one so simple as the brush of his finger along my jaw. "I knew you would come back to me."

"Are you psychic now?" But I loved his faith in me.

His grin faded, and his words took a long time to come. "I don't have to be psychic to know what I know."

"And what is that?" I really wanted this answer. More than I ever wanted another. And a smile didn't count as an answer, but it was all he gave me.

There wouldn't be time for another answer because the knock came. It was time to meet the elder council.

CHAPTER TWENTY

The council sat at their conference table, Soran in the center, Amaya and Dominic on one side, Gretchen and Tobias on the other, and each was just as I remembered them. Amaya was as dangerous looking as she was soft spoken and supposedly kind, though I hadn't seen it yet. Gretchen the opposite. Soft in appearance, harsh in person. Tobias was the one who didn't speak. And Soran was stoic, but a talker.

Dominic looked at Jax and nodded. We didn't bother with the formal greetings this time. Maybe because this was a continuation of the trial they'd adjourned four days ago when they'd sent me on that errand of theirs. I could tell a few of them were hoping I'd fail.

Never underestimate a Bond Girl.

Jax and I took the same seats we'd had last time. Kendra perched a few chairs away and the enforcers were still at the door. Luke had been escorted back to the hotel. As a human, he wasn't allowed at the vampire palace.

"Congratulations, Hailey. You have proved your worth." Dominic smiled at me, like he knew something already.

I nodded, because I wasn't sure whether I was permitted to speak and because Gretchen was mid-scoff. Plus, I had regained all my energy from the fight. "She cheated. She used a vampire, a demon, and a witch."

Tobias nodded. "And a human."

The human was my brother. Kendra who sat in a chair at the side of the table grimaced and stood. "This *witch* almost died helping to capture *your* rogue. Maybe you should learn to control your… group. And did you know he was killing witches?" She sniffed. "I think the words you're looking for are *thank you*."

It was a clan. She knew it. She was being purposefully insulting.

It was time for me to speak. "You said I wasn't allowed to use my maker. You never said I couldn't use anyone else." I stared at Tobias, who scowled in return. He was every bit as fearsome as any other vampire at the table, but he looked more the part with his face contorted in anger and disgust.

Dominic smiled at me again. "She's right. The laws say she couldn't take any assistance from Jaxon, and she did not." He nodded at me. "Not even I helped her."

Amaya stood. "This woman proved herself worthy when we sent her on a mission to catch a rogue vampire. She's untrained."

Untrained and still kicked ass. Well, I'd been trained a little.

I kind of wished Luci was still around. He would've laughed at my wayward thought.

"She proved she's worthy of her fangs." She nodded at me like we were on the same team. And I hoped so, but I didn't really know how this worked and it was probably too late to ask procedural questions now.

"The fact remains, she wouldn't have been able to bring the rogue in without all the help she had." Gretchen was really hanging onto that one with both hands.

"No. The fact remains that the only rule we gave her said that Jaxon was not allowed to help her." Amaya crossed her arms and glared at Gretchen. The air thickened with tension.

"She did as she was asked." Dominic stood and walked in front of the table. "It doesn't matter who she used to assist her in completing her task. All that matters is that she did complete the entire assignment."

I was usually pretty good at reading a room, but there were five of them and while two were obviously on my side, I had no idea if the majority ruled or how the process worked. Did it have to be unanimous?

I had a feeling it wasn't really the room I needed to read. It was Soran. He hadn't spoken yet. I couldn't tell where his allegiances would lie.

Beside me, Jax watched them, stared from one to another as they spoke, but he remained silent, body so still that if he were human, I might've checked him for a pulse.

The elders conferred almost silently, pointing glances at

me every once in a while, occasionally pointing actual fingers. Seemed like we should've been able to hear them, but they were half communicating with the slightest whispers and half with eye wiggles.

When they broke apart, Soran glanced up. "Miss Whitfield, we have come to a decision."

"It's not unanimous." Gretchen stood and braced both hands on the table. "I dissent."

Oh, that had to be good news. Jax squeezed my hand and mouthed, "Stand."

I stood and resisted the urge to wipe my hands down my pants legs.

"We are reserving full judgment until your maker has been dealt with, but *you* are cleared of any wrong-doing." Amaya smiled at me and nodded. I didn't know if I should speak or just nod, but because I was so happy I was about to cry and speech wouldn't be easy, I nodded.

I looked at Kendra and smiled, then reached for Jax's hand, but his was curled in his lap.

It was time for his trial to start.

CHAPTER TWENTY-ONE

"JAXON PARSONS, Master Vampire of the United States, you are accused of making an unauthorized vampire and murdering a vampire, both without the sanction of this council." Soran spoke without his usual volume or the pomp of his tone. It was as if he didn't agree with bringing Jax to trial at all.

Jax nodded. "Yes, but the vampire I killed hadn't been authorized to be made. And Zara's maker is here in Milan being rehabilitated." He paused and looked at Soran.

Gretchen shot Jax a glare. Either she wanted to punish him for making me, since she hadn't been allowed to punish me, or she had the worst case of RBF I'd ever seen. "You should've known, better than anyone. You sent Leo here to begin with."

Well, that was a completely different situation. Obviously. Leo had been out making vampires to suit his purposes. I'd been made to save my life. Although to the council, apparently, there was no difference. Hell, they might've even favored Leo, since Jax had made me to save my *pitiful* human life.

"Let's not forget that she killed Kalon, also." Gretchen sneered.

Jax held up one finger. "That was self-defense. She had no choice about killing him." He glanced at me and half-smiled then wiped it away as quickly and turned back to the council. "He used my heir to lure me to a fight so he could kill me."

I kept quiet.

Dominic rose, although I couldn't believe the council let him sit for this trial since he was Jax's maker and had strong feelings about Jax. "Jaxon has been an exemplary leader. He's shown courage in battle, defended our causes, and enforced our laws all across America."

I didn't know much about Dominic, but I knew enough to like him despite how scary he'd been when I first met him.

He held Jax's gaze for a few moments, then offered me a short nod. Hopefully, that would be enough.

Jax sighed, like a breather and Gretchen cocked a brow. "I didn't make Hailey for the sole purpose of saving her life. I made Hailey because she is my true mate."

What? True who, now?

My whole body froze. Was that his card? What did that even mean?

He wasn't looking at the council anymore. He'd turned to stare at me. "Because from the minute I saw her, I knew. It was why I brought you the muffins. I had to meet you face to face to see if what I felt from observing you was real." He uncurled his hands and took mine. "If I lost you, I would lose a part of myself."

I was sure my heart started working, it was pounding inside of me, trying to get out so I could give it to him. And it was a bad visual in my head, but no one, not even the guy I was supposed to marry, had said anything remotely like that to me. And no one had ever looked at me the way Jax did.

Warmth rolled up my body, and I wanted to throw myself into his arms and kiss him until neither of us could take it anymore.

And no one on the other side of the table seemed to care that we were having a moment. There were gasps from their side, probably eye rolls to go with them. But I didn't care. I was caught in a gaze so potent, I never wanted to be released from it.

Amaya cleared her throat and with as much reluctance as I'd ever felt before, I looked away from Jax and stared at the council. "If you'd told us that from the beginning, we could've dispensed with all this mess," she said.

Dominic even sent a scowl Jax's way before he looked at me. "You wouldn't have even had to prove yourself if he'd just told us that *any* of the times he was spoken to about this."

I didn't care what they said. I was still asshole-deep in my feels.

True mate.

I didn't really understand what that meant, but it sounded like something I could really get into.

Jax worked his jaw. "You know as well as I do that you

would've still wanted Hailey to prove her worth for the simple fact that she is my heir."

No one denied that. I grunted and crossed my arms, glaring at the elders. All except Dominic.

Soran glanced down the table on each side of him then stood. "Jaxon, you know the laws. You have two moon cycles to complete the mating bond."

Two moon cycles? *Bond?* That was two months, give or take a few days.

And what would we have to do for a mating bond? I liked Jax a lot more than I'd liked anyone else I'd *ever* been with in a relationship, but heckfire! We'd barely kissed. Until a few minutes ago I hadn't known how he felt. I wasn't sure I understood it. Did he feel things for me because I was his mate? And only for that reason?

We hadn't even had sex and *mating bond* sounded an awful lot like something more permanent than I was ready for. No freaking way was I mating-bonding with anyone. I had a life. My own place. A job. I didn't know if I even had room for a mating-bonded mate in my life. I'd almost married someone recently, too soon, too fast, and he'd burned me, *bad.* No way was I rushing into anything again.

My emotions were in charge of my lungs again, and I might've started hyperventilating. Shit.

Soran wasn't finished issuing edicts and doing his level best to change my life. Obviously, I couldn't be sure it was his best, but if he had better, I couldn't see how. "If you don't complete the mating bond"—maybe he considered my crazy nose breathing as a rejection of his order to *mating-bond*—“you will be punished.”

Oh, for hell’s sake. They were going to keep threatening me with death. Enough, already. “If I don’t, let me guess, I’ll be killed?” I was haughty and indignant. Annoyed, too. I curled my fingers into my fist and waited.

“Of course, not.” Amaya smiled, softening her RBF a bit. “You went through the challenge. *You* would be allowed to remain a vampire.” She shot a pointed smile at Jaxon, and the implication would’ve been clear even if she didn’t continue. “Such isn’t the case for you.”

I sighed because… breather… and, though it pained me, I didn’t wipe the self-satisfied smile off Gretchen’s face.

I saved that privilege for another day.

CHAPTER TWENTY-TWO

As we walked out of the council chamber, I shot Jax a side-eye. "Mates?" I spat.

He didn't reply.

"Could've mentioned it to me."

Before we made it to the hallway, he stopped, pulled me against him. "You don't feel it? Feel like your heart is going to explode? Like you need big gulps of air when we're together? Like you can't stand the thought of being away from me?"

Of course, I felt those things. "New relationships are full of exploding hearts and labored lungs and fantasies of forever, but a mating bond?"

He grinned and caressed my cheek with the back of his hand. "It doesn't change anything. You can still be you, and I'll still be me. We'll just be us, too."

As much as I liked the sound of it, I couldn't shake the

uneasiness of connecting my life in such a quick way to someone else's. We only had two months to make it happen.

I swallowed hard, making the gulping sound, and he chuckled, then threaded his fingers through my hair. "We'll spend a lot of time together, and if you don't want to do this, we won't. All right?" For such a confident guy, his uncertainty was adorable.

Not complete the mating bond? While I wasn't sure about what it was, I also wasn't sure about what it wasn't. There wasn't anyone I'd ever liked more. Ever wanted more. And no way I'd allow him to be killed, but...

He grinned again. "We'll figure it out. But if I don't kiss you right now…"

I didn't hear the end of his sentence because I pulled him down and pressed my lips against his, waited for him to urge my mouth open, then caressed his tongue with mine. When he pulled back, I smiled. "Maybe we could do it in stages." I paused. "And practice the stages before we get to the last one."

"Don't you want to know what the stages are?"

I shook my head. "I trust you."

And I really did. Even if we only had two moon cycles to figure it out.

"Should we get your stuff from your room?" I could've gone for a few more kisses, but I wanted to get as far away from the council as I could and fast.

He shook his head. "Nothing there is mine."

"I know what I'd like to do," Luke said. "Head back to Heaven."

I rolled my eyes. "That place was too much for me."

"There's a similar club here in Milan," Nash said. "Great dancing. It's called Amnesia."

Everyone seemed eager, so we headed out the door and onto the private subway car. Similar to how we were brought to the vampire palace, we rejoined a regular subway car, then walked up the stairs to street level, emerging down the road from the club.

My heart hadn't felt this light in what felt like years. "What about feeding?" I asked.

Jax winked, and a few seconds later, Dominic appeared beside us like a shadow turned light. "Shall we?" he asked.

"Hey, Gramps," I said brightly. "Glad you could join us."

He rolled his eyes, but they each took an arm, and we marched up to the bouncers.

Just like at Heaven, they let us in without a word, but this time, it was obviously Dominic doing all the influencing. No doubt he was well known around the clubs in the city.

Just like when we went to the other human bar, the atmosphere inside was almost too much for me. But also like Heaven, we were able to go straight to a VIP section.

"They have a special menu for us," Dominic said. "I have several bartenders in my pocket."

"Bathroom?" Kendra asked a few minutes later.

Dominic snapped his fingers, and a woman walked over. He said something in Italian and the woman smiled at us. "This way, please."

But as we walked down the hall, Kendra pulled out her phone. "Hello?" she said. After a second, she stopped me and put her phone on speaker. Luckily the hallway was behind the VIP section, so the music of the club was very muted. “It’s Cleo’s daughter.”

“Hey, Tracy!” I hadn’t talked to her in a while.

“Hailey, I need your help.” She sounded frantic and her breaths came loud through the phone.

Red flags waved like they were caught in a gale force wind. But I kept my own fear behind a wall of calm. “What’s up?”

“It’s Mom. She’s missing.”

MASQUERADING IN THE MIDLIFE

CHAPTER ONE

A FEW MONTHS AGO, I was a woman who'd been stood up on my wedding day by a man who'd never made me a priority, never been honest, never been worthy of my time, but I'd been living a typically normal life. I'd gone to work, I'd come home, generally, I'd watched a little TV and had gone to bed with a man who'd slept soundly without so much as giving me a second glance. As far as self-esteem went, it'd been soul-crushing.

In stark contrast, having a neighbor who had proposed a mating bond with me was a big boost in the how-I-viewed-myself department. I loved the idea of being someone's forever, someone's life partner in all things that mattered. I know, I know, when I started this new chapter in my life at the ripe old age of forty, I'd said I would never love again.

Well, suck it up, buttercup. Things change. However, that didn't mean I liked the fact that the vampire elders had put Jax and me on a ticking time clock to complete our bond. It crushed all the romance out of the whole meet my mate and fall in love thing.

Really, how well could I get to know someone after a few months when those said months were filled with one crisis after another? We'd barely had a moment to breathe, much less bond.

At least my future mate was hot, with his shoulder-length strawberry-blond hair, big hazel eyes that changed colors depending on the color of his shirt and mood, and a body that could've made a grown woman weep with joy at just seeing him shift a shoulder or clench a muscle. Believe me, I'd had to resist the urge a few times. He had a way of wearing jeans that made me grateful I had eyes.

Despite his bodily excellence, Jaxson Parsons was so much more than eye candy. He was a strong, fierce leader of the United States vampires and a compassionate friend. Friend, not lover, because we hadn't yet done the deed if you know what I mean. You… you know what I mean, right? The deed. The big kahuna. Bumping uglies. Taking a trip to Pound Town. Knocking boots, checking the oil. Two-person push-ups, the no-pants dance.

Oh, sorry. You did understand what I meant. Sex.

The idea of mating with the beautiful brooding vampire from across the street, the guy who'd saved my life, the guy who looked at me like I used to look at dessert, wasn't a completely unwelcome thought. At least, not when I was alone in my room in the dark of night fantasizing about it. About him.

As far as fantasies went, rolling through the sheets with him was one of my faves, but knowing the choice was out of my hands was on the ugly side of overwhelming.

During all this chaos, I'd also started a new business with my best friend, and that took up a significant amount of time. We were the Bond Girls Recovery Agency; skip tracers. Move over Dog, the Bond Girls were on the case. And we were good. Like, really good. We'd learned most of what we knew from Cleo, a seasoned bounty hunter who was happy to teach us everything she knew. Of course, a little magic and vampire speed helped too.

I thought about all of this as I lay in the bed on the jet flying us home from Europe because Cleo had gone missing. Missing. Our mentor was MIA, and it was going to be on me, on the Bond Girls, to find her.

As far as my new vampire status, time was on my side. Or would have been if I hadn't wasted so much of it in Milan having to justify my existence to a council who blamed Jax for turning me without permission. Never mind I would've died from Zara draining me. They'd rather I had died.

More wasted time in the air when I should've been sleeping, but couldn't because…mating bond, missing friend. Sleeping wasn't exactly something I was going to be able to manage until this was all handled, at least. The pull was still incredibly strong, though. This was the first time I'd been able to resist it.

When the plane rolled to a stop on the tarmac, I rolled out of the bed, ready to face whatever I had to in order to get Cleo back.

I followed Jax through the airport with my phone pinging notifications as if I'd been out of touch for weeks, months even, rather than the hours I'd been in the air from Milan. We had to meet Luke and Kendra—they'd accompanied us to the council meeting—then we could be off to find Cleo. They were on the same flight but didn't have to be confined to the light-tight rooms.

I saw Kendra first. She was tall in her heeled boots and her hair was pulled back in a long cascade of ebony—she'd had a spa day in Milan that included a chemical refresh of her hair color—but since she was as close to Cleo as I was, her face was drawn with worry.

"I did a spell on the plane." She kept her voice low because we were in public. "I sensed Cleo, so I'm almost certain she's alive."

A WEIGHT like a cinder block lifted from my chest. This was good news. Her spells were at least sixty percent how we found our skips and she was hardly ever wrong. "I have at least ten missed calls from Jordan and Tracy combined."

Tracy, Cleo's daughter, had brought the abduction to our attention, and she was understandably frantic. Jordan, as Cleo's boss and the possible reason she was abducted, was also understandably hysterical.

Without Cleo, he was twenty percent down in terms of his workforce. And teeny tiny Jordan, who had Michael Jackson's voice and Danny DeVito's comb-over, needed his entire work-force to keep him solvent. Plus, I suspected he had a thing for

Cleo. For her badassery, her class and her ability to shoot the wings off a fly in the dark just by hearing it flap its little wings. There was a lot for Jordan to admire about Cleo. A lot for all of us to admire, but he took it to ever-flirting extremes.

Luke walked up to us, not quite as worried. He knew Cleo, but only in passing. "Come on," I said. "We'll drop you off on the way."

Nash and Grim—part of Jax's creatures-of-the-night team —were going to meet us at Jordan's office, so off we went. Jax drove, because it was his car, and he didn't mind driving, although as vampires, we could run like the wind, and it probably would've been faster than battling traffic. However, that kind of speed through a very busy city was a bit hard to explain to humans who chose to act as if witches and vampires and fae were the stuff of folklore, not living right under their noses.

I texted Cleo's daughter, Tracy, to let her know we were going straight to Jordan's and then on to finding her mama.

"Where are Paige and Ransom?" I asked as Jax navigated the streets of downtown Philadelphia, heading for Jordan's.

"Dealing with my kingdom," he said. "Just normal stuff. Property rights disputes, a petition for a new club in Seattle. That sort of thing."

I touched his hand on the gearshift. "Thanks. I'm glad you're here, helping with this." He easily could've delegated finding Cleo to his subordinates or left it to me. It was my problem, not his.

He cared because I did, and that meant a lot to me.

By the time we arrived, Nash and Grim were stationed

outside like trench-coat-wearing secret service agents. Except these guys had fangs and were cold to the touch. They didn't care much for taking chances in the sunlight. Hence, our movements tended to be under cover of darkness. It gave us the element of surprise. The ability to sneak better than we could in daylight excursions.

I walked inside and stared at Jordan, who had bitten his nails down to the knuckle. Not really, but you get the point. When his eyes met mine, he started talking in fast, high-pitched sentences. "Where have you been, little lady? Do I not have enough to worry about with Cleo missing? Then you take off, too? And no call, no email, no word whatsoever."

I would have interrupted and told him that I definitely informed him that I was going to be away by phone and email, but he hadn't taken a breath yet.

"I left you eleven voicemails," he squeaked, his voice higher than normal, thanks to his worry.

It'd only been seven, but Jordan was prone to exaggeration. "I was ready to file a second missing person report."

He was on a roll. I hated to interrupt his tirade, but I had questions. "You filed a missing person on Cleo?" That meant cops would be involved, which would make finding her much harder because we would be limited about how involved we could be, or at least, how much we could let them know we were involved.

He huffed out a breath, folded his arms, unfolded them and rubbed his hands over his hips then folded his arms again. "Well, no. But I wanted to. I just thought you might have a better chance of finding her. Your success rate is a hundred percent better than theirs."

I would've basked in the praise had Cleo not been missing. "Jordan?"

"Yes, yes." He fastened his fanny pack around his waist. I didn't know what he kept in that thing. I'd never had the courage to ask, but he never left home without it—assuming, and I did, that the back room here doubled as his living space. He was going somewhere. It took a second for me to figure out he meant to go with us.

"What are you doing?" I wasn't as high-pitched as Jordan, but it had been a while since he'd gone out on the streets, although Cleo had repeatedly vouched for his greatness. Still, it worried me. Plus, he didn't know how the Bond Girls had such a high success rate. And if he went with us, we'd have to act totally normal.

"I'm coming along." He cocked a brow. It was his version of a silent dare.

"No, no. That's a bad idea." I didn't know why. Gut feeling, maybe. And I trusted those a lot more than I trusted a hobbit to be helpful. Plus, the whole, we needed to be able to use our powers thing.

"Hails, can I see you outside for a minute?" Kendra laid a hand on my shoulder, intervening before Jordan and I came to verbal or physical blows.

The office wasn't small but looked like it was because of the amount of furniture in the place. Chairs, tables, desks, all in such disarray that Kendra and I had to maneuver around because Nash, Grim, Jax, and Jordan were positioned in the empty spaces.

I walked out first and the bell on the door jingled. I'd made Jordan put it on the door after the first time we walked in on him half naked so he'd know when we arrived, giving him time to put on a shirt and pants before he came out of the back room. I turned to Kendra as she asked, "What do we do?"

"About what?" Like I said, I'd spent a few hours too many on a plane. My brain was fuzzy.

"Jordan can't go with us without finding out that you have a very specific skill set these days." She made it sound like I was the guy from that movie. "He'll know you're… special, and he has no inside voice. No filter. He'll tell everyone in a ten-mile radius just by breathing."

I nodded because her point was valid. Plus, I'd been thinking the same thing.

"What do you want me to do? You know how he feels about Cleo." Being left behind wasn't an option for Jordan. He wouldn't listen if we told him to stay. Pfft. We wouldn't even be able to keep him semi-quiet.

Moonlight glinted off of Kendra's shiny hair as she sighed and tossed it behind her shoulders. "Maybe we should just tell him. Get it out in the open. Here. Now. Let him see it isn't a big deal." Her idea made sense. We could use his own walls to contain his enthusiasm about me. He was sure to freak out one way or another.

"You can't tell him about vampires." The voice came as a whisper inside my head, a sexy, low purr of a whisper that traveled down my body like a caress. Jax. He couldn't read my mind or hear my thoughts, nor could I read his. However, we could send our thoughts to one another like telepathy. Another of those handy new skills for this amazing skillset was the hearing of a bat or a moth.

"Jax says we can't tell him about my personal… abilities," I whispered.

She did a full spin. "Oh, Jax says, does he?"

"Easily agitated, isn't she?" Jax's voice made my body vibrate, and I lip-twitched away a smile. I loved hearing him whisper like that. It was so dang sexy.

I let my head wave from one side to the other, then crossed my arms and assumed an all-business face. No need to make her think I wasn't taking her seriously. "He does."

"Well, maybe you could ask him what we should do here? How we should force Jordan to stay here."

"You should tell him that Kendra's a witch." Holy catnip, this man had a way about him. A voice. A body. Intelligence. He was the full package. But no way was Kendra going along with that idea.

Still, it was my duty as a vampire to protect the identity of my kind, because there were predators. The Salem witch trials ended a long time ago, but since that danged Buffy and those Winchester boys on TV, amateur fang hunters were everywhere. "Jax thinks we should tell Jordan about you."

"I hope you mean that you're going to tell him that I cook a mean linguine alfredo, that I can ballroom dance, that I know the value of a dollar in ways that a lot of women don't when it comes to buying designer shoes." Her eyes flashed then went dark with the challenge.

"Yes, Ken, I'm going to give Jordan the headlines from your Tinder profile." I rolled my eyes and tapped one foot.

"Listen, sister, just because you're getting the goods from Count Hotpants doesn't mean you should demean my online dating." Now she was getting huffy, and we were so far off-topic I was going to need a tractor-trailer and a crane to bring us back around. And for goodness sake, he could hear us and was chuckling in my ear. Well chuckling in my mind via telepathy.

"I'm not getting the goods from anyone." Sweet holy hominy, getting the goods? I wished.

"Could be." It was him again. And he knew we were talking about sweeping the proverbial chimney. And he wanted me to know we could be sleeping together. Thank goodness he couldn't read my mind unless I let him. Cause then he'd know I'd be bright freaking red right now if I were still a human.

"Hush."

Kendra's head jerked up. "Did you just tell me to hush?"

"No, I…" Lord. I couldn't tell her he was listening. Although maybe she knew already. "I would never. What I'm saying is…" What the hell was I saying? "What I'm saying is…" I came out stronger, still didn't have a big finish. "What I'm saying is that telling Jordan about vampires is dangerous, but letting him see you do a simple spell, maybe scry for Cleo's location is enough to keep him watching you in case I give myself away."

"Nice. Way to keep it focused on her." I didn't need the

cheering section, but I didn't mind the praise, even if it was in a whisper and only I could hear it.

Kendra sighed, then threw her hands up, and growled. "Fine. We'll tell him I'm a witch."

She turned and walked back inside. To myself—more to Jax—I muttered, "You'd better hope this works."

We walked inside. Jordan was still fumbling with his fanny pack and Nash and Grim were as focused as ever. Jax wore a smirk and ridiculously, even that was endearing on him. That wasn't something I wanted to unpack right now, so I slipped it in with all my other Jax thoughts to be contemplated at a later time.

I glanced at Jordan. He'd finally managed to fasten his belted bag around his waist and huffed an impatient sigh. "Why are we all just standing here?"

Kendra had never been shy before about who she was. For those of us who knew about her, her powers were just a part of what made her the fun-loving, slightly eccentric, always beautiful woman she was. But she was looking at Jordan as if we were sending her in front of the firing squad.

"Oh, fine." Finally, she stepped forward. She took Jordan's tiny shoulders in her hands and spun him to face her. "I'm going to tell you something." He pulled his head back as if she'd just threatened to kill him. "And if you ever tell anyone, I will yank your ears off and use them to make tiny man soup before I shove you in the pot. You hear me?"

He cocked an eyebrow, and the unflappable Jordan looked ever so slightly flapped. "I hear you." This was the most solemn I'd ever seen him.

Instead of explaining, Kendra took a piece of paper and wrote Cleo's name in bold, black marker. Then she closed her eyes and waved one finger over the page so that the words rose off the page and into the air. The letters straightened into a line that formed an arrow and then pointed outside. "Let's go."

Jordan stared hard. First at the arrow then at Kendra. He didn't move more than a couple of inches and then only because Nash stepped around him and bumped Jordan's shoulder. "What in sam blasted hell is going on?" Jordan yelped.

I moved forward. "Jordan, you know that there are things in the world that happen that people think are unexplained?" He nodded but kept his gaze on the arrow that was scrunching then straightening as if telling us to get out the door. "Kendra is one of those unexplainable explanations."

Blinking rapidly, Jordan braced himself on a nearby chair with one hand and waved the other in the air as he spoke. "So you're like that wizard kid in the movies? The one with the round glasses and the warthog?"

His details were fuzzy, but I knew who he meant. Unfortunately, being compared to that kid was something that set Kendra's hair on fire. She narrowed her gaze and stared hard at Jordan.

A lesser, smaller man would have shriveled, but this guy lifted his chin. "What?"

"Not at all like the kid." Even though she kind of was.

Her eyes flashed, and I shrugged at Jax whose smirk had flattened into a thin line that was still adorable.

Jordan hadn't stopped staring at Kendra. "Can you wiggle your nose to cook dinner?"

"Why would I do that?" Her gaze pinched.

"Can you grant me three wishes?"

"That's a genie, Einstein." Every word he spoke deepened her frown.

"Can you teleport? Transform into a dragon? Do you dine on the souls of little children?" He rattled off a couple more Hollywood versions of witchy powers. I had to bite back giggles at his reaction. He'd taken it like a pro.

"Yes, you butthead. I breakfast on seven-year-olds or tiny little men with screechy voices." She shrugged like the difference didn't matter.

I hid a smile behind my hand. "Maybe we should go. Cleo's still missing."

Jordan nodded at me. "Yes, we should."

We drove to Cleo's house because to scry for her location, we needed something of hers along with the city map I'd pilfered from under the counter in Jordan's office. Jax drove me and Jordan while Nash and Grim followed behind with Kendra. She'd ridden with them because leaving her in the back seat with Jordan wasn't safe for him.

When we arrived, Kendra stopped me at the door as I was about to put my key into the lock. "What about Tracy?"

She wasn't aware of the supernatural, and the fewer people who knew—it was bad enough we'd had to tell Jordan—the better. Jax took the key from my hand and looked inside the apartment. "She's asleep on the sofa."

I nodded. "I'll just run inside for a second."

It was all too easy to stay quiet, thanks to my preternatural powers, and soon came back out with a necklace of Cleo's and handed it to Kendra. We didn't have to be inside the apartment. The hallway would work. Heck, anywhere would work as long as we had an item of Cleo's. Nash stood guard on one side, Grim on the other, as Kendra kneeled on the floor to work her magic with the map and necklace. Jordan chortled and giggled as the necklace pointed us to Cleo's location.

"I have got to learn how to do that." Then he looked up at me. "This is how you catch them all, isn't it?"

I chuckled. No way was I telling him anything. "Sorry, Jordan. A girl has to have her secrets." I smiled as we walked to the stairwell. There were some things he didn't need to know. How we were going to manage to keep them from him, I had no clue.

CHAPTER TWO

We ended up at a little cottage on the not-so-good side of town. There was once upon a time I'd have feared for my life entering a high-crime area like this one, but not now. Not mostly.

I was a vamp, and I could kick butt, thanks to Jax keeping up with my training.

Plus, the man…vampire in question, was there with me, along with two enforcers and a witch. So I was confident that we were all good.

Studying the small dwelling, I noted that one window in the front had a piece of plywood covering the opening. The siding had been torn off by either the wind or vandals, and there was a gaping hole in the porch near the front door. "Well, it's not a summer getaway, but let's go see if we can find Cleo," I muttered and slipped out of the car.

Nash went around to the back while Grim stood to the side

of the front door. Apparently, we weren't going to knock first. He turned, kicked the flimsy wood door, and it fell in a puff of dust. We were in.

Cleo sat bound and gagged in the center of the room, but she didn't seem injured. Just pissed, jerking her body left and right trying to break free of the bindings. Underneath the gag, she was cursing. I couldn't make out the exact words, but they weren't prayers for a swift release.

Nope, not injured if she was fighting to get free. Of course, she could've been hopped up on adrenaline. We'd figure it out when we had her out of there.

There were five guys in the living room with her, who apparently hadn't heard us break down the already broken door. Cleo was making too much noise, so the men were ignoring her.

Not that our presence went unnoticed for long.

The three men playing poker at a table turned toward us in unison. It was kind of creepy. The one sitting on the sofa removed his feet from the table and stood while the other man sitting in a chair took the last swig of his beer. None of them seemed particularly surprised to see us, but I didn't have time to care because Jordan pushed past me and walked into the room.

The little man with the big personality ninja kicked and karate chopped his way to them, not stopping even when the big one by the sofa came at him. Jordan punched low, used his knees, his elbows, and his big ol' melon head to disarm and disable the goon.

When the three at the table stood, I moved to rush in to

help Jordan, but Jax stopped me. I glanced at my maker-soon-to-be-mate with a stern look. Jax shook his head. I didn't have time to voice my concerns about letting Jordan die at the hands of Cleo's kidnappers before the little man started kicking ass without taking names.

He humiliated the men. Big, brawny men who should've been able to kick his tiny ass. When Cyclone Jordan was finished, nary a man was left standing. Kendra and I stood there with our mouths open while Jax, Grim, and Nash looked impressed.

Jordan dusted his hands against one another then gave us each a satisfied smirk before he glanced at Kendra. "Can your magic do that?"

"Is it a competition?" she asked with a hint of a smirk.

He smiled. "Could be."

She rolled her eyes and walked out. "Oh, for goodness sake."

Jax took over for Jordan who was untying Cleo. She pointed to one of the big guys who was still prone on the ground, his hands covering whatever of his man bits Jordan hadn't crushed. "He's the guy in charge here."

I nodded as Grim jerked the guy to his feet. He groaned—the guy, not Grim—and held onto his crotch when he noticed Jordan was still eying him.

I smiled at the small man, now wondering if he was some sort of supernatural creature himself. "Why don't you help Cleo out to the car. Get her a bottle of water?" There were always emergency supplies in Jax's cars, and I needed Jordan out of here so I could compel this guy into giving up the information we needed. No way would the man in charge of the kidnapping let himself be caught here. So we had to know who these asshats were working for.

When Jordan had Cleo safely outside, I stepped in front of the guy Grim was still holding upright while Jax checked on everyone else. I pointed my gaze into his and stared hard until his eyes glazed over. He wouldn't be able to lie now.

"Who is the man who hired you to kidnap Cleo?"

The guy looked at me. "There is no man who hired me."

I glanced at Jax who lifted his head, brow pinched, to stare at me. Focusing back on the goon, I tried again. "Why did you kidnap Cleo?"

"I was hired to kidnap her."

"But you just said..." This wasn't working. Dammit. It always worked. Maybe my compulsion power was on the fritz. "Give me the name of the man who hired you."

He sighed and clamped his lips closed. What the eff?

I glanced at Jax. He shrugged. "Maybe he doesn't know. He can't be compelled to give you information he doesn't have."

"Son of a bitch." I was swearing, not name-calling. Neither of which made me feel any better about myself or my lack of vampire prowess. This should've been easy. "Tell me."

The guy let his head fall forward. "I was hired by someone who is sick and tired of you throwing all the low levels into the clink. You think you're so smart. So good." He shook his head. "Pfft. You ain't nothing but some tiny little woman. We were supposed to grab you, but I couldn't find you, so I took her instead."

Oh, no. If they'd hurt Cleo because of me, I would never get over it. The fact that they meant to get me instead of her didn't sit well in my gut or my heart. But I pushed all those feelings into a small box in my brain so I could deal with them later. Right now, I had to get to the bottom of who wanted me out of the way.

"What's his name?" I wasn't about to give up. I needed to know the ringleader.

The guy rolled his eyes at me.

Rolled. His. Eyes.

The nerve of him. Anger bubbled up, pulling my fangs out.

"I told you what I know," he said flatly.

Jax nodded to Grim. "Put them all in the van and we'll take them to the police."

Grim and Nash brought the kidnappers out while Jax checked the table for any clues. He held up one of the hands of cards—four aces. "With a hand like this, you'd think the guy would've fought a little harder."

I smiled, but there were no happy feelings put into it. They hadn't meant to get Cleo. They'd meant to get me, to use her to draw me out. I shivered. This could've been me. Although, I doubted any of the gorillas in this room would've been much of a match for my speed, my strength. Big and bulky didn't mean much against a vampire. Especially a young one with strength to spare.

Jax drove the rest of the crew back to Cleo's while I rode with Grim and Nash to the police station. They knew me there.

I sat in the back with the prisoners. In turn, I stared at each one. "You will confess to kidnapping Cleo Jackson and holding her at your hideout." I wouldn't get a skip trace fee for this one, but no way did I want these fools running the streets either. I hadn't even remotely done it for the money, anyway.

While they were processed into custody, I stood at the sergeant's desk chatting with Officer Dell Prince. He chuckled. "You're making us look bad, Hails." He nodded to the line of thugs I'd just delivered. "How'd you find Cleo?"

I tapped the side of my nose. "I'm like a bloodhound, Dell. I can sniff out trouble a mile away." I couldn't very well tell him Kendra had used magic to find most of the perps we brought in.

He laughed. "Well, Philly PD is grateful for your dedication. Makes our lives a lot easier." His smile faded and he blew out a slow, semi-loud breath. "I was thinking. Maybe we could get a coffee? Or dinner? Maybe a movie?"

Oh freakin' frack. He was asking me out. Warmth crept up my neck to my cheeks. Dell was young. Maybe twenty-five with black hair and gray eyes. If I had a daughter, he would've been exactly the kind of guy I would've wanted her to date. Honor rolled off of this kid, and he was too young to be jaded yet by a job that gave little and demanded much. He was still idealizing life. I liked that. But not enough to date him. Besides, I had the whole mating bond thing going on with Jax. "Thank you for the offer, Dell. But…"

"You're not interested. I get it. It's totally cool." Despite his calm demeanor and kind words, a little dot of light in his eyes died. Oh, what a sweetie.

"I'm involved with someone." True enough, I supposed. If I wasn't now, I would be very soon.

And the light was back. He grinned. "If that goes south…"

"You're my first call." As soon as I learned to turn back time and become twenty years younger. Also, how to not be a vampire anymore. Speaking of the mating bond and the someone I was involved with, I took a step back. Then another. "I'd better get going…gotta check on Cleo. See you around."

He waved and smiled. "I hope so."

The invitation had been crazy flattering. And maybe if it wasn't for Jax, I would've considered it, even with the age difference, but I had enough to deal with right now. The agency kept me busy. Now, some crime kingpin wanted me out of the way and there was no telling how far he would go to make sure that happened. No doubt the reign of terror wasn't going to stop with a foiled kidnapping. And then there was the mating bond.

Mating. Bond.

The matingbond, matingbond, matingbond. Didn't matter how I said it. Or how many times. The thought still gave me alternating chills and shivers. And though they might've sounded like the same thing, they were very different. One stemmed from fright, from the idea that if I didn't do this, the council would act in a way that was meant to end Jax's life and-or mine in one way or another. It came from the panicked part of me where my soul should've been.

But the other, the shivers, came from anticipation, from an eager hope, from a keenness to make it happen, and make it happen right now. It was the part of me that remained in a constant state of excitement. The part that made being in the same room with Jax a challenge.

As I rode back to Cleo's with Grim and Nash, I tried to put all thoughts of mating out of my mind and concentrate on the matter of Cleo's kidnappers.

Paige appeared out of the shadows as we stepped out of the car. "Hey," I said brightly. "Where'd you come from?"

She grinned and fell in step beside me. "I had some business at Catch and Release, so I walked over." It wasn't that far from here. Not for a vampire, anyway. "I wanted to check on Cleo."

When we walked into Cleo's apartment, she,Tracy, Jax, Kendra, and Jordan were all sitting in the living room. Cleo stood, gingerly, as if in pain, then pulled me into a tight hug. "Thank you, girlie."

I nodded, hugging her back. I should have apologized to her, not accepted her gratitude. She could've been killed. And it was my fault.

I pulled back and looked at her. I couldn't let that go. And I damn sure wouldn't let it happen again. And to make sure it didn't, I needed to know all the details. Every bit she could remember. "What happened?"

"I was home, snug like a bug in a rug in my bed." She looked at each of us in turn. "I thought I heard something, but this is my home. My safe space. Doors were locked. Windows closed. Security system on. This place is like Fort Knox." I nodded. She liked her deadbolts. "So I thought, maybe the building was creaking, or something, you know? Some wind. I got up to check just in case. When I got to the living room, there he was. That fat bastard who took me."

My heart clenched. "I'm so sorry, Cleo."

She waved me off and kept talking. "He had a gun, forced me into his car and drove me to that terrible little house. Fed me burgers three times a day." Ah, she would've hated that. Cleo was on a health kick. Burgers three times a day was probably enough to make her want to kill them herself. "I fought back when I could, but I'm still not running on full cylinders since the shooting."

I'd initially met her because she'd been shot and before I was a skip tracer, I was a caretaker. Specifically, hers. She got me into the skip tracing.

"Maybe you should rest now, Mama." Tracy laid a protective hand on her shoulder then looked at me. "Can one of you guys stay with her? I have exam prep."

Paige looked toward Jax, and he nodded once. "I can," the lead enforcer said. "Now that Jax is home I'm free."

Jordan, who'd been blessedly silent since we returned, nodded. "And I'm not going anywhere until you're right as rain again." What about Jordan? It turned out he was quite the fighter. I was beyond impressed.

Cleo looked at Paige. "I have a light-tight room you can use."

Jordan's eyebrows formed a tight line across the lower edge of his forehead. He had a sudden Bert from Bert and Ernie thing going on. "Why does she need a light-tight room?" Uh-oh. His voice was chock full of suspicion.

Paige glanced at me, then Jax, then Jordan and faked a

yawn. "I can't sleep in anything but a pitch black room." She shrugged, and even I was convinced. "Pitfall of working the night shift."

Jordan accepted that excuse readily. Even now that he knew about witches, most humans were eager to take any reasoning that meant their world wasn't insane and full of monsters.

Something about all of this was bugging me. We had Cleo back and that was great, but for a kidnapping, it had been mighty easy to find her. Easier yet to bring her home unscathed. And for me being the one they'd wanted, I'd walked right in and no one had even flinched.

Too easy. That was what was bothering me. I was waiting for the other shoe to drop.

I hugged Cleo, then followed Jax out the door. Kendra walked beside me, her voice soft as she asked, "Is it just me, or was that a little too easy?"

I swung my arms up, prepared to talk with my hands, as I vehemently agreed, but Jax beat me to it. "I was thinking the same thing."

Oh, okay. I wasn't the only one.

Thank goodness.

CHAPTER THREE

We dropped Kendra off at home because she was tired. Mostly tired of putting up with Jordan, but it was mixed in with jetlag.

If I were still human, I'd be just as tired. But I wasn't, so I wasn't. Heh.

Even though I didn't sleep much on the plane, and despite the pull of the coming sun that usually knocked me out cold, I was pretty wired.

"You want to go to Catch and Release?" Jax asked before putting the car in reverse.

Catch and Release was a bar Jax owned where vampires and humans mingled and vampires fed. Most of the humans who hung out at the bar knew about vampires and were sworn to secrecy. Those who didn't know got compelled to forget everything they saw when they left. It was a great set up and much safer for vamps to feed. They didn't have to hunt, which could quickly become dangerous.

I nodded, hungry for the first time since we'd arrived back in the states. My focus had been on getting Cleo home safe. "That sounds great, if you don't mind backtracking to downtown Philly."

"Anything for you." I froze and watched in almost slow motion as Jax lifted his hand and stroked my cheek with one finger before time sped up and he backed out of Kendra's driveway. A shiver danced down my spine.

He twisted the steering wheel, and I couldn't stop staring at the muscles in his arms, the clench of his fist on the wheel, the laser focus as he weaved in and out of traffic.

We hadn't gotten our drink in Milan before I'd found out about Cleo, so it was half past feeding time and approaching time to feed again. The urge was strong.

My new life was all about urges and reactions. Part of me responded as a human would—gasps or groans, anger, happiness—with appropriate emotional responses. That same part expected the visceral human reactions that were no longer there—racing heart, rapid breathing, surges of adrenaline in my blood. I kept waiting for my body to respond, hoping it would, having the phantom sensations Jax had told me would fade. So far, that part of me still existed. And right now, watching Jax, without even bothering to hide it, gave me the phantom racing heart, the feigned need for extra oxygen. Although the urge to run my hand over his forearm was very real.

I curled my fingers into my hand as he pulled the car into the lot at the club. The pull I felt toward him was real, even without the physical responses.

When he shut off the car, he waited to get out until Nash and Grim were already waiting, then glanced at me. “I know this mating bond is a whole, ah, thing for you.” I’d never seen him stumble over words before, and that he was doing so now was endearing.

The unexpected announcement of the mating bond caused a tidal wave of confusion. I wasn’t ready. Or was I? I was undecided. My mother would’ve called it flighty. My father would’ve called it ridiculous. I was sticking with undecided.

The real problem that pissed me off was the council putting a deadline on our courtship. My past relationships had all moved too fast and ended in heartache. My first husband, Howard, and I were friends now, but it had taken a while to get to the place we were currently at.

“We don’t have to talk about it,” he offered, but I knew it was only a temporary hold on the subject. We had two months to figure it out. Just thinking about it made my indecision fade to unhappiness, and I had a strong suspicion unhappiness was going to morph with a distinct lack of ceremony to straight up anger. Then again this could’ve all been the result of hunger and lack of sleep. “No, we should. But let’s go in. I can't think while I’m so hungry.”

Before I reached out to grab the handle of the car door, Jax cupped my face and kissed me.

My dead heart reanimated and was about to leap out of my

chest. That's how it felt, anyway. Every inch of my body heated and tingled and craved Jax's touch. Was this because of the bond? Fate?

Wowza.

Much too soon, he pulled away and got out of the car, leaving me panting in the passenger seat. It was a darn good thing I didn't need to breathe, because that kiss left me breathless.

We walked inside together. His cologne hung around me like an enticing, spicy cloud of come-get-me. I breathed through my mouth out of habit. His hand at the small of my back was another tool in his arsenal of mating bond seduction weaponry. I walked faster because the lack of blood added to my confusion. I was about to lose my shit. Either violently or sexually, either way, publically.

He matched me stride for stride until we were at the bar, waiting for a bartender's attention. "In a hurry?" His smirk said he knew exactly the problem.

Jaxon Parsons was the epitome of a cool guy. The perfect hair. The body. The way he wielded his smile, used his voice. And he knew exactly what he was doing and how it affected me.

"Not at all. It's just that I'm capable of making it through a crowd without your guidance." Smirk at that, big fella.

"I like touching you." His voice purred next to my ear, and I almost groaned out loud.

Oh, and I liked being touched. By him. But the more I thought about the mating bond and the way I found out about it…

“Jaxon, you know the laws. You have two moon cycles”—sixty-ish days—“to complete the mating bond.”

Soran was the member of the council who’d called us to Milan so Jax could explain why he’d made me. He was old. Soran, not Jax. Although Jax was pretty old, but Soran was ancient. He was also stuck in the old ways, insisting if Jax and I decided not to mate and bond, Jax would be put to death. And there was some serious work involved in parting a vampire from its life force.

Beheading—the council go-to form of permanent death. It took a big knife wielded by someone strong, but the council had reserves of folks for this sort of purpose.

It was a worthy fear. Probably a quick way to go unless the guy swinging the ax-knife-machete-thing wasn’t strong enough to do the job the first time.

Death by sunlight was another way to end a vampire's existence. It was a painful and lengthy process that lacked the showmanship of a good beheading.

There was always staking. Wood through the heart was tried and true, the layman’s way to kill a vamp, but also took a lot more strength than Buffy made it look like.

No, nothing said punishment like a literal rolling head. And despite noses and jagged neck bones, they rolled. It was almost magical. I’d done my research, on the plane when I couldn’t sleep.

Sixty days-ish and fading fast.

Something inside of me snapped. Or maybe it was the music. The song, anyway. A slow one. Marvin Gaye’s smooth deep voice talking about sexual healing. My body swayed of its own volition, my hips like they'd been attached to a pendulum. My shoulders joined the party.

Jax's eyes darkened. "Come with me." Instead of guiding me, he moved a few steps ahead, turned, and crooked his finger. Crooked his finger.

Of course, it worked. A finger wag was my kryptonite. Melted my panties every single time. It was the ringing bell that made me look around for the feast. How'd he known?

When we were in the middle of the dance floor, he held out his hand and pulled me in when I laid mine over his. His hips gyrated. Swirled. Circled. Turned. And it was divine and glorious, not to mention the most magnificent thing I'd ever seen. And so telling of his knowledgeability on the use of said hips. It gave me ideas I couldn't push away and fantasies I wanted to make reality.

Mating bond. Mating. Bond. Matingbond! Dammit. All I wanted was a quick tumble through the Egyptian Cotton, but as soon as I did it with this guy—this delicious specimen of man-vampire…manpire?—we would be bonded, forever. Mated. Bonded. And forever was a pretty long time for a couple who could never die. Unless of course we decided not to mate and bond.

My mind was as twisty as his hips. And not nearly as decadent or fun. He made it feel as if we were one. A single entity driven by desire, and I had damp panties to prove it.

If I caved and went along with the mating, would this feeling fade over time and we'd grow to hate each other?

"You smell like heaven." He leaned in and breathed. When

his inhale was complete, he moaned softly, and all the good parts of me clenched. All of them. At once. Yeah.

"Have you been?" I was trying to be witty. Trying to make him see how ridiculous his line sounded, let him know it damn sure wasn't going to work, and my panties, damp or not, weren't going anywhere.

But he lowered his head again, brushed my ear with his lips, his breath warm, and my phantom heartbeat kicked into high gear.

"I have now." Annnnd he pulled me closer. Damn it all to hell.

"Jax…" His name was a moan, a sound of desire slipping from my lips. It snapped me out of my Jax-induced psychosis. This was a ploy. A way to see if he could use all his allure to convince me that mating and bonding was inevitable. And if it was, fine, but I needed to make that decision while not clouded by his sex appeal, his smile and his ability to bundle and use it as a weapon.

Bad news, buddy. Nothing sexual going on here, healing or otherwise. That door is closed. I pushed away, walked off of the dancefloor, and went back to the bar.

I was too strong to succumb to his charms. But someone was going to have to have some kind of chat with my lady bits because they were screaming in unrequited need.

Within a hot second, Jax stood beside me. "I know it's a lot."

"A lot? It's… it is, yeah. A lot." I could agree without falling into bed with him to consummate some ritual from a gazillion years ago. At some point, someone was going to have to explain it to me, exactly how it would work, but I wasn't in the mood to listen tonight.

I picked up my drink , threw it back like it was a tequila shooter—man, I missed those—then turned to look at Jax. I could've asked him if there was a possibility of sex without completing the ritual of mating for life, explained a girl had needs. Hell, I could've hauled him into one of the club's dark corners, flashed him, then put his hands right where I wanted them, but I wasn't brassy enough for that. Sigh. A girl could dream.

None of it was going to happen, though. I was still a little pissy about Soran being the one who'd forced Jax to share all the mating bond news. Heck, I couldn't help it. In my mind, the headline should've come privately from the guy who thought this bond was such a spectacular idea.

But Jax's scent wrapped around me as physically as the hand he used to stroke my arm where it was resting on the bar. I watched his finger go up and down my arm, across my skin. The touch was perfect—neither too hard or too soft—and I wanted more. So much more.

"You want to get out of here?" His voice brushed warm against my ear and a lesser woman would've let her eyelids fall shut, would've leaned back into him, would've fallen prey to his very persuasive seduction techniques.

I wasn't a lesser woman. Maybe a little less since I did, in fact, almost close one eyelid when I let my head rest against his shoulder, my face going kind of wonky with my eyes trying to close as I fought it. Eventually, I found my backbone, straightened, turned, kept from tilting my head more than a couple of degrees, then nodded. There was no smile. No acquiescence. It was a nod.

I saved myself by adding a yawn. "I should get home." I hadn't slept enough on the plane and it was going to be morning very soon.

He grinned and motioned for me to walk in front of him. I didn't want to think about the grin, but I, of freaking course, did. Ever since I'd heard about the mating bond, the attraction I'd felt for this guy was nearly overwhelming. Certainly almost more than I could resist. I didn't know if science or magic or some sort of ritualistic mojo was involved. That was what confused me by the whole thing. Were the feelings real at all?

He followed me out of the club, guiding me with that dang hand against the small of my back to his car. Again, I couldn't get over the potency of his touch, the way it made my stomach quiver and my phantom heart race.

Only to save myself the disgrace of commenting on it, or worse, begging him to pull over for a round of backseat boogie, I pretended to sleep. I even threw in a snort and a snore for good measure. If he wanted to bond, he needed to know exactly what he was getting.

When he pulled up to the house and shut off the engine, he laid his hand on my shoulder and gave a squeeze. "Hey, Hailey." The softness of his voice, the touch, the scent of him in his car were all a lot to process.

I turned my head and added the eyes to my list of things I was going to have to develop a shield against. Holy hot tamales he was a lot of man.

And then he was out of the car—which he'd parked on my side of the street in front of my house—walking around to open my door and hold out his hand for me to take so he could help me out. It wasn't that I needed help, but this wasn't a guy who did things based solely on what I needed. There was something old school about him. Bygone from one of the eras he'd lived in.

I walked beside him to the door, free hand in my bag for the key, but stopped. I knew what was coming.

"Hailey." He was still beside me and curled his finger under my chin to turn my head toward him. Everything this guy did intensified how much I wanted him.

But I looked into his eyes and smiled because he'd pulled me in, so my chest was against his and his arms clasped at my back. "I'm sorry Soran is the one who told you about the mating bond."

Aw. He went right to the heart of what was bothering me. I nodded, accepting his apology, though I needed a bit more to move past it.

It wasn't entirely his fault. Well, it depended on how much he knew and how comfortable he was about talking to me about this kind of thing before I knew about it. I could give him the benefit of the doubt, but I needed to work around to it and being in his arms helped.

But some part of me couldn't let him off that hook. I

couldn't just look up and say it was okay. I wasn't born to be Absolution Annie. People had to face their actions and the consequences thereof. So, instead of speaking, I pursed my lips and nodded.

He wasn't finished, though. He lowered his head and brushed his finger from just under my earlobe, along my jaw to my chin. "I wish I could've explained it before he busted out the directive. I wish I could've done it in a much more satisfying way." The way he said satisfying induced… thoughts. Fantasies was probably the more accurate word.

"How would you have explained it?" I might've sounded breathy. At least a little throaty.

His smile slid across his lips. "I would've started with this."

Jax took a hand from my back and threaded it through my hair, used a gentle nudge to tilt my chin up and then lowered his head and claimed my mouth. This was the kind of kiss dreams were made of. Slow and decadent, sweet. A full body experience.

Heat spread through my veins. Emotional heat, really. And my heartrate, the phantom pounding in my chest, kicked up. His fingers and mouth caressed with equal potency, though the kiss was languid and unhurried. It was like we had all the time in the world, though daylight was closing in.

When he pulled back, I opened my eyes. "That would've been a good start." Maybe it wasn't his fault that Soran busted out the super secret mating bond before Jax had the chance. Honestly, we hadn't known each other so well that I would've been comfy talking about a mating bond. So maybe he hadn't either.

We were still pressed together, his fingers still massaging my scalp, his lips still hovering, eyes searching.

There was something decadent about kissing this man. And he certainly knew it. Of course, he had years of experience to build his skills. I was personally very grateful, but part of it felt deceitful, like he was using all this skill against me.

Of course, that was probably in my own head, but I didn't have a lot to trust except my own instincts. "I should go in."

He smiled. "Or you could stay with me. No pressure, just, you know, I could hold you."

Oh.

And oh. How sweet. But I couldn't. I had to think it through. Make sense of it. Figure things out before I jumped into spending my days sleeping with him. Even where sleeping with him meant actual sleep.

Besides, if I got in bed with Jax: bow-chicka-wow-wow. "I should…" I nodded toward the front door of my place.

His smile was soft, probably as convincing as he meant it to be. I nearly faltered. Nearly kissed him. Nearly agreed to head across the street with him, but I couldn't. Not like this. Not until….

Until what? What was my tipping point?

I'd almost married not one, but two lesser men. Well, one I did marry and the second was definitely a mistake. Two men who cared nothing for me. Who'd offered me nothing but a new last name. Thoughts like these worked through my brain. Maybe I was being foolish. Maybe there was nothing wrong with wanting Jax. Maybe fate and destiny started working the minute he turned me, the minute we'd seen each other, or even before, when I came to this town. Maybe this was all planned, and I was powerless to do more than to go along.

And maybe after a good night's sleep, I'd have more of an answer.

CHAPTER FOUR

By the time I walked into the house, I was ready for a few good hours of uninterrupted sleep. Sleep not haunted by dreams of Jax, although I had no idea how to manage that.

I was halfway up the stairs to my bedroom when my cell rang. Frowning, I pulled it out to check the screen. We'd dropped Kendra off at home a few hours ago. A little ball of apprehension rolled in my belly. She should've been asleep, and that she wasn't told me something was going on. If there was one thing Kendra didn't skimp on when it came to self-care, it was sleep. She could've fallen asleep in the middle of a rock concert. I knew because she'd done it before. I'd actually been impressed.

I answered before it had the chance to ring again. "Hey, what's up?"

She didn't bother with hello. "I had a dream."

The Sandman didn't have as many dreams as Kendra.

"Okay." But I also knew that because she had so many dreams, she wouldn't call unless this one was important. It must've been major, because it had her huffing and puffing through the phone.

"A storm. It was about a storm rolling in."

Hmm. "Was it a dream or a premonition?"

The difference was important. Dreams were musings of the mind, a way for the brain to process events and ideas of a day. But a premonition, especially of a storm coming our way, was fearsome. I had no reason to believe one of her premonitions wouldn't come true. They always had before.

Always.

"Something bad is coming." When she said it, I didn't doubt it. But I couldn't ask questions. She wouldn't have the answer about more than what sort of clouds signaled the storm in her dream.

"Okay."

"I'm outside your house." With a sigh, I hurried back down the stairs and looked out the window. Sure enough, she was standing in the middle of my yard, staring up at my bedroom window. I walked to the door and opened it with a sigh. "Come in, then," I hissed. Dawn was on the horizon, the sky starting to turn purple, and there wasn't much I would be able to do until the evening, but she was freaked enough to be here, so I waved my bestie in.

And she waved me out.

In our respective spots, we each flapped our arms about, trying to get the other to move, until finally she shrieked,

"Would you please get the hell out here? We need to warn your boyfriend."

Sometimes her premonitions came with intense feelings that told her who was involved. If she said it was Jax, then I had no reason not to believe her, but shouting in the street when the not-quite boyfriend of mention had the hearing of an owl. Better than an owl, actually.

"Keep it down, would ya?" I sighed and looked around like he was going to walk out and be convinced this was further proof of our need to complete the mating bond. It was the predominant thought in my head, anyway.

She lowered her voice to a hiss of a whisper as she marched across the yard and pointed. "We need to warn your boyfriend."

I rolled my eyes because even her whisper was as loud as a scream for me. "I'll be out in a second."

Not that I needed to do much more than calm down, but I couldn't very well head outside breathing like I was one huff from hyperventilating. I concentrated on slowing down, clearing my mind, not picturing Jax, who was likely getting ready for bed right then. That sparked a whole other set of thoughts—if he slept naked, if he hugged a pillow the way he would a lover, if he snored—none of which would make the phantom beating of my heart settle.

I couldn't keep standing inside waiting for my body to get with the program. There was a storm rolling in and, if Kendra had a feeling that Jax needed to know then Jax needed to know. Now. Plus we still needed to beat the dawn.

I walked out, and together we headed across the street to

his house, and the nerves inside of me, the apprehension, and more, the anticipation hurried me along so I was a few steps ahead of her when she reached the porch to his place. Heck, I'd already knocked on the door. Dang it! It was like I just couldn't wait to be near him again.

I easily heard him moving around inside, but I wasn't prepared when he opened the door bare-chested, smiling, and flirty. "Change your mind?"

Tempting as it was, I shook my head. "No." Oops. The word erupted from my mouth, abrupt, sharp and loud.

He smiled and looked down. "Damn."

His gaze burned its way up my body, smoldering, hot in ways I'd never noticed people look at me before. Then his gaze cleared and he nodded at Kendra as we walked inside.

"Did we wake you?" I asked. Of course we hadn't. We'd just gone to our respective homes a few minutes before.

Kendra began frantically pacing. Back and forth. One way then the other in front of the blackout curtains at his window. "I had a dream."

Jax looked at me, but I was still ogling the abs. He cleared his throat, and I looked up.

"Her dreams are a big deal."

Kendra nodded. "Right. You don't know this, presumably, but when I have a feeling so strongly connected to a dream, it's not just a dream. It's foretelling."

"Is that like foreplay?" His voice was smoky and suggestive as he stared like a heat-seeking missile, and I was on fire. We knew where his mind was.

I didn't have time to answer because Kendra had stopped

pacing again to glare at him. "Not at all like foreplay." She shook her head but not enough to make her scowl waver. "I dreamed of a storm rolling in."

Jax glanced at me then back at her. "I need a little bit more than that."

"Storms are bad. They're indicative of danger. I can't speak to what kind." More to herself than to either of us, she continued, "Of course the dreamweavers wouldn't let me know what kind. They're evil that way."

I'd heard her speak of dreamweavers before, and until then I'd always assumed the idea was a fiction, a song from the seventies. According to her, they were the ones responsible for her premonitions. She'd never lied about anything so magically related before, but I had no firsthand knowledge of them. My dreams were never vibrant or indicative of danger. Since I'd met Jax, not that I planned to share this information with either Kendra or him, they were mostly about Jax.

Jax nodded at her, his brow pinched. "Dreamweavers are the senders of messages." His tone said he believed her, or he'd already known that.

"You know about dreamweavers?" She swirled her head to look at him, black hair fanning out behind her.

He nodded. "Back in the day"—and with as old as he was it could've been anywhere from pre-revolutionary to the 1980s– "dreamweavers were blamed for all manner of catastrophe and disaster because the messages they sent weren't clear. But they were doing what dreamweavers do." He spoke as if dreamweavers were real entities.

I looked at him. "Dreamweavers." Not questioning. Just restating. Clarifying.

He nodded. "Someday, I'll tell you about the dreams they send me." The eyebrow wag wasn't entirely necessary, but I liked it anyway.

"Can we please?" Kendra's voice had risen to an octave that made Jax and me each wince. Volume was not our friend when wielded as a weapon. And that was exactly what she'd done. "Can we please talk about the storm rolling in?"

We could've but none of us knew exactly what it meant. Jax shrugged. "Okay. Exactly what did you see?"

She blew a breath out of her nose. "I was a leopard, and I know it was me because I was wearing a collar with my name on it." She looked at me. "Dreamweavers are crafty like that."

"Okay. Does being a leopard have a meaning?" She'd paused and my question seemed pertinent to the situation.

"I don't know." She shrugged and tilted her head for a second. Then stared at me again. "I don't think so." She sighed like I was inconveniencing her with my interruptions. I held up a hand and mouthed sorry as she continued. "So, anyway, I was a leopard, and I was running down this street, and I stopped in front of this house." Even her arm gestures were dramatic. "I could see the storm clouds, the dark horizon, the way the storm seemed to be coming just for this place, this house." All of a sudden, she was a dramatic actor. "And then a single cloud broke free and swirled into a tornado over this house. Whipped the roof off. Took the papers and books into the funnel."

From behind her, Nash snorted. "A dream?" I whirled

around. The enforcer was good. I hadn't even heard him come in.

She shot him a look so potent the big bad vampire enforcer wiped the smile from his face and stepped back. Her magic wasn't the only powerful thing about her.

"A dream." She nodded at him. "And you'd all do well to take heed." Kendra'd never seemed so witchy before.

I nodded at Jax. "When Kendra says something bad is coming, you can bet your million dollar mansion that your video doorbell is going to find a reaper or maybe even a hungry snow leopard who dines on the soulless bodies of vampires at the door."

Jax chuckled. "Nice."

"And serious." I couldn't reaffirm enough how urgent it was that he pay attention to her.

She huffed out a sigh and turned toward the door, like she was about to leave.

Jax stood and put his hand on her arm. "I believe you." And then he glanced at me like I could help him.

"It's all right, Kendra. He's going to listen." I had no idea if she cared what I had to say at that moment. Her anger was written in her eyes.

A wobbly smile was the only reassurance that came from my friend, and it did very little to settle the rumbling in my stomach.

His voice, on the other hand, was a balm for my lack of soul. "Do you have a theory about what the storm means?"

She looked from him to me and back to him. "I do. I think it's connected to this mess with Cleo."

"Connected how?" Jax watched her as she fiddled with the zipper on the jacket she'd worn over, since the spring nights were chilly and we were still at the edge of the night before dawn. Judging from my heavy eyelids, perilously close to dawn.

"I don't know, but while I was dreaming, I had a sense of Cleo." But since Cleo hadn't appeared in the dream, Kendra seeing her might've been relative to having just come from rescuing her. I didn't want to say that, though, since I knew so little about her process of dreaming other than they were usually spot-on accurate.

I nodded. "Whether or not we connect Cleo, there's definite danger surrounding her, since we just now rescued her from the kidnapper guy." Not that Cleo couldn't defend herself, or more surprisingly, that Jordan couldn't protect her until she was back at full-strength.

I yawned, and Jax smiled. "Maybe we should sleep on it." He didn't say the word together, but it was where my brain went, and I nodded.

His gaze traveled up my body, and he pulled his lower lip between his teeth, although it didn't hide his smile. If I wasn't completely sold on the mating bond, I was definitely smitten. Definitely in lust, if not in love.

"Do you want to stay?" Jax asked. "We could talk it through after you sleep."

I nodded because the words were jumbled somewhere between my throat and my mouth. I couldn't get past the thought of sleeping here. With Jax.

He held his hand out, and when I took it he smiled at me

then looked at Kendra. "The Wifi is strong here. If you want to do some research?" It was like he was asking her to stay, and I wondered if it was to make me comfortable or her.

It didn't matter, because she hid her wink to me with a slight turn of her head as she answered him. "That would be great."

Jax and I walked toward the steps. "Is this okay?" he asked.

I liked that he was cautious, that he sounded less than confident. "Yeah. It's not like we're going to…" I shook my head. No delicate way to say this one. "We're not going to."

He grinned. "Yeah." He gave my hand a squeeze, and I would've liked to have known what he was thinking, if knowing we weren't going to mate made a difference in whether or not he still wanted me to stay.

"Do you want me to go home?" There was enough cover of darkness I could make it if I hurried.

He stopped in the hallway outside his room and linked our free hands together. My phantom pulse could've powered a hundred fifty horse engine.

"No. Not at all. I don't want you to leave." He pulled me closer. "I just want to hold you."

Maybe it was the tone of his voice, the softness, the cadence, but I wanted him. Wanted so much. "Okay." If he'd asked me to walk into fire, so long as he'd said it in that voice, I would've happily grabbed a flame retardant suit and started sauntering toward the blaze.

When I pulled his t-shirt over my head, one that hung to my knees, I breathed in the scent of his laundry soap, of him, which was in the air in his house, in the blankets he slept in, in the drawers and closet where he kept his things. My stomach clenched.

I crawled beneath the sheets, cool and crisp, again scented by the man himself, and I wanted to turn to face him, to look into his eyes, to lay my hand on his bare chest, to kiss a trail from his throat to his belly button. Maybe lower, even.

Instead, I stayed on my side, facing away, even when he slipped an arm under my head, and settled the other over my waist. When he moved closer, his chest pressed against my back and his legs curved behind mine as he kissed the back of my head.

Many hours later, when the sun set, I woke up with his hard body still pressed against mine, except some parts were more prominently harder than others. To his credit, he didn't mention it, ask for me to help relieve it, or read my mind when I visualized doing just that.

I was only moderately let down by his conversational lapse. Not let down enough I stopped immediately visualizing. But it did hover a bit too near the idea of mating, so I pushed back the blanket and stood, pulling the T-shirt down as I did.

Then, like I was a proud confident woman who only wanted the benefit of his shower, I walked to the attached bathroom, started the water and undressed. And even after waking up with him, wanting him, yearning in ways I hadn't in years, the shower was uneventful. Boring even. And I stepped out, wrapped myself in a towel and used another on my hair.

Holy freaking crap, this was the most daring I'd ever been.

And without a thought to the mating bond, I stepped into his bedroom wearing nothing but a towel and a bit of hope on my face.

His empty bedroom.

He'd sent someone to my place for clean clothes which were now laid out on his already made bed. I dressed and found him in the dining room looking over Kendra's shoulder at her laptop screen.

The poor witch was bleary eyed, like she'd spent the entire day surfing the internet or databases or whatever websites led her to whatever she was showing Jax when I walked in. He looked up at me and smiled, slow, like he'd never seen me before or like he'd never seen me like this—wet-haired and in clothes fit for jogging. The shorts were actual running shorts I'd outgrown a year or so ago before being turned and the top was part of a Halloween costume the year I'd dressed as a Honkers waitress.

Kendra chuckled. "Can I get an order of hot wings and a pitcher of beer?"

I mimed a big, fake laugh. "Is this your doing?"

This time she giggled. "I got bored. I did also bring you a real outfit. It's in my bag."She pointed to a paisley print overnight bag on the sofa. "Help yourself."

I nodded. "Yeah. You bet." I shot Jax a glare. "What are you looking at?" I walked to the bag with my head held high.

Kendra tilted her head at me as I peeked inside the bag at jeans and a Bon Jovi t-shirt that wouldn't pack the punch of a Honkers tank top and my running shorts, but was probably more appropriate for time inside a mate's house until we truly were—if it ever happened—mates.

"The guy we brought in wasn't the kingpin we thought," Kendra said.

"Do tell?" I hefted the bag over my shoulder so the meaty part hung over my back while my hand gripped the straps.

"Rodney Coleman. Low-level drug dealer." She turned the screen around so I could see his mug shot.

"Low level? I didn't get that vibe from him." He'd been more confident than low-level. "Are you sure he's not at least mid range?" I seldom missed the mark on reading people.

But she shook her head with her eyebrows up. "No. Even his arrest record calls him low level."

Hmm. "Maybe it's a false clue." Now I had their attention and nothing to do with it. They didn't know what I meant. Sheesh. "Maybe he's keeping his kingpin-ness on the down low."

Kendra shook her head. "You shouldn't say down low. It just sounds wrong coming from you."

"You prefer hush-hush?" I didn't have a preference but apparently she did. "On the QT? Under wraps? Off the record." I smiled at them, still dressed like I was about to slap an order of wings on the table. "Do you suppose this could be where the phrase 'off the record' came from?"

Jax grinned and pulled his lower lip between his teeth as he blatantly looked me up and down. "Smart and sexy."

Man, he'd really stepped up the hitting on me game since the formal announcement of the mating bond ritual's participants, and I didn't know how I was supposed to resist him or if such a thing was even possible.

"Why would some low-level thug want to kidnap Cleo?" He spoke as if he thought he knew. Wasn't that just the million dollar question, though? "And why would he make it so easy to get caught?"

Well, if I knew that, I'd be able to solve the whole damned thing and concentrate on what to do about the mating bond. Oh, well. That would make life a bit too easy.

CHAPTER FIVE

I pondered my current life choices right up to the minute a new skip trace came through. Brad Bointon. Arrested for theft of a tractor trailer full of adult undergarments meant to supply the local stores and nursing homes, senior living facilities and oddly, Carmella Quitman, a millionaire marketing mogul who wrote some genius commercial jingles in the 1980s and now lived off residual checks and royalties.

They found Brad in possession of the trailer, wearing a pair of the underwear on his head, and blowing the horn like he was parade worthy as he drove naked through town. Well, naked, except the undergarments on his head. The crime scene photos had been posted on the town's tourism website which the mayor claimed was accidental.

Not that the pictures being online were incidental to his escape or had any bearing on how we would catch him. It was just interesting and really weird trivia. His jail break was much less entertaining than the story of how and why he'd been arrested. Brad had been bonded out, then just skipped court. Three times his trial was reset because the judge liked him, said he was charming. But now, he was on the loose and townsfolk were hoarding their adult intimate wear because there was no telling if he would cause another shortage.

Paige and I were about to get in her car when Jax's front door whipped open like a tornadic wind had caught it, and he stepped onto the porch looking like an ad for a cat burglar. A sexy cat burglar if I could add. He'd dressed in all black, even covered his moonlight-catching strawberry blond hair in a black beanie cap I suspected he could pull down into a mask.

With a sigh, I shut the car door and put one hand on my hip. "What are you doing?" I met him half way back to the house because somehow whenever he was walking toward me, it inspired me to walk toward him. More like I couldn't control my feet. Couldn't control my want. Couldn't control me. The unseen force that drew us together as fated mates was in control. That scared me.

There, I admitted it. The whole not being in control of my own future scared the bejesus out of me. That was the holdup.

"A storm is blowing in." Jax repeated Kendra's premonition. "Until it makes landfall, when you chase a skip, I'm chasing with you. See? Running shoes." He went so far as to lift his foot so I could see a pair of black trainers. "You go grocery shopping, I'm pushing the cart. You go to the movies, I'm buying popcorn and guessing the ending." He grinned, entirely too pleased with himself. "Now, shall we go?"

Nope. Nuh-uh. "You can't go. This is my work." I didn't

have a reserve of money built up from centuries of life. "I have to work."

He nodded. "And so you shall. I won't be in the way. I won't speak."

He didn't have to utter a single syllable. He would be the distraction I couldn't afford. The loss of my focus. But I was already wasting precious minutes with this argument. These were minutes I couldn't afford to lose in the great skip-chase game.

"Fine. Just stay out of the way." He would, and it wouldn't freaking matter. I wouldn't even be able to blame him. Not unless I figured out how to stop the phantom throbbing that had moved from my chest to…lower. Much lower.

I stomped back to the car, pretending I didn't know he was looking at my ass and pretending I wasn't shaking it more than necessary because I wanted him to look. Also that I didn't see Paige's smirk when I slipped into the back seat because when Jax and I went somewhere, he drove. Paige moved around to the passenger side.

"Shut up," I murmured when I scooted over. Seconds later, Kendra climbed in beside me with her map and the email printout of the skip's photo. She scried as Jax drove out of our neighborhood.

Within minutes, we had a location and I didn't speak as Jax sped off in the direction Kendra indicated. The tracking spell took us to Brad's house. At least, I thought it was his house. We got out of the car and Pagie went around the back of the house in case Brad decided to run.

Kendra had a few hex bombs made up and was ready to

use them. I didn't have any weapons. I usually didn't need them, because I depended on my vampire senses and strengths.

Holding a finger up, I silently counted down while ignoring how close Jax was to me. This was a bad idea. He may have ruled the vampires in the US, but he didn't know a thing about catching a human skip.

I had no idea what was up with his sudden need to protect me while I worked.

Instead of knocking, I kicked the door in and entered the midsize home, freezing at the sight. Brad—I knew it was him from his mugshot on the skip report—stood in the middle of the living room in a pink lace babydoll nighty with a pair of matching lace panties on his head. At this point, I wasn't sure if Brad needed to go back to jail or a psych ward. Or a lingerie store, I mean, to each his own. Where wasn't my choice to make. I got paid to bring him in, and that was what I was going to do.

However, ol' Brad wasn't about to give up his freedom for a refusal to appear. He whirled around and let out a surprised squeak before darting across the room to the dining room table.

At that moment, Paige rushed in from the kitchen, having entered the house from the back door. Brad tossed a bag of feminine napkins at Kendra while grabbing an empty soda can to launch at Paige, but before he could pick a weapon to throttle me with, Jax moved forward, presumably intending to help. Instead of being an asset, he tripped Kendra, whirled around to help her and knocked me down. "Sorry," he yelped as he tried to back away. Unfortunately while moving back he inadvertently blocked Paige from intercepting Brad.

The skip's eyes grew larger as he got a look at Jax, then he bolted toward the kitchen and out the back door.

By the time we untangled ourselves and made it outside, there was no trace of this mostly naked guy. Closing my eyes, I focused on my sense of smell and hearing. Unfortunately, there was a rank pile of trash at the corner of the house, overwhelming my olfactory senses, and the neighbors had loud music playing. I couldn't focus on trying to discern footfalls running away.

I shot Jax a glare. "You said you would keep your mouth shut and stay out of the way."

I kept looking around in every direction to see if I could see Captain Psycho Crossdresser, but there was no sign of him. Dang it.

Jax sighed. "I was trying to protect you." And there it was. The protection I didn't need, but the idea of which said he didn't think I could handle myself after all these months of chasing and catching skips, of learning to wield my power. "It was an accident."

Giving up on finding Brad right this second, I whirled and stared daggers at my supposed mate. "The effect, but not the action. The action was purposeful." I huffed out a breath and wheeled to look at him. Had my anger not been driven by his overprotective misbehavior, I might've been swayed by his pretty face. But anger won the moment. "And unnecessary."

"I realize that now. I'm sorry." He looked around me at Paige. "See? A good mate knows the power of the apology?"

"What?" My brow squinched. My eyes narrowed. What was he on about?

He yanked a book from his back pocket. It had a half-naked man on the front and a woman in an old-style corset-dress kneeling in a half-swoon pose in front of him. "It's from a Rogue's Guide to True Love. And I figure a mate has to be a good gentleman." He flipped to a random page. "She unbuttoned his trousers and stuffed her hand inside. 'You will apologize to me, right now. It's the measure of a gentleman,' she said, stroking gently. He inhaled deeply, filled his chest with air he sorely needed as his manhood swelled in her palm."

What in the actual… Oh Lord, could this man read a passage. It gave a girl all kinds of thoughts. Imaginings. Mental images.

"He looked down at her. 'I think you have the measure of this gentleman in your hand.' When she looked up, her emerald eyes flashed, and she smiled the smile of a vixen. 'I'll need your apology, sir, and with it, the power of the apology will restore my good faith in you.'"

Gaping at Jax, I tried to think around the desire him reading historical porn fiction brought up. I didn't know what the apology had to do with sex, because he hadn't read the entire scene, but I too could visualize the power of the apology. And it was…mesmerizing. I saw a trip to the library in my future. There was lots more historical porn for me to enjoy.

"Oh, the power of the apology." That part slipped out. I didn't mean it. I mean, I meant it, but not for him to hear it, not to be said aloud, for certain.

Kendra snickered, and Paige widened her eyes. The words mating bond flashed in my head in neon colors, and I did a full body shake to get rid of the thoughts. "Can we please concentrate here? I have a job. A bond jumper to apprehend, remember?" I pointed like little Napoleon and walked on down the alley behind the house.

It dead ended at a building on one end, and a street at the other. It was lined by chain link fences and old cars better junked than as lawn ornaments, but such was the neighborhood. I didn't judge.

Instead, I looked over at Kendra as she laid her scrying materials out on the hood of an old Ford with a battered front fender. "That's strange." She glanced at me. "Says he's right here."

She looked under the car. I checked the inside. Then we both looked at the green dumpster sitting at the end of the alley, close to Brad's house. The source of the stink a few minutes ago. Paige sniffed the air then looked at the dumpster. Nodded.

I smirked at Jax. "I'll hold your book." He had to make it up somehow.

And so he did. It took about three seconds for him to haul Brad out of the garbage and bring the pink teddy-clad felon to stand in front of me. I looked up from page ninety-three and watched Kendra slap the cuffs on him. Paige dragged him to the car. Teamwork at its finest.

Jax leaned in and whispered, "You should read it from the beginning."

I handed the book back and almost glared, but I just didn't

have it in me. He was so cute. And sexy. "Or you could finish it and give me the Cliffs Notes version."

He grinned. "Maybe I could do a Power Point? Make a little demonstration video."

I chuckled. "Based on that scene you read, I think they might call that porn."

He didn't answer, because we'd reached the car. He moved closer. Much, much closer.

So much for focus. I didn't have a prayer, at least, not while I was pinned between him and the side of the car. "I'll bring the top hat." He nuzzled my neck with his nose. "You smell like cinnamon and apples. And I miss food."

Oh, Lord. Even if I wanted to resist, there was no defense to a guy who said things like that. I managed an, "Oh," before he moved away and walked around to his side of the car. Damn it. My knees weren't working. At all.

If it wasn't the mating bond making me and my hopeless damp panties react to him, then if that thing ever kicked in, I was screwed. And hopeful to be so multiple times.

I sat in the back beside Brad. Paige, as the other super-strong vampire of our business, boxed him in on the other. Kendra and Jax sat in front. As always, Jax drove.

When I'd first spoken to Kendra about this case, and any other we might get, we'd agreed to use certain gifts we had to elicit information during transport from whatever skip we ran across. I looked at Brad and made my voice sultry and as sexy as I imagined I could be. "Brad, look at me, sweetheart." He did. Big sparkling blue eyes as blank as a new canvas stared into mine. I probably didn't need to use my seduction voice, but Jax was watching me in the rearview, and I didn't miss his low moan when I spoke to Brad.

When Brad tilted his head, I smiled. "I have to ask you some questions." My eyelids were half-mast, and my voice sounded like I smoked a pack a day and loved it. "Word on the street is that you're the man. Are you, Brad? Are you the man?"

He nodded. "I'm the man."

"They all say you keep your fingers…" I grabbed his hand, rubbed it with mine. It was gonna take three or four showers to get this ick off me, but I was a woman with purpose. "On the pulse of the city."

He nodded again. "It's how I knew which truck was the one I needed."

"Ooh. I could sense that about you." A shoulder shimmy, because Jax was watching while we sat at a stoplight. "Have you heard about any big crime going down soon? Something big and naughty."

Oh, Lord. I was going to need a brillo pad and bleach to clean the filth off me after this. But I pressed on, because I wasn't a quitter.

"Naughty?" He breathed in sharp on the tail end of the word.

"Oh, yeah. So naughty."

My mind wandered as I attempted to draw information from Brad.

What I knew about this night: Jax was reading one of those olden days, tawdry romance novels in the hopes of gleaning information on how to manage our new relationship dynamic.

He cared enough to stop a guy from throwing a box of adult incontinence underwear at me and to dumpster dive after the same guy when he got away. And he was a big fan of my acting skills.

"I don't know anything." Not only was I using my power to compel, the slutty investigator thing would've probably worked by itself with this guy.

"Nothing about someone putting a hit on bond agents?" I prompted.

"You're a bond agent?" I nodded and he batted his lashes at me. "I can't imagine anyone wanting to hurt you. Unless you asked real nice."

Ugh. I concentrated on not throwing up then tried one last question as Jax slammed the car into park in front of the police station.

"What about crime lords? You know any of those?"

He shook his head.

I glanced at Paige. Me playing the vixen hadn't gotten us new information, really hadn't done much more than make me feel like I needed a bleach bath, but at least we knew this guy—one in a city of 1.5 million, give or take—wasn't involved in trying to kill bond agents. That was something.

CHAPTER SIX

ARE you still at Count Chocula's?

Count Chocula was Kendra's cute little behind-his-back nickname for Jax. Although with his hearing, and how close he'd been remaining at my side, he probably knew about it.

ME: *Sigh* Yes. Although if I don't find a way to get out of here soon, I might try a back window escape.

Not that he was keeping me hostage. He wasn't. But everywhere I went, he went. If I watched a show on his rather impressive TV with surround and some high tech 3D picture capacity, he watched, too.

Right. Beside. Me.

And don't get me wrong. He smelled divine. Made me want naughty things. But so long as those things meant I was linked to him for life, we were on hold. I had to psychologically come to grips with this first. And I had to find a way to do it before the deadline.

It'd been a couple of days since the mess with Brad, the underwear-stealing, diaper-wearing, nut job skip. I needed a big-time distraction or an excuse to escape my overprotective mate.

Yes, I'd admitted he was my mate.

My phone buzzed again with another text from Kendra.

Wanna hit a club later?

Yes, that sounded fun and might be the distraction I needed. I wouldn't be drinking because, vampire, but neither did I want to go to Catch and Release.

We could go to the new one in Bradbury?

Her reply was quick and enthusiastic.

Yessss!

I'll call you later. Chocula is lurking. I looked up at Jax as I typed.

He'd walked in and sat beside me on the sofa. "Hello."

It wasn't like I hadn't just seen him ten minutes ago.

Rubbing my hands on my thighs, I sucked in a deep breath. "Can we talk for a second?" I needed to make some things clear, and now was as good a time as any.

"Sure." No matter how irritated I was by his constant presence, his smile still made dead heart go ga-ga.

I looked down at my hand, now, somehow, clasped with his. When had that happened? "I like you. On a personal level. Maybe even on a romantic level."

He grinned. "I like you, too." He didn't elaborate on the kind and that was good. Last thing I needed was to be distracted by his perfect words and smooth delivery.

"Good." I paused. Frustrated or not, it was hard to tell him how I needed my space. Because my space, with him in it, smelled rather heavenly. I couldn't waver. Had to be strong. No matter how good he smelled. "I appreciate your help and your protection these last few days." He opened his mouth to speak, but I put a finger over his lips. His soft, full lips. Crim-iny. "Please, let me finish before you say something that makes me not want to finish." And that was a very real possi-bility since I'd tried a couple of times already to say this and failed. "You're getting in the way. I have a job to do and I need to do it. I can't… I need to do it alone."

"Getting in the way?" I ignored the hurt in his eyes. "I appreciate that you want to protect me. It's very sweet." And he was strong and fast and kind of scary when he went full vampire, but I had skills of my own, and me and my girls had a process when we were chasing a skip. For this, I didn't need him. "But I need to…" I sighed. "If I was in the bathroom right now, you'd be standing outside the door with the toilet paper offering to help me wipe."

Not that he had, but these days, nothing was out of bounds. In his mind, anyway. And that was why we so desperately needed to have this conversation.

"If this is about the other night—"

"If I'd lost Brad, a really high value skip, Jordan would've called in another hunter, and I would've lost that fee."

He tilted his head. "I can give you money."

Argh, what wasn't he getting about this? "I can make my own money. I just need the space to do it." I didn't want to hurt his feelings, especially since he'd been so sweetly attentive lately, but he was crowding me, and I was about three seconds from blurting it in a not so nice way.

"I didn't know if the guy had a gun or what." His voice was soft and his eyes were dark. "I don't want you to get hurt."

I didn't want me to get hurt either, but there had to be a balance. "First of all, if he had a gun, he wouldn't have bothered throwing the bags of underwear and second, I can handle myself." I grinned. "I'm not quite as fast as a speeding bullet, but his aim wasn't true enough to pierce my heart." The only way a bullet could kill a vampire.

"I couldn't stand the idea of you being hurt." Somehow, he'd managed to tangle his fingers in my hair and was urging me ever so gently forward.

Instead of going for the big kiss, he leaned his forehead against mine. I sighed and said, "I'm a vampire. A bullet can't hurt me." I didn't even bring up the point that we hadn't actually seen a gun, and yet he'd jumped in like he had Wonder Woman's bracelets to deflect the shots. "I need some space, or I'm going back home."

Which was just across the street, but there was a point to be made, and I was making it. I hoped.

He sat with his forehead on mine for two seconds, then sat back. "Fine. I'll back off. But if the shoe was on the other foot"—his brow pinched and he looked down— "you would do the same thing. It's part of the mating bond." A lot of things were being chalked up to that damned thing. "I've tried to give you space but now that you know, I just can't lose you."

Well, crap in my cereal. When he put it that way, I felt like pooh for asking him to step back. But I was still confused by the whole thing and felt completely out of control. "What else is part of the mating bond?"

He pulled his lower lip between his teeth and backed up a few inches, but kept his hand cupped at my cheek. "It's the way I have to touch you. The way I go to sleep thinking of you and wake up thinking of you. It's attraction and need."

"Desire?" I was using the voice again, but this time, it was accidental.

He nodded.

"Yearning?"

"Yes." It was a whisper, a hiss, and my phantom heartbeat was hard at work. Again. But then he blinked and cleared his throat. "It's as out of control for me as it is for you."

If he kept making admissions like that, no way was I going to be able to go home. And that was as big a problem as the fact he'd, for a second, looked as freaked out as I felt about it.

I contained the hurt. Why was I hurt? I'd been resisting it from the get go! "Is there anything else?"

He nodded. "You'll be stronger. Faster. And we'll be tuned in to each other."

Tuned in. "More so than now?" I was already pretty tuned in to Jax.

He shrugged. "It's not like it's an actual measure."

"And stronger?" I didn't need all the details, but some clarification would've helped. Maybe even helped me lean more to the side of making the bond happen, but I didn't want to say that. I couldn't.

"Yes."

Another sigh slipped from my lips. "And it boils down to the fact that I have no choice in the matter." I decided to be honest about my deepest fears. The thing causing me to hold back as long as possible me. "What if a year from now or ten years from now you wake up and decide you don't want me anymore? What happens then? Could the bond be broken?"

I already knew the answer to the latter question. One of the vampire elders had said it was unbreakable.

"The bond will be unbreakable. But you do have a choice." He moved his hand from my cheek to grab my hands and hold them to his chest. "I know you've been hurt before and it's not easy for you to trust your own heart. If you need space, then I'll give you some, but we need to at least date and act like a couple, get to know each other."

He had a point.

"Deal." I smiled, then slid my hands from his and picked up my phone to send Kendra another text.

Getting ready. Will pick you up soon.

Luke's coming along. Oh, yay. My brother was always fun in a club.

I hadn't realized she'd added Luke to the chat until he replied. Wild cowboys couldn't keep me away. But let's hope they try.

He sent the fingers crossed emoji and I laughed before returning my attention to Jax. "I'm going out with Kendra and Luke tonight." I didn't have any skips to trace, Cleo was doing much better since her rescue, and I just wanted to get out.

"I should stay home?" He sounded more curious than hurt, and I didn't want him hurt, but I needed the time away from him to clear my head, sort my thoughts, and make sense of my new life.

A nod had to be easier to take than a full-on yes. I added a wry smile for good measure.

"All right. But Nash and Grim have to go."

I nodded for a couple seconds until his words sank in. "What now?"

He sighed, and for a guy who was quite used to not having to breathe, he made it sound convincing. "Look, you're my heir now, so even if there wasn't all this dangerous detail going on around Cleo, you would still be a mark for every vampire who wants my power. My money. My lifestyle and…" He paused like he was Brad Pitt delivering a line. "My mate."Oh, the drama.

"I'm not your mate." Yet. We hadn't made an official announcement to the vampire world, so I hadn't seen the point of the increased security he placed me under.

"Not yet, not officially, but you're still my heir, and therefore, in danger. And we don't know who the council might've told. Anyway, Nash and Grim won't 'get in the way.'" I could've done without the air quotes, but I didn't interrupt because I was busy trying to figure out how to lose his bodyguards. Then again, I'd worked with Nash and Grim in Milan. "You'll never even know they're there."

Now, I sighed. And it really did help dispel some of the anxiety that manifested itself in phantom heartburn. "Fine."

Jax's new overprotectiveness was starting to make sense. I hadn't thought about what it meant to be his heir.

He grinned and pointed his most earnest gaze at me again.

"I'll see you later, then." He stood and walked out of the living room so I was alone for a second thinking that this, too, along with finding Cleo, had been way too easy.

I went home to get dressed.

By the time I walked over to Kendra's, right next door to me, Luke was there in a Gold lamé suit with glittery gold platforms and a Coach bag on his shoulder.

"When I heard my biotches were going out and didn't invite me, I didn't get mad. No, girl. I pulled out the outfit." He ran his hands down his sides to show off the suit before doing a little turn.

That was my brother, diva on a mission. I wasn't sure what the mission was, but he was on it.

"Oh yeah, you did." I laughed, loving his style. One that only Luke could pull off.

Kendra walked out in a sleek skirt with her hair slicked back into a neat braid. By comparison to these two, I needed a better wardrobe.

We walked out and headed to my car next door. For the first time in what felt like weeks instead of days, I was Jax free. I slipped behind the wheel and off we went.

"You know, I did some research on the mating bond." Kendra looked over at me while I watched the road. "If you submit to him, he gets control. All the control and you're his property."

"Oh, that sounds hot," Luke moaned.

Ignoring my brother, I glanced at Kendra. "Who told you that?" Jax sure as hell hadn't mentioned any of that to me. "Who said I would be his property?"

Luke leaned forward from the back in a cloud of floral perfume to pat me on the shoulder. "It's common knowledge, honey."

"If it's so common, why don't I know it?" I didn't have any other answer.

"Because you read romance novels instead of Anne Rice, instead of Bram Stoker, instead of Stephanie Meyer." Luke loved those stories these days. His Kindle looked like a who's who of vampire lore. "And I binged all the seasons of True Blood. You, my pet, have your own Eric Northman, and if you think for one second he's going to let you be the boss in bed or out, you are so wrong." He shook his head and fanned himself with a white gloved hand. "I love me some Eric."

"I haven't agreed to do the mating bond yet. I'll wait and see how it plays out." Big words. I knew darn well I'd end up giving in. But, it was as good a plan as any other. Vampire fiction was a good source of real life vampire lore. Now that the idea was planted in my head, it was one more thing to worry about. But not tonight. I needed time with my girl and brother.

Besides, we'd arrived at the club, and I was trying to fit my car into a space between two badly parked SUVs.

When we walked inside, Nash and Grim were already there. Luke bee-lined for the bar and Nash followed him. Kendra and I stood beside Grim. She was already swaying to some Bruno Mars, and she pulled my hand. "Let's do this thing!"

While Luke distracted Nash by trying to hook him up with a Kardashian look alike, Grim danced with Kendra and me.

She laughed. I twerked, dropped it like it was hot, backed that ass up into Grim who, surprisingly, danced like a Latin lover who'd been long denied the company of a woman.

Nash nudged Grim. "Jax is going to kick your ass."

Grim laughed. "His woman is always safe with me. Jax knows that."

And for a just a second, the words, his woman, shot a warm thrill through me and I missed him. Since I'd been annoyed by his presence only a few hours ago, I chalked this up to the mating bond. Of course, it could've been that I just missed him because I truly liked him and enjoyed being around him. But admitting that opened a whole can of emotions I didn't want to examine. Not until I had to, anyway. Certainly not tonight.

CHAPTER SEVEN

MANY HOURS LATER, we walked out of the club. Well, I walked and my inebriated brother and my tipsy BFF stumbled and laughed. Since I couldn't get drunk unless I fed off a human who had been drinking, I was the DD–designated driver. There was something to be said for being the sober one in the group, but this wasn't it. Pouring my brother into the car while steadying Kendra was my own fault because I shooed Nash and Grim away when they tried to help. Kendra, Luke and I had survived many a night without the help of any super-powered vampire enforcers-slash-babysitters, and I wasn't about to surrender to one now. Especially since I was a vampire.

After Luke was secured in the back, I put Kendra in the front passenger seat and then walked around to the driver side and fell into the seat. I breathed like I'd run a marathon and fatigue was settling in. Sunrise was close, and it always made me a bit more tired than nightfall had made me when I was human. It was okay. In a few minutes, I would be with Jax, safe and sound and asleep in his arms.

The missing him hadn't stopped throughout our night, and now I was anxious to see him. It felt like we'd been apart for days, not hours.

Yes, I admit that. The attraction to him had always been there. That was no secret or surprise.

"Luke, you're sleeping at my house since it's so close to sunrise."

He mumbled a reply that I didn't understand, nor did I care if he didn't want to. We made it home fine, and I let Kendra let herself in. She wasn't so far gone she couldn't get herself to bed. Luke, on the other hand, I practically carried to the guest bedroom, then brought him a trash can, glass of water, and three ibuprofen. He'd be needing it.

After making sure both of them were safely inside the houses, I crossed the street to Jax's. Why? No idea. I could've just stayed at my own place, but that felt uncomfy. Like I'd been been snubbing Jax. And I wanted to see him.

Not bothering to knock, I opened the door and smiled when I found my unbonded mate in the kitchen reading the newspaper. He wasn't waiting up, since he did this routinely. Obviously his schedule didn't follow anything resembling normal.

I shut the door and leaned against it, waiting for him to look up. When a few seconds slipped by without him so much as raising an eyebrow, I surrendered, walked to the fridge, and pulled out a bottle of O neg.

When I poured it into a mug and slipped it into the microwave, he murmured, "You lose nutrients that way." He still hadn't looked up.

I waited for the beep. "I'll be fine."

"Did you have fun?" And still he had his face buried in news he'd probably already watched on the TV.

"I did. Danced a lot." He still didn't look up. I fanned myself. "Phew. I am exhausted." Not nearly as bad as I was acting though. I slumped against the refrigerator door and slipped off my heels. "Oh, that is so much better." He still didn't look up and it rankled. "What the hell, Jaxon? Why won't you look at me?" More than that, I needed to know why it mattered so much to me.

I ignored that nagging voice in my head because now he did glance—no, it was a gaze—up from his paper at me. "Because when I look at you, I want to touch you. I want to be near you. I want to be close to you." He paused and let out a short breath. And a little part of me sighed because I wanted to believe he was breathing because he had to, because his body's response to me was visceral and emotional and defied his vampire ability to not breathe. "And you want your space."

"Oh." He had to have some kind of cheat sheet for things to say to make me melt.

"And I know you aren't ready yet for the mating bond."

I nodded, a little more ready with every minute that ticked off the clock. "Jax?" He tilted his head and looked at me, his face as beautiful in honesty as I'd ever seen it. At least, I hoped he was being honest. "I'm not ready for the mating bond, but I like being here with you and sleeping beside you." It was the best I could do for now.

He nodded and held out his hand, smiling now. "Good. The sun is about to come up and in no way do I want you to go home." When I slid my hand over his, he gave me a little squeeze, then brought it to his mouth for a kiss against my knuckles, and all the while his gaze stayed locked onto mine. It was a swoon-worthy moment. And when coupled with, "Let's get ready for bed," a girl could get ideas.

Stirrings.

By the time I showered and settled in beside him, the ideas had taken on the shape of a fantasy. He was gorgeous. Built like a statue of…a really well-built guy. His body had more angles and planes, ripples and valleys than a topographic map, and I imagined myself touching every single one. Tasting every single one.

But even if I wanted to, right now, I really was tired. Exhausted. And being held while I drifted off to sleep wasn't a hardship.

He pressed a soft kiss against my shoulder. "Goodnight, Hailey."

"Goodnight, Jax." I laced our fingers together, then was just about asleep when my phone vibrated on the other side of the bedside table. Groaning, I stretched out and snagged my phone to find a text from an unknown number.

Unknown to the phone anyway, but I knew the number. I'd very much known it for years and had simply deleted it from my contacts.

My ex. Howard Jefferies.

Hey, babe. It's been a while, but I heard you're in the biz now. I'm coming your way on a big $ skip.

I sighed and went ahead and replied with Jax reading over my shoulder. Skip tracers are like teenage girls with their gossip.

I didn't know why Howard was bothering to tell me he was coming my way. I didn't care, not really. We hadn't been friends when we parted. It got a bit better after he'd remarried, but we hadn't talked much since. At best I could say it was now an amicable unfriendship

Well, if it helps, they say you're kicking ass and taking names. LOL. A few seconds went by while I decided what to say back. Another text came in while I deliberated.

Anyway, offering you a chance to join forces on this skip. The $ is huge. Would split it. What do you say?

I would've liked to have said a lot of things that would've taken way too much energy to type into the screen. Instead I went with simple. Meet me at my place tonight at 8.

I sent the address and let the phone slip to the floor as blessed sleep fell over me.

KENDRA, out of friendship and probably morbid curiosity, dropped in a few minutes before Howard was due to arrive. As did Jax. Nash and Grim were across the street, on Jax's porch like a couple of dads polishing their shotguns while waiting to

meet their daughter's date. Although, polishing their fangs would be more like it.

Howard arrived right on time, and I had to race Jax to the door. "Go sit. He's my ex for a reason, there's nothing to worry about."

Jax stared at me for a long few seconds before taking a seat on my sofa with a stiff neck and ramrod straight spine. Kendra sat in the armchair and pretended to read. It would have been believable if she wasn't holding a freaking dictionary.

Jax was overprotective, but Kendra was just a plain old Nosey Rosey.

I opened the door and smiled a genuine smile when I saw my ex. Howard looked exactly the same. Like an accountant: cardigan and pocket protector a part of his daily uniform. He was older, but still the same, if that made any sense.

Jax, on the other hand, was alpha and wanted everyone to know it. He stood and somehow made himself seem taller as I stepped back for Howard to walk in.

I could've sworn Jax growled when Howard hugged me.

"Long time, no see, Hails."

I pulled back as soon as was polite and looked him up and down. "Yeah, it is. You look…" To lie or not lie? "Great." I went with the truth because he did look good. Jax needed to man up and accept that I had a past. Howard was a part of that past.

He blushed just a bit, then raised his eyebrows at me. "You too. A little pale though. You getting enough sleep?"

Howard's answer to all of life's ails had always been more sleep.

"Oh, you know…." It was all the answer I was prepared to give. "I do most of my hunting at night when the criminals are criminalling."

"Not a word, Hails." It took Howard three seconds to correct me. He was slipping. He used to do it before my made up words hit the air around my lips.

"Anyway, I sleep fine." Jax moved closer, coming around the back of the couch to slide his arm around my waist. I didn't move away, but neither did I return the gesture. The move was some serious chest-beating, and I wasn't going to be part of it.

I did, however, make the introductions. "Howard, this is Jax. He's my…" They both looked at me. "My very good friend."

Jax smiled, predatory and way too damn sexy for him to get away with this level of possessiveness.

Howard smiled, too, the smile of the oblivious.

Kendra chuckled and stepped forward, holding out her hand to Howard. She was sparkling. Like… sparkles. "I'm Kendra. Best friend. Oh, but you know that."

Howard smiled at her and she smiled back. So many teeth.

This wasn't awkward at all.

"How have you been, Howie?" I'd never called him Howie before, but we were on a different playing field now. More social. Less married. It made a difference.

He didn't miss a beat. "I'm right as rain, Hails. Right as rain." But he was still smiling at Kendra. Interesting.

"How about a drink?" I offered. Not that I would have one, but there was no need to let him know everything that was going on in my life.

I went to the kitchen and came back with a couple of glasses of wine I'd started keeping because O-neg and B-positive weren't on my big brother Ollie's approved beverage list. After our original meeting, I'd started keeping a few other things in the cabinet.

Howard took his and Kendra hers while Jax sat in a chair with his arms crossed over his massive chest. It only made his chest look broader. I couldn't stop looking.

Not that it mattered. Howard was speaking to Kendra. More accurately, giggling with her like they were sharing some secret joke. This was quite the intriguing development.

Kendra sat in one chair, Howard in the other while I sat beside Jax on the sofa. "So, Howard. How's the wife?"

He'd married at some point—I couldn't remember exactly how long ago—and that he wasn't mentioning it to Kendra didn't sit right in my stomach. Howard hadn't been a great husband, but he hadn't been a cheater.

He looked up at me and smiled, more teeth, but it wasn't as bright as it had been earlier. "The divorce was final three months ago."

I said, "Oh," but Kendra's eyes lit up.

"Ooh." Then she glanced at me. "Er, sorry."

I shrugged and went back to listening to Howard speak.

"It just didn't work out. We were essentially two very different people."

I knew that song and dance. That was essentially why

Howard and I hadn't worked out. He needed to find his person.

Jax slid an arm around my shoulders, pulling me closer while Kendra leaned toward Howard with her chin on her hand, her face a mask of sympathy. "That's terrible."

Howard shook his head. "No. Not really. We parted most amicably."

Howard did everything most. Most amicably wasn't unexpected. I stared at him as he stared at Kendra. Most interesting.

"So where are you from, Howard?" Jax squeezed my shoulder, and when I glanced from Howard to him, he was more relaxed. Looser. Laid back. The smile was real, and I was torn between watching him and watching Kendra and Howard. Kendra and Howard won.

Whatever he'd just said made her giggle again. Kendra hadn't giggled since we were in high school. She wasn't a giggler. "Tell me all about it." And now she sounded like Mae West.

I suddenly found myself most fascinated by the mating habits of North American witches and their prey.

Howard adjusted his cardigan, smoothed his eyebrow with the tip of his pinkies, and then turned his most charming smile her way. "Maybe another time." His smile, teeth and all, said he meant that sincerely. "Ivan Markovich is the skip I'm here to capture. He's not quite international—that's mostly what I do now." He lifted one eyebrow at Kendra and half-puckered then winked.

She chuffed out a short, shallow breath and glanced at me. "Sorry."

"And who is Ivan Markovich?" I glanced at Howard, hoping he wouldn't pucker again. That was just disturbing.

"He's accused of theft. Jewel theft that totals into the hundreds of thousands of dollars. Bail is three million." He shrugs. "Ivan"—he said it like EEE-von—"is an escape artist as well. Slippery as a wet peapod."

I had no first-hand knowledge of wet peapods, but I knew Howard. He was either off his meds, or he was trying to impress someone in this room. And it wasn't me. Or, I strongly suspected, Jax. The eye contact between Howard and Kendra was almost obscene.

"And from me…?" I prompted.

"From us," Kendra corrected and smiled at Howard in her best Miss Scarlett impersonation until suddenly we were center stage at Basic Instinct's famous interrogation scene. "What's our cut?"

"Fifty-fifty. Right down the middle." He stared at her. "Us?"

Kendra blinked slowly. "Hailey and I are two-thirds of The Bond Girls. We catch skips together. When do we start?"

"Wait!" I held up my hand. I liked Howard. We'd become sort of-kind of friends since our divorce, which seemed like eons ago.

He ignored me and looked at her. Probably trying to show his version of the smoldering seduction gaze.

Bless him, it looked more like he was constipated, but since I'd seen both looks—mostly the second from him—I wasn't judging. He definitely was pulling out the stops, playing his A game. "Tomorrow night?"

"Howard!" I needed a minute to look over EEE-von's file jacket. I needed the details. The information.

Kendra did not. "Absolutely."

"Whoa, whoa, whoa." I held up my hands to two people totally ignoring me.

"He frequents a nightclub in downtown Portsmith," Howard said. A couple towns over, not bad. "I can pick you up at eight?"

"I'll be ready." She took his wine glass. "I'll just get you another. Hailey, would you mind helping me?"

It really wasn't a question. I stood. When we were alone in the kitchen she whirled and handed me the glasses. "Is this weird for you?" Surprisingly, it wasn't. Not at all.

I shook my head, but she'd already turned and pulled the wine bottle from the fridge. "I hope it isn't. Please, say it isn't. I've never been so instantly and wholly attracted to anyone in my life."

"Howard is...something." I didn't want to rain on her parade. Different strokes for different folks but I wasn't sure I'd really been fully attracted to Howard even when we were married. He was just so blah.

"Yes, yes, he is." She poured the wine. "He's amazing." She took one of the glasses, handed me the empty bottle, then threw back the drink like it was a tequila shooter. When she reached for the other, I pulled it away.

She clasped her hands together. "I want to ask him to dinner. Is that okay? Please let it be okay."

I'd known Kendra for years, since her kids were small. I'd seen her in lust. Seen her through break ups. I'd even helped her create a dating profile, though why she needed one was beyond me. She was one of those women who made men stop and stare.

But I'd never seen her like this, with stars in her eyes. Over Howard. Howard!

With a hand on her shoulder, I look deep into her eyes and smile. "Kendra, nothing would make me happier than you and Howard each finding happiness in each other. I wouldn't have guessed it, but I like it." At least I knew he was trustworthy. And he'd never hurt her. He might bore her, but not betray.

She reached out and pulled me into a hug. I was happy for them. "I'll keep you posted," she whispered.

When I nodded, she laughed and pulled back. "But not too posted."

I didn't need any more detail than that she was happy. Ew.

CHAPTER EIGHT

SINCE I DIDN'T HAVE any skips to trace until tomorrow and Kendra and Howard went out for a late dinner, flying the coop within seconds of Kendra inviting him out, I was free to do whatever. I decided to spend the evening with Jax. Only he didn't know that yet.

I turned to Jax, who was hovering by my front door as if unsure if he should leave or not. Crossing the room to him, I asked. "Have you DVR'd anything good this week?"

A slow seductive smile tugged at the corner of his lips. "We could go to my place and check."

I wasn't home enough to justify paying for cable TV, and I spent a lot of time at his place, so I watched his TV.

I nodded and his smile widened while his hand settled on the small of my back. Instead of resisting, I let him spin me into his arms, against his chest. Not that I didn't want to be there. Part of me wondered why I resisted at all. The mating bond. The lust. The desire to spend hours looking into this man's eyes. Seemed kind of silly to fight it. Watching Kendra and Howard meet, then run off on a date night within a few hours made me think about—really think about—Jax and me.

Another part of my brain reminded me that I wasn't aware of all the aspects of the mating bond. I didn't know if he would suddenly be the boss of me. This was a lifetime deal. If he thought for one damned minute that I was going to let him tell me what to do, except during sexy times when sometimes I might like being told what to do, then he had a whole other shock coming for him.

However, the latter part succumbed to the one that loved holding his hand, sleeping in his bed, wearing his shirts. That part of me was bad ass enough to take out any wayward parts that were rebelling. He'd already told me once he wouldn't become my master or anything like that. I'd ask him to clarify, just to be sure, before we went through with it, but for now, I pushed all the hesitation out of my mind as we walked across the street to his house. I was still in control when he turned on some island challenge show that I happily ignored to make out with him like a teenager on the sofa.

He was halfway around second base when his cell phone rang. Then, when he ignored it, it pinged three times in rapid succession. Whoever had called was now texting. That was when the kissing turned into a weird kind of staccato pecking before he finally pulled away.

I adjusted my shirt while he checked his messages as the

phone rang again. "Hello…Okay." I could only hear his side until I focused on the other voice with my vampire super hearing.

"The vampirism secret is out." The panic made this person's voice high-pitched. "I was in Wyndmoor, and I was hunting." If this guy had a heartbeat, it would've been loud and proud right about now. "The old fashioned way."

Jax groaned. "And?"

"I found a girl. It was fine. But a kid caught it all on video."

"Video?" Jax stood and started pacing.

"Yeah. And then the kid got away. I followed him to his house, but he went inside and locked the door. I suck at compulsion, so I couldn't get the owner to open the door, and I couldn't figure out how to break in without causing a call to the cops." Oh, no. If the secret got out…there would be no peace. No safety. My new life would be changed in ways from which I would never be able to recover.

Jax got the address then spoke firmly. "Stay where you are, and stay hidden." He hung up and turned to me. He eyed my second base area, then sighed. "Come on. We have to go."

I might've given my second base area a shimmy. Not because this wasn't a big deal, but because my second base area didn't get a lot of action these days, and I wanted to let him know it might be available later if he so decided.

"Isn't this something you usually delegate?" I cocked my brow because if we could resume make-out activities, fine by me.

"Nash and Grim are at Catch and Release, Paige is with Cleo, and Ransom rushed over to Luke's about an hour ago." He smiled. "Besides, we can handle this." He looked me up and down. "You're able bodied. And as my heir and mate, you should know how to deal with our people and situations like this."

"You are able bodied." I shot him a smoldering look of my own, and he grinned. I didn't comment about being his heir and mate. That was who I was, for better or worse. Or would be if I ever stopped being a big baby.

"Finding out exactly how able bodied I am means completing the mating bond. You ready for that yet?" He didn't ask often, but every once in a while he found a way to work it into conversation.

"We have a vampire rumor to stamp out. Then we can talk about bonding later." I added a smile to my usual avoidance tactic, happy I had an actual reason the mating bond had to wait. When he didn't move, I cocked my head. "Sooner we leave, sooner we get back."

He smiled as we walked outside. I went for the car, but he froze and looked at the street. "It's time you learn some of the perks of being a vampire."

I already knew about the hearing, the keen ability to know the exact moment a pin dropped before it hit the ground. And yeah. Even if no one was around to hear the tree dropping in the woods, it still made a sound. I'd heard it.

Before I could reply, he took off, running out of the house and through the night. To show me the perk of super speed, I supposed. I followed though I couldn't see him. He stayed just out of sight. But it was okay. I could sense him, and I was close enough that I smelled him. Another perk of being a vampire.

We were little more than a blur, and I doubted a human would be able to process what they were seeing if they happened to catch a glimpse of us. Not only were human bodies slower, human brains were, too. Pity.

We stopped at the entrance to a neighborhood divided into culs-de-sac and streets named after storybook characters—Pan Drive, Finn Avenue, Darcy Street.

I smelled another vampire. Close. When he stepped out of the shadows, he was nothing like Jax or Nash or Grim. He was more like a younger version of Howard with glasses and a pocket protector tucked inside his cardigan.

"Jax, I broke my glasses," he whimpered.

Jax shook his head. "Peter, I told you that you don't need them." He took the wire rimmed eyeglasses and straightened the frame for the boy, but one of the lenses had already popped out.

This guy was nothing more than a kid. Old enough for high school, too young to drink or vote. And he was the vision of what the teenage girls were all dreaming of. A dark-haired Bieber. His hair fell over his eyes and he pushed it back, removed the glasses and tucked them into his pocket. "Chicks like them." Then he turned and presented his butt. "Between the glasses and this thing, I get all kinds of action."

I burst into laughter, but Jax rolled his eyes. "You'd be a

great vampire if you could figure out how to stop getting yourself into all this trouble."

The confidence fell from the kid's face. "I'm sorry. But I was just taking a little sip from that chick"—he pointed to one of the houses—"when her boyfriend came out. He videoed it." He sighed. "I tried to scare him into giving it to me, but he wouldn't give it up." He looked at Jax and there was no disguising the hero worship in his eyes, the sadness that he'd let Jax down. "Now they're both inside, and I can't get in."

Jax shook his head. He glanced at Peter. "Stay here." To me, he said, "Watch him. He seems to have a special talent for finding trouble." He kissed my cheek then turned and made his way toward the house. The kid and I watched from the side of the porch.

"Police!" Jax rapped his knuckles against the door and a second later a light flipped on and the door swung open.

"What's going on?" The guy stood framed in the doorway and Jax smiled.

"Got a call about a disturbance. I was in the neighborhood. Just got off shift." Clever. To explain the lack of uniform. The guy who'd answered the door was a greasy, second rate version of Johnny Depp and the woman was small, with long blonde hair piled on her head. I could easily see the teeth marks on her throat. The kid hadn't even healed her. Then again, he had said he was interrupted.

Jax was mesmerizing to watch. Every flex of muscle, every tick of his jaw as he spoke. "You will let me in and show me the video you took of the vampire." He was gorgeous, and if he'd spoken to me that way, I would do whatever he wanted.

Jax walked inside and Peter and I followed. And by that I meant, Peter followed Jax, and I followed Peter. So much for staying where we were.

The guy led Jax to the living room and flipped on the television. He screen-mirrored the video from his phone and there was Peter, live and in full living color, blood dripping down his chin, eyes rolled back in ecstasy. I wondered if that was what I looked like when I fed from a human. There was a certain euphoria to it.

Jax smiled and held out his hand for the phone. The guy passed it over and Jax tapped the screen a few times. "There we go, now it's gone. Did you email it or send it by any other means to anyone or save it to any other device?"

The guy shook his head. "No, sir, not yet."

Jax looked up and smiled at me. "Peter already ate. Do you want to…" He nodded to the guy. Then looked him in the eye. "Offer her your wrist." He turned back to me. "A crying shame to waste all this compulsion."

I moved in, took the guy's arm. There was a moment of indecision, a couple of seconds of guilt for not knowing if this guy would mind, then the smell of his blood was so strong that I couldn't stop myself. I couldn't let this moment pass without tasting him.

Jax brushed my hair aside and kissed the back of my neck as I fed, then he fed near where I'd bitten the guy. And this was the new most erotic moment of my life. Feeding together was arousing in ways no simple touch could compete with.

When I looked up, he was finished feeding, watching me with his lip pulled between his teeth.

Free will.

Turned out, I didn't have to make a decision because the wail of a police siren—these folks had obviously called the cops before we arrived—shattered the silence.

Jax healed the wound on the guy's arm, and then looked at him. "You will tell the police you were having an argument and that you thought you saw someone skulking outside. You will forget about the video and us. Vampires don't exist."

The guy nodded, and Jax repeated the words to the girl. Peter must've healed her neck while we tasted her boyfriend. I moved with Peter to the doorway, Jax right behind us. We left, running for the next street over as the cops turned into the neighborhood. Once we were safely away, Jax stopped, grabbed little Peter by the shirt and held him off the ground with nothing more than a couple of fists full of shirt and leather jacket.

"Listen to me. If you do this again, I might not be able to save you." Despite holding Peter up off the ground, Jax sounded fatherly. Kind. Then his face darkened, and he jerked at the kid's shirt. "And I will kill you myself if you compromise the safety of the vampires under my care." The moon caught the point of his fang and it made a bright, little starburst in the darkness. And seeing Jax so fierce, so ferocious was hot. H-O-T.

The chant of free will ringing in my head silenced. Suddenly, I didn't care.

Jax was the sort of leader his people came to, knew it was safe to turn to when they made mistakes. "They all come to you when they mess up?" I whispered as Peter disappeared into the night.

He nodded. "Yeah. The first couple of times I can let it go. After that…" He shrugged. "It's another story."

I didn't have to ask the ending of that particular story.

CHAPTER NINE

THE WAY back to Jax's house—short as it was—was fraught with longing and desire. I wanted Jax, and the words free will didn't matter anymore. Well, they didn't matter as much. All I cared about was the vibrating of my body. The heat. The desire to have his body next to mine. Inside mine.

"Want to finish watching the show?"

I shook my head and chewed my lower lip, moving closer to him. "No." I smiled at him and ran my hands up his chest to tangle in his hair. "The mating bond is more than sex?"

He nodded as I stroked my finger down his carotid artery. I didn't know at first if it would do to him what it did to men with a pulse, but his eyelids drooped and his lips parted. Oh, yeah. It worked.

"There are words that have to be said. A promise made."

"But we could…you know…without sealing the bond?" I pressed a kiss against his throat.

"Oh, yeah." He slid his hand down to my hip and pulled mine closer to his. "If you're sure?"

Was I? There was something so decadent about having this power to decide for both of us. I watched him as passion flared in his eyes. If I said no, it would take all of the power, all of the strength inside of him to pull away, but he would, because undead didn't mean dishonorable. It made me want him more.

"I'm positive. But no bond. Not yet."

When he nodded, I pulled him down and kissed him with all the passion, all the yearning rolling through me. My phantom heart throbbed and my breaths—habits that could possibly have been a need—were shallow and fast.

"Hailey."

I yanked his shirt over his head and whipped it to the side. I was powerful. Sensual. Smart. And I wanted him more than anything.

He kissed a trail down my neck and let his hands glide across my skin, my belly. Fire burned inside of me, through my veins, through every cell. I didn't know the mechanics of a vampire's body more than there was no heartbeat, no life force, but tonight, I begged to differ. Tonight, in his arms, I was alive.

We made it to his bedroom, sank onto his bed, kissed and touched, moaned and begged. I was by no means a virgin, and I made fun of those women who said, "It's never been like this before," whether it was a book, a movie, or a person. But at this moment, I understood.

Now, I got it.

I'd never felt so much. Never been so alive.

He kissed me, hard and deep, so passionately I felt the kiss to my bones. Powerful and vibrant. My body trembled in response.

I fumbled with his buttons, my shirt, zippers, even elastic bands seemed a bit harder than usual, but I managed, and he managed and soon he was inside me, his lips still melded to mine, and his hips thrusting. Over and over he pressed deeper and harder. I clung to him. I urged him on, wanted him so deeply in my soul.

His body made mine sing. Made mine respond. For those minutes, he was the center of my universe, a focal point for everything I was.

He kissed me over and over as his body drove into mine. His hands were almost reverent as he caressed and stroked until the trembling turned to quaking.

A symphony of sensations—every hard breath, his and mine, our eyes locked on one another, the gentle kneading of his hands, the taste of his mouth on mine—washed over me. I wanted to savor every moment, and I wanted more.

Then, in one breath, the moment changed and all the tenderness ebbed into frenzy, a frantic push and pull. Beautiful chaos right up until his body went rigid and mine tensed. Until together, we cried out, came hard. Explosive and desperate.

And there truly was nothing like it.

When my body was my own again, I looked over at him and smiled.

"There are things you need to know." He grinned. "It's always going to be like that because we're connected."

I sighed. While I was basking in the afterglow was not the

time to try to convince me to agree to the mating bond. "Because you need something from me?" If I sounded bitter, it was because he'd taken away everything else. My emotions were on vacation after that orgasm.

"No. Because we're connected." He smiled, all charm and sex appeal. "A vampire and his heir are connected in ways no one else can connect with them. I can feel your emotions. You can feel mine." He grinned and wagged his eyebrows. "Wanna feel them again?"

"You can feel my emotions?" I sat up and looked at him.

He nodded. "It's a good thing, Hailey." His voice dropped lower when he said my name, and I was there for it. It made my name sound like a plea. "Watch."

I'm in your head. If you let me in your heart too, we can have everything.

I looked at him. "You're in my head again."

"And you can be in mine. Try it."

"I wouldn't know how." And this was a little bit closer than I really wanted to be.

"Yes, you would." He sat up beside me, kissed my shoulder, and put his husky voice, his warm breath, his hot lips against my throat. "Try."

Fine. Stay out of my head.

Without his making a sound, I heard his laugh in my thoughts.

I mean it. You are not invited into my thoughts.

He grinned and cocked an eyebrow. "We're connected, Hailey. There's no getting around it." He shrugged. "I can't just jump out."

I nodded. So much had changed in the weeks and months I'd been here. On a regular occasion, I was pretty good at adapting. Although most of the things that had happened hadn't required much adaptation or acceptance. They just were. This, though, was going to take some getting used to. Between my conscience and that little voice in my head that told me I was tired or hungry or horny, it was already pretty crowded up there. Last thing I needed was Jax in there, too.

"So, no matter what I do, you can poke around in there whenever you want?"

He pointed an earnest look my way. "I won't."

Time would tell unless I could figure out a way to keep him out. And that was something I was going to work on as soon as possible. But first, I wasn't quite ready for bed yet. Not to sleep anyway.

CHAPTER TEN

I WOKE up to about ten messages from Kendra. Urgent messages. Call her immediately messages. Gotta talk ASAP messages. I dialed her back and waited for her to answer.

"Oh, my God. I've been calling you since sundown."

I overslept. It wasn't like I'd spent the whole night sleeping. I had a couple of other things going on. And one of those things was still nestled against my back.

"Sorry. I just woke up."

She huffed out an exasperated breath. "I know, but Howard is chomping at the bit. He has been trying to call you since dawn. He's all itchy about not being able to get ahold of you while he's working on this skip." The words came at about eighty miles an hour and I was still on ten miles an hour comprehension. "What should I tell him?" she asked.

I took a second and tried to figure out what to do. "I don't know. It isn't like I can just tell him about my new lifestyle." I didn't even want to imagine how that conversation would go. *Howard, I'm a vampire.* And he would turn to me, wide-eyed and gaping mouthed, and then he would keel over trying to figure out how it worked, how he could make it work for him. We would both lose the skip and make no money.

She blew out an exasperated breath. "I don't know, Hails. But you're going to have to tell him something. He's freaking out. This skip is huge, and he's like a wind-up toy repeating himself about all the ways you're being irresponsible. We need this skip."

We didn't, not really. We already had money. Cars. She even had a Prada purse and Louboutin shoes. But when it came to hauling the bad guys back to the cop shop, Kendra had turned into an addict. She liked the adventure, the excitement, even the danger.

"Okay. Just tell him I only work nights because that's when criminals come out of their holes, so I sleep all day." It was easy enough and the same thing I'd told him the night before.

"All right." And she hung up.

I set the phone back onto the table and smiled when Jax kissed my shoulder. "You know, you can tell him if you think you can trust him with it."

Could I trust Howard? The news would probably kill him, which would solve the problem one way or the other. "I'll think about it."

"I trust your judgment." Good news. "I know you wouldn't compromise our safety." He smiled, and I could've swooned.

I held it together because there was another matter at hand—whether or not to tell Howard. Plus, it kind of seemed like he was ready to start a thing with Kendra, who would have to tell him about her special skills. Which could in all likelihood would shed light on mine, which meant the decision was essentially out of my hands.

I sighed because that was what one did when one was facing a crisis of vampirism. Which this definitely was. To tell or not to tell. That was the question, and Shakespearean or not, I had to figure out the answer.

If I made a pro-con list, my friendship with Howie would have been on the pro side. Him being a bounty hunter on the con because he would be like a dog with a bone. He would want to research. Would want to know everything, and I didn't even have all the details yet.

He would do the research though, and that was a pro. I wouldn't just be able to turn to Jax. Howie could give me the legends and the lore, too.

I dialed Kendra. "I think we have to tell him." I didn't bother with hello. "I think he'll take it well."

She breathed a couple of quick bursts through the phone line. "Yeah. But are you taking it well?"

"Taking what well?" I trusted Howie. Howard was nothing if not reliable, sensible, decent. He was also tenacious, stubborn, tireless in his determination to gather facts.

"You know, that I'm attracted to Howard." She was tentative and for a minute, just one split second, I considered teasing her, making a big deal of it, but I thought it was possible that could backfire in the worst way.

"Call him. Tell him to meet me at my place in an hour." There was only so much reassurance I could give until I saw how he handled everything. I had no doubt he and Kendra would be good together, but whether or not we could tell him was the issue.

In any case, it was decided and we were going to try. If it went south, Jax could do the compulsion not to remember thing. Hopefully, that wouldn't be necessary.

I took a quick shower, did my hair and then walked across the street to my place and made a cheese plate. Howard was a cheese connoisseur. And even though I didn't eat anymore, I kept snack food on hand in case Ollie checked the fridge again.

Jax arrived first. Then Kendra. Howard came last, and he sat beside Kendra. She did the nervous giggle, adjusted her position, smoothed her shirt, and fidgeted. Gone was my uber-smooth best friend. She was like a nervous teenage girl.

"Hi, Howie. Cheese plate?" I gave the platter a little nudge toward him and he smiled, settling in to use the small knife to spread some garlic cheese onto his cracker. As he sat back to enjoy his snack, Kendra made a hiccupping sound I ignored. "We have to talk."

He set his cracker on a napkin and leaned forward. "About what?"

I was distracted by a chunk of cracker sitting on the chest of his cardigan. I couldn't form a single word while that tiny chunk was staring up at me, growing by the second until I pictured it as a boulder on his chest. I leaned forward and brushed it away.

Beside me, Jax growled low in his chest. Oh-ho, Mr. Mate. I couldn't even touch Howie? Turning while still leaned forward, I shot Jax a warning look, then remembered I could just say it in my head. Back off, Kujo.

I sat back more because the boulder was gone and because of Jax, but he relaxed. "Howard, do you believe that things exist that cannot be explained? Magic and the like?" I sounded stiff, not at all like myself, but telling Howard this wasn't nearly as easy as I thought.

"Like Houdini?" He cocked a brow and stared at me like he was daring me to contradict him.

I glanced at Kendra. "More like Gandolf or Sabrina."

She blew out a breath through her puffy cheeks then cracked her neck with a tilt to one side then the other. It took her a second, but she flicked her fingers out and a couple of small sparks lit the air. Then she made a flame appear in the candle on the table in front of him.

"Nice."

I expected surprise from Howard, but he only nodded, then looked at me and whatever he saw on my face wiped the smile from his. He pulled his head back as if he thought I might assault him and rolled his eyes. "Am I supposed to be surprised?"

"A little, maybe." He'd been more surprised on our wedding night when he'd discovered the hundred or so little buttons on the back of my dress had been functional and not decorative.

Howard screwed up his lips. "Look. You can't be a bond agent in this town, or any other, for that matter, and not be aware that witches and shifters exist. You're going to have to work a lot harder to surprise me." His body language was arrogant and cocky. It was part of his charm, usually. Right now I wanted to thump him. "There are even rumors that young Mr. Redford over there"—he nodded toward Jax—"is running his own coven of super witches."

I chuckled then looked at Jax. This was either a hold-my-beer moment in terms of the surprise I was about to deliver or a pick-up-my-toys-and-send-Howie-packing situation while I kept my secret to myself.

Jax nodded at me. Apparently, we were going with hold my beer.

I glanced at Howard. He had a particularly sweet smell, and it didn't take much effort at all to let my fangs drop. "Not witches, Howard. Vampires."

For as well as he took the reality of the supernatural, this wasn't the same. His eyes went wide, and he backed up, propelling himself back until he fell off the end of the sofa. Somehow, the arm of the damned thing was no obstacle for his terror to overcome.

He scooted across the floor backward on his ass.

"No! No, no. Vampires?" He looked at me again, shrieked another, "No!"

"Howie. Calm down, Howard." I used my stern voice, but when it came down to it, the only thing that calmed him was compulsion. By Jax. I sat back and waited for my new mate-to-be to calm my ex-husband down.

Once Howard was over his terror, with a lot of help from

Jax, he looked at me, tilted his head and reached out a finger he tried to stick into my mouth.

I jerked back. "The hell are you doing?"

He drew his hand back to his side. "Just, you know, checking."

"They're sharp. Trust me." And he was looking more and more like a T-bone. I was getting hangry.

"Sharp enough to bite me?" He had a glimmer in his eyes. A dare. He wagged his eyebrows, and I gave him a little shove.

The shove wasn't much. Playful even, but Howie reeled backward and through the drywall. Not completely through it, but there was a Howard shaped dent in the wall now. "Crap," I muttered.

When he was dusted off and standing again, he looked at me. "I imagine that helps when hauling a skip to the cop shop."

I shrugged. "We each have our own skills." I meant the Bond Girls.

He blew out a breath. "Yeah."

Kendra stepped forward. "Maybe we should talk about the skip?" She laid a hand on Howie's arm and then pulled it back, tentative. "Sorry."

But he smiled at her and her cheeks flushed red. She ducked her head. There was something to be said for a new attraction. It was pure before all the real-world concerns set it off.

"Do you have anything that belongs to the skip?" I asked the question because Kendra was busy silently gushing over

Howie's smile at her. I knew her well enough to recognize when she was off the deep end.

Howard nodded. "I have a shirt with a few spots of his blood on it."

I didn't ask how he'd come by such a thing because it didn't matter. "You're sure it's his?"

"Yeah. It was bagged and tagged from the crime scene and DNA tested." He nodded and walked to the messenger bag he'd walked in carrying, pulled out a plastic bag sealed with a red piece of tape with the word evidence in bold black letters.

"Are you supposed to have that?" The note of reproach in my voice elicited a familiar narrow-eyed look from Howie.

"Not my fault if the police had it messengered to my place by accident."

Fault no, but it certainly was about to work to his benefit.

Kendra picked up the bag and stared at it.

Howie looked at me, confused. "What's she doing?"

"Watch." I shook my head at him and moved him back so Kendra could work. She spread her map on the table and began to scry. It took about three seconds before we had a location.

She pointed at the map. "There."

"Wow." He smiled at her, his charming, ingratiating smile. She gobbled it up, cheeks flushed, her own smile almost shy. I'd never seen her like this before. "You ever get tired of this Bond Girl thing with Hailey, give me a call. I'll put you right to work."

She grinned at me and shrugged her shoulders.

"Don't even think about it, Kendra," I growled.

We had a location, and that was enough for now. I had my own romantic issues to solve. I couldn't get involved in theirs. "Oh, I hate to break up all this mutual admiration and eye-flirting, but we should go get our skip." I cocked an eyebrow at Kendra and she flushed again.

"Yep." She had an extra spring in her step, a sashay, and I was happy for her. I wouldn't have put her and Howie together as a couple but seeing it up close was convincing.

When we arrived at the apartment her scrying led us to—one of the swanky condo complexes with marble foyers and a doorman—Paige and I went to the fourth floor and Kendra and Howard waited in the lobby.

We came back a few minutes later with the skip in his cuffs. Easy-peasy. This had gone off without any curve or bend in the plan. And when we brought him to the police station to collect the bond ticket, I handed it to Howie. "What is this?" he asked, confused.

I winked at him. "On the house. Least we can do for an old friend."

Beside me, Paige snorted. "I'm not his friend."

But she winked. She knew what I knew. Now Howie would be back with his big money skips, and we would all benefit. Other than that one complaint, she kept quiet and we went home.

CHAPTER ELEVEN

I WOKE at dusk to the bare chest of a semi-chilly, gorgeous vampire. We were in his bed, because I hadn't slept in mine since we'd stepped up our relationship a week ago to include as much sexy time as possible, because…have you met Jaxon? No? Well, let's just say I'd gotten used to waking up with him. And not sleeping with him before sleeping with him.

He was watching me.

"Hello." I still hadn't worked out whether I should say good morning or good evening. Easier to keep it simple.

"Hello." His morning voice was husky and deep, sexier—I wouldn't have thought it possible—than his regular voice. "Your phone is blinking."

Of course it was.

I usually left it face down because Luke had installed an app that worked around my do not disturb feature and made my phone strobe when he called or texted or left a message.

And it didn't stop until I entered a six digit code that he chose when he left the first message of the day.

He said I'd ignored one call too many and this was my reward. Today it was face up and lighting up the darkness.

My brother really didn't have a concept of time.

Moaning, I shielded my eyes. "One of these days, I'm going to kill him." But I picked up my cell and stared. "Eleven texts, nine missed calls, and a voicemail." I listened to the voicemail first because I could listen to it without the code.

"Hails!" His voice was a screechy shriek. "I'm desperate. Took on a big gig and need your help! Your muscle! Your support! Honestly, come quick! Kendra's already here." Every word was high pitched and a decibel louder than the last until by the time it ended, I was holding the cell away from my ear. "Help!"

I looked back at Jax who'd started kissing my shoulder and now stopped.

"I have to go." I sat up and by default, it pushed him away. I might've practically moved in here—had clothes in his closet and a toothbrush in his bathroom—but I wasn't quite ready to call it what it was. I needed to keep my place because I needed the time to work it all out. Baby steps.

But right now, Luke needed me. I didn't bother explaining why I needed to leave,because he'd heard the message with his vamp hearing.

Then again, with how high Luke's voice had been, the whole house of enforcers had almost definitely heard it too. I hurried into the shower.

This last week had been a doozy. Ups and downs. Highs

and lows. Howard had gone home to Jersey. I didn't have a particular feeling about it, but Kendra was still in the throes of new relationship bliss and when he left, it took her a few days to remember that cellphones had a video call feature, which took her phone sex with him to a whole new level. I'd reminded her planes flew between here and there, which would make actual sex easier. One of these days.

Anyway, she'd set him up with a witch in Jersey who agreed to help him with his skips—for a fee, of course.

The shower door opened, and Jax stepped into the stall behind me. "What are you doing?" I didn't mind, really, but I didn't have time since Luke was so frantic.

"Just starting the day." His innocence didn't extend to his penis that pressed intimately into my back as he reached around me for the soap.

The feel of his flesh against mine was so tempting. It felt amazing, like we were meant to be together, which was true since we were fated mates.

Luke was waiting on me, though. It would've been selfish… to take more than a couple kisses. To give into the desires to indulge in the pleasures my mate offered. I turned to face him, torn.

Ah, to indulge or not to indulge.

"Jax…" I glanced down, which was a mistake. A long and girthy mistake. A moan escaped me.

But no. Luke never let me down, and I wasn't the kind of woman who put her man before the people she'd had in her life before the man appeared. Then again, this was Luke we were talking about. If the roles were reversed, Luke would definitely indulge. "What the heck, Luke can wait a little longer."

Jax flattened me against the cold shower wall and claimed my mouth in a fiery, passionate kiss. The rest of the world melted away. There was just me, Jax, and Jax's little undertaker. Well, not little. Definitely not little.

Twenty minutes later, we were out of the shower, and I dressed and dried my hair. By the time I finished, Jax was beside me, dressed and smelling like a dream. "I thought I'd tag along."

Typical Jax. But if Luke needed help, then two vampires—no, four since Paige and Ransom were sure to be coming along—were better than one. "Great. Let's go."

Ransom drove with Paige riding shotgun and Jax sat beside me in the back, holding my hand, using his thumb to stroke the inside of my palm, stirring up all kinds of emotions. This man had all kinds of magic in him. Touch was but one.

As we drove through the city, lights flashed past the car indicating that the city life was alive tonight. Saturday nights brought the people out. If we were hunting rogue vampires, tonight would've been a good one.

We weren't doing anything that exciting. We were heading toward Luke's gallery to see what drama was unfolding there.

Over the last week, we'd continued chasing skips and questioning them about the person who might have been targeting us and other skip chasers. So far, we'd come up empty. We'd used intimidation and interrogation, glamours and compulsions. Still. A big fat lot of nothing. Well, not nothing. We'd made a lot of money.

But the lack of info was frustrating and disappointing, to say the least.

Ransom pulled up in front of the gallery, and I was the first one out of the car and in the front door. Not that it mattered, but I needed to show Luke I was here for him. Despite my new personal life issues.

After the obligatory hug and air kiss, I looked at Luke, noticed things about him that normally escaped me because I loved him. His coif of hair was in an artfully arranged man bun and he wore loafers sans socks with his Miami Vice/Don Johnson white suit and coral t-shirt combo, and he was fragranced with what smelled suspiciously like my Kate Spade eau de toilet. But it was the worry lines in his face that worried me.

"Luke, you have to calm down. All the moisturizer and hyaluronic acid in the world aren't going to get rid of those stress lines if you don't chill."

He shot me a side-eye then a grin. "I'll Botox later. Right now, I'm in the midst of a crisis." He drew out the final S so it sounded like a hiss.

"What's the crisis, Luke?" He was going to have to ignore my dry skepticism. He had a penchant for the dramatics. I doubted his crisis was literally an emergency.

"The crisis is that I, Luke Whitfield, master of the party, king of the promenade, have agreed to host the annual Philadelphia School fundraiser which this year is a masquerade ball. And my location—that country club bitch—fell through with four days to the gala."

"I thought you said it was a ball?"

"A ball, my poor uneducated sister, is a gala when the most influential and wealthy patrons in the city are on the guest list."

Uh-oh. Luke was huffier than usual. That meant his struggle for control was very much real. He was about to lose it.

"Okay. Have it here." Problem solved. "What do we have to do?"

"Wha—?" After sucking in a deep breath, Luke began rattling off a list. "Caterers, decorations, flowers, a band since the country club employed a house band, and bar service. I need these paintings moved, and there is a process." He spoke with bite. "It's a bit more than yanking them off the wall and stacking them in the back. They need to be wrapped and prepared for storage." I nodded. I knew that. "And I need to send each of the guests a new invitation that must be printed still with the new address." He squeaked. "They'll have to be hand delivered since it's in four days."

"All right." I looked at Kendra. "Kendra can start making calls. Ransom will help your staff with the paintings." I leaned in to chat a bit quieter with my brother. "That keeps Ransom right here where you like him. Just saying." Then I straightened. "Paige and I will help with flowers and decorations." I held up a finger. "Securing a vendor, not actually arts and crafts." With Luke, every distinction was vital. Had I not added that clause, he would've handed me a glue gun, some glitter, a box of flowers, and expected miracles. That was not happening. "And you can work with Jax on the caterers and bar service." Jax had access to all manner of bartenders and servers since he owned a club."

Luke nodded. Maybe even smiled. Sometimes, he just needed someone to show him the plan. "Okay. Yes. I'll hire a courier to pick up the invitations and hand deliver them."

When we had all the details in order, Luke hugged each of us. He got around to me for my second go, and held me at arm's length. "I knew you'd come through for me."

"Of course." He'd been a wonderful brother every year of my life. I could do this for him.

He nodded. "Thank you for saving me." He grinned. "Again."

It wasn't terribly late by the time we left, so we stopped at Catch and Release for a drink and a dance. This one was a slow one. A head on Jax's shoulder while he swayed with me and John Legend crooned in the background slow one. A soft kiss in a dark shadows slow one.

This mating bond—whatever it meant—attraction was strong. I wanted to be with him. Wanted to fall into his arms and never leave there.

And like he could read my mind, he bent his head to whisper in my ear. "Become my mate."

I sighed. Not because of the words, but because of the way he said them. Voice low, husky, aroused. It did… things to me. Made my fake heart throb and my very real panties damp. But then the words broke through the lusty haze.

"Jax."

"Shh. Just think about it. Don't think about the fact that we have a timeline. Think about how right it feels." He put his finger over my lips then replaced it with a kiss. When he pulled back, he leaned his forehead against mine. The moves in this guy's arsenal were potent, and day after day, wore down my defenses.

But the hard part of me, stubborn and resistant to the idea of belonging to him from now until forever—which was a lot longer now that I'd been turned—wanted the ability to make the choice unruffled by his kisses, by the sea of emotion that shouldn't have been so potent.

"I can't do this." I turned and walked out of the club.

It took a second or two for him to follow me to his SUV and we climbed in. He drove silently home, emotions running a marathon in my mind. When we climbed out, he came around to my side and stared for a second.

"I'm going to stay at home tonight," I said while looking anywhere but at Jax.

He nodded. "I figured."

I sighed. "Jax…"

"The emotions are bigger because of the bond and that we haven't completed the ritual." He kissed my forehead. "It's okay. I've learned how to be patient."

His understanding only made me need to get farther away because I was close to saying the hell with it and braiding my life into his whether I was ready or not.

"Thank you." I wasn't sure for what I was thanking him, but the moment required I say something and shouting my undying devotion seemed a bit counterintuitive to my current plight.

He smiled at me like he understood every emotion I was fighting. Maybe he did. "I'll call you later. Say goodnight?"

I nodded even though the rational part of my mind said that a call would cloud my judgment, said he was trying to sway me toward him and he was doing whatever he thought I would fall for. But he wasn't trying to trick me. He wasn't being duplicitous. He simply wanted to be my mate.

"I would like that." He smiled and chewed his lower lip then turned to go into his house. "Jax?"

He looked back over his shoulder. "Yeah?"

Maybe I just wanted to see his face one more time. Or maybe I just wanted him to look at me. I didn't know. "Is the indecision supposed to be bigger, too? Is my confusion part of the process?"

He smiled, shook his head. "No, you're supposed to be madly in love with me and falling at my feet." If only he knew how close I was. And the way he stepped closer to me again, cupped my cheek with his hand and stroked my skin didn't make it easier. "Because it's everything I can do to not fall to my knees and beg you to love me, to want me, to mate with me." And then he kissed me with all the tenderness and gentility a kiss should have when it meant something solemn, something honest.

It scared the bejesus out of me. Because I wanted the honesty. I wanted the emotion. I wanted him. And that was why I turned and went home, walked into my house and sat on the sofa staring at the nothingness of a white wall in my living room.

I cleared my thoughts, tried like hell to put them away,

until finally I gave up, popped a melatonin gummy with no idea if it'd work or not, and went to bed. Just as I was about to fall off to sleep, the front door hinge squealed as it opened then again when it closed. I listened, hoping it wasn't Jax and hoping it was.

The footsteps were too light, too close. It was Paige and she walked into the guest room and closed the blinds. His solution to keeping me safe when he wasn't here. He knew I wouldn't mind Paige. I would've bristled more if he'd sent Grim, Nash, or Ransom.

I was glad that Jax had respected my space, but lonely without his arms around me. My gosh. I was all conundrum.

CHAPTER TWELVE

KENDRA SKIPPED into the kitchen at my place. I'd spent the last couple nights at home, and it was going swimmingly, except I missed the softness of Jax's bed. I missed the smell of his cologne on his pillows. I missed his body pressed to mine while I slept. Oh for goodness sake, I missed the man. Why was that so hard for me to admit?

Because I'd been hurt, badly, before. Because I'd had my heart ripped from my chest, and it had happened not all that long ago. This was going too fast for my heart to be able to wholeheartedly accept it.

"What's up?" I asked.

She waved a fax in my face. "From Jordan. We've got a skip to trace." I took the paper and looked at the picture of the skip. These days, the skips looked like dang fashion models. Hell, there was even a convict I'd seen who'd come out of prison to a modeling contract and several offers of marriage.

This guy probably had a whole line of women waiting to bail him out of jail. "You have anything of his?"

Paige took the fax from me and stared for a second. "Wow. He's…" She fanned herself with her free hand while she looked. "Hell, I might put up a few bucks myself."

Kendra took the page back. "Down girl."

"How are we going to find him?" I supposed we'd engage in some of the tried and true old-fashioned nose to the pavement work, but I wasn't especially optimistic since we had a last known that had already been checked, according to Jordan's note on the bottom of the fax. It simply said, "Already checked his last known, no dice. It's a warehouse in the industrial district. Need my gals. XOXO The Big J."

"I saw a thing in a chat room online." Kendra pulled out her Philly city map.

"Witches have chat rooms?" How did I not know this? Maybe because I wasn't a witch and wouldn't be welcome in their chatroom, but my best friend, witch extraordinaire, hadn't mentioned it either. Of course there were things I hadn't mentioned to her either about being a vampire. I thought so, anyway… Maybe. I pretty much told her everything.

"Of course we have chat rooms. Don't vampires?"

Now that was something to think about, maybe check into. "I don't know." I glanced at Paige. She shrugged. These weren't vampires who were big into computer usage. It was probably a good thing they'd adapted to using touch screen cell phones and microwaves for heating up blood.

"Give me a minute." She took the fax page and began using it to scry the locale of our target. She stopped when she got to the end of the map. "I need another map. Outside of this one."

I went to my laptop and printed another with a radius ten miles wider.

After a few minutes, she looked at me again, shook her head. "Maybe go out a little further."

I printed another and finally we had a location. An hour east of Philly. Near Chadds Ford.

Paige glanced at me, and I looked at Kendra. "It's going to be dawn soon."

Kendra nodded. "Call your boyfriend."

I pursed my lips and made a clicking sound with my tongue. "We can do this without him." Having him around so much wasn't helping me figure out—logically—what I wanted to do about the mating bond. His nearness tipped the scales his way.

We walked out to the car Ransom was already leaning against. "Jax sent me."

I rolled my eyes and shot a glare towards Jax's place. "Of course he did."

It was getting harder to assume that he had faith in my abilities, the same abilities he'd taught me to use. It was starting to become an issue. But I let it go and climbed into the car.

I sighed and Paige chuckled. "He has to keep you safe. It's part of the mating bond."

That damned thing. It was not only responsible for all my confusion, but every single one of my sleepless nights of late, a wide range of hormonal eruptions, and now the constant shadowing of his cronies. I wondered if vampires could suffocate. Probably something I could find out in a chat room should vampires have one.

"What do you know about this mating bond?" I looked over my shoulder at Ransom and Paige, who had climbed into the backseat of the SUV. "Truth please."

"I know that without it, Jax is going to die." Paige's pointed look—her wide-eyed, scrunched brow, don't-screw-over-my-friend-look—spoke volumes to how she felt about my hesitancy. And now I felt like the world's biggest asshole. Of course I'd do it to prevent Jax's death. But I still had a few weeks to learn all about it, come to terms with it, and hopefully decide for myself that it was a good idea, and not just to save Jax's or my life. Forever was a very long time.

"But that isn't her problem. She has to do what's best for her, too." Ransom chiming in on my side was a surprise, since my not complying would also mean his death and hers, probably. They'd go down with the captain. "Why's it all have to be laid on them? There has to be a loophole."

Right? That's what I needed. A loophole.

With a scoff, Paige shook her head. "It isn't like Jax isn't hot or that he's an asshole. He's a great guy who can get any woman he wants. What's wrong with attaching her wagon to his car?" I had no idea Paige felt so strongly about this. People, vampires or not, were seldom who we thought they were. It was a hard lesson, but I'd learned it a long time ago and now it didn't seem like that big a deal and they seldom surprised me. This did. Jax did, too, but this was more.

Back to my defense, Ransom said, "Maybe she's after more than a pretty face. Maybe she wants a life partner."

Paige scoffed. "Don't we all?" She shook her head. "Don't get me wrong. If she isn't into him, fine. Move on. But stop doing the hibbity-dibbity with him. Stop sending him the signals."

The signals? "What?" I asked.

She scoffed again, added in a head shake, popping out one hip and pointing her finger at me. "You know what I'm talking about. He thinks you're going to choose him."

But…Of course I was. Eventually.

"And every day you don't, something in him changes."

Oh my. This was a spiral I didn't want to go sliding down. "Paige…"

She wasn't having it. "No, I know this is your decision, but every day you put it off hurts him. And he's doing everything in his power—"

Ransom interrupted, "To suffocate her. To force her away from him, to show her how it would be if they did this ritual. He would own her. He would force her to live the way he thinks is safe." I had no idea Ransom felt so strongly, either. Wow. It was like I had Luke here defending me.

"She would be safe," Paige pointed out.

Definite pro.

Ransom fired his own shot. "She would be his prisoner."

Con. I filed that one in the con side.

Paige spoke softly, and if I wasn't mistaken, with stars in her eyes. "He would be devoted to her."

Pro.

She wasn't done. "What woman doesn't want a guy like Jax devoted?" Oh yeah. She had the whole milky way in her big baby blues. She wanted a mating bond, too. I'd never gotten the slightest into-Jax vibe off of Paige. It wasn't that. More likely she wanted to be presented with this opportunity. For her, it was a dream. For me, a nightmare.

But Ransom wasn't buying it. "And expect her undying devotion to him. And that's for eternity. Because that's their life expectancy." Con. Con. Con! "What if he stops loving her?"

"Stops?" I whispered. Did that mean he already loved me? That gave me some major warm fuzzies.

"He isn't the kind of guy who would stop loving her. But if he did, he would set her free." I glanced over my shoulder at Paige and her hard gaze found mine. Locked on. "You would be so lucky to be loved by him."

"I know that already!" What I didn't know was how he felt, straight from the horse's mouth, and maybe that would make it easier. I knew he lusted after me. He definitely wanted the bond.

But did he love me? I had no idea.

I also didn't know that Paige was so painfully aware of all of this. But her tone said what her words didn't. "Paige…" I tried to warn her to stop and let me process this.

"No. He isn't my mate and that's fine. I have one out there somewhere. I'll find him, and when I do, I won't hesitate. There won't be anything more important to me than he is." She sounded so sure.

"Jax is important to me." And that was all I wanted to say

about it. I was going to do the right thing for all of us. Eventually, but I had to give some talk time to the independent part of me, the part that said I could conquer anything, and also some to the part of me that said I'd been hurt a lot. Often. In ways it was hard to look past. That part of me deserved her say, too.

The fact my decision was hurting him shouted in my mind. It stood loud and proud in my head. Spoke in harsh, angry tones. I wasn't a person who hurt other people. I also wasn't a person who could decide where and when or if this was going to happen while I was kneecap deep in finding a skip. A shift in focus here could be dangerous. Get us all killed.

Kendra pulled the car off the road near a farmhouse. "We're here."

Ransom got out and sniffed the air. "He's in the barn."

Of course he was. Probably waiting for us with sharp farm instruments. Paige, Ransom, and I walked to the barn in a horizontal line while Kendra followed close behind us, protected. We stopped at the entrance and Ransom opened the door then rushed inside. As he took a sharp left, Paige took the right, and I went straight. Ransom found our skip, overpowered him, and hauled him to the wide open where I was waiting.

"Look at me, fool." He did, apparently taking no exception to my cute pet name for him. I compelled him for the truth and asked the standard what do you know about the bad bananas in Philly.

He was quick to talk. "I know the masquerade ball is a trap."

Oh. Well. Finally. We'd struck gold. "How so?"

"I don't know more than the word on the street." He didn't blink which was true of those bound by compulsion.

"Which is?" The down side to compulsion, I had to drag every detail out.

"A kingpin will be in attendance and that kingpin is going to finish this. Whatever it is."

Word on the street wasn't what it used to be. Back in the day, everyone knew the kingpin and just kept it hush-hush. How could a person even be a kingpin if no one knew who they were? Anonymity kind of undermined the entire idea of king anything.

I shook my head. Somehow, I knew I'd gotten everything out of this guy. "He doesn't know anymore than that." Ransom smacked the cuffs on our skip and we walked back to the car.

The ride back was silent. The skip sat in the center between Paige and Ransom while Kendra drove, and I sulked in the front seat.

We brought him to the police station without incident. The incident was just a flirtation waiting to happen and Jordan stepped up to the plate. He looked at Ransom. Batted his eyelashes. Said, "Hey big boy." And Ransom was a big boy. He stood at a muscular six-five at least. Probably weighed in at about two-eighty. "You ever let a little guy on for a ride?"

Not that Ransom sparkled his gayness, and he sure as hell didn't flame, but Jordan must've picked up on something. I'd never seen him flirt with another man, ever. Jax included. He did seem like he was head over heels in love with Cleo. Okay, well, whatever floated his boat. It was none of my business, despite the fact that I was insanely curious.

Ransom chuckled but didn't answer.

Jordan looked at Kendra then. "Hey witchy woman, you know any growth spells?" He wiggled his eyebrows and shook his hips. This was Jordan at his flirty best, and he was good. And for just one minute, I smiled. Maybe I should've asked her for a love spell or something that would wash away any doubt left inside of me so I could open-heartedly be with Jax and complete the mating bond ritual.

If it came down to it, at least I had a plan.

CHAPTER THIRTEEN

We gathered at Jax's because he needed to know what little information we'd gathered. It had nothing to do with anything that was said in the car or the fact that I wanted to see him because not seeing him was hard. H-A-R-D.

And we waited for Luke to arrive because this affected him. The masquerade had to be canceled. It was a matter of urgency. Of a life. Because whoever that kingpin was after, this masquerade was about getting that person.

When Luke breezed in the door, he walked near Ransom, gave a sniff and cocked his head. "You smell like little-man-gay."

He had a thousand names for Jordan. This was but one. I couldn't tell if it was a play on a Jodie Foster movie title or had something to do with hemorrhoid cream. I didn't much care.

Ransom gave Luke a weak smile. He'd had to endure

Jordan practically humping his leg until I'd finally threatened Jordan with not working anymore so he would write our check. Ransom leaned into Luke and whispered, "You can help me wash it off later."

Luke's eyes rounded and his cheek tinted. "I sure can."

I watched the two of them and my heart melted. Their relationship has really turned into something serious in the last few weeks. I was really happy for my brother and Ransom.

But we had more pressing issues at hand. "The masquerade ball is a ploy. The kingpin is going to make his move then."

"Well, isn't this just a bit of over-acted dramatics?" Luke rolled his eyes as he sat on the sofa and crossed one knee over the other then smoothed a hand down his pant leg. "Kingpin? Ploy? Make his move?" He threw in a shoulder shake in mocking. "Fancy talk coming from the girl version of Dog the Bounty Hunter."

I sighed. He had all of the defense mechanisms out for show and tell. "Luke…"

"It's gotta be Hailey they're after." Paige's tone was sharp. Apparently she's had enough for today. "This Kingpin didn't show up until she did."

"Show up isn't really a fair assessment. I've been around." And why was I defending myself? I wasn't sure I liked her tone. I thought she was my friend. Did this have something to do with me not completing the mating the moment Jax and the council sprang the news on me?

"Maybe we should cancel the masquerade?" Jax looked at me like it was my call. The truth was, it wasn't any of our calls. Not even Luke's. He was the organizer, the person providing the venue, but the city council, some arm of the government or the governor himself was throwing this shindig. They were the financiers of this whole thing.

"Hell, no!" Luke was on his feet now. "I'm making more off this charity gala than I've made in the last three art sales."

"I'll double security," Paige said with a sigh. She wasn't happy about it.

"Maybe if you can provide a few more vampires, we can station them as servers in the room." Luke was conceding some points. It was a good sign.

"And we can put a tracker on Hailey." Ransom shot me a smile like he was doing me a favor.

"A tracker? Really?" It came out as a screech because my stress often came out through my voice.

"I'll put it in a diamond necklace. You'll never even know." Jax smiled, kept his voice soft.

"You just told me." And beside the point altogether. Although, diamonds…

He turned to me and took my hands in his. "If they're after you and something happens because I can't sense you or because I can't get to you, I need to know I'll be able to find you." I blinked twice, and he tilted his head, reading thoughts he had no business reading. "I know you aren't ready for the mating bond, and I'm trying to give you space, but I am ready, and I have honest feelings for you. Whether or not you feel the same, I don't want anything to happen to you."

Oh, no. He thought I didn't care about him. That wasn't the case at all. If I leaned in one inch, I could've kissed him.

But first, I had to have my say. "I love that you want to protect me. I do. And I love that you're all in right now. But this is all new to me. I need to work my head around everything." Honestly, I was talking myself into doing whatever he wanted. "Vampire or not, you're a good man and I appreciate it. I don't need a diamond necklace." Want, sure. Need, no.

"A ring then?"

I chuckled. There was a charm about this man that wasn't fake or dishonest. And I liked it—and every other thing about him—enough I could smile. I could take the suffocating care a while longer. "If that's your idea of a proposal, the answer is no. Just get me something I can wear under my costume."

He took my hand, brought it to his lips, and softly kissed my knuckles. "I hate how little we know about what's going to happen. And I hate that all I can do is be prepared to react to it instead of stopping it, but I will react. I promise."

And I didn't doubt the sincerity of his promise. I just didn't know if I should be flattered or offended. I chose flattered and smiled. Feminism was fine. I liked it. But I like him, too, and for it to be insulting, he had to intend it that way. He didn't. He meant it as caring.

It was a lot to digest.

I nodded and stood. It was time for a fast getaway. I needed to get away before I did something untoward, like professed my undying devotion to him. I was no way near ready to profess anything undying.

"Hailey?"

I waved a hand behind me. "I'll talk to you all later."

Right now, I had sorting to do. Mind sorting.

When I walked into my house a couple of minutes later, I pulled my cell from my pocket and dialed Cleo. She was an early riser and she was wise. World wise. And even if she didn't have an answer, she would let me vent.

When she answered, I launched. It was verbal vomit but it got the facts out there. I told her everything including the meeting with the elders in Milan who informed me of the mating bond and the ramifications of denying it, and then all the long looks, romantic pauses, the sleeping with him and then the sleeping with him, and all the ways Jax was and wasn't the answer to my romantic issues.

She mm-hmm-ed and uh-huh-ed at all the right spots and when I ran out of words, she said, "My, my. That is quite the quandary."

"You're telling me." I wished I understood how to handle the problem without dragging everyone else into it, but at least Cleo didn't have an iron in this fire. Her opinion would be unfettered by the threat of death if her advice was not to comply.

"Well, Hailey, if it was up to me, and I was the one in your shoes…" Here it was. She was about to tell me to run. To get the hell out of here before they forced me into vampiric servitude. "I would seal that bond at the first opportunity and then every single one after that. He's beautiful, and you're beautiful, and you're obviously head over spiked heels for him."

My jaw dropped. Out of everything I'd told her, that's what she took away?

Well, hello fuzzy. She was right. It was just a matter of

wrapping my head around it. Of changing my perspective. "You're right," I whispered. "I'm in love with Jax."

"I usually am." She chuckled. "And if you don't snag me an invite to that masquerade ball, I will never speak to you again which means you will no longer have the benefit of my knowledge and intuition." She wasn't finished. "Which, by the way, is always spot on. So my being there and reading the room is an invaluable resource at your disposal to ferret out the kingpin."

She was hard-selling what I would have eventually agreed to anyway, and I was ashamed I hadn't thought of on my own. "Absolutely you're invited." And if anything went down, there would be enough vampires there to keep her safe. Hopefully enough to keep both of us safe, because I had a mating bond ritual to complete. And maybe, just maybe, the sooner, the better.

CHAPTER FOURTEEN

THE NIGHT of the masquerade didn't just approach quickly. It sped forward like a bullet train. I'd found a dress with Kendra's help. It looked amazing and was form-fitting, which I wasn't sure I'd like until I tried it on. The dress was light blue with silver beaded accents. It showed off my curves and flared out at the bottom. I think Luke called it a mermaid cut. Whatever the cut, it made me feel like a princess.

I walked to the living room where Jax was waiting for me. He stood with one hand in his pocket and he was looking into the fireplace, back to me. What this guy did for a tuxedo made my girly bits stand and applaud.

I was having unholy thoughts. The naughty, naked kind. I only hoped he wasn't poking around in my brain because I wanted to go to the ball and not miss it on account of I couldn't control myself around him.

That was the thought I forced into my mind anyway, just

in case he was taking a tiptoe through my mind. But when I cleared my throat and he turned, his eyes flamed with desire. Made the fire beside him look dim by comparison.

"You're beautiful." It didn't sound like a line—although nothing he said to me ever did—and I hoped he meant it, because I felt beautiful. Also exhausted, because feeling beautiful took time and a suitcase full of products that aided in the transformation. But who needed sleep when I had a guy like Jax looking at me like… that.

My phantom pulse had a life of its own and it seemed to be connected by telepathy and every word he said, every touch. That didn't matter. It was a phantom and a heart attack couldn't kill me, so I just rolled with the thrill of knowing he had an effect on me.

I smiled. He smiled. I pictured his pants disappearing just as he answered his cell.

"This is Jax." And my, oh my, it certainly was. "Yes, I see. I'll be there as soon as I can." I didn't like the sound of that. I liked less that his smile had faded. He sighed and hung up the phone. "I have to go to Milan."

"Tonight?" Since he'd promised me a dance at the ball, I'd been able to think of little else. Not seriously anyway. And I'd practiced. Watched seven episodes of dancing with the stars. I could waltz, cha cha, paso doble, and I was working on my jive. God bless that pretty blond Hough boy.

Jax nodded. "Dominic is sick, and they can't figure out why. The council wants me to do a blood exchange." A blood exchange? And a sick vampire?

I furrowed my brow. "I didn't think we could get sick."

"We can catch a very few things." He shrugged as he scrolled through screens on his phone. "Apparently, we're susceptible to whatever it is that he has." He looked up at me and smiled sadly. "I can't not go." Like it would entice me, he added, "If I go, I might be able to buy us some more time for the mating bond ritual."

Even though more time wasn't any longer what I wanted, I hadn't told him yet. I'd wanted tell him tonight. Might have even convinced the other more resistant parts of me to do it tonight. Alas, it wasn't to be.

Because it would've been wrong to tell him now when he had to do this for Dominic, I smiled, took his phone, and dialed the magic number. "Luci!"

"Hails! Just a minute, sweetheart. I'm on the job."

And when my new-old pal was silent for a second, I covered the phone and smiled at Jax. "I'm hanging on." On the job to Luci could've meant any number of things. None of which I really wanted to know. He was rather an enigma.

And then, Luci was in the living room with us, zipping up his fly. Annnnnd on the job took on a slightly less savory meaning. "Hello, handsome." He adjusted Jax's tie and winked. "I love the new look." After giving Jax's tie one more unnecessary adjustment, he turned to look at me. "And you. Dahling, you are divine, if one believes in such nonsense." He air kissed me, then immediately spun back to Jax. "I heard you need a ride."

How he'd come across that knowledge, I had no idea. Like I'd asked the question out loud, Luci smiled. "Oh, you sweet naïve beauty, you. Creatures of the night such as yourselves are solely my dominion." He grinned. "Want to ménage à trois with my dominion?" He turned from me to Jax then back again. His smile faltered when we didn't bite. "Pity. Another time, then. Allow me to ferry you to Italy, love. Did you want to hop on?" He bent and patted his ass as he looked over his shoulder at Jax. It was hard not to laugh at his antics. I'd worked with him long enough in Milan to be fairly sure he was messing with Jax, but Jax hadn't really gotten to know him, since he'd been imprisoned the whole time. If we could call being put up in a luxury suite imprisoned.

Jax chuckled. "Let's save that for another time." He kissed me softly. "I'll be back as soon as I can." I nodded, because he had to go and I couldn't, wouldn't, say anything that would deter him from this trip. He sighed as if he knew what I was going to answer before he asked. "If I asked you to stay home tonight?"

I shook my head. There were a lot of things I would do for him. That wasn't one of them.

He sighed a sigh of the resigned. "Okay, then please say I don't have to tell you to be careful."

"I'll be careful." I didn't want him to worry. "I have my tracker and my hundred or so vampire protectors. Just hurry back." I didn't tell him to make sure the council didn't have its way with him and our mating bond agreement, but I couldn't because this time when he kissed me, he went all in. Hands in my hair, hips aligned, tongue stroking mine—all in.

When he pulled back, I was dizzy. Heck, I was still off-kilter when I walked out to the limo with Kendra. I'd barely caught my breath—it was a phantom breath but still hard to catch—when I slid into the backseat of the limo beside Grim, who sat beside Nash.

Kendra was in a black dress with a lot of layers underneath. It took up a lot of space in the car, but she was lovely in a way that made me happy for her. She spent hours and days and weeks working on spells that helped others. Doing things that made our business better. Finding skips. She's even started making love potions she sold in an online store and had about a thousand five-star reviews already in only a thousand sales. If anyone deserved to look this good it was her.

"That dress is…"

She smiled as she fluffed the skirt and it smacked Nash in the chin. He pushed it down. "It's jeweled and, best part? It has pockets!"

"Well, it's gorgeous. And you look amazing."

Grim agreed with a smile.

Nash grumbled next to her and patted the skirt again, but it seemed to be expanding the closer we get to the event. "Kendra, is this an enchanted garment?" he asked.

She nodded and smiled, adjusting the sweetheart neckline so she didn't bust out—and I suspected the dress wasn't the only thing she'd enchanted for this evening's event.

Since Ransom and Paige were already at the gallery helping Luke set up, which mostly meant reminding him to breathe and fanning him when his nerves got bad and he forgot how, we stopped to pick up Cleo.

She walked out of her building's foyer on the arm of a mesmerized door man. Not undeservedly either. Her hair was swept up into a delicate chignon with tendrils curling around her face, and her crimson mask was feathered on one side. She held it up by the attached stick as she made a kissy face at Grim who would've flushed if not for the lack of blood flow.

Her dress was deep crimson and showed off her long expanse of leg which looked longer in her four-inch heels and the diamond sparkles on her bag could've been real for all I knew.

She'd been hunting skips for a long time and had a rumored fortune amassed, according to the whispers I'd gotten from Jordan. She certainly looked like a million bucks.

A slightly smaller, equally bedazzled gay man the size of an eight-year-old with the combover of a man much older followed her. "You didn't really think I would let you push me out of an opportunity like this one, now did you?" He looked at Kendra. "And my witchy-woman." He purred. "Stone cold fox is more like it."

But it was Grim who captured Jordan's full attention.

It was Nash's lap, though, that he fell into. Face first. He lifted his head without the slightest hint of embarrassment. "Oh my. Big boy you really are."

Nash pushed Jordan away and he moved to stand between my knee and Grim's. "Slide over, soul sister."

I moved as far left as I could, and Jordan climbed in. "Now, tell me, Mr. Grim. Is there room on your dance card for a Rumba?" He drew the word out and added a snap of his fingers.

Grim nodded. "Maybe, little dude. Maybe."

It was a fine start to a fine night. Even if Jax couldn't be there.

CHAPTER FIFTEEN

By the time we arrived, Kendra's dress had grown to occupy more space in the limo than any of the rest of us and it was almost a relief to climb out. Nash took my arm, as if he'd been told to stand in as my date, and we walked to the entrance on the plush red carpet where photographers were stationed.

The red carpet flair was Luke's idea. He wanted the sanctity of the masquerade with the glam of a Hollywood premier. From the smiles, the social media postings, and the gushing from guests, it looked as if he'd succeeded.

Nash and I posed for a few pictures. The first was a normal, stand side by side pose. The next few were a little more silly. Nash even dipped me in a semi-romantic kind of pose. I laughed and pushed him back a little. "You definitely have a death wish."

He flashed his brilliant smile showing a hint of fangs. "Jax knows me better than that. He told me to make sure you are safe and have fun. So we're having fun. While it lasts."

His latter statement was how I felt. The fear that this night was going to end badly churned deep in my soul.

The interior of Luke's gallery had been transformed to an homage to twenties Hollywood. Gold lamé tablecloths, a sparkling marquis on one wall, up-lit movie posters, all added to the ambiance Luke had managed to create. It was like stepping back in time, and he was the belle of the ball. Taking the praise. Basking in the adoration. This was my brother in his glory. His finest hour. His big moment.

And I was so proud of him and happy that he was on cloud nine.

There was a well-coiffed pompadoured Elvis with a pair of blue suede shoes and mask to match, a Marilyn Monroe in her platinum wig and platform heels. There were costumes and masks, ball gowns and veils, tuxedos and masks. The costumed characters were part of the décor hired by Luke.

As Nash and I took our first stroll around the room, he kept his hand at the small of my back, much the same as Jax did when we went anywhere together. "Did he tell you to stick to me like glue?"

Nash grinned down, nodded once then looked away. "Yes, but a man would be lucky to be by the side of such a beautiful woman all night long."

"Did he tell you to say that, too?" It sounded like something Jax would say.

Nash chuckled. "You already know him so well."

We stopped in front of the silent auction table. Each item

had an iPad in front where the bids would be entered. It was more efficient than the former bid in a basket style of auction that required someone to tally said bids. There was less margin of error this way, and Luke had insisted.

Nash picked up the tablet in front of a painting of a landscape—could have been Monet, but wasn't—and bid twenty grand. A two with four zeros behind it. Twenty-thousand American dollars.

"Nash?" I gasped.

He glanced at me. "Yes?"

"If you win that painting, they're going to expect you to pay twenty-thousand dollars."

He nodded. "I'm aware."

"You have twenty thousand dollars, liquid?"

He chuckled and patted my head which should've been insulting but for whatever reason wasn't. "Yes, but I'm bidding with Jax's money."

I nodded. "Oh." And then it hit me. "Jax's money?" I didn't know a lot about art, but I knew that this painting wasn't worth twenty grand. "You spent twenty grand of Jax's money on a finger painting of some lily pads?"

His smile was the kind that said he'd expected—had probably been told to expect—this reaction. "It's only money, Hailey. Jax has had plenty of years to build a…let's call it a nest egg."

"Nest egg." I couldn't do more than parrot his words.

"Nest egg." He moved us along to another table. "He told me to find something and bid twenty thousand on it."

I nodded, not because it made sense, but because it wasn't my money. I had no claim to stake.

He glanced at a woman in a silver dress with sequins. "She looks a bit like a mirror ball." He did the John Travolta finger point and pose. A second or so later, he nodded to a guy who, like Jordan, hadn't quite mastered the art of the comb-over. "Does no one spend the money for toupees anymore?"

Some of his comments made me laugh, sometimes behind my hand because I felt like I'd be going straight to hell.

There was a woman with a brick colored dress with sleeves that started up by her cheeks and rounded down to her shoulders so it looked as if her head was captured inside the sleeves. She resembled a dilophosaurus in red. I knew the specific name because I'd wanted to be a paleontologist once upon a time. Some things stuck.

"Someone escaped Jurassic Park." He was a sniper, and no one was safe. When she walked up, he made a caw caw sound and flapped his arms behind her back.

"You must be Hailey Whitfield," she said in a regal voice.

I had no idea who she was or how she knew me, or how she'd managed to get into that dress. I wanted to investigate to see what held those sleeves so rigid.

Eesh, I might've been a bit distracted while she spoke. Missed a question while my mind ran through a list of possibilities. It could've been wired. Or some kind of piping—the plumbing kind not the sewing kind—or boning, this time the fabric kind.

"Ms. Whitfield." The sternness in her tone made sense as

it finally registered that she was the Director of Schools for all of Philly.

Her sleeves did more to obscure her face than her mask. She was obviously beautiful—porcelain skin, features I couldn't find a better word for than pleasant, full lips, and a nose that probably cost her as much as Nash's bid of Jax's money. She had a softness about her that belied her sternness of tone.

"I'm sorry. I was admiring your dress." And dying to get a feel for the arc on one of those sleeves.

"It's a Mendez. I got it at a celebrity auction." Her smile spread across her face. "That's where I got the idea for this."

Ohhhh, Luke was going to maim her if he found out she was taking credit for his idea. "The glamor of Hollywood right here in Philly." She held out her hand. "Anyway, I don't think we've been properly introduced."

I smiled and shook her hand. "You're Linda Hull. I've read so many good things about your work. The amount of personal care you put into your job." She wasn't just revered, she was loved. Adored, by all of Philadelphia.

"And you're cleaning up the streets of Philadelphia and the surrounding area." She smiled, and we finally stopped shaking hands.

"I'm doing what I can." I was about to tell her about our team of Bond Girls because I was proud of the job we did, but she patted my shoulder.

"I have to make a speech, but let's talk later." She turned before I could answer. Then she was up on the dais, mask on the podium beside her written speech. The gurgle of voices in the room faded to silence as people took their seats. "Thank you all for coming here. I thank you. The children of Philadelphia thank you."

She waited a moment for the light applause. "When I took this job"—she'd campaigned her butt off to win—"I knew this school system needed an overhaul. It needed to be more child-focused with a stronger curriculum that is tailored to the children." She went on for a few minutes about a school system that she revamped—yup, she used that word—and that she, in her role as supreme educator—used that one, too. She was loved, but she was cocky—happily oversaw and directed, and by directed she meant insisting that the local school boards implement her plan of action.

I stopped listening, because this was more of a reelection campaign than it was a fund raising, let's-support-the-kiddos speech.

Instead, I tried to scan the room, to feel for any ill intent, bad tidings, but I didn't have that kind of power. I wondered if Kendra could create a spell...hmm. I looked around for her. I checked every place setting and she was nowhere to be seen.

Somewhere in the back of my mind, a red flag started blowing in the breeze, but I ignored it and continued to glance around for my friend.

CHAPTER SIXTEEN

AFTER THE DIRECTOR'S SPEECH, I stood, ready to look for Kendra, with Nash at my side, when someone poked her spindly fingers into the soft tissue of my upper arm. Instinctively, I jerked away and stared at the woman who had grabbed me, aghast. What the hell was a member of the council doing here?

Nash leaned in. "Hailey," he said in a warning tone. When I shook him off, too, he gripped the opposite arm's soft tissue and gave his own little squeeze. "That's Gretchen."

I shook my head and jerked away from him, too. "I don't care who she is. The only person allowed to grab me like that is Jax."

"Which"—even her voice was spindly—"brings me around to the question as to why the grabbing hasn't already occurred?"

I chuckled but it was false. As fake as her eyelashes. "I assume you're using grabbing as a euphemism for our mating bond?"

She smiled, but there was nothing jolly about it. More like the dead grin of a serial killer. "Might I have a word?"

I sighed. She was on the council. The woman wanted me dead. And she wasn't asking to speak to me, whatever her words had been. She was demanding it.

I was as happy as she was to pretend it was my choice. "Sure," I said in a sickly sweet voice.

This was my brother's gallery, and I knew every square inch of it. And the only place we were going to be able to have this word without the wealthy and financially endowed in Philadelphia overhearing was Luke's office. I led her there, Nash still close by my side. When Jax told him to stick close, Nash took it seriously. For once, I was glad.

I showed her to the office, opened the door and let her step in first.

Knowing Luke, the place was spotless, a show of white lines and angles, a piece of art in actual art's absence. Luke took understatement literally. His desk, the focal point in the room, was white marble, as stark as an operating room and as clean, but there was a speck of black suit in Luke's sleek, white leather chair.

Soran. Not a small man, but the chair was huge.

"Hailey Whitfield," he drawled. "Is there a reason why you aren't mate-bonded to Jaxon as ordered by the council?" His voice dripped with accusation.

But Gretchen saved me from the deficiency of an answer.

She stepped around me and crossed her arms, shooting a potent glare at Soren. "I thought we agreed you were going to wait outside."

"We didn't agree. You dictated. I am not subject to your edicts, Gretchen." He chuffed out a breath. She walked forward and leaned down on her fingertips which were going to leave yucky fingerprint marks on Luke's desk, and he wasn't going to be one bit happy about it, but I wanted to see this through before I went for the cleaning wipes. Plus, I had Brangelina, er, Gretoren, or maybe Sortchen, to deal with, and no matter their argument, they were here for a purpose that apparently involved speaking directly to me. As soon as they worked out who was the Alpha dog in their relationship.

Soren looked at me again. "Miss Whitfield, you were given an order by the council, and I demand to know why you haven't mate-bonded yet with Jaxon."

I didn't like his tone. And his council knew jack diddly about me. About what their demand meant to me. About anything other than that they saw themselves as almighty. And threatening my death sure as peanut butter loved jelly wasn't the way to get me to carry out their orders.

Undoubtedly, Soren had been pinned in place by others, much more powerful, and I wasn't likely much by comparison, but I glared defiantly anyway. And he stared back. So I advanced, and he stayed put. But I wasn't deterred. "I appreciate that you're prince of the platters or king of the cuckoos—"

"He's the council leader." Nash leaned in like I was really confused and not being flippant.

When I cocked a brow at him, Nash straightened and held up his surrender hands. I continued as if he hadn't spoken because his words meant nothing. "...or whatever your official title is, but you aren't going to kill me, and I think we all know it." My tone was even. No malice or threat even though I was full of malice and wanted more than anything to issue a threat or two. But I didn't have their strength or their speed, and I didn't want Nash to have to step in. Today, I had to use my words.

Fortunately, I was up to that task. "Your deadline is meaningless."

"No, no, of course it isn't." Nash leaned in again. "For hell's sake, Hailey. Could you stop daring them to kill you so Jax doesn't kill me? I like it here. I like life."

"They aren't going to kill you, Nash." Gretchen opened her mouth but I refined my glare, and she snapped it closed. More out of shock than intimidation. "Just like they aren't going to kill me. I am Jax's fated mate."

"I'm not his fated mate, so..." Nash shrugged at me.

I rolled my eyes. "I will bond with Jax when I want to, when it's convenient for me. And if you don't like it...kill me." There. I'd finally gotten the dare out. I'd decided to call their bluffs.

Nash put his body between me and Soren. "She's under so much stress. She helped with this party and that was huge..." He paused and if he breathed, this was the place where he would've sighed. "And she's hunting bad guys to make money because... baby vampire." He said it as if making money was reserved for those who didn't have three hundred years of vampiracy behind them.

Soren lifted his hand to silence and if he thought Nash was just going to shut up, well, he was right. Nash clamped his lips together with an audible clack.

"Maybe you should all ask yourself why I would want to mate with Jax." I looked at Gretchen. "And you, especially. I'm surprised you would be willing to force this." We were supposed to be sisters in this fight for equality. "Why do you, of all people, expect me to tie myself to someone so much more powerful than I am? It will take hundreds of years before he and I are equals."

Soren pulled his head back as if he no longer had command of the English language and needed a translator. Gretchen, on the other hand, laughed like I'd just told her that Jax slept in one of those sweet little bunny onesies.

After a couple of long seconds of listening to her cackle, I shot a sterner than any before it glare at her. "What?"

"He didn't tell you." She shook her head. "Bonding would bring you up to his level. You would have equal power. Equality in all you do." She chortled again, and I wasn't above waiting until I had my power then smacking a little of her arrogance right out of her. "That Jaxon is such a naughty boy." More than her arrogance, I hated the way she said naughty. It was sexual and knowing.

But she was also the bringer of information he seemed to have neglected to tell me. "Equal?"

Gretchen nodded.

I was shocked to say the least. Now that I thought about

the conversation on the plane where he'd explained the mating stuff to me, he had told me, but in his defense, he'd explained it so badly. Maybe because he was nervous, too. I didn't know why, more than that since he obviously wanted me to mate with him, so he wouldn't have kept a fact like that from me on purpose. It was an oversight.

Still. "I'll do it when I'm damned good and ready."

"I'll doubt good."Soren made a joke. At my expense, granted, but a joke. I wouldn't have thought it possible.

I shook my head, eyes still narrow. "When I'm ready. Have a problem with that?"

I stared at Gretchen. She sneered but Soren smiled.

"You are a fiery one." He walked around the desk to hold out his hand. "Miss Whitfield, you might make a decent vampire yet."

Then like they were never there, Soren and Gretchen disappeared out of the window in a blur of black.

"I didn't even see them move." When I turned to Nash, he scowled at me. "What?"

"You! Your mouth!" His nostrils flared and he threw his hands up, spun away then turned back. "You could've gotten one or both of us killed. And even if they only killed you, Jax would've then killed me."

Oh, wow. He was gearing up for a right snit. "No one's dead."

I imagined the top of Nash's head was going to pop off. "They're the high council of all vampires." He shook his head. "You're unruly. That's what you are. Unruly."

He crossed his arms and tapped his foot. I shrugged. "I've been called worse."

Poor Nash didn't appreciate my humor.

"Aw, Nash, they wouldn't have hurt you. Or me. The rest of the council would've killed them for acting without everyone's vote. Something fishy is going on here." I patted his back. "C'mon. Don't be mad at me."

I should've been somewhat contrite, but I wasn't. The council couldn't kill me because I was the solution to some long-ago problem they hadn't managed to fix back in the day and they weren't likely to fix without me now. Why Jax's mate mattered I didn't know, but apparently, it did, and I'd seen it.

We were all safe and my contrition to Nash wouldn't matter. I needed this win. This moment of glory.

He let me have eleven seconds before he took me by the arm again and pulled me out of the office and back to the party. I pulled away. "Look, Nash, I appreciate the security. I am capable of deciding where and when I walk anywhere without you doing anything to aid me."

He flared his nostrils at me. "Could you just wait right here for ten seconds?" His frustration was palpable. One poke, and I probably could've made him explode, but I refrained because I had no reason to want one of Jax's closest friends to explode. And Nash was really growing on me.

"Fine." I was near the bar, and I happened to know that thanks to the sheer number of vampires in the building, we had some AB negative in the storage room right behind the bar.

I slipped behind the bar and into the backroom, opened

one of the room-temperature bottles and drank. It was a matter of safety. The last thing we needed was a picture of me on the front page, sipping from the neck of the Philadelphia Educational Director while the rest of the guests ran screaming from the building. Plus, Luke would never forgive me.

When I walked out, full and happy, Nash had murder in his eyes and Grim audibly sighed.

"Do you ever listen?" Nash asked. "I said stay right here!"

"And here I am." I smiled. If he had a blood pressure, all of his veins would've been bulging. But he didn't. He was still safe.

Paige came to stand beside me. "You're with me, now. You're driving them crazy. The boys will shadow."

I nodded. "Fine with me." She wouldn't guide me like a child, at least.

We walked ahead. "So, are we worried about the sudden appearance of the council?" I assumed that was why they'd decided to close ranks around me.

Paige smiled. "You enjoy the evening. Leave all the worrying to me."

Oh, sure. Because I had that kind of self-control. The High Council of Leeches had made their appearance. Whoever the kingpin was—nope, hadn't forgotten the purpose of our being here—hadn't made his. And Jax had accidentally kept a pretty vital piece of information from me that would've been useful when trying to make a decision. Sure. Paige could do all the worrying, and I would work on my moonwalk with Luke.

If I rolled my eyes any harder, I was going to see the inside of my own brain. But there was honestly not much reason I couldn't work on my moonwalk.

I looked at Paige and opened my mouth to ask her to dance, and no sound came out. I tried again. Still nothing.

Well, this was just one more unexpected wrinkle I was going to have to deal with and fast.

Because there was a woman— one I'd never seen before— herding Paige and me back down the hallway to Luke's office.

CHAPTER SEVENTEEN

THIS WAS the opposite of good. This woman—a leggy blonde with gray eyes and no mask— had some sort of magic in her that was making the vampire in me respond. Or not respond.

She wasn't a witch, but this wasn't a spell. I didn't know how I knew it, but as certain as I knew my own name, I knew this. Whoever she was, this woman was a…what were they called? Those critters that had power over the dead. Over zombies and vampires. It was going to bug me until I thought of the word. The lady I bought my house from, Ava, was one. Dang it! What was the word?

I would've asked Paige, but her eyes were wide with terror, too, and knowing what this broad was wouldn't help free us from whatever bond she'd placed on us. Instead, I needed to figure out how to break the magic, how to free myself and Paige from her mind control, but the truth was, Jax had never gotten to this chapter—if there was one—in our training manual.

I turned to face the woman, but that was the most control I could exert over my body. I couldn't even wave an arm at Ransom, who was standing at the end of the hallway. He apparently couldn't tell that we weren't moving of our own volition.

As soon as I was free, this chick—who and whatever she was—was going to feel some vampire power in the fingers I planned to wrap around her neck.

She shoved open the door to Luke's office and pushed us inside. It was overkill since whatever mind control she was using could've directed us inside, and we were powerless to stop it, so the shove went on the list I'd started of her wrongs. Every step went on the list. And the fact I couldn't turn around and throttle her took top spot. These were crimes for which I would punish her. At my earliest convenience and as soon as I could control myself.

She shoved again, and I ended up on the ground, which was how I saw Ransom slip in behind her. Then Nash, then Grim. Two others behind him. Oh yeah. The odds were in our favor.

Ransom moved first, ready to attack. Hands out, fangs bared. She turned him away with one pointy little finger. And he walked into the wall, face first, pressing his nose against the white paint.

Then Grim tried. Nash went next. The others as a team. As she directed and held one, another could move. I tried moving and waved my arm. Paige tried too. We looked like cheerleaders in very sparkly dresses, but we could move and that was what mattered.

She could only keep a couple of us locked in her grip at a time. The others were able to move. She shifted her focus enough to keep herself vampire free, but she was dancing like she was possessed by the spirit of ol' blue eyes.

And it gave Kendra time to run in and throw a potion, one of her special potions that induced immediate sleep. The woman—a necromancer, that was the word!—fell and conked her head on the floor. Her magic—the necromancer's—went away in a poof of air, and we were all free. Linda, superintendent extraordinaire, ran into the office with Luke just after her.

He groaned and shot me a look, because his office was a disaster now, but as we stared at one another, Linda pulled a gun that made Dirty Harry's look like a cap gun.

She jerked him close and shoved the barrel of the gun against Luke's temple.

"Whoa, now, hang on." Luke held up his hand. "This really doesn't have anything to do with me."

"Shut up!" Her voice was coated in steel. "We don't need an audience for this, now do we?"

I swallowed hard. She had my brother in her grasp, and even if I couldn't see her with my own vampire-strong eyes, I would've known she had an itchy trigger finger. "Wait, please!"

"Stop right there. You move, and I'll shoot him where he stands." I didn't doubt her.

She jabbed the barrel so that his head moved and honest fear glistened in his eyes. Ransom growled and moved, but he was no match for the speed of Smith & Wesson. His sudden movement spooked the hag, and she pulled the trigger.

Luke went down, shot. In the head. Shot.

A scream bubbled up in my throat.

Grim and Nash moved, because Linda had even surprised herself. Certainly, she didn't expect that the crowd wouldn't hear a gunshot. They took her down, but I didn't care. My brother was on the ground, bleeding from a gunshot to the head. The skin on the left side of his head was loose, as if it'd come detached from his skull.

I knelt beside him, afraid to touch him, afraid not to, afraid to move or breathe. "Luke!"

"He isn't dead." Ransom breathed the words in a whisper. "He's alive."

I looked at Luke's chest. It rose and fell.

Ransom used a fang and ripped his wrist open then pressed it to Luke's mouth. But Luke was motionless, neither accepting or drinking from Ransom. "Oh, no." He tried again, but I pulled his arm away.

"You'll turn him." The truth was, I didn't know that to be true. All I knew was that if a human took in too much vampire blood it could start the process. It could also turn him into a vampire zombie of sorts.

Plus, we already had the council on our backs over my rebirth as a vampire. Luke was still human, and human medicine was going to have to save him. We had to give it a chance, at least.

CHAPTER EIGHTEEN

When I looked up, sobs ripping up my throat and tears splashing onto my brother, Jax stood in the doorway, jaw slack, eyes wide. Luci stood beside him. Man of action that he was, Jax took charge. He nodded to Linda and spoke to Grim and Nash. "Get her to the house and restrain her. I'll deal with her later."

He spoke with force, but it set his people moving while I waited for someone to come to save my brother. I held his hand, begged, cried because I couldn't help it. My brother was shot in the head. And whether he lived or died, I was going to kill Linda. She would know every second of Luke's pain and more. So much more.

The thought of vengeance was the only thing that kept me sane while I waited for the ambulance to come.

Luke's pristine white office was red now, with blood sprayed all over his desk and the far wall.

I didn't leave my brother, and neither did Ransom, until the EMTs asked us to give them room to work. Even then, I hovered. I stayed close, still wavering on whether or not to turn Luke. His heart thumped hard in his chest. That was all that kept me from doing it, consequences be damned.

I walked beside the gurney out to the ambulance and held his hand until they loaded him into the back of their rig. "Can I…?" I looked into the back. If something happened, and he didn't make it to the hospital, I didn't want him to be alone.

The EMT was a young guy, but that was all I could say about him. The only thing I could really see was the bright red blood—Luke's blood—on his blue gloves. "We're going to be working on him in the rig." But he let me climb in behind him.

True to his word, they kept Luke alive, and there were a couple of touch and go moments, but they rushed him into the hospital, and I followed, then was pushed into a waiting room where I sat alone until Jax, Ransom and Kendra arrived just a few minutes later.

I couldn't speak, couldn't cry, couldn't do much but wait, holding Ransom's hand. Neither of us could console the other because we were both beyond consolation. The only thing that kept me sane was the idea of Linda paying for what she'd done to Luke.

"Why is it taking so long?" Ransom's voice was little more than a whisper.

I wanted to say something helpful, but I couldn't manage the words. Instead, I shrugged.

"No news is good news in a situation like this." Kendra

spoke from behind me, and I nodded. She was trying to help, and I loved her for it. But she also loved Luke.

I looked at Jax, who sat in the chair beside me. "The council was at the gallery." When he cocked an eyebrow, I clarified. "Soren and Gretchen, anyway."

"They wanted to know about the bond?" He didn't sound surprised so I assumed he'd expected they would come eventually. But that was another of those things that didn't matter anymore. I just spoke about it because I needed to focus on something other than the anguish churning in my stomach.

I nodded. "Gretchen said that the bonding would make me as strong as you are." I didn't mean it to sound like an accusation, but the words were sharp, and he tilted his head.

"I told you that." His voice was soft, his words meant to cajole me, but I was so deep in my anger and hatred of all that had happened and all involved, that he could've used his sex voice, and it wouldn't have mattered to me.

This probably wasn't the time to have this discussion. "No, you didn't." I kept my voice low. "It would've made a difference."

"I'm sorry, Hailey." He looked aghast, but I didn't have the emotional capacity for it.

I shook my head and waved him off. It was water under the bridge now. "Jax, why couldn't I save him before the bullet got him?"

"Sweetheart, you're fast, but you're not Superman. None of us are."

Then what was the point of all of this if I couldn't save

Luke? Not that we could go backward and change time, but... "Should we petition the council? Just in case?"

Jax glanced at Ransom who was now paying close attention. "If we petition the council and Luke comes out of this whole, he might not want to be a vampire and we will have taken his choice away from him." He swallowed as if he was unsure, but I was already shaking my head. Luke would be happy to be his young and beautiful self for eternity. "If he's... not right when he wakes up, that's how he would be until he dies."

No. No, that couldn't be. "I thought he would heal." I couldn't even get a paper cut now. Vampirism healed.

"He would heal from there forward, but what he starts with when he's bitten is the way he would be. If there's brain damage..." His explanation was gentle, but the rage inside of me was desperate for an outlet. I wanted to set it free, but his hand rubbed small circles on my back. This wasn't the news I wanted, but it also wasn't Jax's fault. I had enough mental clarity to know that much.

An hour later the doctor came out and I stood, breathed out a real and very necessary breath, then walked toward him.

"Miss Whitfield? Your brother has sustained severe cerebral trauma. Obviously, we need to get the bullet out, but the swelling in his brain is preventing us."

"The bullet?" I asked weakly. "But the side of his head. It looked like it came out."

He shook his head. "It almost exited, enough to cause the damage you saw, but it's still in there. Right now, he's stable but he's very weak. We've removed a portion of his skull to accommodate the swelling. When it's safe, when he can handle it, we'll go in and remove the bullet."

I had a thousand specific questions, but I couldn't think of one. So, I nodded. "Can I see him?" Finally, one I could manage. Probably the most important question I could've asked and understood the answer.

He nodded. "For a minute. He needs to rest to heal and rebuild his strength so we can operate."

This was too much. I wanted to pound my fists into his chest, to demand he tell me that Luke was going to be okay, but I hadn't asked that question, and I was too scared now.

I nodded and held out my hand, looking back at Ransom. We followed the doctor down the hall to a glass cubicle with machines—five of them— hooked to my brother. I steeled myself against the fear, against the sadness, and walked inside.

Tubes and wires were attached to every visible part of him. He would've been so pissed off to know the bullet had ruined his three hundred dollar haircut. And it would've driven him crazy that the blanket lying over him was at an angle, dangling off one corner of the bed.

If I ever got my hands on Linda What's her name, I was going to tear her apart one tiny piece at a time.

The whoosh of the ventilator and the beep of his heart monitor were good sounds, because they meant he was alive, and I focused on the thought, ignoring the straight line coming off of the machine with the electrodes attached to his forehead.

I pressed my hand over his and gave it a gentle squeeze. "Luke, it's me." Ransom stood on the other side, looking like a lost puppy.

I looked back at the strip of paper and the solid, unwavering line down the center. "I'm here. And I'm going to call Oliver." I should've done it already, but I didn't know what to say to him. "I don't know what to do here, Luke. The idea of a world without you in it..." The thought itself choked me. "I can't fathom. I don't want to live in that world."

We stayed until the nurse came in and reminded us that Luke needed his rest, then we went back to the waiting room and sat between Jax and Ransom. "He's too weak for surgery and he's in a coma, on life support. There's brain swelling and it's all very medical and technical."

Ransom nodded, looking around at our friends. "Is he going to live?"

Oh, God. I hadn't asked because I couldn't face the answer if it was the wrong one. "I don't know." I wished I did. I wished being a vampire came with the power to see into the future. I needed to find a seer, someone who could tell me the future, but again, I wasn't sure if I was strong enough to hear the answer.

Jax wrapped his arm around my shoulder, and Kendra crouched in front of me. "If anyone can come out of this, it is Luke Whitfield." She spoke with authority and confidence.

It wasn't me, but Ransom who asked, "What if he doesn't?" He looked around me to Jax. "We have to turn him. We have to." For all of Kendra's confidence, Ransom was equally desperate.

"We can't. We have to wait. You know we do." I wanted to believe this was as hard for him as it was for me and Ransom. He'd worked all week beside Luke, and it was absolutely the fault of someone other than Jax that Luke'd been shot. And in the absence of taking the blame myself, I blamed Jax for not making sure Luke was protected.

Which wasn't fair, and it wasn't right.

"We could petition," I said again. "I don't understand why we aren't."

And I would've asked harder, insisting Luke wouldn't be at all unhappy to live forever whether he was himself or had to learn another way to be, but the waiting room door opened and Oliver rushed in, past us to the desk. I pushed to my feet and ran toward him. "Ollie!"

He turned and opened his arms. I fell into them, sobbing.

All would be okay now that Ollie was here. I told myself so, anyway, and I believed it, even though I knew better than anyone that it was a lie.

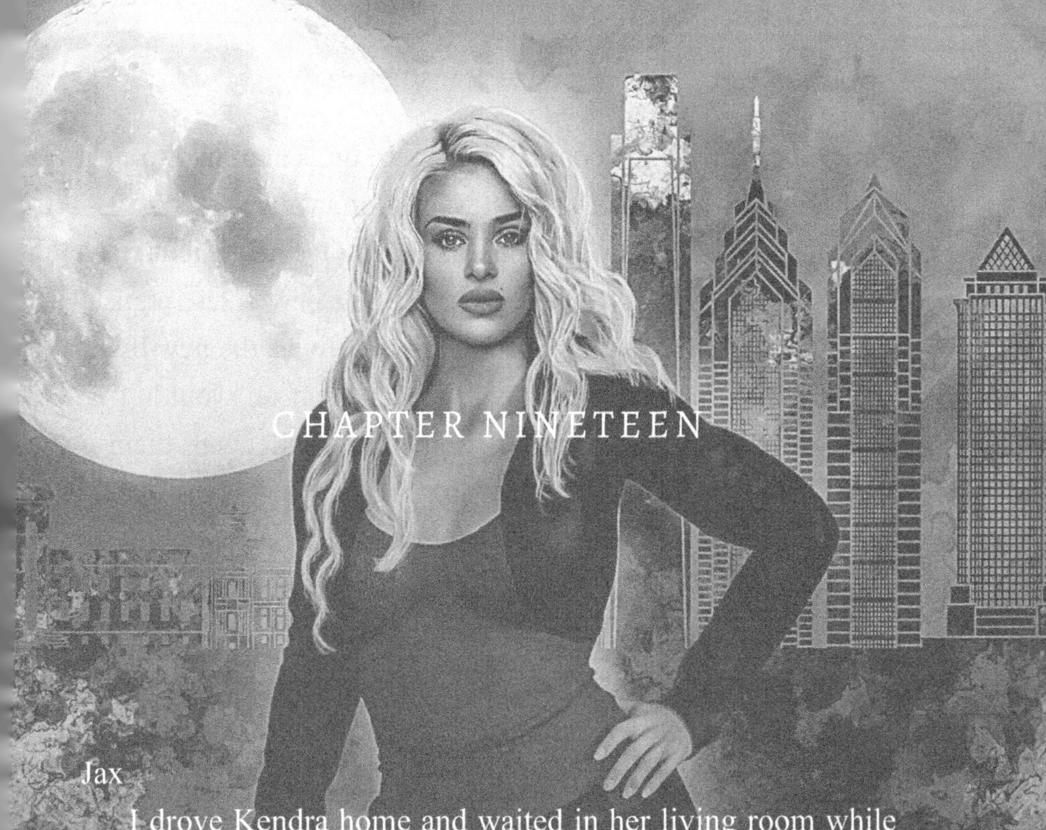

CHAPTER NINETEEN

Jax

I drove Kendra home and waited in her living room while she worked at her kitchen counter to create a potion we could use on Linda Hull. If anything was ever going to kill me, leaving Hailey at the hospital had almost been enough to do the job. But I had important things to take care of and she had her brother and Ransom with her.

Maybe the idea of going to the council had merit. This newfangled way of petitioning the council for permission to turn an heir was lengthy. They took too long to weigh their decision and by then, it was possible Luke would be in such a state that we couldn't prevent the damage done by doctors when they went in for the bullet. Or worse. He could be dead.

There was a time when vampires could make a decision without facing the big walk into the sun. I didn't want an outright war with the council, but come on. There had to be a way around waiting six to eight weeks for an answer.

The council was old school, had clung to the ancient ways in some respects, but then started making new rules, punishments, ways to exert their absolute power. I was the new breed of our kind. Democratic. Maybe taking them on wouldn't be such a bad thing. Maybe if someone challenged them—someone with the sort of backing I could get—they would open their minds to other ways of governing.

It was time to move our kind into the current century. But if I won, would that make me the leader of all vampires? That was a lot of responsibility. A lot of time. I wasn't sure I wanted all of that. I liked being a leader, but the head wore a lot of crowns.

Kendra tapped my shoulder, and I looked up, startled. "What?"

She towered over me, and it would've been intimidating if she'd wanted it to be, but she smiled. "It's done."

"Wow. That was fast." She was an impressive little witch.

Her cocked brow said she doubted. "Not at all. It's almost dawn."

I looked outside. There were streaks of amber across the horizon, low in the sky. I hadn't realized how much time had passed while I sat in her living room mulling over the council.

"We'd better hurry." She handed me the crystal bottle and nodded to the door.

"It's okay, Kendra. I'm a lot older than Hailey. As long as I'm out of direct sunlight, I'm fine. I don't fall asleep like

Hailey does." She had an adorable penchant for not being able to stay awake for even a minute after sunrise.

Even though this felt like a solemn moment, considering the night we'd had thus far, Kendra snorted and mimicked Hailey falling asleep like a narcoleptic. I chuckled, thankful for the ease of all the tension. I got the impression that in a crisis, Kendra was one of the people who helped others get through. Someone I was glad to have around.

We didn't hurry across the street. We had the potion and plenty of time. I couldn't do much with the answers until tonight, but I had to know now. I had to give Hailey something because she would be back soon and she would need the answers only Linda could give.

Linda looked up when I flicked on the overhead light. She'd been left for me, strapped to a chair in my basement, her eyes covered in case she was a necromancer, like her sister, who was still out cold in the next room. I couldn't take a chance of her seeing me and exerting her control. I needed answers, and I needed them now.

Kendra stepped back out into the hallway. "I'm going to check on the sister, maybe give her another dose to conk her out."

"Thanks," I muttered. I moved closer and pulled up a chair so I was facing the venomous woman. "I have a potion. You can either drink it, or I can inject it." I didn't want to have to exert my power over her, but I would. My physical strength, necromancer or not, along with my age would be extremely difficult for her to overcome.

She opened her mouth, eyes still covered, so I could pour

the potion down her throat. I obliged, she drank, and her head bobbed forward a couple of times as if she was drunk. But then she jerked upright, perfectly straight.

"You can take her blindfold off. Not only is she bound by the truth, but she's powerless. I bound her magic with the potion." Kendra had returned to the doorway. I looked over my shoulder and cocked an eyebrow.

She shrugged. "I don't care one way or the other, but I just thought you might like to face the woman who tried to kill Luke, who would've killed Hailey." Her voice was hard, angry, like steel, and her anger was a sentiment I could appreciate. Kendra was a formidable enemy. I'd have to work hard to keep in her good graces.

And she was right. I damn sure wanted to look at Linda. I reached to remove the blindfold. "Who the hell are you?"

"My name is Helen Hull of the family Hull of Cambridge, Massachusetts. My family are necromancers." That much was obvious, thanks to her sister's show of power.

"I don't care about your family." I did, but I wanted to talk about why she'd nearly succeeded in trying to murder Luke. "Who are you?"

She smiled like she was proud. "I'm the Director of Education and Schools in Philadelphia and…" She paused, shook her head as if she was moving the hair out of her eyes, but there was none, so maybe it was for effect. Or she might've been trying to fight off the potion, which didn't work. "I am the kingpin of Philadelphia. I don't have the necromancy magic of my family, but I am the mastermind of organized crime in this city. And I'm immune to your compulsion, Vampire," she spat out the last word like it made her physically ill. Her disgust was almost as visible as what was running through my veins.

"I used my charm, of which you can already see is immeasurable"—her conceit made my stomach roll—"and is part of the small bit of family magic I was blessed with, to build an intricate network of criminals to do my bidding."

"Why did you attack Luke?" I snarled.

She sniffed. "I didn't mean to shoot him. I wanted his sister. She's the one who is disrupting my operations all over the city. Sending my workers to jail."

As I'd thought. She was the one after Hailey. I didn't care about the details. Not even a little bit. I glanced at Kendra. "How long is this potion going to last?"

"About twenty-four hours."

Twenty-four hours to get her to the police station and before someone who could take her confession. "We should go now."

I dressed in my sunshade clothes which made me look like I was heading out in a snowstorm on a mostly spring day, but there was nothing else I could do. We put Linda in the car and Kendra drove while I guarded Linda Hull, Philadelphia criminal kingpin, in the back seat.

When we arrived at the station closest to my place, I compelled an officer to interrogate her. I fed him specific questions and then went on my way. She was still being questioned when we left.

It wasn't much. But all I had to offer Hailey in terms of justice for Luke.

CHAPTER TWENTY

HAILEY

OLIVER AND RANSOM were at the hospital with the twins. Ally and Avery had sped here from New York as soon as they heard the news and were apparently here for the duration. The girls, Mom and Dad's late-in-life children, were currently not working—their Broadway show had just closed—which meant they had plenty of time to spend with Luke, sobbing at his bedside, holding his hand, tik tokking and snapping it to their social media accounts. Fawning over him, which he would've wanted, for sure.

Ollie had yet to reach his tolerance level with them, but it was his turn. I'd spent the last couple nights with them. Our parents had flown in yesterday, and Mom was managing

Luke's sponge baths, while Dad made sure my sisters didn't post all the details online. All in all, Mom's job was easier.

After several days, Luke lay still. Barely breathing. Hooked to machines that did all his body's work. I had a thousand new powers and yet, I couldn't do a damned thing to save him. Couldn't convince Jax to do it either. It was a bone of contention between us. Although, he was wavering. And before I celebrated, I had to be sure it was what Luke would want. That even if he wasn't the same bright and beautiful man he once was, he would still be happy. And I didn't have the power of foresight to know for sure.

I couldn't tell the future, but I could remember every minute of our past.

The party was for the happiest six year old in all the land. Luke was on one side of me, Ollie stood with his usual sulk face on the other side. Mom and Dad, Grandma and Grandpa, my Aunt Shirl, cousin Bree, and my Uncle Will were all standing at the opposite side of the picnic table in the backyard waiting for me to blow out the candle.

I was six and thought they should keep singing the birthday song, so I was mid-meltdown. Luke, who was always so much cooler than Ollie, leaned in. "If you don't blow it out, Hailey, I'm gonna do it." I didn't move because I was in the middle of a spectacular melting down. "Better hurry." He puffed his cheeks. "Last chance." And then he blew out my candles. All six of them.

The meltdown rolled on, more so when Luke picked up a corner piece of cake and icing with his bare hand and smushed it in my face. Mom laughed. Grandma gasped. Dad grabbed the camera, and Luke and I covered each other in cake before chasing Ollie around the yard. We were a team, and if we were both going to wear the icing, so was he.

It was the last birthday year Mom stood across the table from us. From then on, she stood close by and swooped in to grab it up before a single crumb could be tossed by one of us.

The images in my head flashed. Most of my best memories included Luke. He'd been my best friend since I was born. That wouldn't ever change.

"Hails, sit." He pointed to a chair and when I sat, he breathed out, slow, swiped his fingertip over his eyebrow. "I have to tell you something and I don't know how you're going to take it."

"Are you dying?" I'd just watched a movie where a guy sat his sister down much like we were and he told her he had cancer.

"No." he shook his head, his brow pinched. He was fifteen now. Practically a grown up. Would be driving soon and we wouldn't have to beg Ollie for rides everywhere. But if he was dying… "Look at me, Hails." I turned my head and met his gaze. "I'm not dying."

I nodded. "Okay. Then why the drama?"

"I'm dramatic. It's who I am."

I nodded. Yes, he was. If he'd been a woman, he would've been a drama queen. I wondered for a second what they called guys like him.

"I'm gay, Hailey."

I looked at him and grinned. "Fine. You can have the basketball team, but I get football. They have better butts."

He threw his head back and laughed. "That's it? You're not surprised?"

"Luke, you're my best friend. I've known probably longer than you have."

He pursed his lips and cocked out one hip which meant he was mulling something over. "Think I should tell Ollie?"

"He won't care. Ollie only cares about Ollie." I stood and hugged him. "Thank you for telling me, officially. And I'm very happy for you."

The thought of losing him was unbearable.

Luke was a man who was confident in who he was. He was kind. A wonderful man on all fronts—professional, familial, person to person—he was always upbeat, good in every way.

"I'm nervous, Hails."

I put down the shears, and spun the barstool he was sitting on to face me. "This guy—"

"Brent." Names were so important to Luke.

"Brent is so lucky to be your first date." I smoothed an errant strand of hair. "You're the whole package, Luke. You're handsome, witty, smart. If you weren't my brother and if you didn't like boys, I would date you."

He looked me up and down. "And if you had a penis, and you weren't my sister, I would probably let you wash my car."

My eyes went wide. "Did you really just insult the girl cutting your hair?" I spun him away. "Bad move, if you ask me."

"I'm sorry, I'm sorry, I'm sooooo sorry." When he tried to

turn to face me, I put a hand on each side of his head and made him hold still. "I'm sorry, Hailey."

"Mm-hmm."

This was his first date and he was going to look amazing. I just needed him to hold still.

I couldn't lose him. Not now. We had centuries of life left to live. Mistakes to make.

"Are you sure you want to do this?" Luke wound my hair around the iron and held it. But he looked at me in the lighted mirror.

"Of course I'm sure."

"He wears a pocket protector, Hails. Does he wear it during sex, too?"

I smiled at him. If that was Luke's biggest complaint, I'd done all right. "Of course he does. The question is, why don't you?"

Luke chuckled, then his face pinched and he hid his mouth behind his fist. "I thought I was your guy. It's you and me against the world."

I nodded and turned to face him. "Of course it is, but you've spent years dating pretty boys and having a life outside of our family while I spent Saturday nights at home with Mom and Dad." He shrugged and looked at his fingernails. "I want to get laid, too, Luke."

"Fine, but I'm your bowling partner. Not him."

"You got it. If ever I go bowling"—I'd gone years without even trying it—"you're my guy."

"That's all I ask."

And then a few years later…

I held it together as long as I could and drove the hours to get to Luke, where the hugs would be sincere and the coffee horrible, where he would be angry with me, let me cry and never once say the words, "Buck up."

When I walked into his place—a cute two bedroom condo in the center of the city—he opened his arms and I fell into them. "Want me to kill him for you?"

I shook my head.

"Want me to run over his foot? You know pain, a little maiming, but he gets to live to torment you another day?" His offers would only get more outrageous until I put a stop to it.

"He got rid of his pocket protector and bought a red Beemer with a convertible top." I was whining.

"That bastard."

I didn't want Luke to hate Howie.

"Should we do wine or coffee?"

I sniffed and wiped my eyes. "Wine." He kissed the top of my head and pulled me into the kitchen. "Why would he leave me, Luke? Do I have bad breath?"

He discounted all of my concerns. No B.O., or pit stains, no stench of any sort, no confusing behavior, no inept conversations, no parking or speeding tickets. No reason to explain why Howie didn't love me anymore. I hadn't yet admitted to myself that I didn't really love him, either. We'd grown apart. He'd just been the first to figure it out.

"Can I stay here for a while?"

He hugged me. "You can stay here as long as you like." He nodded. "I promise to be insulted when you leave."

"Good." I could use someone being insulted at the idea of losing me.

And I'd been there for his big moments.

I looked out the window of Luke's condo. The limo was here. We were only driving a few blocks, but appearance was everything on a day like today. He'd seen to all the small details and agonized over all the big ones.

Everything was perfect.

Except Luke. He had a giant ketchup stain down the front of his shirt. "Luke? Did you eat that hotdog after I specifically told you not to?"

He huffed and puffed and I flashed on a three little pigs moment from the cartoon, but then refocused as he stomped his feet. "Help me, Hails! I don't have another white shirt."

Until today, the day he'd insisted I rush out to the boutique and buy him a ruffled, white shirt the likes of which would've been suitable for any pirate or a performance by Prince, Luke only wore colors. He refused to wear any garment—black or white—that could've been argued as the lack of color.

"Your suit jacket is purple?" And Prince-spangled. He had an image he wanted to project.

He was red-faced and dark eyed. Tears were a very real possibility.

I checked my watch. "Okay. I have twenty minutes to get to the boutique and get back here, get you dressed and get you to the gallery before the crowd is scheduled to arrive." It could be done. If I could fly, but for Luke, I would make it happen.

I walked out the back door to where my car was parked and called ahead as I drove to the Ruffled Man boutique. The owner met me at the door with the shirt already bagged and my receipt inside. I had five minutes to get back.

I dialed Luke. "Get in the limo. Go to the gallery. Don't get out. I'll slip you the shirt, you get dressed in the car before anyone sees, then the rest of the night, you sing the praises of your wonderful sister, without whom this night wouldn't be possible."

"I love you Hails. This night aside. You're the one person I know I can count on no matter what. You're my heart."

I didn't give a damn about the council or their edicts. My brother would not die.

Hurry on to Volume 2

LIFE AFTER MAGIC WORLD

Life After Magic World

Math After Magic

New in 2023: Middle-Grade Fiction Set in the Life After Magic world! Now your kids can read hilarious adventures as well. Or you can. We won't judge. <3

Witching After Forty

A Ghoulish Midlife

Cookies For Satan

I'm With Cupid

A Cursed Midlife

Birthday Blunder

A Girlfriend For Mr. Snoozerton

A Haunting Midlife

An Animated Midlife

Faery Odd Mother

A Killer Midlife

A Grave Midlife

A Powerful Midlife

A Wedded Midlife

An Inherited Midlife

A Fiendish Midlife

A Witching Babymoon (A FREE Witching After Forty book)

A Normal Midlife

A Grand Midlife

Fanged After Forty (Paranormal Women's Fiction)

Volume 1 (Books 1-3)

Volume 2 (Books 4-6)

Bitten in the Midlife

Staked in the Midlife

Masquerading in the Midlife

Bonded in the Midlife

Dominating in the Midlife

Wanted in the Midlife

Sleighing in the Midlife

Awakened in the Midlife

Ransomed in the Midlife

Hoarding in the Midlife

Hunting After Forty

Midlife Hotspots

Midlife Sight

Midlife Accomplice

Godmother Training Academy

With the Wand in the Library

Wears Valley Witches

Volume 1

Next of Twin

Twinnin' Ain't Easy

Keep Your Twin Up

Clash of Twins

Twin Eater

OTHER HILARIOUS FICTION FROM L.A. AND LIA

Life After Magic World

Math After Magic

New in 2023: Middle-Grade Fiction Set in the Life After Magic world! Now your kids can read hilarious adventures as well. Or you can. We won't judge. <3

Witching After Forty

A Ghoulish Midlife
Cookies For Satan
I'm With Cupid
A Cursed Midlife
Birthday Blunder
A Girlfriend For Mr. Snoozerton
A Haunting Midlife
An Animated Midlife
Faery Odd Mother

A Killer Midlife
A Grave Midlife
A Powerful Midlife
A Wedded Midlife
An Inherited Midlife
A Fiendish Midlife
A Witching Babymoon (A FREE Witching After Forty book)
A Normal Midlife
A Grand Midlife

Fanged After Forty (Paranormal Women's Fiction)
Volume 1 (Books 1-3)
Volume 2 (Books 4-6)
Bitten in the Midlife
Staked in the Midlife
Masquerading in the Midlife
Bonded in the Midlife
Dominating in the Midlife
Wanted in the Midlife
Sleighing in the Midlife
Awakened in the Midlife
Ransomed in the Midlife
Hoarding in the Midlife

Hunting After Forty
Midlife Hotspots
Midlife Sight
Midlife Accomplice

Godmother Training Academy

With the Wand in the Library

Wears Valley Witches

Volume 1

Next of Twin

Twinnin' Ain't Easy

Keep Your Twin Up

Clash of Twins

Twin Eater

***

Packless in Seattle

The Midlife Prelude

The Midlife Shift

License to Midlife

Primetime of Life

COMPLETE SERIES

Series Boxed Set

Complete Series Volume 1

Complete Series Volume 2

Borrowed Time

Stolen Time

Just in Time

Hidden Time

Nick of Time

Howling Creek Paranormal Cozy Mysteries

Familiar Magic and a Dead Wolf

Magic Mishaps and Hidden Agendas

Magical Midlife in Mystic Hollow (Paranormal Women's Fiction)

Karma's Spell

Karma's Shift

Karma's Spirit

Karma's Sense

Karma's Stake

Karma's Source

Karma's Spice

Cornellis Island Paranormal Cozy Mysteries

COMPLETE SERIES

An Otterly Secret Scheme

An Otterly Ridiculous Riddle

An Otterly Laughable Lie

Midlife Magic Dating Service

Monsters Matchmaking

Trying the Trickster

Vetting the Vampire

Testing the Troll

Bellarose Cat Cafe

Secret Witches

Suspicious Wizards

Scheming Warlocks

Sisterhood of the Stones

COMPLETE SERIES

Citrine Wishes

Sapphire Omens

Onyx Interruptions

Wears Valley Witches

Volume 1

Next of Twin

Twinnin' Ain't Easy

Keep Your Twin Up

Clash of Twins

Twin Eater

Shifting Into Midlife

COMPLETE SERIES

Pack Bunco Night

Alpha Males and Other Shift

The Cat's Meow

Midlife Mage

Complete Series

Complete Series Special Edition

Unfazed

Unbowed

Unsaid

Uncaged

ABOUT LIA DAVIS

Lia Davis is the USA Today bestselling author of more than forty books, including her fan favorite Shifter of Ashwood Falls Series.

A lifelong fan of magic, mystery, romance and adventure, Lia's novels feature compassionate alpha heroes and strong leading ladies, plenty of heat, and happily-ever-afters.

Lia makes her home in Northeast Florida where she battles hurricanes and humidity like one of her heroines.

When she's not writing, she loves to spend time with her family, travel, read, enjoy nature, and spoil her kitties.

She also loves to hear from her readers. Send her a note at lia@authorliadavis.com!

Follow Lia on Social Media

Website: http://www.authorliadavis.com/
Newsletter: http://www.subscribepage.com/authorliadavis.newsletter
Facebook author fan page: https://www.facebook.com/novelsbylia/

Facebook Fan Club: https://www.facebook.com/groups/LiaDavisFanClub/

Twitter: https://twitter.com/novelsbylia

Instagram: https://www.instagram.com/authorliadavis/

BookBub: https://www.bookbub.com/authors/lia-davis

Pinterest: http://www.pinterest.com/liadavis35/

Goodreads: http://www.goodreads.com/author/show/5829989.Lia_Davis

ABOUT L.A. BORUFF

L.A. (Lainie) Boruff lives in East Tennessee with her husband, three children, and an ever growing number of cats. She loves reading, watching TV, and procrastinating by browsing Facebook. L.A.'s passions include vampires, food, and listening to heavy metal music. She once won a Harry Potter trivia contest based on the books and lost one based on the movies. She has two bands on her bucket list that she still hasn't seen: AC/DC and Alice Cooper. Feel free to send tickets.

L.A.'s Facebook Group: https://www.facebook.com/groups/LABoruffCrew/

Follow L.A. on Bookbub if you like to know about new releases but don't like to be spammed: https://www.bookbub.com/profile/l-a-boruff

Made in the USA
Coppell, TX
24 October 2024